Eileen Townsend is t̶ ̶ ̶ ̶ ̶ ̶ ̶ ̶ ̶ ̶l novels *Of Woman Born*, *In Love and War*, *The Love Child* and, most recently, *Child of Fire*. With her husband Colin Townsend she compiled *War Wives*, the highly acclaimed story of women in the Second World War.

Born in Scotland, Eileen spent most of her childhood in Cumbria. She is an MA graduate in Modern History and Political Science, and now lives in the Midlands.

By the same author

Of Woman Born
In Love and War
The Love Child
Child of Fire

Non-fiction

War Wives (with Colin Townsend)

EILEEN TOWNSEND

The Other Woman

Grafton
An Imprint of HarperCollins*Publishers*

Grafton
An Imprint of HarperCollins*Publishers*
77–85 Fulham Palace Road,
Hammersmith, London W6 8JB

Special overseas edition 1992
This edition published by Grafton 1992
9 8 7 6 5 4 3 2 1

First published in Great Britain by
GraftonBooks 1991

ISBN 0 586 21277 9

Set in Meridien

Printed in Great Britain by
HarperCollinsManufacturing Glasgow

For Anthony

Book One

'THE BREAD IS CAST'

Cast thy bread upon the waters:
for thou shalt find it after many days . . .

In the morning sow thy seed,
and in the evening withhold not thine hand:
for thou knowest not whether shall prosper,
either this or that,
or whether they both shall be alike.

ECCLESIASTES 11: 1

Prologue

It seems only yesterday, but seventy years have gone – three score years and ten; the Book of Life is nearing its end. When we are young we imagine that we can turn the pages slowly, pausing every now and then, to dwell for a moment on a paragraph here, a page there. But life is not like that. As we grow older, the pages get caught by the wind and are whipped through our fingers like autumn leaves from the trees when summer has gone.

It is autumn now, and that wind grows strong, and it carries with it echoes of places and loved ones long gone. Gone from this life, but not gone from the heart.

And the place that has remained dearest to my heart is a special island that lies off the coast of the Western Highlands of Scotland. To its own, the Isle of Skye is known in their Gaelic language as *Eilean a' Cheo* – the Island of Mist – and its sons and daughters are the Children of the Mist. And as a Child of the Mist, I knew I was one of the chosen ones, for had not God Himself rested on the seventh day and made Skye on the eighth?

For me, to live on Skye was to open a door through which you looked down past the centuries that are dust, and to know that the breath that breathed o'er Eden breathed still over *Eilean a' Cheo*. It was to lie as a child on a hilltop on a hot summer's day and watch the sun go down over the Western sea. Like a flaming torch held by an unseen hand, it set the heavens ablaze, crimsoning the waters beneath, that dazzled like a mirror broken by spears of amber light. And far above me, like a speck of gold caught in the dying rays of the sun, a bird winged its way upwards, like some homeward-bound angel seeking the Immortal Gate that led to the Gaelic heaven of *Tir-nan-Og*, the Land of the Ever Young.

To know my island was to know the very essence of life itself. But since my birth in that beloved place, two world wars have wreaked their havoc on two generations of my people; great empires have crumbled and new ones been born. But it is not the great events of history that leave their mark on us; it is the people and places we come to know and to love, and sometimes to hate.

There is a saying in the West of Scotland that the Gael is a creature of extremes: his sadness is despair, his joy is rapture, and perhaps that is how it has been for me. I have known the dizzying heights of ecstasy and plunged the depths of despair, and I would not have had it any other way.

> I sent my soul through the invisible,
> Some letter of the afterlife to spell,
> And by and by my soul returned to me,
> And answered, I myself am Heaven and Hell.

Chapter One

Isle of Skye
October 1886

The day they buried her, a dense mist lay low on the surrounding hills, clothing them in a dripping white shroud. For the seventy-two hours since her death there had been neither night nor day, only the lifeless gloom known as the haar, and the infinite, weary weeping of the rain that fell as chill and silent as the grave on the small knot of mourners that had gathered to pay their last respects to the dead woman.

Those that had made their way along the stony path to her last resting place knelt and prayed by the graveside, their knees sinking into the damp spongy peat that had been her native sod for all of her twenty-six years. Then, when they had done with praying, the four brothers of the dead woman, who had shouldered her coffin up the rough road from the front room of the cottage where it had lain for three days, lifted the two oars of their father's old boat and pulled taut the ropes as they lowered the rough-hewn casket into the black earth.

And all the time the minister's voice was continuing in the child's head: '. . . May the Lord have mercy on the soul of our dear departed sister Mary Anne McLeod; may He in His infinite mercy forgive her for her sins in this life and grant her eternal peace in the life hereafter. May He lay His hand in the hand of the child in our midst this day – the fruit of her sins – and may He walk with this child in the paths of righteousness all the days of her life . . . *An ainm an Athar, a Mhic, 'S an Spioraid Naoimh* . . . In the name of the Father, the Son, and the Holy Ghost . . . *Mar a bha, Mar a tha, Mar a bhitheas, Gu brath* . . . As it was, As it is, As it shall be, Evermore . . . A-men . . .'

'A-men . . .'

'A-men . . .' It was the child's voice, piping and clear, that sounded after the others had raised their bowed heads and closed the Reverend Donald McDonald's prayer in hoarse unison.

'Give me your hand, child.' The old man at the head of the grave, his craggy features betraying little of the emotion within, held out his hand to clasp that of his granddaughter.

The child stared up at him, her dark eyes wide with wonder and not a little fear as she glanced back down into the gaping darkness of the grave. 'How long will they leave Mama in there, Grandfather? When will Jesus come and take her?'

'Wheesht, Mhairi.' The old man tugged at the child's hand as the procession, led by the Minister, began to wend its way back down the hill.

But the nine-year-old girl stood firm. 'I'm not leaving till Jesus comes for my Mama. I'm not leaving her here all by herself.'

'Quiet, child. Your mother's already gone to Our Lord.' The old man gave his granddaughter's hand an impatient jerk and started off down the hill behind the others, dragging the small figure behind him. It had been a bad idea to let her come in the first place. Funerals were for grown men and women, not wee lassies like this.

The child squinted up at her grandfather through the thick grey mist that still swirled around them. He wasn't telling her the truth. He had that look on his face and that tone to his voice that meant he would say anything to keep her quiet. But she would not be quiet. For how could she? She was still in there. Her Mama was still in there, in that dark hole, trapped in that box, waiting for Jesus, and they were leaving her alone in this awful place.

She began to wail – great heartrending sobs that made the others who had gone on in front turn their heads to see what was the matter.

'It's only the bairn,' someone muttered, head down against the chill wind from the sea. It was to be expected, wasn't it? Wee Mhairi being Mary Anne's only child, and not having a father and all. The poor wee thing was to be pitied, right enough, having only a crabbit old man like Long Rob, and his four sons, to grow up to womanhood with.

Every child had a father, of course. Only some were not married to the mothers. Some fathers would not even acknowledge the tie of blood that bound them to their offspring. And – even harder for any small God-fearing community to come to terms with – some mothers would not confess as to the father of their child, and the wages of sin were to be dearly paid for in such places as Ballintuim. In the Free Kirk they would make you appear before the elders and all the congregation and confess your sin – make you crave their forgiveness as a fallen woman.

But Mary Anne McLeod had not had that ignominy to contend with; as a member of the Established Kirk of Scotland, she had simply the whispers and shaking of heads to put up with, and the ill-concealed condemnation of her father and four brothers. In fact, the old man had not spoken to her until the child was almost six months old; by which time the head of dark curls and rosy cheeks of the infant had melted the ice in the coldest of hearts within the small cottage where Long Rob McLeod lived with his younger daughter and four unmarried sons.

His only other child, Belle, had gone off years before – first to Glasgow to work in service, then, to the family's great concern, all the way across the border, and down to Manchester to work in the great cotton mills of England's foremost industrial city. There she had married an Irishman by the name of Finbar Rafferty and had had several children by him in quick succession. The family in Ballintuim heard little from her, for Belle never was a great one with the reading and writing. But tonight, once they had seen her younger sister laid to rest, over the teacups and whisky glasses, the talk in the McLeod household was all of Belle and her Irishman, in far-off Manchester.

'It's the only sensible thing, Rob, and that's the God's truth. It's not an old man's place to be bringing up a young bairn – especially a lassie. You'll have to send her down to Belle, in England, there's nothing else for it.'

'Och, away with you! Wee Mhairi belongs here, not in some God-forsaken town south of the border. You send her down there and we'll never set eyes on her again. She'll be gone for good, just like Belle herself!'

Long Rob listened to all the arguments and kept his peace. But in the end, despite the initial doubts of some, there were none in favour of his keeping the bairn, and in his heart he knew what they were saying was the truth. He would be seventy next year. He had done his three score and ten; who could say how much longer he was for this world, and then where would that leave Mhairi? Certainly the thought of her ending up as a skivvy for those four great hulking lads of his was not the future he had in mind for the girl. Nor did he want her skivvying for the Gentry, in their castles and big houses. He had little in this life, but he had his pride. His granddaughter deserved better than to end up scouring pots in the kitchens of Dunvegan or Dalriada. But what was the alternative if she stayed on here? His own health had been worrying him of late, and without himself around much longer to keep an eye on her, who was to say she might not end up like her own mother in years to come, if she remained here? He shuddered at the very thought. A disgrace such as that once in a lifetime was more than enough for any family.

The furrows on his seamed brow grew deeper and he

puffed thoughtfully on his pipe as the talk went on around him. All were eager to have their say, and no one was aware of the small pair of ears listening from the depths of the box bed in the back room beyond. Just who was this Belle they were all suddenly talking about? And where was Manchester? It was not on Skye, that was for sure.

But more important than either Belle or Manchester — had they all forgotten about her Mama all alone in the kirk graveyard down there by the shore? What if Jesus hadn't come for her? What if she was still lying there all alone in that awful hole waiting for Him?

Mhairi's dark eyes grew bigger with fear in the semi-darkness. She could not bear to think of her mother all alone out there waiting for Our Lord to come and take her. Someone should be with her . . .

Silently she slipped from the box bed on to the rag rug and padded barefoot over the stone slabbed floor to where the door to the next room stood slightly ajar. She pushed it open even further. They were all in there: Long Rob, her grandfather, in his usual chair by the fire, Dougal, Hamish, Neil and Ian, his four sons seated round the table, and next to them on the wooden stool on the other side of the hearth, her Great-aunt Jessie McLeod sat, her arthritic fingers busily negotiating the heel of a woollen sock. It seemed to Mhairi that all Skye women came on to this earth with knitting needles in their hands. A motley collection of other friends and relations who had come from the four corners of the island for the wake, perched on various items of make-do seating around the room. Not one noticed her at the door.

'I want my Mama!'

All heads turned.

'I want my Mama!' The childish voice piped louder this time. 'Somebody take me to my Mama!'

'Wheesht now, Mhairi!' It was her Uncle Dougal who came across and put an arm around her shoulders. 'Your

15

Mama's gone to Jesus. You know that fine. Were you not hearing what the Minister said?'

'Get you back to bed, bairn. You'll catch your death standing there with bare feet on that stone floor, and one death's more than enough for any family to contend with in a week.' Her grandfather tapped the bowl of his pipe on the iron bar of the grate and glowered across the lamplit room. 'Put her back and close the door behind her, Dougal,' he commanded his youngest. 'It's overtired she'll be. She'll sleep soon enough.'

But Mhairi did not sleep. Instead she lay quite still and silent in the darkness beneath the coarse blankets of the box bed and thought of her mother all alone down there in that graveyard. She could hear the wind whistling through a crack in the window pane above her bed. It was cold out there – cold and dark. What if Jesus was busy? What if He did not come for hours yet?

She bit into her bottom lip and an upper tooth wiggled. She poked at it with her tongue and then her little finger. She had lost one last week and her Mama had said to put it under her pillow for the fairies who would pay a farthing for it in the night. But there were to be no fairies and no farthing, for that very night had seen her mother taken ill with another bout of what they called 'the consumption'.

It frightened Mhairi when her mother had the consumption for she sweated and coughed, and spat blood into a little white bowl she kept specially by her bed, and the whole family seemed to speak in whispers for days, until she was well enough to rise and go about her usual household chores.

Mhairi had shared this bed with her mother for as far back as she could remember. And now she was alone. The bed felt much too big, and cold. She shivered and remembered the nights before her mother had taken ill, the nights when she would lie safe and warm here beside her and listen to the wondrous tales of Ossian and the other Celtic bards who had inhabited these islands a thousand years ago. And her mother's voice would take on a strangely mystical tone as it gave life to their stories and poetry; and she would tell tales of her own and weave magical fantasies out of words such as the child had never heard from another human being.

Yes, with all her heart Mhairi looked forward to the nights, with just the two of them lying safe and snug beneath the heavy weight of the coarse homespun covers, when she would be transported to that other world that inhabited her Mama's mind. And Mary Anne McLeod would tell her young daughter of the pride she should feel to be born in this most special of places: the Isle of Skye – this island they all knew as *Eilean a' Cheo* – the Island of Mist – and they its children, she reminded her, were the Children of the Mist.

And she would tell her of their people – the Gaels – and of the Gaelic heaven of *Tir-nan-Og*, the Land of the Ever Young, which lay somewhere beyond their island and the others of the Hebrides, away out towards the place where the sun sets over the Western sea, where the night waves speak with a voice like thunder, as the grey mists drift eastward from the great Atlantic Ocean itself to engulf their small island home.

And there on the shore of the great sea the Gaelic soul waits patiently for the coming of the White Ship which, since time immemorial, has ferried the chosen ones across the waves to that special place, *Tir-nan-Og*. And that great ship needed neither wind nor sail, nor rudder, to speed her on her way, as she glided like a bird over the sea, for her power comes from the mists of Fate that guide her on her sacred journeyings.

And she would tell her of the sacred bird, the white merle, who long ago had flown out of Eden to settle on these islands, and though many claimed to have heard its song, only those who had glimpsed the shimmer of its

17

white wings could count themselves truly blessed, for they were of the chosen ones; their place was already awaiting them on that great White Ship.

But when her mother talked of the White Ship her voice would not be quite the same; sometimes Mhairi could sense it in the darkness; something would be wrong; it was as if she knew it was already out there in the bay, awaiting its next passenger.

It was such a night when the child placed her tooth carefully beneath the shared bolster for the fairies. There had been no story from the bards that night and her mother's face had been pale and drawn as she slid beneath the covers. Instead she had told her of awakening that morning and going up to the hill pasture to fetch Betsy the cow for milking; she told it in words that were more beautiful to Mhairi's ears than any poem from Ossian, as she hugged the child to her breast:

'Today, my heart, I watched the coming of the day, when on the rowan trees at the foot of the hill the grey leaves of dawn turned to leaves of rose. When beneath the scarlet splendour of the heavens, a ripple of golden sun came out of the narrow corrie at the summit of the hill and ran like the running tide through the flushed grey, washing in amongst the sprays of silver birch beside me, and among the clusters of rowan berries, as I carried the milk-pail down the hill for your breakfast.

'Then later, when I returned, the tide of noon was upon the hills, and amid the purple heather and pale amethyst ling I stopped to rest on one of the great granite rocks that mark the path you take to school each morning. From there I could not see the shore, nor the great ocean beyond, where your grandfather's boat had already been since long before daybreak. And in the vast blue of the heavens above me nothing was visible save a speck of white where a bird drifted above that invisible sea; and I knew then, as sure as the Good God gave us breath, another ship was waiting . . .

'And through the hot tide of noon went a yet hotter breath within me as of the heart of flame. And as I rested there on the cold grey granite, far, far beyond that place, beyond the dim hills of dreams, there my heart hung suspended as that sacred white bird longing for home.

'Then, when at nightfall I climbed the hill for the last time, at the setting of the sun the golden ripple was an ebbing tide, and the sprays of the silver birch were as a perishing flame, and the rowan berries were red as drops of blood. And there I paused once more and watched the flaming splendour of the rose-coloured sky's slow fading into the grey veils of dusk. But my heart no longer sang as those grey veils obscured my rose-lit heaven, for my thoughts were all of that bird – that sacred white creature – that had pierced the azure of my noonday heaven, and in so doing had pierced my very heart . . .'

And then her Mama had cried . . . And there were drops of blood as red as the rowan berries on the pillow the next morning.

'Your Mama is not well again,' the child was told. And she was taken to live with her grandfather's sister, her Great-aunt Jessie McLeod, in her cottage down by the shore beyond the kirk.

For four long days she was not allowed up to her grandfather's house to see her mother, until on the fifth day her great-aunt had lowered the blinds at all the windows facing the street, and she was taken by her grandfather's hand up the winding path to their home.

Her mother was lying stretched out in a long white dress in a wooden box on the table in the front room. Her heavily-lashed eyes were closed, and her dark auburn hair was combed out over her shoulders, a sheen on it like the strange amber-gold of the harvest moon rising through a sea of mist beyond the Cuillins. Though her skin was pale, its pallor was that wrought by the sun and wind, and her cheeks still had the glow of sunlit hill-water that the child

19

would play in on her way to and from the high pastures. Her hands, that had wiped away so many tears from the small face that peered down at her from her grandfather's arms, were clasped as if in prayer on her breast. She looked more beautiful than the child could ever remember. 'Mama!' she had cried and had made to reach into the box, but her grandfather's arms had held her fast.

'Your mother's not in there, child. The Good Lord has taken her.'

And they had told her that ever since. But they were wrong. Jesus had not yet come, for she was still lying there in that box where they had left her this day in the kirkyard.

The child glanced through the darkness towards the closed door. A faint chink of yellow light from the oil lamp in the next room showed beneath and she could just make out the faintest hum of voices. The whisky bottle had been on the table and they were still talking; they would be there for hours yet.

Silently she slid out from beneath the bedcovers and stood up at the small window above the bed. The haar had lifted and the stars stood out bright against the dark canopy of the heavens. Carefully she pushed open the window and the wind that whipped the hair back from her face was chill. She shivered, but wasted no time looking for her coat as she pulled herself up on to the rough wood of the window ledge. There was just enough room to squeeze through.

She landed on the grassy bank on the other side of the house with a soft thud, the coarse ground causing her to wince in pain, but there was no going back for shoes now.

The wind caught her nightdress, and it billowed around her as she made for the path down towards the graveyard by the shore. The moon was high in the night sky, an orb of stilled pale fire that lent an unearthly glow to the landscape around her. 'I'm coming, Mama. I'm coming!'

She began to run, then stopped, for suddenly she felt no fear. It was as if her mother were there with her, her hand in hers.

As she approached the kirkyard the wind from the sea grew stronger and the stars seemed as wind-whirled fruit, blown upwards from the treetops that swayed and whispered to her in the moonlight. Then she stopped, her heart thumping in her breast, for she was not alone.

As she stood by the wooden gate she could make out the figure of a man standing by the grave. A man wrapped in a long dark cloak, standing hat in hand, his head bowed. Mhairi caught her breath. It was HIM. It had to be HIM.

Slowly she opened the gate. It creaked wearily on its hinges. The grass felt coarse and damp beneath her bare feet. Silently she stole across the graves between until she was standing directly behind Him.

She stared at Him for a long time. He was just as she imagined. Tall and dark and mysterious. But was it all right for her to speak first? Her grandfather had told her she must never address any grown-up before being spoken to first. But if it was a sin to speak first, then He would forgive her, for had not her mother taught her that He forgave all sins?

She cleared her throat. 'Hello, Jesus.'

The man whirled round to face her. 'What the devil!' He stared down at the child as if at an apparition.

Mhairi took a step back, startled at his outburst. 'You — you *are* Jesus, aren't you?' she whispered. 'You *are* Jesus come to take my Mama?' Her bottom lip was quivering and she was shivering now, half from fear, half from cold.

The man stared down at the tiny, nightdress-clad figure in a mixture of astonishment and concern, mingled with a much deeper emotion. 'This is your mother buried here?'

The child nodded.

The tall stranger knelt down beside her, slipping the

21

cloak from his shoulders to wrap around her shivering body. 'And what is your name, child?'

'Mhairi Anna McLeod, if it please you, Jesus.'

The semblance of a wry smile crossed the finely-hewn features of his face, beneath the dark red of his beard, but nothing was said to disillusion her. 'Your mother was a fine woman, Mhairi Anna McLeod. I want you to know that and remember it.'

The child nodded. 'And you will be taking her with you, just like Grandfather said? . . . I didn't want her to be alone, you see. I didn't want her to be all by herself down here waiting for you.'

'And so you came to keep her company.'

Again Mhairi nodded. 'She didn't like the dark, you see. She would never go out without a lantern.' She looked around her. 'They don't have lanterns in the kirkyard, so I came to wait with her. But I can go now – now that You've come.'

The stranger glanced round up the hill beyond the gate. 'Your grandfather's cottage is the last one up the hill, am I right?'

'Yes, Jesus.' It was right that He should know everything.

'Then I'll take you home first.' And with that he bent down and swept the child into his arms and set off in the direction from which she had come.

It was several long years before Mhairi Anna McLeod realized that the tall figure who deposited her silently outside her grandfather's door that night was not her Saviour. And it was several years later still before she realized if he was not her father in heaven, then, as sure as there was a God somewhere beyond this godless world, he was her father on earth.

22

Chapter Two

For the days and weeks that followed her mother's death Mhairi continued to live with her Great-aunt Jessie in the small two-roomed cottage by the shore. And as the darkening days of autumn gave way to winter, and the pain of losing her mother lessened to a dull ache within her, her life returned to the regular routine of life at home helping her Auntie Jessie, and then each weekday morning, the long, lonely trek to the schoolhouse two miles over the hill at Auchindoir.

She had started school in the September of that year, only a few short weeks before her mother's death, and it had come as a shock to her to find herself spending her days with others of her own age. In common with so many Highland communities, the Clearances of previous generations had seen most of her own village of Ballintuim reduced to only one or two families. And now, apart from her uncles, almost all that was left there were the old and infirm. The young and healthy had had little option but to leave the island in search of work, and spend the rest of their days in far-off cities like Glasgow or Manchester, or to make the long journey across the sea to North America.

Mhairi was the first child to be born in Ballintuim for almost two decades and it was to the adult world that she related best. To find herself seated on a long bench in the single classroom of the school beside almost a dozen other children of varying ages was a daunting experience. But the dominie was a kindly man; Mr McPherson taught all ages by himself and was strong on the Bible. 'Purity of heart, children. Purity of heart is what's required in this world. Faith can move mountains.'

Mhairi would listen and gaze out at Craig Mhor, the great hill that stood between herself and home. If she had faith maybe one day, if she prayed hard enough, Craig Mhor itself would move. Just a wee bit over towards Auchindoir, that was all that was required; a wee bit over so that the walk up its steep slope in the morning was not quite so tiring. But no matter how hard she prayed, Craig Mhor would not budge, and after a few weeks she gave up trying. Maybe faith was not such a wonderful thing after all.

They had said a special prayer for her after her mother died, and Mr McPherson had prayed that God would lead the motherless child in the paths of righteousness. She had felt honoured by such attention and during the dinner break, when they were allowed to eat their sandwiches by the stove at the far end of the big room, she had asked Jean-Belle Morrison, the oldest girl in the school, where these paths were to be found. It had taken her all her time to keep back the tears at the giggling and mockery that followed.

'I don't see why she should have special prayers said for her, anyway,' a plump girl from one of the hill crofts said indignantly as she turned to Mhairi. 'It's only your mother that's dead, isn't it? You must still have a Dad.'

Mhairi had stared at her. In all her nine years the thought had never occurred to her. It was something that was never mentioned at home. After all, she had her grandfather and the uncles; there were plenty of men in her family already.

'Aye, everybody's got a Dad!' someone else chimed in. Then, 'Where's your Dad, Mhairi McLeod? Where is he?'

She had sat in the middle of the sea of faces, clutching her jam sandwich, as they all joined in. Mouths full of bread and sticky with homemade jam took up the chant: 'Where's your Dad, Mhairi McLeod? Where's your Dad?'

And she had no answer for them.

She walked home slowly that evening, dragging the bag with her books behind her. Suddenly she wasn't like the others. She was different. She had no Dad.

Her Auntie Jessie was making pancakes on a griddle hanging on a hook over the fire when she got back to the cottage. The old woman saw at once there was something troubling the child. 'What is it today, bairn? You've not been getting yourself in trouble with the dominie?'

Mhairi shook her head as she sat down heavily on the wooden settle by the fire.

'What is it, then? Are you no' feeling well, is that it?'

Mhairi ignored the question as she looked intently at the old woman. 'The dominie said a prayer for me today . . .' she began.

'Well now, that was a Christian act.'

'He said I was a motherless child and they should all pray for me. But when dinnertime came, the others said I shouldn't have had a prayer said for me because I must have a father.' She could see the jeering faces now in her mind's eye. 'They all laughed at me, Auntie Jessie, and said I should have a Dad. Everybody's got a Dad, they said.' Her lower lip was trembling now. 'Where is he, Auntie Jessie. Where's my Dad?'

Jessie McLeod lifted the last pancake from the hot surface of the griddle and placed it in the middle of the clean teacloth with the others as she avoided the child's eyes. It had to come sometime, this question. She should have been prepared for it.

'Tell me, Auntie Jessie, *please*. Where's my Dad?'

The old woman sighed and turned to the child before her. 'That is something I canna tell you, bairn. It's something only your dear mother, God rest her soul, and the Dear Lord Himself knows for certain.'

'But my Dad must know. He must know who he is.'

Jessie McLeod looked down at the pair of hazel eyes looking up into her own. Trust a bairn to get to the heart of the matter. She sighed. 'Aye, Mhairi, so he must. But he hasn't told me, that's for sure.'

'But he'll tell me, won't he? If I find him, he'll tell me.'

The old woman put a hand on the youngster's shoulder as she hobbled over to the table to prepare the tea. 'Aye, bairn, when that day comes, as come it must, I hope he has the good grace to tell you.'

And so the school year moved on, and the subject of Mhairi's parentage passed into the mists of dinnertimes past, and new matters took up the attention of the young ones who gathered round the stove at one o'clock each school day to eat their jam pieces. But for Mhairi far more worrying than anything that occurred at Auchindoir school was the fact that she was having to stay much longer than she expected with her Auntie Jessie.

When her mother had died, her grandfather had taken 'a turn', as her great-aunt put it, and had taken to his bed the day after the funeral. 'It's only for a few days more,' Mhairi had been told by her Uncle Ian as he walked with her down to the shore to her great-aunt's cottage. But it was turning into much longer than that – weeks in fact, and now there were mutterings amongst the family that he would never rise again. Death was no stranger to those who lived by the sea, but losing his favourite daughter at such an early age, and the imminent departure of his grandchild for England, seemed to have knocked the heart out of the old man.

Mhairi did not mind the woman in whose home she now found herself for there was something of the mystical about old Jessie McLeod that reminded her of her own mother. Her great-aunt had never married: 'Passed all the bonnets looking for a hat!' Long Rob, Jessie's twin brother, would say as he shook his head; but for her part Jessie would simply smile that quiet smile of hers and go about her business. She had quite enough with the Good Lord in her life without any mortal man to be behoven to. In her seventieth year, despite her arthritic knees, she still did a full day's work: gathering mussels from the foreshore for bait for the menfolk, tending her own strip of land at the side of the cottage, which provided her with vegetables for most of the year, and spinning her own wool.

Her daily tasks kept her busy from dawn till dusk and she never ceased to thank God that she still had the health to carry on and had not been plagued with the heart trouble that had dogged her brother Rob over the past few years. She worried about him more than she cared to admit and never more so than over these past few weeks. It appeared that Long Rob had neither the will nor the strength to pick up the pieces of a life that seemed to have ground to a complete halt when Mary Anne died, and Jessie had even stopped taking Mhairi up to see him, for the sight of his grandchild seemed to upset him even more.

It was a stormy night in late November, just after the supper dishes had been washed and replaced on the dresser shelf, when there was an impatient knocking at the door of the cottage by the shore.

'Co tha sin'? Co tha sind?' The old woman's brow furrowed as she glanced first at Mhairi then at the door. 'Who can that be at this time of night?' she muttered, making her way to answer it. But in her heart she already knew.

The door was opened to find the tall, lean figure of Ian, Long Rob's eldest son on the step.

'Ian, is tu.' There was no surprise in Jessie McLeod's voice as she stood aside to allow her nephew to enter.

His tall frame seemed to fill the small room. He had a natural stoop that gave him rather a furtive appearance, and there was a wild look to his eyes that was strangely at variance with the pallor of his face as he looked from one to the other. 'You'd better come,' was all he said.

His aunt reached for the peg on the back of the door to pick up her shawl and wrap it around her shoulders. It had to happen sooner or later. Her brother had been failing visibly over the past few days. She did not bother to change her old slippers for the shoes that were kept mainly for the kirk on Sunday.

'You'd better bide here, bairn,' she said quietly, turning to Mhairi, who sat silently on the wooden settle by the fire.

'No, let her come.'

The two adults looked at one another.

'It's as bad as that, then?'

'Aye, it is.'

'May the Lord have mercy on us.' Old Jessie reached for a smaller shawl from the nail on the back of the door and handed it to the child. 'Put this on, bairn.'

Mhairi obeyed, her usual cheerful chatter stilled by the looks on both their faces. There were times for asking questions but this was not one of them.

With her thumb and forefinger the old woman extinguished the candle that sat on the shelf by the fire then followed the others out the door. A gust of wind from the sea plastered the long fringes of the shawl across her face as she bowed her head against the elements and followed the young man and small child up the steep path to her brother's home.

Mhairi's hand was clasped tightly in her uncle's fist as they made their way steadily up the hill, stumbling occasionally on the loose rocks that lay in wait for the unwary on a dark night such as this. Normally he would have offered to carry her on his back, but somehow the child sensed this would not be right tonight, and, save for their laboured breathing, the three of them continued their walk in silence.

28

The thunderstorms of the day had rolled away, but their echo could still be felt in the hills that glowered above the village. A stiff wind was blowing from the sea, and the tumult of the breakers caused the great ocean to moan and sigh behind them as they made their way, heads down into the gusts, up the winding path to the old man's home.

Long Rob McLeod was lying in the box bed in the kitchen with his other three sons gathered around a table at the far end of the room, by the fire. They acknowledged the new arrivals with grim faces which softened slightly at the sight of the child.

The room was lit only by the peat fire which glowed in the open hearth and caused flickering shadows to appear on the rough walls of the cottage as they entered the low-ceilinged room.

Mhairi remained close to her Uncle Ian as he ducked his head to avoid the dark oak beam that straddled the centre of the ceiling; then, removing his cap, he walked over to the figure lying motionless in the bed. There was a strange look to his eyes as he gripped the worn tweed bonnet tightly between his fingers and looked down at the old man who had sired him. All his life he had yearned for but received no real love from his father, and the love that had flourished within the child's soul had withered during adolescence, and died with manhood. But now as he stood looking down at the shell of what had once been a proud, God-fearing man, a strange feeling took shape in his heart, and a great sorrow and pity welled within him for what never was, and now never could be between them. 'It's Jessie and the bairn here to see you, Father,' he said quietly. He knew the old man felt more for his sister Mary Anne's child than he ever had for any one of his four sons. He motioned for Mhairi to join him by the bed.

The old man's head turned on the pillow. His face looked grey and sunken in the firelight, and the week's growth on his chin was as white as the hairs of his moustache and side whiskers. On his head was a Fair Isle nightcap that had been knitted by Mary Anne, two Christmases past. In the white linen nightshirt his once brawny body seemed half its usual size. A hand reached out, almost imploringly, towards the child.

Mhairi shrank back at first, then, nudged imperceptibly from behind by her uncle, she reached out and placed her tiny fingers in the great fist.

'You've come, bonnie lass.'

'Aye, Granda, I've come.' She wanted to rush into his arms as she had done on so many occasions in the past when worried or upset about something. She wanted him to tell her everything was fine and she would soon be allowed to return home. 'I wanted to come afore but Auntie Jessie said you weren't well.'

The old man sighed. 'Your Auntie Jessie was speaking the truth, bairn.' His voice was faint, so Mhairi had to strain to pick out the words. It had a harsh, guttural sound to it that was unfamiliar to the child's ears, and there was a strangely wistful look in her grandfather's eyes as they burned into hers. 'Sing for me, bonnie lass. Sing for your Granda.' His granddaughter had the voice of an angel, like her mother before her – aye, and even her Auntie Belle away down there among the heathen of Manchester was blessed with the same talent for melting the hardest heart with song.

'What shall I sing, Granda?'

The old man closed his eyes for a moment and no more was he here in this painracked body; he was out on the hills with the bairn at his side, and they were standing on the summit of Craig Mhor looking out to sea.

Slowly his eyelids flickered open, and a fine mist had covered the faded blue as he gazed on the child who was his all. He knew only too well what he would see waiting for him if they were on that hilltop now. As sure as there was a God in heaven it would be waiting, way out there in the bay. The white ship would be weighing anchor long before he ever trod those hills again with the child at his side. 'Sing our favourite song, bonnie lass . . .'

Mhairi glanced at her Uncle Ian, who nodded his head in encouragement.

She took a deep breath and began, haltingly at first, then seeing the smile that began to flicker in her grandfather's eyes, the sweet, clear notes began to fill the small kitchen:

'Lassie, bonnie lassie, come wi' me o'er the hill,
Where the burnie runs sae cheerfully by the golden daffodil,
Lassie, bonnie lassie, it's there I love to roam,
Come wi' me, o'er the hills, lassie,
O'er the bonnie hills o' home.

There are those who say that England's fair,
Or have crossed the ocean blue
To that Land of Liberty to build their lives anew,
But we have wealth beyond their dreams
Wherever they may roam,
God grant us peace to live and die on these
Green hills of home . . .'

Mhairi's voice tailed off, the last note hanging in the air and in the hearts of all gathered round the box bed. The old man had closed his eyes. It was not done for grown men to weep. Even old men had their pride. For over half a century he had been the rock his family had clung to. But that rock was now crumbling before their very eyes. His small world was breaking to pieces, and the most precious part would soon be gone. 'Tell me you'll be a good wee lassie, Mhairi. You'll not give your Auntie Belle down in England any cause for concern.'

Mhairi's brow wrinkled. There they were again talking about this Auntie Belle whom she'd never even met, and this place called England that was surely as far away as Portree, for she had never met anyone who could claim to have been there. 'But I don't want to go to England, Granda. I want to stay here in Ballintuim with you.'

The mist clouded the old man's eyes so the child was a mere blur by the side of his bed. 'That canna be, bonnie lass.'

'Why not, Granda? Why can it not be?' Her childish voice rose in indignation. 'I want to stay here. I want to be with you.'

The old man shook his head as his fingers tightened round those of his granddaughter. 'Did they not tell ye, bairn? Your Grandaddy's not well.'

Mhairi looked at her grandfather in frustration. She hardly recognized him as this frail old man lying before her in the Fair Isle nightcap. In her mind he was still the spry, tweed-bonneted figure, in the dark blue gansey, seated at the fireside of a night, sheeling his mussels and baiting his lines for the next day's fishing. Her grandfather was the rock on which her whole world was founded. To see him lying here in this bed, speaking to her in a voice she barely recognized, it was as if the keystone had dropped out of the arch of her heaven. 'But you'll soon be well, Granda,' she protested. 'You'll soon be up and sheeling your mussels. You will, you will.'

The mist that had clouded the old eyes that looked into hers condensed into a single tear that formed on a lower lid to trickle slowly down the white stubble of his cheek, as the old man shook his head slowly on the pillow. She was just a bairn, yet she was his whole world, and he wished with all his heart that it could be different. 'Bonnie lass, my mussels are a' sheeled . . .'

Those were the last words Long Rob ever spoke to his grandchild, and Mhairi's small hand was still in his a few moments later when he closed his eyes to give a last shuddering breath, then breathed no more.

Her Auntie Jessie took her home to the cottage by the shore. The fire of peats in the inglenook was still aglow as they entered the room they had left barely an hour earlier.

Once they had taken off their shawls, the old woman took the child's hand and led her to the fireside, where she motioned for her to kneel. Then, after placing another peat on the fire, she too knelt down, her old bones creaking as she made herself comfortable on the rag rug, then bent her head in the firelight's glow. Long Rob had been more than a beloved brother, he had been her twin, born of the same flesh, wrought of the same sinew. *'Doilghois ormsa, tha mo chridhe briste*, Mhairi my bairn . . . A great sorrow is upon me, my very heart is broken . . .'

As the two of them knelt there in silence for a moment or two a peculiar calm seemed to descend and Mhairi was no longer afraid. It was as if her grandfather was there with them, surrounding them with his love and strength.

Then, as the child continued to kneel silently by her great-aunt's side, the old woman began to croon an unfamiliar song, the sweet-sounding Gaelic words falling from her lips to fill the child's whole being: old, long-forgotten chants with melodies more ancient than the oldest pine forests, older even than the Isle of Skye itself.

Then, with arms lifted as if in invocation, her face took on a strange haunted look in the fire's glow as she began to repeat an ancient prayer of her people in a Gaelic tongue so ancient that the child could only listen and not comprehend. But she understood only too well the emotion that was behind the words. It was as if the whole world had shrunk to this firelit hearth, and her love and trust in the old woman into whose home she had been taken was complete. They must not send her away from this place. She had no wish to go to that faraway place called England where the world would be full of strangers who knew no Gaelic, and knew nothing of her beloved island and its people.

Ga'r comhnadh's ga'r gleidheadh
Gus an tig an solus geal a maireach . . .

A white-robed angel shall be with us in the dark, till the coming of the sun at morn . . . Mhairi recognized the last few words and they brought a peculiar comfort, for her mother had used them every night as they said their prayers together in the warmth of the old bed in the back room of her grandfather's cottage.

'It's time you were in bed, bairn.' The spell was broken with the words, and the old woman rose painfully from her kneeling position on the floor, to gesture to Mhairi to do the same.

'What will happen to me, Auntie Jessie?' she asked tentatively, a few minutes later, as she neatly folded her day clothes across the wooden arm of the settle. 'Will I really have to go away from here?'

Jessie McLeod half-turned from her seat at the fireside, and a great pity welled within her for this child she had taken into her home. To be cast adrift in the world at such a tender age did not seem right somehow, yet she knew in her heart it was the only answer, for she herself was too old to cope for long with the needs of a growing girl.

She sighed as she leaned forward to coax some life back into the dying fire. 'There are those in this life who are born to stay in the same place forever, bairn, and there are those of us for whom the Good Lord has decided differently. Some are like trees who put their roots down deep into their native soil and would wither and die should they ever be uprooted from that place, and there are others who are like thistledown – they blow with the winds, alighting on a place only to take off again as the winds of Fate decree. Those, some might say, are the chosen ones, for they are carried to all four corners of this earth.'

Her voice was gentle as she continued softly, 'You are

34

the thistledown, Mhairi. Fly on the winds, lassie. Let them carry you where they will, but never forget who you are. Never forget you are Mhairi McLeod from Skye . . . A Child of the Mist . . .'

And Mhairi listened and thought about the old woman's words, so she would remember them and one day understand. But they did little to relieve the pain in her heart as she thought of the fate that awaited her in that faraway place they called Manchester.

The child slept little that night and the old woman beside her in the box bed tossed and turned and moaned now and again as if in pain. Mhairi obtained no solace from sleeping with her great-aunt for Jessie McLeod's old body had none of the warmth and comfort of her own mother; and where her mother had smelt sweetly, the old woman emitted a cloying, unpleasant smell that was peculiarly her own. She thought of her grandfather lying in that bed in her old home and wished with all her heart she could be with him. But they were now using words about him such as they had used about her own mother all those weeks ago; words that meant only one thing: she would never see him again.

The day they buried him she was not allowed to join the procession from his cottage to the kirk graveyard by the shore. She was told she had behaved badly at the burying of her mother and out of respect for the dead such a thing could not be allowed to happen again.

Her Aunt Jessie was the *bean-tuiridh* – the mourning woman – for the village, and even Mhairi knew this was a privilege not to be taken lightly. She was not quite sure, however, what exactly her great-aunt did that was so special.

'What *is* a *bean-tuiridh*, Auntie Jessie? And why do they need one when somebody dies?'

Jessie McLeod paused as she laid out her best black shawl on the morning of her brother's funeral. Just how did you explain to a nine-year-old child something that had been part of the Highland way of life since time immemorial? 'Well now, bairn, it's something that has been with us as far back as there have been men and women on these islands.'

And old Jessie McLeod went on to tell her niece of how in the old days of lang syne, in the Auld Kirk, the death-croon had been chanted over the deceased by the *anam-chara* – the soul friend of the departed; but later on this sacred rite passed into the hands of the elders of the community, and to the mourning women who accompanied the coffin to its last resting place. But now that rite had itself passed to only one woman, and it was to her that a special veneration was due, for the *bean-tuiridh* was also the *bean-ghluin* – the knee-woman – who also attended every birth, so she was there at the coming and the going, to chant her sacred runes for the souls of the newly-born and the dear departed.

'Yes, and long, long before Bonnie Prince Charlie landed at Moidart, Mhairi bairn, the *bean-tuiridh* would celebrate the sacred rite of *Bealltainn* – and better than Christmas, better than Easter, it was. She would make the *caim*, the sacred circle about herself, and once she had made the sign of the cross in it and blessed it in the name of Father, Son, and Holy Ghost, the people of the village would know that no evil could ever come upon them. They had complete faith in their chosen one in whose hands the souls of the departed left this earth, and into whose same hands new life was delivered.

'And to banish the one who lived in the dark loch – the one the Good Book called Satan – the *bean-tuiridh* would chant:

> Torture, torture, man that be!
> Over there, over there,
> Thou shalt be bound, thou shalt be bound,

A raven above thee, a thistle in thine eye,
A venom-serpent coming nigh, coming nigh,
Over there, over there,
Man that be.
Torture, torture, man that be!
Over there, over there,
Thou shalt be bound, thou shalt be bound,
Wind a-freezing through the willows,
Stinging cold like scalding water,
Over there, over there,
Man that *was*.'

And as the old woman finished, the child shivered as if the hand of the devil was upon her. 'And you will say that for my Grandaddy, Auntie Jessie? You will banish the devil from his funeral today?'

Jessie McLeod nodded her grey head as she covered it with the black shawl. 'Aye, bairn, I will say it for your Granda, for Long Rob was more to me than any other mortal man. Today his soul will sail in the white ship, bound far over the Western sea to *Tir-nan-Og*, where neither death nor sorrow can touch him in that beauteous land.'

And so Mhairi watched alone at the window of the cottage as her great-aunt took her leave to walk at the head of the procession that would wind its way down from Long Rob's cottage to the kirk graveyard by the shore. She had promised to remain in her Aunt Jessie's front room, carding wool while the burial took place. 'Idle fingers make mischief,' her great-aunt had warned her. 'I'll expect that bagful to be done by the time I get back.'

Mhairi had looked at the canvas sack full of wool from her uncles' small flock and made no response. Instead, when they had all gone to follow the Minister down the steep path from her grandfather's cottage to the kirk, she had slipped out and made her way up the hill behind the village, and there she had lain in the long grass and looked out to sea.

For a day in early December it was surprisingly warm, with a pale sun shining from out of a clear blue sky. Far below her the ocean was glittering and the only sounds to be heard were the cry of the seagulls and the faint bleating of her uncles' sheep in the field beyond the kirkyard. Such a day her mother would call a benediction. Mhairi did not quite understand, but knew it to be something holy, for she would go on to say that such a peace as was to be found in this place was borne on the winds of God which blew straight from heaven.

Her Uncle Ian had told her that her grandfather was now in heaven, where he would be at rest with her mother, and she felt strangely close to them as she lay there in the long grass and watched the ceremony being enacted down there below in the graveyard. All that carrying of the wooden box and the saying of prayers by the Minister, and the *bean-tuiridh*, had nothing to do with either of them – her Grandaddy or her Mama; they were here with her now – up here on the hillside, where the wind was blowing through her hair and whipping the colour into her pale cheeks. The wind was blowing straight from heaven and she would be there with them one day.

> Grant us the peace to live and die on these
> Green hills of home . . .

And then she began to cry.

It was three weeks into the new year when they sent her away from her island to make the long journey to the home of her mother's sister in faraway Manchester. They were all gathered to say their goodbyes at the stone jetty of the harbour, where a boat was to take her across to the mainland to begin her journey down the wild west coast of Scotland and on into England, that strange land to which Highland folk often travelled never to return.

She was dressed in her Sunday best, and her Auntie Jessie had packed a change of clothing into a tartan woollen travelling rug which was then tied in a knot, for the child to carry on her back. Her Uncle Ian was to go as far as Glasgow with her, and put her on the Manchester train to be met at the other end by her Auntie Belle's husband, the Irishman, Finbar Rafferty.

She was not quite sure what she was expecting when she got to Glasgow; a place a bit bigger than Ballintuim certainly. Bigger even than Portree. But the reality of Scotland's biggest city defied even the most vivid of her imaginings.

Glasgow was a terrifying place which held more people than she had believed to be in the entire world. And the houses seemed to reach right up into the sky itself. People lived right up at the top of them, her Uncle Ian said. Whole families up there in the sky. She shuddered inwardly at the thought.

And the traffic! So many carriages and horses and carts jostling each other as they travelled over the cobbles much faster than any could go on the rough roads of the Highlands. But worse than the traffic, far worse even than the houses in the sky, was the station itself. There the noise was so bad she could hardly hear herself speak. Not that she felt much like talking, for she knew her time in Scotland was quickly drawing to an end.

Her uncle held on tightly to her hand as they waited on the station platform for the arrival of the cross-border train. He was dressed in his best clothes – the same suit of dark blue fustian that he had worn to the funeral of her mother and grandfather, and a new tweed bonnet rested uncomfortably on his thick mop of dark hair.

Ian McLeod was the tallest and quietest of all Long Rob's

sons, but the one felt to be the most trustworthy, for he neither drank whisky nor smoked tobacco, and had no discernible sins save that of an uncompromising belief in the Scriptures, which often led him into fierce arguments with his less than devout younger brothers.

And now he was all that stood between Mhairi and the unknown.

'What if I don't like my Auntie Belle, Uncle Ian? Can I come home if I don't like her?'

The polished black boots shifted uncomfortably on the station platform. 'It's not quite as easy as that, Mhairi . . . You see your Auntie Belle has very kindly agreed to bring you up. You'll be like one of her own bairns.' The child made no response, but continued to gaze up at him with a puzzled look on her face. He tried to help matters: 'Belle is a fine woman, Mhairi, you'll like her. She was your Ma's sister, remember.'

'What if she doesn't like me?'

'Now that's a daft thing to say if I ever heard it. How could she not like you?'

'Well, you and the uncles don't like me any more.'

'Mhairi McLeod, what a terrible thing to say!'

'But it's true!' Her bottom lip trembled. 'If you liked me right enough I wouldn't have to leave home. I could bide in Skye with you and the uncles, and Auntie Jessie.'

Her uncle shook his head and gave a despairing sigh. 'Oh, bairn, bairn . . . How could a young lassie like you bide where you were with the likes o' us – just four grown men and an old woman to look after you? You need a mother at your age – and other bairns to play with.'

'Auntie Jessie says bairns have to work in mills where Auntie Belle lives.' She was not quite sure what exactly mills were, but they surely could not be as much fun as having the freedom of the island from daybreak till dark.

Her Uncle Ian was silent for a moment, then said

40

quietly, 'Aye, well that's as may be, but you've a few years yet till you come to that stage.'

They were loading the last of the other passengers' trunks into the baggage compartment of the train now and there was a slamming of doors by the guards and shouts of 'All aboard for Manchester'. Her uncle's hand gripped hers even more tightly. 'You'll be a good girl, wee Mhairi. Promise me that. And you'll never forget us — you'll never forget Scotland, or Skye . . .'

He placed both hands on her shoulders and went down on one knee so that his eyes were level with hers. *'Beannachd leat, a Mhairi.* May God go with you.' Then he kissed her on the brow. It was the first time she had ever been kissed by anyone other than her mother.

'Wave to me from the train,' he had said, as he settled her into a seat between a young woman and a baby and an elderly man wearing a plus-four suit. But she could not get near the window for others' feet and baggage as the train pulled out, and her failure to keep her promise ate at her heart as the train pulled out of the station and headed south for the English border and that place called Manchester which was to take the place of her bonnie Isle of Skye.

Chapter Three

It was late at night when the train pulled into Exchange Station, Manchester, and the small girl in the brown, rough tweed coat and bonnet would have continued to sleep on if it had not been for the old gentleman in the seat opposite who, spotting the label pinned to her lapel, shook her awake and said loudly, 'Time to waken up, m'dear. We're in Manchester now.'

Mhairi blinked her eyes and stared about her, then a shiver ran through her as reality dawned. She had been dreaming she was back in the classroom in Auchindoir, and the man in the seat across from her looked strangely like Mr McPherson, the dominie. But he was not Mr McPherson. He was a perfect stranger and he was speaking to her.

'Your label says you get off here,' he said, pulling his own case from the rack above his head. 'Is that all the luggage you have?' He gestured with his head towards Mhairi's bundle on the floor at her feet.

The child nodded, glancing down at the knotted travelling rug on which her brown buttoned boots rested. She had an almost uncontrollable urge to cry. She did not want to be woken up to find herself here on this train. It was like some awful nightmare from which she must soon awaken, and she longed for the security of her Auntie Jessie's fireside back in Ballintuim.

The stranger sensed her misery and his bluff face softened. He had joined the train at Carlisle and had been curious about the small child alone in the seat opposite who had remained asleep for the past three hours. She had obviously come all the way down from Scotland and was tired out. 'Here, let me take your things.' He bent down to lift the bundle from the floor beneath her feet. 'Is there somebody to be meeting you at the station?'

Mhairi nodded, not trusting herself to speak for fear the tears would come. Her lower lip quivered and her eyes filled, but she had promised her Uncle Ian she would not cry.

The elderly man took his own bag in one hand and the child's bundle in the other and headed for the carriage door. 'Follow me,' he commanded. 'We'll find the Station Master. He'll know what to do with you.'

Mhairi followed, stumbling, in his wake. She was still half-asleep and her small body ached from hours of sitting in such a cramped position. Her new friend lifted her down from the high step of the carriage on to the platform. She attempted to look about her but found it difficult to focus her eyes which began to smart from the steam and smoke that seemed to swirl around her like some devilish fog. She had never experienced such a noise or crowd before; with the cacophony of strange metallic sounds, the whistling of the trains, the clatter of the luggage trolleys, and the shouts from those on the platform, it seemed as if they had arrived in the bowels of hell itself.

It took only a minute for her elderly companion to find help and she stood forlornly on the edge of the platform as the older, tweed-suited gentleman approached with a taller, younger one in some kind of uniform. 'Now then, young lady, this here's the Station Master. He'll take good care of you until whoever is coming to fetch you turns up.'

She was aware of being taken in hand by the tall   as the older man patted her head and offered som comfort, before disappearing into the thro   passengers still milling around the Glasgo

'Well now, young lady . . .' Her new co

down at her from a great height and frowned, his brow beneath the official-looking cap wrinkling into two distinct lines. He wore a uniform of the same dark fustian cloth as her Uncle Ian's best suit, and he had full sidewhiskers and a moustache with waxed ends that twirled upwards before turning in towards his nostrils. Mhairi had never seen the like before and stared up fixedly at it. This was a queer place indeed, with some very queer folk. If it really was hell, then this must surely be one of the devils.

She was still undecided whether to allow herself to be taken away by him when they were approached tentatively by a much smaller, thinner man with bright red hair and pale brown blotches all over his face. He appeared much more shabbily dressed than either the Station Master or the elderly man on the train, but he had a kind face despite the funny marks on it. He peered down at the label on Mhairi's lapel and gave an embarrassed half-smile as he addressed the railway official by her side, 'I'm not too good at the reading, I'm afraid. Would that say Mhairi McLeod, by any chance?'

The Station Master looked down at the label himself for the first time. 'Aye, that it might. And who would you be?' He cast a suspicious eye over the shabby attire of the younger man before him.

The new arrival adjusted the knot of the white scarf around his neck and cleared his throat. 'Rafferty's my name. Finbar Rafferty. If this here's Mhairi McLeod, then I'm the wee girl's uncle, and I've come to collect her.'

'Is that so now?' The railwayman had assumed a proprietorial air over his charge. 'Well, young lady, do you know this gentleman who claims to be your uncle?'

Mhairi looked from one to the other, her gaze returning to the stranger with the red hair and freckles. He was looking down at her and when he swallowed his Adam's ~~ple~~ bobbed perceptibly beneath the rough, badly-shaven skin of his neck. He looked tired, very tired, and stared down at her from a pair of pale blue, red-rimmed eyes. He was willing her to say yes, so they could be off and out of this place.

Slowly but surely Mhairi shook her head.

'Aha! He's totally unknown to you, then?' The Station Master gave an almost triumphant smile as he laid a firm hand on the child's shoulder.

Mhairi nodded and shrank back behind her new friend, all thoughts of the devil forgotten. If she failed to admit to knowing of this stranger who called himself her uncle maybe the railwayman would send her back to Skye.

Finbar Rafferty looked perplexed. He had walked all the way from Ancoats at a time when he should have been long abed and he certainly had not bargained for this. 'Come on now, Mhairi, you know fine I was to be meeting you. You're to come home to live with me and your Auntie Belle, remember.'

'I don't know him!' Mhairi gripped tighter on the Station Master's hand. 'I don't know him, Mister . . . Please don't let him take me!'

The official rose to the occasion. 'Now don't fret yourself, child. Nobody's taking you anywhere you don't want to go. You can come into the office with me until we decide what's to be done with you.'

'Now just you wait a minute! That's my niece you've got there. I've walked across half the city to take her home with me tonight!' The Irishman's protest was almost lost in a shrill whistle from the nearby train was shunted along the tracks.

'Have you any means of iden-

Finbar Rafferty shook his

Mother of God, what is th

up and take her home. child claims to know nothing

to be up again at fiv

'That's as may

of you.' The Station Master had the bit between his teeth now as he fixed his eyes on the shrinking figure of the red-haired man before him. They had had enough trouble of late from men exactly like this, abducting young children into the ways of the devil. The station was a favourite haunt of theirs. Who was to say he couldn't read well enough and was simply trying to pull the wool over his eyes by claiming to know the child? This city was full of such rogues. And, if proof were needed, the young girl claimed to know nothing about him. They could not both be right. It was his duty to protect the innocent. 'If you want to claim her, you must come back with proper identification.'

Finbar Rafferty looked helplessly at the small child before him. 'Mhairi, love, for pity's sake tell him – tell him I'm your uncle!' he pleaded. The thought of that long walk home in the middle of the night with nothing to show for his trouble and an earful from Belle waiting at the other end was too much to contemplate. And where in God's name was he to get identification at this time of night? He'd need to go to the priest the next day to get some sort of letter saying he was who he said he was – and maybe even that would not suffice; that Station Master was looking at him as if he were some kind of vermin.

But Mhairi's small face was set as stubbornly as it had ever been. She turned it up to the official whose hand she now gripped tightly. 'I don't know him, Mister. I don't know the man. Don't make me go with him.' If she pleaded enough she wouldn't have to go; she wouldn't have to stay in Manchester. This man who owned the railway would don't let him take her home to Skye. 'Please, Mister, 'You heard, sir. some form of prope... is going with no one until I see The man before the ...ation.' hopeless arguing. To ... d out loud. He knew it was get the better of these the sun hardly penetrated and there was barely a blade of grass or the leaf of a tree to be seen anywhere in the industrial heart of the city that was to be her new home.

The Raffertys lived in the district of Ancoats. It was the area which housed the largest cotton mills, and they lined the canal banks, towering six or seven storeys high over the low back-to-back cottages of the workers. Finbar Rafferty and his family occupied the lower two rooms and a kitchen of a four-roomed house in a narrow alley just south of Great Ancoats Street. The house, which had seen better days, had once belonged to the local coal merchant who had sold it to move his family further out of town in the direction of Victoria Park. It had been bought and split in two by one of the many speculators who made their living by renting out accommodation to the thousands of families who had flooded into the city to look for work in its booming cotton mills.

The area south of Great Ancoats Street was a hilly, barren stretch of land, built over by irregular rows of straggling workers' dwellings. Between the houses the clay soil was an uneven wasteland, a depository for all sorts of filth and discarded household matter, where emaciated dogs and cats scavenged in the hope of securing an edible morsel.

The district was cut in two by the Birmingham railway and by the River Medlock, a stagnant, foul-smelling stream that wound its way through what had once been a green and fertile valley. It was known locally as Little Ireland, and the majority of human beings who inhabited the infested dwellings along the river banks had crossed the Irish Sea a generation or more before to escape the worst of the famines, and to find work in the Lancashire mills. For many, the poverty-stricken conditions they found on their arrival differed little from those they had left behind; there was to be no escape from the near starvation and deadly disease that had been part of their daily life. And the man in whose family Mhairi found herself was no luckier than most.

Finbar Rafferty had arrived as an infant at his mother's breast in the winter of 1851, thirty-five years previously, and with the passing generation he had seen his mother and father both dead before the age of forty, and his younger brothers and sisters not live to reach either man or womanhood.

Perhaps it was that that made him fall in love so quickly with the young Scots girl, Belle McLeod, when she first arrived in the city seventeen years ago. They had both been lonely and little more than children. In fact Belle had not yet reached her sixteenth birthday when they plighted their troth that night on the banks of the Irwell as the whole world celebrated the ringing in of another new year.

They had made love for the first time that night, in an alleyway behind the local Methodist Church, and Fiona had been born almost exactly nine months to the day later: a squalling red-faced mite that brought reality home with a vengeance to the young lovers.

Father O'Sullivan had been a fresh-faced young priest then, newly arrived from Cork to tend the flock who had fled the homeland for pastures new across the Irish Sea, and he had remained much more than a local cleric, for he had been as staunch a support as any young couple starting out in life could have wished for.

They had been married in his church when the baby was almost six months underway, for it had taken Belle that long to realize she was about to become a mother. Her own mother had died shortly after the birth of her young sister Mary Anne, and with no other female in the family with whom to discuss such things, Belle had arrived in Manchester almost totally ignorant of the facts of life. In fact, if it hadn't been for the other women and girls in the mill commenting on her growing girth, she would have remained in total ignorance until the moment of birth itself.

Their daughter Fiona had been followed in quick succession by three more children, two boys and a girl, none of whom survived infancy, and then, just when Belle had believed the Good Lord had been merciful and had decided not to put her through it again, the twins, Seamus and Shona, arrived two days before her twenty-fifth birthday.

That was all of eight years ago, and the news, just before Christmas, that she was to be landed with her sister Mary Anne's wee girl, Mhairi, was not exactly met with great rejoicing. There was barely enough to go round as it was, and one more mouth to feed, and back to clothe, was the last thing the small family needed; especially with Fiona presenting them with her own surprise present that Christmas: a baby son who was the spitting image of the younger son of the millowner, Edward Ashton himself.

That young Barnaby Ashton was the baby's father was a fact that was acknowledged but seldom referred to aloud outside the home, for Fiona's father, Finbar, had neither the strength nor the inclination to have it out with the young man in question, especially as Ashton Senior paid all their wages. With the city undergoing a slump in cotton manufacturing at present, there was no question of finding work elsewhere.

The baby, a boy, had woken and was howling for its next feed by the time Fiona and Mhairi arrived safely home from the Exchange Station. The door was opened for them by a thin-faced, perspiring woman, wearing a large canvas apron on top of her dark worsted dress. Her fairish hair was pulled tightly back from her face in a knotted pigtail at the nape of her neck, and her sleeves were pushed up to reveal rough red hands on the ends of scrawny wrists. She reached out and took the infant from its mother and made cooing noises to it as Fiona prodded the reluctant Mhairi through the open doorway.

The scullery they entered was full of steam from a large copper which hissed and spluttered ferociously in the corner; a huge, cast-iron mangle stood alongside it, and a tin bath full of wet, newly-mangled clothes sat on the stone-slabbed floor beside it. Various items of laundry hung from a long wooden pulley above their heads, and through the steam Mhairi could just make out a shining black range on which two flat irons were heating. The fire itself was almost obscured by a wooden goffering stack, in which an item of fine linen was being pressed, and just visible, on the fire behind it, there simmered a large black pot.

'It's broth,' the older woman in the apron said, seeing the child's eyes alight on it. 'Good Scotch broth. Just like your Mammy, God rest her soul, must have made you.'

For some reason Mhairi resented her mother's name being mentioned in this place and she shook her head defiantly, as if to negate anything else the woman might say.

Belle Rafferty handed her grandchild back to its mother and knelt down beside her new charge. 'Well now, Mhairi McLeod, it's tired you'll be from your long journey, I'll be bound, and no' a wee bit frightened into the bargain. But there's nothing to be afraid of here. I'm your Auntie Belle, your Mammy's sister, and your own flesh and blood, and yon poor red-haired galoot you sent packing from the station last night was my man – your Uncle Finbar. He'll not take kindly to you making such a fool of him again, I'll warn you that. But we'll say no more about it. We don't want to get off on the wrong foot now, do we?' She gave a weary smile and there was something about her face that reminded Mhairi of her Uncle Ian: a gauntness, and a trace of wistfulness about the eyes, as if life had dealt one blow too many.

'Uncle Ian says you're to be my new Mama. But I don't want a new Mama.'

'Well now neither you should, for I'll never even try to take her place,' her Auntie Belle said firmly. 'I'm your Auntie Belle and your Auntie Belle I'll stay. Your Mammy's with the Good Lord, bairn. And, if you ask me, she's a damned sight better off than the rest of us poor blighters still toiling here down below!'

As she spoke two small faces appeared at the door that led into the room beyond, and a boy and girl of around Mhairi's own age crept into the room. Despite the freezing cold weather, they were barefoot on the stone slabs, and both had the same bright red hair and freckles as their father.

Their mother turned her head in their direction as she took Mhairi's bundle and set it down on the scrubbed table. 'And these two taurags are the twins, Seamus and Shona. Apart from Fiona, and wee Bobby her bairn, that's our lot – and thank God Almighty for that!'

Mhairi stood in the middle of the floor and looked through the steam of the boiler to the fearsome-looking contraption of the mangle beside it, then looked in turn at the strange faces that were all turned on her. Her gaze turned lastly to the two freckled faces on the same level as herself, and, in unison, two red tongues poked out in her direction. And, for the first time since leaving Skye, she broke her promise to her Uncle Ian and began to cry.

Chapter Four

Mhairi's first few weeks in the Rafferty household passed in a dull haze of glowering skies, cold weeping rain, and the damp, steamy warmth of the family kitchen where her Auntie Belle carried out her trade as laundress to the better off of the parish.

The portion of a house in which the Rafferty family lived consisted of two rooms and a kitchen. Her cousin Fiona informed her that they were more fortunate than the family in the other half of the house for they possessed their own Iron Parker pump in the kitchen, therefore did not have the inconvenience of queuing with buckets to await their turn at the street pump. 'That's where half the scandalmongering in this parish is carried on,' Mhairi was informed bitterly. 'The less we have to do with the rest of them as lives round here the better!'

Fiona also showed her young cousin how to make soap with lye, for her mother's washing. 'This is one of my jobs at the moment, but once you've got yourself settled in, I'm sure you could manage it.'

Mhairi nodded gravely, but made no reply. It seemed there were so many strange things to take in that she wondered how she would ever manage to 'settle in' as Fiona called it.

For some reason she could not quite fathom, one of the two small back rooms was always referred to as 'the front room', denoting it to be the best room in the house. But that rather grand name referred to nothing more than a space ten feet by ten that held only a battered horsehair settee on which the twins slept, three rickety, rush-seated hand chairs, and a dresser of sorts where the family's Sunday clothes were stored.

The focal point of the room, the fireplace, was a mean cast-iron affair which was never lit, to save precious fuel for the copper in the kitchen next door. And, for Mhairi, the one chink of light in the gloom of her new home was the single white china dog which sat proudly next to a Staffordshire figure of Prime Minister Gladstone on the mantelpiece above the empty grate; its opposite number had sat above her grandfather's own fireplace back home in Skye.

Pinned to the wall above the dog was an embroidered sampler with the words: 'How far that little candle throws its beams! so shines a good deed in a naughty world', with the name William Shakespeare carefully picked out in blue wool beneath it. Then beneath that illustrious name, in neat cross-stitch, was that of Isabelle McLeod, aged seven years.

It came as a shock to Mhairi to realize that her Auntie Belle, of the careworn face and rough red hands, was a McLeod like herself. Although her family back in Ballintuim had been at pains to point out that it was to her mother's elder sister she was being sent, somehow the child found it difficult to believe that the woman with whom she now lived had also once belonged to *Eilean a' Cheo*, and had herself been one of the Children of the Mist. There was little in her speech or manner to remind her young niece of Belle Rafferty's origins in that beloved land. And humble though her grandfather's and Auntie Jessie's cottages had been, they were possessed of a homely warmth that was sadly lacking in the abode of Finbar and Belle Rafferty.

Whilst the parlour floor could boast a covering of cracked oilcloth, the other room had merely the bare boards underfoot, but this scarcely mattered for the only

55

floor-space to be seen was the few inches which separated the two iron bedsteads squeezed between the dank walls. One was slightly bigger than the other and that was the one shared by her aunt and uncle; the other more narrow one Mhairi found herself sharing with her cousin Fiona and Bobby the baby.

The mattresses were what her Uncle Finbar referred to as 'donkeys' breakfasts'; they were straw-filled and uncomfortable to the point of pain, and the room itself had a dank musty smell which seemed to clutch at the throat and remain in the nostrils long after it had been vacated in the early morning.

Beyond the windows of both rooms the perpetual rain dripped from a cracked gutter upon the sour soil of the backyard, where a broken cartwheel lay protruding from a pile of rubble which had to be negotiated in order to reach the brick-built privy – or 'the contemplator' as it was commonly called.

The sanitary arrangements for the whole household, and that of the Hogan family who shared the other half of the house, consisted of a tin bucket that was emptied every day into the local midden. This was a job usually carried out by the womenfolk of the households, and one which Mhairi was informed she herself would be able to do just as soon as she was tall enough to lift the pail clear of the ground. 'We're hoping to persuade the landlord to have one of yon new-fangled "thunder-boxes" put in before too long, then the earth and muck'll be removed twice a week by the night cart,' her Uncle Finbar informed her, and Mhairi hoped fervently that this great event would happen quickly, before she grew big enough to carry the pail.

She usually saw little of her Uncle Finbar or her cousin Fiona, for both worked in the nearby Ashton's Great Ancoats Street mill, and, with her Auntie Belle spending all of her days and most of her nights doing other people's washing and ironing, Mhairi found herself left to her own and the twins' devices for most of her waking hours.

Back home on Skye, she had never imagined that such a place as Ancoats could exist, with no grass or trees or flowers, no sight of the sea glimmering in the distance, and no blue canopy of the heavens above. Here the sun seldom shone, and if it did it was impossible to see it through the thick haze of grey smog that hung like a foul blanket above them.

On Skye she had had the gullies and ravines as her playground, and streams and springs where naiads and kelpies dwelt; and sea caves wherein dwelt the monsters that the heroes of Fingal slew. Every sithean and grassy knowe on her island had had its own place in elfin lore, for had not her mother told her that great heroes such as Cuchullin and Fingal had walked its shores? And when she had wandered those grassy knowes with her mother, every glen had whispered a memory of those heroes of long ago.

And now far from those beloved glens, as she sat with the twins on the stone step in front of her aunt and uncle's house, Mhairi told Seamus and Shona of her mother's stories, and of how there was not a sea loch in the whole of Skye that had not played host to such great galley ships as the Reindeer of the North, or the Rider of the Storm. And it was these stories of the great ships that particularly appealed to the twins, for they had never seen such a thing as a ship, nor caught sight of the great expanse of blue water that was called a sea.

And, as the twins' eyes grew wide with wonder, she told of how if you stole down to the edge of the sea at the dead of night, when the tide was high and the moon was full, in the twinkling vault of the heavens one night you might catch a glimpse of a fleet of those white warships, and of the tall, fair men of the North who would guide their white-masted fleet into the glistening stillness of the great bay on which their village stood.

And the twins would beg her to tell them more, for Mhairi's stories were like nothing they had ever heard before. Their own mother was always far too busy and too tired to tell them tales, and they doubted if their father even knew any. 'Tell us more, Mhairi,' they would beg, but their cousin would shake her head, for to talk too much of Skye and its legends was to make the ache within her for her island almost unbearable. So she would shake her head and feel a great pity in her heart for Seamus and Shona who had never known any home but Ancoats, where there was only the drab greyness of each passing day.

'Will you ever go back to Skye, Mhairi?' they asked her and each time she resolutely nodded her head.

'Oh, yes. One day I will go back.' There was nothing of which she was more certain.

'But where will you live, with your Mammy dead?'

Mhairi would close her eyes and see again the grandest castle on their part of the island – far bigger and more splendid than anything they had here in Manchester, far more beautiful even than Dunvegan Castle itself, the family seat of their clan chief, McLeod of McLeod. Her mother would often walk with her over the great hill of Craig Mhor and gaze upon it as it stood there proud and stately, its turrets disappearing into the blue of the heavens above the forests of tall green pines that surrounded it. 'One day I will go back and live in Dalriada,' she would state in a quite emphatic voice. 'It is the most beautiful place in the whole world and one day I shall live there and you shall come and visit me. I shall send my carriage, drawn by four white horses, and you will say, "Oh, Mhairi, for sure this is a wonderful place." And we will eat chicken every day and sleep in a brass bed with clean white sheets, and we shall have shoes for winter *and* summer . . .'

And her voice would tail off at the wonder of it all, and

the twins would look at her and nod sagely back and believe it. Their cousin Mhairi was barely a year older than themselves but she had brought a new dimension into their young lives that made her almost an enchanted being. Whatever she told them must surely be the truth.

And for Mhairi herself, it was only her dreams of returning to Skye that kept her going, for now her world, like theirs, had shrunk to the dirty alley down which they lived and the incessant hissing, steamy cauldron of the small house they all shared.

She still prayed every night like her Mama had taught her — prayed with all her heart that one day soon she would be able to leave this awful place. But just how soon that wish was to be granted, no one could have guessed.

Notice that her world, and that of the whole family, was soon to change dramatically was given one day in mid-March, when it was brought to the attention of old Edward Ashton, of Great Ancoats Street Red Rose Mill, that he had a bastard grandson born to one of his own millworkers, and that not only the child's mother, but also the child's grandfather worked for him. They were actually saying that he shared a grandchild with one of his own operatives! The thought was enough to bring the stout figure of the millowner to a state of near apoplexy.

As Belle Rafferty toiled in the steam of her kitchen half a mile away, and as Mhairi played in the alleyway outside with her cousins, and their father and elder sister Fiona toiled amid the clattering looms of the factory floor, unknown to them all, all hell was being let loose in the oak-panelled office on the first floor of that Great Ancoats Street mill.

Edward Ashton was more than one of the biggest millowners in Manchester, he was little short of God Almighty himself to both his employees and his own family. A tall, proud man who believed in speaking his mind, he was not used to being the recipient of news which all but left him speechless. But speechless he was when his senior clerk, Mr Redway, confronted him with the gossip that was now rampant in the area.

'I wouldn't sully my lips with such lies, Mr Ashton sir, but it's reaching such proportions that I believe it's only a matter of time before your good lady wife, Mrs Ashton herself, hears of it.'

Edward Ashton's normally ruddy complexion heightened even more as he listened to what his senior clerk had to say, then he dismissed the man far more curtly than was merited, instructing him to send for his younger son without delay. 'We'll put a stop to this scandalmongering once and for all in two minutes flat!'

And that was how long, he was certain, it would take young Barnaby to refute the rumours. In fact, he fully expected his younger son to vehemently deny all knowledge not only of the charges laid against him, but all knowledge of the Rafferty girl herself; and that being the case, they could then all go about their business without such damn-fool gossip taking up any more of their time. Why, the lad couldn't knock the skin off a rice-pudding, let alone knock up one of the lasses from the shop floor, where they were a right rum bunch, the lot of 'em.

But, as the young man in question listened, ashen-faced, to the charges laid before him, to his father's amazement, no such immediate denial was forthcoming. On the contrary, in a voice that betrayed little of the emotion within, he admitted that yes indeed, not only did he know the operative Fiona Rafferty, but he could not deny she was the mother of his child. 'I – I realize it must come as a shock to you, Father, but you could not expect me to deny the truth, could you?'

The millowner's brows rose in a mixture of incredulity and barely suppressed fury as the words sank in. Come as a shock to him? Come as a shock to him? 'It's come as more than a bloody shock to me, lad, I'll tell thee that for nowt!'

He drew a hand across a stray lock of grey hair on his balding crown and stared at his son who stood facing him with his back against the window. The young man's naturally pale face was drained of all colour, and, despite the covering of light down on his upper lip that passed for a moustache, he looked far too young for such a charge to be made against him. There had to be some mistake. His father's eyes narrowed as he shook his head. He must keep calm. He was a fair man. The lad must have a fair hearing. 'There's nowt wrong with my hearing, lad, but I cannot believe I'm picking this up right. Art thou actually standing there telling me that this tittle tattle that has reached my ears not ten minutes since is THE TRUTH?'

The last two words were spat out as Edward Ashton rose from his seat behind the desk and rested his weight on his two clenched fists on the blotter before him. 'You are asking me to believe that a son of mine has – has . . .' he searched for the right word, 'has consorted with a slut from the mill floor? And not only that, but has produced EVIDENCE of such goings-on?'

The young man by the window stood his ground, although his insides quaked. 'Aye, Father, it sounds like that's exactly what I'm telling you.'

A low rumbling sound came from the throat of the older man as he rounded the desk. 'By God, lad, have you any idea what you are saying? Have you paid any heed to the consequences of this – this unholy occurrence should it become public knowledge?' His pale eyes protruded in horror at the thought. 'Why your poor mother could never hold her head up in decent society again!'

Barnaby Ashton's expression altered perceptibly from one of virtue at speaking the truth to one of consternation. Trust his father to hit the nail on the head at the first attempt. His mother was precisely the reason why he had not dared to be honest with his family at the outset; he would do anything to avoid hurting her.

'Well, lad, have you nowt to say? . . . Think on, will you? Just imagine what this scandal will do to your mother. By God, it will finish her and no mistake, if it gets out!'

His son stared out of the window, his face totally expressionless, save for a nerve that twitched at the corner of his mouth. This was the moment he had been dreading for almost a year – ever since Fiona had confided in him she was in the family way. The knowledge had staggered him, for at barely twenty he knew almost as little as she did about the reproductive process and had somehow imagined that as it had only happened between them on two or three occasions, there would be nothing to worry about. His elder brother Ted and his wife had been trying for a family for over four years now without success.

'Hell, Hull and Halifax, may the Good Lord deliver us! Even dogs have the sense not to mess their own doorstep,' his father's voice was continuing to boom in his ear. 'To think my own son could be so stupid, so bloody stupid . . . Nay, it's worse than stupidity – far worse – it's crass bloody incompetence!'

He was spluttering and drops of saliva clung to the whiskers around his mouth. He took a linen handkerchief from his breast pocket and dabbed in the general direction. All thoughts of keeping calm were forgotten as he confronted his son. 'Dost thou care nothing for the family name, lad? Are you not bothered if you see your mother into an early grave? Because, mark my words, that's what this'll do to her should it ever get out!'

The two men looked at one another across the square of Indian carpet. 'What do you suggest I do, Father?' Barnaby Ashton spoke the words through gritted teeth for, despite his shame, and concern for his mother, he still had a more than passing affection for the pretty, golden-haired daughter of Finbar Rafferty, and in his heart he had nurtured the dream that somehow they could go on seeing one another without it becoming common knowledge around the town.

'What do I suggest *you* do?' His father gave a derisory snort. 'And just what is a young whippersnapper like you capable of doing, may I ask? . . . Nay, lad, thou's done more than enough already by casting your wild oats in places where they've no business to be.'

Edward Ashton dug his thumbs deep into his waistcoat pockets and shook his head. 'It's a pretty hole you've dug for yourself and no mistake, and I've half a mind to let you bury yourself in it . . . And if it wasn't for your sainted mother, I do believe I would. Bloody queer in the garret you must be to have done such a thing with ne'er a thought for the consequences!'

He walked over to the mantelpiece and stared down into the flames of the fire that burned in the hearth at his feet as he tried his best to think calmly. Never in his wildest dreams had he bargained for such a thing happening within his own family.

As his son watched silently from the other side of the room, he took one of his favourite pipes from a rack on the mantelshelf and a wad of tobacco from a nearby jar, and pressed it into the briar bowl of the pipe with his thumb. His head shook slowly from side to side as he flattened the golden-brown shreds. Never, never had he imagined the young bugger had it in him. 'I'd never have believed it – you of all folk a Jack-the-Lad!'

His son grimaced. He was well aware of his father's opinion of him and that he could never measure up to his elder brother Ted no matter what he did. Then, for the first time since entering the room, the fleeting suspicion of something resembling a smile flickered across his face. But he *had* just done something that Ted seemed completely incapable of doing, hadn't he?

His father's eyes were far from his son's face as, resting a booted foot on the brass fender, he took a spill from the holder on the shelf beside him and bent down to light it from the flames of the fire. As Edward Ashton puffed the tobacco into life, he pondered a moment longer on the problem facing him. There was one thing for sure, he could not have a bastard grandson growing up here right under the very noses of both his beloved wife, and his son Ted and his wife, Cassie. Talk about rubbing salt into an open wound. Poor Ted and Cassie felt bad enough already about failing to provide an heir. For it to become common knowledge that young Barnie here had gone and produced one on the wrong side of the blanket, and by a millgirl at that . . . Well, he shuddered to think of the effect it would have on the family. 'No, there's nothing else for it, they'll have to go!'

His son stared at him. 'Go? What do you mean – go?'

'Go, lad . . . Do I have to spell it out for you? G-O . . . Bugger off. Disappear. Out of Manchester at least – the lot of 'em!'

Barnaby Ashton's face grew paler still. 'But how can they go? They've no other work than what the mill provides. For pity's sake, Father, they've no money to *go* anywhere!'

The briar pipe was puffed thoughtfully. 'Then they'll have to be provided with some.'

His son was silent. Was there nothing in this life that his father's money could not buy? But he knew it was no good arguing; he himself had not a bean and no prospects other than those provided by the man who now stood before him planning the future of a whole family – and a family that included in its number Edward Ashton's own grandchild at that. Barnaby Ashton's lips tightened, and he wished with all his heart that he was a stronger character, that he could tell his father to go to hell and take his money with him. Instead, fighting to keep the bitterness from his voice, he said quietly, 'And where would you suggest they go with this money you're so thoughtfully providing?'

It was his father's turn to remain silent as he turned his mind to the question. Then he nodded slowly to himself as the decision clarified in his head. He would get in touch with his brother, that's what he would do. The young blighter owed him a favour or two anyhow. 'Your Uncle Arthur's always looking for reliable staff.'

'My Uncle Arthur? But he's in New York!'

'Aye, and it's a grand place, New York. So I've been told.'

His son slumped against the window ledge as he stared at his father. New York . . . New York . . . That was miles away across the Atlantic Ocean. In the United States of America . . . They might as well be on the moon.

And that was exactly what Finbar Rafferty himself thought when he was called into that same office less than half an hour later and had the proposition put to him.

His employer did not offer a seat and chose to stand himself as he laid his terms out in a brusque, no nonsense voice that brooked no interruption. He had determined to be fair, but wanted the whole sorry business over as quickly as possible. 'A hundred pounds is a lot of money, Rafferty. More than most can save in a lifetime. But it's on the strict understanding that you all go. There's to be no one left to prolong the gossip more than one day longer than necessary. I'll not have it reaching my wife's ears, I warn you of that.'

The Irishman's legs felt as though they were about to give way. First he was called to the boss's office – a place no ordinary worker was liable to see the inside of in a lifetime at the mill – and then he is told that both he and his daughter have lost their jobs. But before the shock can properly sink in, he is offered a hundred pounds to take his family to America. His mouth was dry and the question came out with difficulty. 'By "all" I take it that you mean Fiona in particular?'

His employer's face darkened at the mention of the

young woman's name. 'Aye, that I do. On no condition is she to remain here in this town. I have the family name to think about.'

Finbar Rafferty looked at him. Not once had the word baby been mentioned between them. In fact no reference had been made at all to the grandchild they both shared, but there was no doubting that it was the birth of young Bobby that was at the bottom of it.

'Well, will you agree, man? Will you go? If you don't, I'll warn you there'll be no other job to be found around here. All t'mills in Manchester will all have closed doors to the pair of you from now on.'

Finbar's lips tightened. He did not have to be reminded of that. The millowners might be at each other's throats where business was concerned, but once one had blacked a worker he might as well pack his bags and say goodbye to this city for good.

'A hundred pounds, Rafferty. Think on, man, it's a lot of money. A helluva lot of money.'

A hundred pounds: it *was* a lot of money. More, much more than he could ever expect to put past after a whole lifetime at Ashton's mill. Savings were something he had never had, and had never expected to have. Just to have enough to put bread in his family's stomachs was enough to ask these days. He thought of Belle slaving away at that washing and ironing till all the hours of the day and night, and with young Mhairi recently arrived in their midst, there was now another mouth to feed and back to clothe into the bargain. 'There would be work guaranteed at the other side, you say?'

'That's what I said, and I'm a man of my word. My brother Arthur's got mills himself in Lowell, and a big house in New York. He's always looking for reliable staff from home. It'll be all settled up with him before you set sail.'

Finbar's pale-lashed eyes blinked twice, then he nodded

slowly, digesting every word. 'I'll have to talk it over with Belle, my wife.'

Edward Ashton's brows puckered. He had not bargained on such a delay and his irritation showed. 'She doesn't work here any longer, so I'm told?'

'No, she takes in laundry these days. She gave up work at the mill when the twins were born. They were sickly at first and . . .' But he had no need to explain to this man or anyone. 'Anyroads, my wife's at home.'

'She'll have no objection, I take it?' The question was put gruffly, but there was a noticeable nervousness in the voice. 'I mean she'd have no reason to gainsay it? Good God, man, it's Hobson's Choice! Either you're out wi' nowt, or you leave here with a hundred pounds in your hand. Surely no woman is daft enough to turn down an offer like that?'

Finbar Rafferty's narrow shoulders shrugged. 'That I cannot say,' he answered truthfully. 'My wife's a proud woman, Mr Ashton, and she's stood by the girl. We both have.'

'Aye, well, there's no need to go into that.'

Finbar ignored the comment. 'As for Fiona herself . . .' The Irishman looked his employer straight in the face. Edward Ashton may well wish to avoid any mention of his daughter, but she existed just the same, and her opinion was perhaps the most crucial of all. Just how Fiona would take this proposal he had no idea. For all he knew she still had a yen for the young man, although if she had any sense she would know that was as far as it would ever go. He had better clear it up though, so there could be no mistake. 'Fiona will need to know . . . Is your son in full agreement with these proposals, may I ask?'

Edward Ashton cleared his throat and his tone was resolute for the young woman must be left in no doubt. 'Aye, that he is. They were put to him this very day in this office. He stood where you are standing now and he did not gainsay them.'

Finbar replaced his cap on his head. Well, that was that, wasn't it? Just as he thought. The lad was obviously a weakling and Fiona could pin no hopes on him, now or ever. 'You'll get our reply in the morning.'

Edward Ashton came round from behind his desk. It wasn't quite the immediate result he'd hoped for, but things certainly looked more promising than they had ten minutes ago. 'You can let me know when the pair of you come to collect your wages.' It was just as well to remind him that he and his daughter would be out of a job from tonight. 'If you're agreeable the other money will be here waiting for you in new £5 notes and my secretary can arrange the sailing.' He cleared his throat, 'The price of the tickets will, of course, be deducted accordingly.'

'Sure and you think of everything, don't you?'

Edward Ashton ignored the irony in the other's voice and gave a benign smile. 'I'm a fair man and I like to think I do my best by my workers, Rafferty, and I expect them to do their duty by me.'

And so the two men parted company. There was no handshake and no polite leave-taking. Finbar Rafferty did not even attempt to hold out his hand. He merely adjusted his cap and turned to walk, head high, out of the door. He did not possess much in this life, but what little pride he had left he was determined to hang on to.

Chapter Five

'Well, Belle, what do you say to it?'

Belle Rafferty looked up from ladling the broth into the plates on the table before her and met her husband's eyes. She paused, replacing the ladle in the pot, and setting them both down on the edge of the range. America . . . It had always been one of her unspoken dreams. What was it they called it – the Land of the Free? The New World where all men were created equal, and no man or woman need feel inferior to another.

She passed a hand over her brow and her red-rimmed eyes moved to the copper still bubbling in the corner of the kitchen, and the pile of newly dried clothes waiting to be ironed in the wicker basket beside it. She glanced down at her hands; they were never anything these days but red-raw and chapped from being in water the whole day long. God willing, in America there would be no more slaving with hard soap and soda in order to keep the hands of other women lily-white. 'New York, you say?'

'Aye.'

'And there'll be work waiting?'

Her husband nodded as he picked up his spoon. 'Ashton guarantees it. I haven't got all the details yet, but I believe he's to fix it up with his brother Arthur.'

Belle Rafferty turned her gaze to her elder daughter. 'And what have you got to say on the matter, Fiona?'

Fiona Rafferty had been silent ever since returning home from the mill with her father. After leaving their employer's office he had made straight for his daughter to tell her what had passed between himself and Edward Ashton, and the news had struck a blow from which she had not yet recovered.

'You never really expected the lad to marry you, now did you, lass?' It was her father who spoke.

Fiona shook her head and pushed back an imaginary strand of hair from her forehead. Avoiding all their eyes, she fixed hers on the curtain rail of the window opposite.

'Young Bobby will have a better future over there than he could ever have here, that's for sure. And that goes for the twins and Mhairi too.' Finbar Rafferty glanced across at the three young members of the family who sat silent and wide-eyed at the other side of the table. 'What chance have they got here? Your mother and I have already seen too many bairns into an early grave in this place.'

Before her daughter could respond, Belle Rafferty pushed the last filled plate in the direction of Mhairi and said quietly but firmly, 'Well, I'm for it. I haven't got that much pride that I'd let it come between me and my wits. I say we take the money and go. There would be no virtue in staying here and starving.'

'Well, that's that then, isn't it? It seems like your minds are already made up. There's not much point in me giving you my opinion!' Fiona pushed her untouched plate from her and rose from the table to rush to the bedroom beyond.

The slamming of the door resounded through the kitchen. There was a moment's silence, then first Shona began to cry and then Bobby, the baby.

Finbar and Belle Rafferty looked at one another, but neither made a move to go after her. The decision had already been made in both their minds, and they knew there could be no going back on it. They could only pray it was the right one.

It was a cold, blustery day in early May 1887, when the

family set sail from Liverpool's Albert Dock aboard one of the Inman Steamship Company's newest vessels, the packet *City of Paris*; and it was a crisp, sunny morning two weeks later when they caught their first sight of the New World.

It had not been a happy trip, for the baby had taken ill when they were barely two days into the crossing. Young Bobby had kept them all awake for the next four nights, before finally succumbing to the fever on the fifth day. Fiona herself had been almost unable to raise her head through a bad bout of seasickness caused by the heavy swell, and the job of nursing the ailing child had fallen mainly on Mhairi. The infant had never been a thriving child to begin with and it was with growing apprehension that she watched as the crying and fretting gradually subsided and the bundle in her arms grew lighter with each passing day.

Somehow to watch the angel of death hovering over so innocent a being as little Bobby seemed to symbolize all that was wrong, all that was unjust in this life. 'In the midst of life there is death, child. It is a fact we must accept. The Good God gives and the Good God takes away. It is not for us to question His motives in so doing,' her Auntie Jessie had told her after her grandfather's funeral, but as she sat with the pale, quivering frame of little Bobby in her arms, she wondered if she could ever be like her Auntie Jessie, if she could ever accept the unacceptable.

> 'Bobby Rafferty's gone to sea,
> Silver buckles on his knee,
> When he comes back he'll marry me,
> Bonnie Bobby Rafferty . . .'

She would sing the old sea shanty, as she rocked him in her arms, personalizing it just for him.

71

'Bobby Rafferty's fresh and fair,
Combing back his yellow hair,
He's my love for ever mair,
Bonnie Bobby Rafferty . . .'

And tears would come to her eyes and spill down her cheeks as she smoothed the damp strands of fair hair back from the sweating brow of the infant in her arms. 'Bonnie Bobby . . . My bonnie Bobby . . .' she would whisper into his tiny ear. And he was a bonnie bairn, as bonnie as his young mother, who would watch silently from her own sick-bed and curse the God who had brought it to this, and bless the child in whose arms her own son lay, as hour by hour the life ebbed from his tiny frame. There seemed to be an affinity between the two — two small human beings to whom fate had dealt the blow of being born fatherless in a world where every child needed all the love, all the support it could get. And a great love welled in Fiona's heart for not only her beloved Bobby, but for the little girl who spent long, lonely hours softly singing in the voice of an angel, into ears that were no longer hearing. Yes, long after he had breathed his last breath, Mhairi crooned her lullabies to the still, small frame in her arms.

He was buried at sea, in a coffin so tiny that his grandfather could carry it under one arm. There had been a short service on deck, attended by the Captain, four senior members of the crew, and the family.

The priest who officiated was a Father Docherty from Omagh who had befriended the family early on in the voyage. He too was travelling out to New York to take up a position in a new church that was being built to cater for the squalid Irish shantytown that was going up on Fifth Avenue at 116th Street.

Although Belle was not born a Catholic, and her husband remained loyal to the faith more by habit than conviction, in times of trial they both turned with open hearts to the Church as their one rock in an uncertain world. Father Docherty's short sermon on deck, before the infant's coffin was slipped overboard into the restless waves, meant a great deal to them both; and for their small niece, Mhairi, the occasion also made a deep impression for quite another reason: it was the first time she had heard her Auntie Belle sing.

The priest sought to comfort Fiona, the young mother, by reminding her that her child would be waiting for her in heaven, where all souls would one day be united in Christ's love. He likened the journey that the dead child was now embarked upon to their own journey to the New World. '. . . And we must remember as we stand here on the deck of this ship that the hope of heaven in a time of trouble is like wind and sails to the soul.'

Then he took as his message the words from Revelation 21, verse 25: 'the gates of it shall not be shut at all by day; for there shall be no night there.'

And as he closed the Good Book, and his words echoed in the minds of the small group gathered by the ship's rail, Belle Rafferty's fine contralto voice had rung out quite spontaneously as the tiny body of her first grandchild, encased in its cheap pine casket, disappeared beneath the ocean's swell:

> 'There is a gate that stands ajar,
> And through its portals gleaming
> A radiance from the cross afar
> The Saviour's love revealing.
>
> Oh, depth of mercy, can it be
> That gate was left ajar for me . . .'

The solitary voice, quavering slightly from lack of practice, and with the emotion of the moment, touched the hearts of all who heard it. It was the voice of an angel coming from the lips of a woman whose careworn face and body belied her age of not yet forty years; and as Mhairi gazed up at this woman who was her mother's own sister, it was the first time she thought of Belle Rafferty as truly beautiful.

When the song was ended, there was a long silence, for no one seemed inclined to break the spell that had been woven by the strange, haunting beauty of the moments that had gone before.

Father Docherty cleared his throat. 'What we have just heard is a hymn of faith. Faith in Our Lord and the life to come. Cling on to that faith as you leave this place of sorrow. For what is faith? Faith, dear friends, is an image of eternity. All things are present in it – things past and things to come. It converses with angels and antedates our hymns of glory. For every man, woman and child who has this faith the path is straight, for that light has been given. Go onward in faith, dear friends, and leave the rest to God . . .'

Then, after the priest had given his final blessing, and the last prayer was said, Finbar Rafferty shepherded his family before him. The three remaining children held hands as they walked quietly back towards their quarters below deck, to leave Fiona alone to say her own goodbye to her child.

Mhairi paused at the top of the wooden steps for a last glance at her cousin. Fiona was standing alone against the rail of the ship, her fair hair flowing free of the black woollen shawl, and she was gazing far out beyond the horizon. But she was no longer weeping. There was a look of almost defiance in her face and the child puzzled on it as she lingered at the top of the staircase.

She had been strangely moved by what had just occurred. The offering of the infant's body to the waves had seemed right somehow. And the service that followed – it had all fitted in. Her mind went back to the stories her

74

mother had told her on Skye, and to her Auntie Jessie who was always present at times like this, and who said words – magical words – to the evil spirit they called Satan, who lived in the dark loch.

But Bobby's small body had not been offered to the dark waters of the loch, it had been offered to Jesus, and the sea. The sea . . . It was that same sea on which the White Ship sailed, and the sky above them was that same sky in which the white merle flew.

She gazed up into the scudding clouds as the salt-wind whipped the colour into her cheeks. Suddenly it was all One. It all fitted into place. Jesus, Satan, the sea, and the winds of Fate that were blowing all around her at this moment. A shiver ran through her, and she clasped the edges of her coat tighter around her slight frame as she turned from the lone figure of the bereaved young mother on deck, and walked slowly back down the steep stairs to join the others.

Fiona sank into a deep gloom after little Bobby's death and the only person with whom she could share her feelings was Mhairi. The two shared a bunk that now seemed silent and empty without the presence of the infant they had all grown to know and love. As she set about the painful task of packing up her dead child's few possessions, the young mother looked across at her companion. 'I'll pay them back for this, Mhairi McLeod, you see if I don't,' she vowed. 'One day I will return rich and famous to Ancoats and spit in the face of Edward Ashton and his fine family for killing my son.'

She was convinced that they were responsible for Bobby's death and now hated with a passion the young man she had once loved. And Mhairi wondered at the strange world of grown-ups whose affections could change so suddenly. She had loved only two people in her young life, her mother and her grandfather, and they were both dead, like Fiona's baby. The thread between life and death had never seemed more fragile.

'Will it be better where we're going, Fiona?' she asked. 'Will life be better in the New World?'

And Fiona had taken her young cousin's hands in her own and said with a vehemence that surprised them both: 'We will make it better, Mhairi, love. You see if we don't.'

When the ship finally docked at New York, because there had been a death in the family on the voyage, they were kept much longer than most of the other passengers at Castle Gardens. The Emigrant Landing Depot, as it was officially called, was based at the very tip of Manhattan, near the Battery. It had been built originally as a fort, just after the war of 1812, to defend New York against an attack by the British, Father Docherty informed them before taking his leave, with an exchange of addresses and promises to keep in touch. It consisted mainly of a huge rotunda into which the newly-arrived immigrants were disgorged, and on the day the *City of Paris* docked and released its cargo of exhausted passengers, it seemed to Mhairi that half the world was already there milling around waiting to gain entry to their new homeland.

Most of the people from their own ship were Irish women and children arriving to join their menfolk who had travelled on before to find work, and used as she was to the sight of poor people, Mhairi's young heart went out to the wretched condition of most of the emigrants, with their pathetic bundles and often shoeless children. Almost all, like themselves, had travelled steerage and she knew for a fact that many of the infants and one or two of the mothers had met the same fate as Fiona's Bobby on the voyage.

It was almost twenty-four hours before they had cleared all the formalities, including the indignity of being officially deloused, and the carriage and cart that had been sent from the household of Arthur Ashton to meet the boat had been forced to return to their owner's mansion and come back the following day.

The carriage that was sent by their new employers was not as grand as that used by the family themselves, but it was far grander than anything ever ridden in by anyone in Finbar Rafferty's household before. And, as it clattered past the Battery Gardens and on into the wide thoroughfare known as Broadway, Mhairi could only gaze around her in wonder.

Unlike Manchester, here the sun was shining from out of a cloudless blue sky and even the very cobblestones seemed to shine far brighter than any she had known back in the old country. Many of the houses were of brownstone, but those of redbrick seemed of a deeper hue than those that lined the streets back home, and the iron railings were most surely a brighter shade of green.

And the traffic! She pulled at the sleeve of Shona seated next to her, to point out the different types of transport that jostled for space over the cobbles: omnibuses, hackney cabs and coaches, phaetons, gigs and large-wheeled tilburies all vied with one another for superiority on the wide expanse of street.

'Oh, look at *them*!' Negro coachmen resplendent in finest livery clattered past in control of a coach even grander than their own. Neither the twins nor Mhairi had ever seen a black man before, and the sight of so many dark faces sent a shiver of excitement through them. This was indeed a strange and wonderful place.

All sorts of outfits seemed to be on view; there were black hats, white hats, straw hats, glazed caps, and even fur hats; and coats of every conceivable colour and material: black, brown, red and blue, nankeen, striped jean and linen. And the ladies! Even Belle Rafferty was not beyond a gasp or two at the sight of the belles out in their spring finery of rainbow silks and satins, their parasols a-twirl. 'Did you ever see such ribbons or silk tassels, Fiona? Or such brightly coloured cloaks ... Just look at the linings of those hoods!'

While the cart with their luggage carried on straight to its destination in Amity Place, their carriage crossed Broadway into another long main street called the Bowery. Here the stores looked not quite so grand, the ladies and gentlemen not quite so splendidly turned out as on Broadway, and the lively whirl of carriages and phaetons was exchanged for the deeper rumble of carts and wagons. It was in the Bowery that the coach stopped off to pick up a consignment of fresh oysters from a store boasting a real aquarium in the window, before they continued their journey to the brownstone, Ashton mansion in Amity Place, just off Washington Square.

Once arrived at Lancaster House, the Ashton family's domain, they were met downstairs in the servants' quarters by Mrs Donnelly the housekeeper whom Belle Rafferty was to replace. The housekeeper was an ancient, tiny woman, almost as round as she was tall, with sharp, dark eyes behind her spectacles. Her hair, which was done in a tight bun, was snow white and when she opened her mouth to welcome them to their new home her brogue was as thick as the day she set sail from her native land over half a century before. And to Finbar's delight it transpired the old woman was originally from the very town in County Mayo from where his own family had emigrated to Manchester a generation before.

The housekeeper clasped her hands in pleasure as she smiled up at the new under-butler before her. 'Well now, you couldn't be anything other than a Rafferty with that colour of hair!'

Finbar beamed. 'And would you have been knowing my folks then, Mrs Donnelly, ma'am? Peggy and Seamus they were by name.'

The old Irish woman could only shake her head. 'I'm afraid I was little more than the size of yon three bairns of yours when we landed in America,' she answered truthfully. 'But I have a mind that the wee girl that I chummed was a Rafferty, and I swear to God she had hair the colour of a pile of blazing straw. Did your father have a sister by the name of Bridie, by any chance, for I'm sure her name was Bridget, the same as my dear mother's?'

Finbar shook his head. 'I never knew any of my Irish relatives,' he said regretfully. 'And I doubt now if I ever will.'

'Well now, that's a real shame and no mistake. But I'll tell you this for nothing – coming to America is the best thing you'll ever do!' She looked round the whole family standing just inside the kitchen door. They were a pretty exhausted-looking, bedraggled bunch and her heart went out to them. 'Sure and you'll be too tired to take anything in just now, but it's a grand country you've come to – for them that has a mind to get on, that is.'

Her eyes fell on Mhairi, standing a little apart from the others, a dreamy look in her hazel eyes. 'And you, wee girl, are you glad to be here?'

Mhairi's thoughts were still with all those beautifully dressed ladies of Broadway. Some day she would be one of them. 'Oh, yes,' she replied from the heart. 'I love New York.'

And she continued to love New York for the rest of her childhood. The area around the Ashton house in Amity Place, in particular, she grew to know and love almost as much as her beloved Skye.

But the contrast between the teeming city and her island could not have been greater; even the changing seasons here were marked in different ways. Instead of the rich yellows of the broom setting the hillside behind her grandfather's cottage ablaze every May, here the hurdy-gurdy man's appearance on the streets around Washington Square was as sure a sign of spring as the appearance on the sidewalks of the marbles, hoops and tops, or the tangling of kite lines in the branches of the ailanthus trees that bordered the sidewalk outside their new home.

79

Amongst the boys of the neighbourhood the talk at this time of year was all of baseball, and of the coming season, while down at the Polo Ground, the keepers would be preparing the infield for the season's opener. Was this the year the Giants would take the coveted National League Pennant? In truth, Mhairi herself couldn't care less, but to young Seamus it was fast becoming a matter of life and death.

But for most of the children in the neighbourhood, you knew spring was in the air for sure when at the newly renovated Madison Square Garden, on Fourth Avenue and Twenty-fourth Street, they began preparing for the arrival of Barnum, Bailey and Hutchinson's circus's return from its winter quarters down south.

Mhairi had never even heard of a circus until she arrived in New York, and she could barely contain her excitement at the start of each new season as she stood with the others on the sidewalk and watched P. T. Barnum himself lead his monster torchlight parade through the streets of downtown Manhattan.

There had been a race to look at the pictures in the *New York Herald* the following morning and, being a better reader than the twins, Mhairi was elected to read out the report over the breakfast table. She had cleared her throat and waved her arm dramatically as she declaimed that what they had witnessed the night before was '. . . A grand, glittering, gleaming, glistening, glorious, gigantic coruscation, blinding to the eye and two miles long.'

'What does "coruscation" mean, Mhairi?' Shona had asked, as her mother dished the last waffle on to the serving dish.

Mhairi looked scornful. 'If you don't know that, Shona Rafferty, you don't deserve to go and see the show!' The twins had gazed up at her in awe. For someone only a year older than themselves, their cousin was cleverer than just about anybody they knew.

It was on the way out of the door to school some fifteen minutes later that Mhairi was collared by her Auntie Belle. 'And just what *exactly does* "coruscation" mean, young lady?'

Mhairi had blushed the colour of the twins' hair.

After school there was usually an argument between herself and her cousins about who would do which chores. Running errands was by far the favourite, and not really regarded as a chore at all, for there was a fascinating assortment of stores, all within a short hop and skip of home. For helping around the kitchen they would receive the odd dime or two, and these were always spent in the little shops on the east side of Sixth Avenue, such as Walduck's bakery, with its mouth-watering aromas of newly-baked bread, fresh cracker rabbits, and trays of crinkled gingerbread.

It was to Mr Jones, the stationer, that they went for their new slates each Fall, and even these were fancier than anything they had had back home in England; for these had a place in the wooden frame to hold the stone pencil that would scratch and squeak its way through innumerable sums before the year was out. Very quickly they learnt to soften the pencil between their lips, and the taste of that slate pencil on her tongue Mhairi was sure would remain with her forever. Eventually Mr Jones put on sale the last word in refinement: something called a book slate, which was made of a light, unbreakable, black substance on which a soft pencil could be used; but it was quite a while before Finbar and Belle Rafferty's income could run to such a luxury.

The New York Ashtons proved good employers, however, with the American-born Mrs Adeline Ashton being particularly fair minded and approachable. In no time at all after the retirement of Mrs Donnelly, Belle Rafferty had firmly entrenched herself as a housekeeper to be respected by all, and feared by some, particularly the under-housemaids. For his part, Finbar found himself serving his time as under-butler and personal valet to Arthur Ashton himself, and he had very little but good to say about the man who, by blood, may have been the younger brother of Edward Ashton of Ancoats, but by nature was far more amenable and liked nothing more than to share a joke or two with his staff.

Shortly after their arrival in New York, Fiona decided not to stay on in the Ashton household. Her parents were not happy at their elder daughter's decision to look for employment elsewhere, but Mhairi, young though she was, thought she understood. She remembered what her cousin had whispered to her in the confines of that narrow bunk aboard ship on the way over, and she knew that any house that carried the Ashton name would be an anathema to Fiona for the rest of her life.

Instead she obtained employment with a family by the name of Niemand, who, she informed them, owned a large apartment on Fifth Avenue, and although she volunteered little information about her employers, there was general agreement that they must be generous indeed. On her occasional visits home, Fiona's day-gowns were like nothing they had ever seen on one of their own kind before. Such silks and satins, frills and flounces seemed more fitting on the likes of Mrs Ashton than on the daughter of an illiterate Irishman by the name of Finbar Rafferty, and her mother Belle told her so in no uncertain terms. 'And just where in heaven's name did you get the money to dress like that?' she demanded, the first time her daughter brightened the downstairs kitchen door in such an outfit.

Fiona had flushed a deep pink and adjusted the frill around her slim neck. 'It's not what you think!'

'And just *what* do I think, may I ask?'

Her elder daughter looked at Belle defiantly. 'It's paid for fair and square,' she said indignantly. 'There's a secondhand store on the Bowery that sells the cast-offs of the swells on Fifth Avenue and the like. I save the money from my wages, fair and square, like I said.'

Belle Rafferty looked at her daughter silently for a moment or two, then, biting her tongue, she turned back to checking the linen cupboard. What Fiona had to say might or might not be true, but she would as soon believe the former. Pretty young women who turned out in such fine apparel came by it in one of two ways. She just prayed to God Fiona had come by it in the way she hoped, for the alternative did not bear thinking about.

Fiona's visits were always a high spot in Mhairi's young life, for her elder cousin exuded a glamour not to be found in the life below stairs at Lancaster House. And Fiona was now talking quite differently too, for gone were the clipped vowels of Lancashire, and in had come a quite entrancing American drawl. It made both Mhairi and the twins resolve to master the local accent themselves as soon as possible, for then and only then could they consider themselves to be true New Yorkers, and that was what they desired more than anything else.

Chapter Six

East side, West side,
All around the town,
We played ring o' roses,
London bridge is falling down.

Boys and girls together,
Me and Mamie O'Rourke,
Tripped the light fantastic
On the sidewalks of New York . . .

When all their chores were finished in the big house, Mhairi and the twins would be allowed out to amuse themselves and play street games with the other children in the neighbourhood. There was something exciting about learning a whole new set of rules and rhymes. It was like being initiated into a secret society, one in which grown-ups had no place:

Engine, engine, number nine,
On the old Chicago line.
If the train should jump the track
Do you want your money back?
Y-E-S spells Yes.
But if you do not want to play,
Please take your hoop and run away!

And very often that was exactly what Mhairi would do. She would take her hoop and stick and leave the twins playing happily with the other kids on the block, and she would head towards the north-west of the Square where lived a colony of substantial people of New England stock in their tall redbrick houses.

In one of those houses she had made a particular friend of a pretty blonde girl of her own age by the name of Amy Lowell. Amy's parents were originally from Boston, where her grandparents still lived, and Amy's father Harold was a substantial stockholder in the National Park Bank, along with such illustrious names as the millionaires John Jacob Astor, Cornelius Vanderbilt, Stuyvesant Fish and Isaac Guggenheim. Amy would tell Mhairi how these friends of her father had more money between them than the Queen of England herself. 'Why, just think, Mhairi – my Daddy's friends could go to London and buy Buckingham Palace itself if they had a mind to!'

And Mhairi would listen and wonder about these men who had more money than the old Queen Victoria herself. It gave her a good feeling to know that somehow she was almost within their enchanted circle; that through her friendship with the likes of Amy Lowell, the world of top-hatted millionaires and ladies in beautiful gowns was not now so far removed from her own. It made the dark, squalid back streets of Ancoats seem a very long way away, and she never ceased to thank God that somehow He had found a way to take her out of there and bring her to such an exciting city as New York.

The only trouble with her friendship with Amy, however, was that she was never actually invited upstairs in the Lowell household. In fact, all Mhairi's contacts with her new friend took place either over the garden fence on a Sunday afternoon, when Amy was allowed out to 'give her dolls the air', or on those very special occasions when she was invited down to the kitchen, where Lizzie the cook would reach into her cookie jar and allow them each a brown crispy gingerbread man to eat with the tall glass of fresh milk she poured from the flagon that sat cool and creamy on the cold slabs of the pantry floor.

Mhairi never liked to ask Amy why she was never invited upstairs to meet her family, but Lizzie seemed to know. 'The Lowells ain't like you and me, child,' she once remarked to Mhairi, when her young friend was well out of earshot. 'Them's rich folks — from New England!' She said the last two words proudly, rolling her eyes heavenwards, as if to speak the very name of that part of the Atlantic seaboard was something fine. And Mhairi looked down at her worn boots and checked brown stuff dress and knew in her heart that the cook was right.

These New England people such as Amy's family were considered newcomers, however, and were rather looked down upon by the kith and kin of her other best friend Kati van der Donck. Kati's family was one of those of purely Dutch origin whose association with the city went back to its very beginnings. Never had Mhairi known anyone with as many relations as the plumply pretty Kati, with the high-pitched giggle, and the two long brown braids looped neatly about her ears. And so far back did Kati's New York credentials go, she informed Mhairi, that it was a direct ancestor of hers, a certain *Jonge Heer* by the name of Adriaen van der Donck, who had had the district of Yonkers named after him.

Mhairi had first noticed Kati passing by in the street with either her mother or governess long before Amy introduced them. It would have been hard not to notice the pretty dark-haired little girl who wore such a vicious-looking metal calliper strapped to her left leg above an ungainly brown boot. Whatever could be the matter that forced her to have to wear such a terrible contraption? Mhairi was soon to find out for 'Polio' was the funny word that Amy whispered when Mhairi enquired one day what was wrong with the leg of her very best friend.

When they first met Kati regarded herself as Amy's

'extra-special and bestest friend' and Mhairi was aware of a sense of resentment in the little Dutch-American girl that someone else should be finding her way into Amy's affections. But then a strange thing happened, for Kati suddenly began to make a great fuss of Mhairi, especially when Amy was not around. It was as if she could not bear her friend to have anything she did not have – even if only the friendship of someone who did not wear fancy clothes and have expensive dolls with real hair to show off every weekend. 'Of course, my Heidi's a German Heubach,' Kati informed Mhairi one day, smoothing the wrinkles from the doll's satin flounced skirts. 'Mimi, Amy's best one, is only a French Gaultier her folks brought back with them from Paris last Fall. They are not half so expensive!'

Mhairi looked at her in wonder. All this talk of German Heubachs and French Whatever-the-name-was . . . Why, surely dolls were things to be loved and cherished, and what did it matter where they came from? But then she realized that it did matter to Kati. It mattered very much. In dolls, as in friendship, Kati did not like to be outdone, so Mhairi held her peace and listened with a strange mixture of emotions in her heart when her new Dutch friend took her hand one day and told her, 'You will have much more fun at *my* house, Mhairi McLeod. And I won't be so mean as to keep you hidden from my Mom and Dad.'

Those words first sent an expectant thrill through Mhairi, then realization dawned. Could it be that neither of them really believed all those stories she told them about her own background? Could it be that like Lizzie, the Lowells' cook, they could tell by her lack of pretty clothes, and who knew what else, that she really was not the orphaned daughter of a great Scottish clan chief? Could it be that they had known all along, and although Amy was ashamed to take her upstairs, Kati was a really true friend who, even if she did mainly want her friendship to outdo Amy in Mhairi's affections, at least would not keep her hidden away in the downstairs kitchen? Mhairi found herself puzzling on these matters whenever she was alone in her room back at Lancaster House and it hurt to think she might be considered not good enough to ever be the 'extra-special and bestest friend' of either of them. And the more her insecurity grew, the more she determined to keep their friendship and prove herself worthy and as good as them in every way.

In order first to make friends, and then keep up with the stories Amy and Kati told of their families, Mhairi had had to furnish them with equally impressive information about her own background. They were aware she lived in the Ashton house on Amity Place, but she was careful never to invite them home for tea, for then the tales of her beautiful castle on Skye would be found out for the lies they were. As far as Amy and Kati were concerned, she was determined to have them believe that she was Mhairi McLeod, the orphaned daughter of one of the Lords of the Isles, who, after her parents' deaths, was being brought up by her aunt and uncle, Arthur and Adeline Ashton, and she lived in constant dread of them discovering otherwise.

But the more she began to suspect that, like Lizzie, they might be doubting her word, the more colourful and embellished her tales became until she almost came to believe them herself, especially when she talked of her father. No longer was he a faceless creature; now he was as tall and handsome as they came, in his kilt of red tartan, with his plaid flung over his shoulder, and the cocked hat with the feather from the golden eagle itself, which denoted that this was no ordinary man, but a clan chief: a Lord of the Isles, in fact, and they didn't come any higher than that.

At first Belle and Finbar Rafferty were suspicious of their charge's friendship with children from such a different background to their own, but they put most of

Mhairi's talk of her new friends down to childish imagination, until an unprecedented visit below stairs one day by Kati's mother, Emily van der Donck, brought everything out into the open.

Mrs van der Donck had called upon their employer to invite the child she assumed to be the Ashtons' own adopted daughter on a short visit to their weekend retreat up-country. Only the amazed face and total incomprehension on the part of Adeline Ashton made Emily van der Donck stop in her tracks and enquire further: 'Well, if you yourself have no adopted Scottish child, would there be anyone else in the house who might?'

Adeline Ashton had puzzled on the matter. 'The housekeeper and her husband are the only ones from the British Isles,' she said, shaking her head. 'But they are from England, as I recall, and none of their four children are adopted.'

Emily van der Donck was mystified. 'I was sure this was the address that Mhairi gave Kati.'

'Mhairi, did you say?'

'Yes, Mhairi McLeod.'

The mention of the name McLeod meant nothing to Mrs Ashton, who assumed the Raffertys' children to have all the same surname, but the Christian name of Mhairi most certainly rang a bell. 'I wonder . . .'

And so the truth was out, and Belle Rafferty was mortified. Never had she been so shamed by anyone in her own family.

But, to her surprise and great relief, the two ladies seemed to consider it rather a good joke. 'This is America, after all, Mrs Rafferty,' Mrs van der Donck had insisted. 'We don't hold with such class distinctions as they do in England.'

'You mean it's still in order for Mhairi to join you for the weekend?'

'Most certainly it is. And you may tell her that when she returns from school this afternoon.'

But it was a lot more than that that Belle Rafferty told her niece on her return that afternoon. 'You young devil, I swear I've never been so black-affronted!' she shouted, as a well-aimed slap found the side of Mhairi's face. 'A Lord of the Isles, indeed! I should tan the hide from you good and proper!'

But Mhairi had stood her ground. 'But what for, Auntie Belle?' she cried. 'How do you know my father is not a clan chief?'

Belle Rafferty backed off, nursing her own stinging fingers as she stared at the red weal that was forming on the child's cheek.

'How do you know, Auntie Belle? How do you know?'

And, as the child stared in indignation, the expression on Belle Rafferty's face slowly changed. A look of confusion came into her eyes. This was not a subject she could allow herself to be drawn on. She owed it to her dead sister to remain silent. Aye, and to the child herself, come to that.

'It's possible, isn't it,' her niece's voice insisted. 'It *is* possible, Auntie Belle.'

Her aunt nodded wearily, the fight gone out of her. 'Aye, child,' she said. 'It's certainly possible.'

And so Mhairi's friendship with Kati, in particular, received, if not exactly parental blessing, at least acceptance, and not a little envy from the twins whose lot it remained to see no other world beyond the confines of the servants' quarters and the sidewalks outside their own front door.

The van der Doncks' weekend retreat was a four-roomed log cabin about thirty-five miles north, up the Hudson River, on the banks of the Tappan Zee, and from that weekend on Mhairi was often invited to accompany the family on their frequent trips throughout the summer, when the demands of Wall Street were not quite so pressing on Kati's father.

On their arrival at the cabin, if the weather was in the least bit blustery, and the waves on the water outside their door in the slightest bit choppy, Kati's father, Jan, never tired of telling the girls of how during every gale the ghost of the Storm-ship – a sort of Tappan Zee *Flying Dutchman* – would sail again across the unruly waters of the lake. And he would tell the tale in a low spine-chilling voice, with much theatrical gesturing of the hands, usually late at night as they sat by the water's edge, with the sun setting in a blazing sky behind them.

And, as they sipped their hot chocolate, and the first shadows of evening played tricks with the imagination and the shivers ran down their backs, Mhairi would remember how her mother used to tell her stories of the fair men of the North who had sailed their white ships on the waters of her own land, now so far away.

The occasional weekends spent with the van der Doncks by the lake were something that Mhairi looked forward to all year, for there on the edge of the pine forests, heavy with the scents of summers gone, and with the waters of the Zee glittering in the distance, she could once more imagine she was in the Skye of her childhood.

She felt comfortable with these kindly Dutch folk who went out of their way to make the much poorer little Scottish girl feel at home. And she particularly loved the visits to the small village of Tarrytown, where the great storyteller Washington Irving had once lived. Kati's father had assured them that Rip van Winkle himself had been based on a certain Willi van der Donck, a great-uncle of his, and Mhairi wondered wryly if the beloved fairytale character would have seemed quite the same had he been named Rip van der Donck.

All around Tarrytown legend and truth seemed so intertwined that it proved impossible to disentangle them. But as Mhairi and Kati grew they took delight in feigning disdain at Jan van der Donck's tall tales. No more did they believe that in the hills that surrounded them, Ichabod Crane had once courted Katrina van Tassel, then fled in abject terror before the headless horseman.

But after the two friends had wandered hand in hand through the graveyard of Sleepy Hollow, and past the tomb of Washington Irving, then joined the rest of the family for prayers in the Old Dutch Church, Mhairi could not help but wonder if perhaps, just perhaps, there might be some truth in the stories after all, for had not Kati herself been named after the lovely Katrina, and surely no one would name a child after a mere legend?

And so, as she took her place beside the rest of the family in their own special pew, Mhairi found herself listening intently, for there, in the quietness of that holy place, she remembered the old romancer's own words from her favourite school Reader: 'There are peculiar quavers still to be heard in that church which may even be heard half a mile off, quite to the opposite side of the mill pond on a still Sunday morning . . .'

Yes, so many things happened on still Sunday mornings spent with the van der Doncks. And if Kati was sometimes slow to invite her for the weekend, then her mother Emily made sure the invitation went out, until it seemed that she had found a family circle in which she felt as much at home as she did in her own. And in Kati she had found a companion whose friendship must now surely go far beyond merely wanting to outdo Amy Lowell. Neither of them saw very much of Amy at all these days, and she certainly was not around that never-to-be forgotten weekend she and Kati almost perished together, on Sunday, 11 March 1888, when they were all of eleven years old.

She had been travelling back with Kati and their family maid, Sarah, from a two-day visit to van der Donck relatives upstate in Buffalo. It had been a weekend full of fun, for Kati's aunt and uncle and their large brood of children were a happy-go-lucky crowd. In fact the only cloud on the horizon had been for Aunt Liesel van der Donck as she read Saturday morning's newspapers. Aunt Liesel was German born and feared dreadfully for the 'old country' after the news that the old Kaiser, Wilhelm I, had died the previous day, and his eldest son, Kronprinz Friedrich, who was due to succeed him, was himself dying of cancer of the throat.

The information preyed on her mind all day. 'There will be a socialist revolution for sure, mark my words!' she declared over the dinner table on the Saturday night. 'Then what will happen to *Oma* and *Opa*?' Her voice rose quite dramatically at the thought of her aged parents being hounded by a blood-crazed mob.

'Tosh, my dear! I'll go over to Bremen and rescue them myself, if need be!' her husband had declared, wiping his moustache with a large red handkerchief, and the children had all cheered, including Mhairi. There was something fine about the thought of small, portly Uncle Wim taking on the might of the international socialist movement.

As for Kati and Mhairi, however, they had little personal interest in what was happening in such a far-off land; much more interesting was the *Herald*'s story of *un crime passionnel* much nearer home, in Brooklyn that ran under the intriguing headline: LOVED AND MURDERED HER. WOOED HER AS A WIDOW AND SHOT HER DEAD. Every word was devoured avidly, then the six van der Donck cousins were roped into a re-enactment of the whole gory proceedings, with Mhairi cast as the poor, deceived widow and Kati as the murdering husband, complete with her Uncle Wim's Sunday-best coat and hat. It made a welcome change from the perpetual re-enactments of the Jack the Ripper murders, in far-off London, that had been their staple diet of gore for several weekend visits past.

Yes, weekends at the Buffalo van der Doncks' were always fun and the two girls groaned loudest of all the children when Aunt Liesel called late on Sunday afternoon to say it was time to prepare for the train journey home.

They reached the station with only minutes to spare and were delighted to find they were booked to return on the fast train, the New York Central Flyer, heading for Grand Central Terminal, where Kati's father was due to meet them at seven-thirty on the Monday morning.

It was five o'clock on the dot when *The Flyer*, consisting of four day coaches, a diner, two sleepers, a parlour car, and a locomotive left Buffalo station, and the family were all there to wave goodbye. The weather was nothing out of the ordinary for a March day, although the sky was darkening to the south, and Kati's Uncle Wim had shaken his head and warned there would be rain before the night was out.

The two girls had made the journey several times before, with Sarah for company, and they never failed to thrill at the 'grown-upness', as Kati called it, of taking their seats in the parlour car amongst the dark-suited businessmen, who puffed their cigars and looked terribly important behind the clouds of smoke as they sipped their bourbon and studied their Sunday newspapers.

That particular journey the girls had persuaded Sarah to sit in the seat behind and she was only too happy to oblige, for that was the seat nearest the diner and there she could exchange banter with the stewards without being overheard by her charges.

Left more or less to themselves, the girls' imaginations set to work once more and now they were fine ladies off to meet their 'intendeds' for an evening out on the town. And how Mhairi revelled in the plush atmosphere of thick carpets, soft, comfortable armchairs and oak-panelled walls. And the smell . . . Oh how she loved that rich combination of cigar-smoke, hair pomade, and intoxicating liquor; it was the unmistakable aroma of the adult world and it sent a shiver down her spine as the white-coated negro stewards moved skilfully between the seats, dispensing drinks and bonhomie.

The guards had lit the lamps early that evening because of the darkening sky, and as the two girls gazed out of the windows at the huge drops of rain that began to splatter across the glass, it soon became obvious that not only was Uncle Wim right, but, by the looks of it, they were running into a full-scale storm.

'Ah do declare, Miss Kati, would you take a look at those trees!' Sarah's voice exclaimed from the seat behind as the *Flyer* sped southwards, and the two girls stared in mounting excitement, and not a little fear, at trunks bent almost double by the ferocious wind.

As usual, Kati's father had booked them all a sleeping berth, but when the time came for bed the girls were not at all keen to go. Sarah prevailed, however, but neither of them slept that night as the train ploughed on through the mounting storm. Instead they lay and whispered to each other, their imaginations finding it difficult to keep pace with actual events as their sleeping car was buffeted by the fierce winds and rain until it seemed as if any minute it would be blown right off the track.

Leaving Sarah snoring loudly in the top berth, they crept out of bed before six on the Monday morning, to dress and make their way back through to the parlour car. What they saw and heard sent them hurrying back to waken the maid. 'It's terrible, Sarah. It's freezing in there. The stove has gone out and there's no spare coal to light it. And there's snow everywhere . . . Look, you can't even see out of the windows!'

And so Sarah had looked, her brown face peering hard up against the glass. 'Lord have mercy!' Her eyes grew large with wonder and increasing apprehension as she gazed through the frost-encrusted glass at the mounting snowdrifts on either side of the track. She turned to her charges who were standing shivering in the aisle. 'Where are we, for heaven's sakes?'

The two girls could only shake their heads. All they knew was that it was a white wilderness out there and they were still miles from their destination. By the clock they should be within an hour or so of New York by now, but someone had said the train was already five hours behind schedule and getting later by the minute as the engine made heavy weather through the mounting snow.

'Hey, Mister, do you know whereabouts we are?' Mhairi pulled at the coat tail of a porter who was squeezing past with a bucket of hot coals from the engine in an attempt to rekindle the stove in the parlour car.

'We're some miles north of Albany, I guess, Missy. But the Lord only knows if we'll ever see that town, never mind New York, before nightfall – and it ain't even proper daylight yet!'

Sarah gave a gasp and the two girls looked at each other as the porter's words sank in. Suddenly it wasn't a game any more. Kati thought of her father waiting for them on the platform at Grand Central. He would be worried to death. 'I'm cold,' she wailed, to no one in particular.

'Hush your mouth, child! Complaining don't do no one no good!' Sarah heaved her bulk down from the wooden bunk and straightened her skirts. She had gone to sleep in her outdoor clothes and set about tidying herself as Kati grabbed Mhairi's arm.

'Let's go back to the parlour. They're lighting a fire in there!'

And so, despite a loud protest from Sarah, the two girls made their way back to the car where most of the other passengers were already gathered. The porter had succeeded in getting the stove going again and, despite the fact the whole company was chilled to the bone, they were pushed to the front of the crowd huddled round it, with cries of 'Let the kids through . . . Can't you see, they're half frozen!'

In truth, Mhairi was hardly aware of the cold, for nothing so exciting had happened to her since her arrival in America, but she thanked everyone politely, nevertheless, as she joined Kati at the front of the group jostling for warmth around the small cast-iron stove.

At that point one of the stewards opened the door to announce that they were about two miles north of Albany, but had hit a major problem. The track just up ahead was blocked by a major snowdrift. 'Ah swear to God it's just the biggest you ever did see!'

'Well, we've got several tons of locomotive here, dammit!' someone shouted.

'And I've got an important business appointment in Manhattan at three this afternoon!' someone else joined in. And soon it seemed like that whole company had life and death appointments to be kept in New York that day.

'All right, all right. Keep yo' hair on!' the porter shouted above the din. The driver was going to do his best, he informed them. He would attack the obstacle at full speed, '. . . and trust to God, for there sho' is nobody else to help us out there right now!'

The impact of the crash as the front of the train hit the drift rocked the following carriages on their axles. Most of the passengers in the parlour car were sent sprawling against the oak-panelled walls, and the black cast-iron stove was upturned on to the floor. The burning embers spilled out of its open door, setting light to the thick pile of the carpet as the dazed passengers attempted to struggle back to their feet.

It seemed only seconds before the whole car was ablaze, and Mhairi, who had been knocked almost unconscious by the crash, found herself being half-carried to safety by one of the porters.

Once outside, everyone stood dazed and shivering in the deep snow by the side of the track as they watched the flames leap to the roof of the parlour car, sending clouds of black smoke billowing out of the open door and smashed window. Very soon it was spreading to the other carriages, and a deathly silence fell over the still dazed and shaken group as they watched their only means of transport disappear before their eyes in a thick cloud of smoke and flame.

'Well, there's nothing to be gained by standing here freezing to death,' an elderly man announced. 'There's nothing else for it —we'll have to walk . . . How far did you say it was to Albany?' he asked one of the porters.

'Ah guess it's all of two miles, but those kids, they ain't gonna make it, that's for sure! Specially that one with the leg-iron!'

All eyes turned to Mhairi and Kati, then, as one, the company stared down at Kati's left leg. Then to Mhairi's dismay her friend began to cry: great heartrending sobs that racked the icy air around them. The noise brought Sarah puffing up from the back of the group. 'Oh, Miss Kati, child . . .' She clasped the sobbing Kati to her ample breast as the men in the group turned back to discussing the situation.

It was decided that there was indeed nothing else for it, they would all have to set off, children included, to attempt to walk the last few miles into town.

Spirits were high for the first hundred yards or so as the railmen attempted to clear a path through the drifting snow for the others to follow. But very soon, as energy flagged, so did the spirits of the bedraggled travellers, who found themselves floundering in drifts that towered threateningly above even the tallest in their midst.

In the beginning some of the younger men attempted to carry the two girls on their backs, but very soon this had to be abandoned, although several others did attempt to carry Kati slung between them. In the end, though, both Mhairi and Kati were left to struggle on through waist-deep snow with the others. Every step was an effort and a victory won, although there were moments, with the snow blowing straight into their faces and all but suffocating them, that they were convinced they would never make it.

The last mile of the journey was a nightmare that never seemed to end as, buffeted by the wind and blinded by the swirling, drifting snow, the group, now strung out over several hundred yards, inched their way to safety.

How they ever reached Albany neither Mhairi nor Kati could remember. All they knew was that someone carried them into the nearest hotel and tucked them up in a warm bed where they slept right through till the next morning.

It was only days afterwards when Mhairi was back at home in Lancaster House and recovering from her ordeal that she heard the rest of the story.

It was her Uncle Finbar who told her of the chaos that had befallen their city that weekend. He himself had been injured in an accident on the elevated railway a few yards south of the 76th Street station. He had been up early that morning to make his way through the blizzard to deliver an important package from his employer to a business colleague on Lexington Avenue when another locomotive ploughed into the back of the one in which he was travelling. One person had been killed and fourteen injured in the crash, and he himself had sustained a badly broken right arm and crushed clavicle. The injuries meant that for quite some time afterwards he was only allowed light duties around the house and had time on his hands, much of which he spent with Mhairi.

It was the first time in her eleven years that she had really got to know her Uncle Finbar and to her surprise and delight, on his own, he was not quite the galoot that her Auntie Belle tried to make out.

A firm bond grew between them as she lay on the pillows and listened to the stories he related of conditions outside. Some were awesome, and some tragic, such as the stirring story the head butler had read to him out of a local newspaper that morning, of how milkman Xavier Zwinge had perished serving his customers, after his faithful horse had made its way home with Xavier frozen solid on top of the cart.

'Here you are, Mhairi, read it for yourself,' he said, his soft heart full to bursting as he handed her the folded newspaper.

Mhairi took it and, turning to the page, began to read aloud in a sonorous voice befitting the solemnity of the occurrence: 'Frozen like a figure sculpted of ice, he was still in the driver's seat as the horse drew him up the homeward path. In one hand he clutched the reins, in the other he held the money he had collected from a customer. Alone he had gone to his reward in that blizzard-swept wasteland with only the faithful horse to pity his hapless master and bear him to his home and his loved ones.'

She laid the paper down and uncle and niece gazed at one another. Each was overcome by the poignancy of the moment and had tears in their eyes as her Auntie Belle entered the room. She glanced across at the paper lying open at the page, as Mhairi said, 'Oh, poor man. I bet his family were quite overcome by the shock of it all.'

Her aunt looked from one to the other. They were a pair of softies and no mistake. She gave a pitying shake of the head, for she had heard from the cook the postscript to the tale. 'You can say that again. The old boy wasn't dead at all, but lying drunk as a coot in a tavern while they were all mourning his passing!'

'But the newspaper . . . All that stuff in the newspaper . . .'

Belle Rafferty adjusted her apron. 'Well now, Mhairi,

there's a fine lesson for you — it's not to be believing everything you read, for if you do you'll grow up as daft as your Uncle Finbar there. Only he can't read and that makes him all the more gullible!'

Mhairi looked across at the object of her aunt's derision and she could have sworn she saw a wink in his right eye as her uncle got up from the bed to go about his business. Finbar Rafferty might not be the most learned person on this earth, but he was one of the kindest, and she knew her Auntie Belle thought that too. They were an unlikely couple, but happy in their own way, and if she couldn't have her own mother and father, they were surely as good a substitute as she was likely to get, even if they did not have the money of the Lowells or the van der Doncks.

She lay back on the pillows and closed her eyes as her aunt straightened the bedclothes, tucking them in neatly at her feet. She had become used to not having a real mother by now, but what of her father? Her mind went blank. Just who was the man who had been responsible for her birth all those years ago on Skye? The red flush of embarrassment crept up her neck to suffuse her cheeks as she thought of the tales she had told about him since that cold November day, huddled around the stove in the schoolroom at Auchindoir, when she had learnt that such a man called 'father' must actually exist. No wonder the likes of Kati and Amy believed her — she had almost convinced herself he was one of the awesome Lords of the Isles.

She felt her aunt's hand on her brow. She was murmuring something about how flushed she was looking. 'Are you feeling all right, child?'

Mhairi nodded her head but did not open her eyes as she crept down further beneath the clean white sheets. In her mind's eye she was already far from Lancaster House and the snows of New York. She was back on her hilltop on Skye, and in the distance she could just make out the tall turrets of Dalriada piercing the blue sky above the tops of the giant firs. And beyond Dalriada were the mountains of the Black Cuillin, and the mighty peaks of Gars Bheinn and Sgurr Alasdair, on the other side of whose dark mysteries lay the lands and castle of Dunvegan, the home of the McLeods of McLeod, her mother's people.

But what of her father's? Were his roots too in the rich dark soil of that island, or had he come from afar to sow his seed? Had he gone forever, never to return to *Eilean a' Cheo*, or was he still there in that most beloved of islands? There were so many questions, but so few answers . . .

Chapter Seven

Ibbity, bibbity, sibbity, sa,
Ibbity, bibbity, vanilla,
Dictionary, down the ferry.
Fun, fun, American gum
Eighteen hundred and ninety-one.

As the Eighties passed into the Nineties, the city of New York was growing just as fast as the young girl from the Scottish Highlands for whom it was now home, and as Mhairi gazed about her she never ceased to wonder what her family back on Skye would have made of it all. The majestic towers of the Brooklyn Bridge looming above Manhattan had become as familiar a landmark to her as the dark mysterious peaks of Gars Bheinn and Sgurr Alasdair and the other mountains of the Black Cuillin. And the trains of the elevated railway which rattled down the whole length of Manhattan to belch their way, spewing hot cinders, right around the serpent-like curve at Coenties slip, had become as familiar a method of transport as the pony and trap that had ferried the Gentry from the landing pier on Loch Scavaig to Dalriada, and the other big houses around Ballintuim.

But this was not Ballintuim, and America's biggest city had a vitality about it that struck hidden chords within her that vibrated in her very soul. People had come from all corners of the globe to settle here and sometimes on her many walks around the district she could go for a whole mile and not hear a native-born American accent.

But that there were poor parts to the city too, she was well aware, for Carlo the Sicilian milkboy came from that area of the Lower East Side, north of Canal Street and west of the Bowery, where so many other Italian families had settled, and where poverty was still rife. But Carlo was not always going to remain a milkboy, he had informed her; he had an uncle who would see to that. Uncle Rico, who lived on North Fifth Street and Roebling, was a 'man of honour' and there wasn't a Sicilian in the whole of New York who didn't look up to him.

'One day, when I am also a "man of honour", you will be proud that we were friends,' Carlo told her one morning, as they talked on the back stairs, before she left for school. 'And one day you may want to marry me.'

She had blushed deeply, but made no reply, for Carlo, with his dark Italian eyes and soft, curling hair, had come rather too close to her own feelings. With him she had felt the first stirrings of young love, admitted to no one, not even to Kati, but which merited more than a sigh or two, and blushes into her pillow after dark, when her imagination took flight.

It was Mr Buss, the butler, who first noticed that the two of them were spending rather too long passing the time of day each morning, and it was he who took her aside to inform her that the family to which Carlo Benelucci belonged were not perhaps the poor Italian immigrants she might think: 'In fact, young miss, there are some sections in this town that decent folks don't tangle with — and they're one of them!' The comments made her both puzzled and curious, and she determined to find out more.

'*E una sporca macchia sul' onore di Benelucci!*' Carlo had protested, breaking into his native tongue for the first time in her presence, after she repeated the butler's words to him one cold spring morning in early April. His brown eyes had flashed in anger and injured pride as he set down the newly-filled churn with a vehemence that sent the

104

fresh milk splashing on to the doorstep. 'The honour of the family name is everything to a Sicilian! I spit on a man who would throw dirt on that honour!'

She was to learn how much that honour meant one day early in the long hot summer that followed, when the *Herald* carried the story of the killing of a certain Enrico Benelucci by a rival family in the same Williamsburg neighbourhood of Brooklyn, and she heard for the first time of the expression 'the mob'.

Yes, that there was a seamier side to her city, she was well aware, but this was the first time it had touched her personally. She had deliberately not asked Carlo if the Enrico Benelucci who died was his uncle, for in her heart she already knew the answer. That, however, did little to lessen her disappointment when, shortly afterwards, he informed her it was his fourteenth birthday and he would be leaving the world of milkcarts behind forever, to gain his heart's desire to work for the honour of 'the family'.

She did not see him on the Saturday morning he left, for she was spending the weekend at the Tappan Zee with the van der Doncks, but there had been a single pink rose left on the step alongside the milk. She would never have known if Shona had not told her about it as they lay in bed on the Sunday night.

'What happened to it?' she had asked, her heart beating much too fast beneath the bedclothes.

'Oh, it was put into the arrangement for the dining-room,' her cousin answered. 'They thought the flower-seller had dropped it when he delivered the order for Saturday's dinner-party.' Her voice dropped to a whisper, 'But I knew he hadn't for it was lying there before he arrived.'

Mhairi made no reply. The rose was gone, just like Carlo was gone. Just like so many people had come and gone in her short life. Was it to be her lot that everyone she grew to love would eventually disappear from her life like this?

She turned over on the pillow and buried her face beneath the white sheet.

'Goodnight, Mhairi.'

'Goodnight, Shona. God bless.'

But there was just too much going on in her young life to allow the pangs of first love to last forever. And so, as one decade passed into another and she trembled on the threshold between childhood and adolescence, she threw herself wholeheartedly into a life divided in equal parts between school, home, and that fascinating other world of money and privilege she was allowed to glimpse occasionally through her continuing if somewhat erratic friendship with Kati van der Donck.

Sometimes she wished she had never even heard of Kati, or any of her many relatives, for as childhood blossomed into the questioning turmoil of adolescence, she began to realize that her acceptance into the van der Donck household perhaps owed more to the charitable nature of Emily van der Donck's heart than her daughter Kati's true affection for her young Scottish friend. She had been adopted by them, as one would adopt a stray puppy, but no matter how hard it tried that little mongrel would never be a true pedigree like its benefactors' own born and bred variety.

If her Auntie Belle noticed the strangely discontented air about her on her return from her visits to her Dutch friends, she never let on, but Finbar knew. 'It's hard being poor in a rich world, isn't it, love?' he said one evening, as he caught her pulling disconsolately at the fraying cuff of her best dress on her return from the van der Doncks.

She had looked at him with tears of frustration in her eyes. Yes, it was hard. And it got harder all the time, returning home from a world where you were waited on hand and foot to one that did the waiting. Never a day passed but Mhairi was aware that when her time came, she would be destined for a world very different from that of her friend. Barriers which one could leap effortlessly in childhood grew almost insurmountable with the passing years. Yes, even in the Land of Liberty, young girls were not yet created as equal as they claimed.

'It needn't always be like this, you know,' her Uncle Finbar had told her, one night he had found her sitting up into the small hours mending her best dress. 'Young girls with brains and good looks like you can get on in this world, Mhairi love. Some have the good sense to escape before they get pulled down by it all.'

She had looked at him and smiled, but said nothing. She wondered if he was referring to Fiona, but dared not ask, for the departure of his eldest child from Lancaster House was still an open wound in both parents' hearts, despite his words of consolation to her now.

It was one morning in early August that the unexpected arrival of an envelope bearing the head of the British Queen Victoria made her stop and remember that thousands of miles away, across the vast expanse of the Atlantic Ocean, there was another world apart from America, another way of life that had once been hers, and would have been still if Fate had not stepped in to change her fortunes so drastically.

Her Auntie Belle, to whom the envelope was addressed, opened it sitting at the big table in the kitchen, her face suddenly pale despite the summer's heat. None of her brothers were great ones for letter-writing and it was with a shaking hand that she tore open the wax seal. Mhairi and Shona were the only members of the family in the room at the time and the two girls looked at each other in apprehension as the page of thin white paper was extracted and smoothed out on the table-top before them.

The words the letter contained were written in a wavering, unsure hand, for her Uncle Ian had never been one for the reading and writing:

107

Dear All,

It is with a heavy heart I write to you today, for it is sad news indeed this letter must bring. Today our dear aunt, Jessie McLeod, was laid to rest after an illness lasting several weeks. Pray for her soul.

The brothers and I send our best wishes and pray for your own continued good fortune and health.

Yours in sorrow this day,

Ian McLeod.

The news of her Auntie Jessie's death had a profound effect on Mhairi, for next to her mother and grandfather, it was with her great-aunt that most of her memories of her old home were enshrined. She had always felt an affinity with the aged, for they seemed to offer a security and continuity that her own young life had lacked, and it was through telling her friend Kati of her sadness at the news of her Auntie Jessie's death that someone else came into her life who was every bit as old, and, in many ways just as fascinating as Jessie McLeod.

The old lady in question was one of Kati's great-grandmothers, a lively, doughty old lady who lived alone in an apartment high up in one of the new buildings overlooking the East River.

'A relic of a bygone age, child, that's what I am,' Catherine Dearborn van der Donck had stated quite emphatically to Mhairi on her very first visit. 'Should be in a glass case and stuffed by now like one of them mangy old polecats in the City Museum!' But to Mhairi there was nothing in the least bit mangy, or old come to that, about Grandma Cate. And she could tell a story better than just about anyone she knew.

She had moved into the apartment shortly after she was widowed in the spring of 1883, and just a few weeks before that momentous day of 24 May, when the President Chester A. Arthur declared the new Brooklyn Bridge open.

But Grandma Cate was not, in fact, a New Yorker; she had been born and brought up in the small village of Chicago, Illinois. Yes, a real frontierswoman was how Grandma Cate liked to describe herself, and to her great-grandchild Kati and the young Scots girl who accompanied her on the visits, that was an exotic breed indeed.

'Born in 1809, the same year as Abraham Lincoln,' she informed them, as her lace-mittened hands smoothed the fine needlepoint cushion she was stitching on her lap. 'A vintage year, my Daddy used to say — him being a really staunch Republican and all. But . . .' and her eyes would twinkle as she leant forward over her sewing and added in a confidential tone, 'as far as 1809 goes, I always thought it much more exciting knowing that was the year that Napoleon divorced Josephine!'

Mhairi and Kati looked at one another, then back at the old lady. 'Oh yes, Grandma Cate, we do too!' Mhairi breathed. Such a spicy morsel was far more interesting than hearing of Old Father Abraham, even if he did grow up in a log cabin and free the slaves.

And Grandma Cate's conversation was full of just such spicy morsels. Her bright eyes would twinkle behind the pince-nez that perched precariously on the end of her nose and the two girls would shiver in anticipation on the carpet at her feet as they begged, 'Tell us more, Grandma Cate. Tell us about being a young girl out there amongst the Indians.'

And the old lady would shake her head and say, 'Those were rough days out there in the West, children, make no mistake. Rough and hard, especially for the women, and heaven knows there were few enough of them. In fact, there was such a terrible lack of young ladies of marriage-able age in Chicago in those days that they took to advertising for them in the likes of the *New York Star*!'

'And did they get replies?' Mhairi asked, agog with the thought of finding your life's partner in such a way.

'Mercy, yes. In fact, when the boats arrived from New York, you should have seen the rush to the docks. Why the whole town closed down for the day just so's the menfolk could go and grab themselves a young woman. And some of them that arrived weren't so young, I can tell you! There were some sights to be seen coming down that gangplank.' Her shoulders shook with suppressed mirth at the memory. 'Not that it mattered, mind. Most of them didn't give a hoot for the cut of the jib, just as long as it arrived on two legs and in a skirt, that was good enough. Some pretty queer matches were made, but beggars couldn't be choosers – not in those days.'

'Did you answer an advertisement too, Grandma?' Kati asked, as the old lady reached for a new length of silk thread.

'God love you child, no! If the truth be known, my Pa didn't intend me marrying any young man. After my Mama died he thought it would be right and proper for me to stay on and keep house for him, what with the boys up and gone and all . . .'

'But you didn't,' Mhairi said hopefully.

'No, I did not!' Grandma Cate said vehemently, looking from one to the other of the young faces that gazed up at her. 'Not that it was easy to meet a decent young man out West back then.' She took care to stress the word *decent*, for there were certainly plenty of the other type around the frontier towns in those days. 'Well, as I said, it was real hard to meet a decent beau, and the only public dances in Chicago in those days were held in Mark Beaubien's hotel. Very proper affairs they were too.'

'And you met Great-Granpa at one of those dances?'

'I surely did.' Her seamed face glowed with the remembered pleasure of those dear dead days. 'Visiting from New York, he was. His bank was considering setting up a Chicago branch and he was boarding for the few days in the hotel. He just looked in out of curiosity, I guess. He certainly wasn't on the lookout for a wife, that was for sure!'

'And was he a good dancer?' Kati asked, unable to visualize the stern old man whose picture gazed down on them from above the mantelpiece as ever being a young man with dancing on his mind.

The merriment gleamed in her great-grandmother's eyes. 'As good as it's possible to be, dressed in a high-buttoned linsey wool coat and a pair of thick-soled broughans on his feet the likes of which I hope to never see again.'

She dabbed an eye behind the pince-nez as she continued, 'Not that his rig-out stopped us, mind, for we *dos-à-dosed* the whole evening — after being properly introduced, that is.' She could see the scene now as if it were yesterday. 'Not that I would recommend doing a chassez cross in a pair of satin slippers with a partner in shoes like that. As I recall, I told him the poor lost feet of the Colossus of Rhodes must have served his cobbler as a last!'

'But you married your banker,' Mhairi sighed. 'Big feet and all.'

'Oh yes,' the old lady smiled. 'I married him all right, and you, Katrina, can thank the Good Lord for that, or you wouldn't be sitting here today.'

Kati raised her brows and looked thoughtful. 'I'm not going to marry a banker,' she stated flatly. 'I'm going to marry an English prince or lord!'

Her great-grandmother raised her brows. 'Well, is that a fact? And it wouldn't surprise me one little bit . . .' After all, weren't just about all the daughters of New York's top 'Four Hundred' families doing just that? And certainly the van der Doncks had as much right to their place amongst them as any one. 'But how about you, Mhairi?' Her gaze turned to the other young face looking up into her own. 'Who will you marry?'

But before Mhairi had a chance to reply, Kati had answered for her. 'Oh, Mhairi's going to marry either Henk Smitt or Billy Boyle!'

Mhairi looked across at her friend, her face stricken. Henk Smitt and Billy Boyle were the sons of her father's under-butler and head groom.

'Well, is that right now? And a fine match I'm sure one of them will make,' the old lady's voice continued in her ear.

A cold empty feeling entered Mhairi's soul as all the doubts and fears that had been growing in her heart were confirmed by those few words, so lightly spoken. It was accepted, that was all. It was the way of things. Kati could marry the European princes or lords of this world, whilst she, Mhairi, could have her choice of the servants' sons. Now, more than ever, she was aware of the real gulf that had already opened up between herself and her friend.

The summer of 1889 when that conversation took place turned out to be the last summer Mhairi ever spent with the van der Doncks at their cabin by the shores of the Tappan Zee. It was a weekend in early Fall, towards the end of September, when she joined the family party for the trip north. They were all in good spirits that day, particularly Kati's father, Jan, for he had just taken delivery of a new boat that week and could not wait to try it out.

As the trip coincided with Kati's twelfth birthday celebrations, as a special treat the two girls were allowed to join Kati's elder brother Andreas and their father on a trial sail as far up the Hudson River as Haverstraw Bay. Neither of the girls had ever been that far up-river before and excitement ran high as they set off. It was the most memorable time either had ever spent on the water. The wind was in their favour and Jan van der Donck took great pride in identifying all the well-known landmarks to the girls and Andy as the boat sped across the waves.

High Tor and the Dunderberg Mountain, the great precipices that lined the river's western shore, were both pointed out, and as the small craft negotiated the narrow, dangerous channel between the Dunderberg and the peak called Anthony's Nose, Kati's father told them of the sudden violent storms that often occurred there. They were caused, he said, by the bulbous-bottomed Dutch goblin who lived on top of the Dunderberg, bellowing orders to the four winds, and it was only through dipping their sails in homage to the goblin could sailors hope to pass in safety. 'But of course, children,' he went on to say, 'being Dutch ourselves, he would not dream of harming us in any way . . .'

Those words were to return to haunt Mhairi on many occasions throughout the rest of her childhood, for Kati's beloved father, Jan, was to lose his life barely one month later when his new boat capsized during a particularly bad squall on that very part of the river.

Mhairi tried to tell herself it was pure coincidence, and all that talk of hobgoblins and the like was pure fantasy, but there remained something deep within her – a distant memory of her mother's tales on Skye perhaps – that did not scoff, and made a shiver run down her back in the wee small hours of the morning when sleep would not come, and when she would lie awake and wonder just what exactly life would have in store for her once childhood was over.

Yes, despite an uncomfortable feeling of being *with* but not *of* her Dutch friends, how she had loved those enchanted summers of her youth, spent with the kindly van der Doncks before Kati's father's death. They had given her back, at least in part, a childhood she had thought she had lost forever when she left her beloved island. And perhaps it was for that reason that she went on visiting Grandma Cate in the flat above Brooklyn Bridge right up to the old lady's death in the Fall of 1891.

After her death, Mhairi grieved not only for the old lady whom she had grown to love, but for the times she had spent at the tall windows of her apartment gazing out at the awesome edifice that was Brooklyn Bridge. The reason Grandma Cate had chosen that apartment was because of its view of the bridge, and it was one of the delights of both their lives to gaze out on its massive Gothic arches and awesome towers that spanned the fierce tides of the East River. For Mhairi it seemed to symbolize everything she felt about her new home; it was a cathedral in the sky, a glorious paean in granite and steel to the people of this town who, like herself, had made that journey from the Old World to the New, and were determined to grow tall and strong in its shadow.

The city itself had become her world far more than the claustrophobic confines of life below stairs in Lancaster House, and every spare moment was spent walking the streets she had grown to love, particularly the fascinating, meandering Broadway that north of Twenty-third Street took a slantwise westerly course as if searching for the Hudson River and an exit to that countryside so beloved of those such as Washington Irving, and which within living memory had been quite wild and open after Bloomingdale was reached.

Her Auntie Belle was always threatening her with incarceration in the notorious insane asylum there. 'It's Bloomingdale you'll end up in, my girl, mark my words. Wandering about the streets like that. No good comes of it. There's work enough here to be getting along with without spending your time raking the sidewalks like you do. Wasting precious time watching the world go by,' she would scoff impatiently, but her niece would smile quietly to herself for she knew it was far more than that. But her dreams she would share with no one but God.

It was in the Church of the Messiah, on Broadway, just opposite Waverly Place that she would slip into a pew at the back and say her silent prayers. It was there that she would pray with all her heart that she would find a way to get out of the life below stairs that seemed to be the only destiny she was to be allowed.

Often in quiet moments such as those her Auntie Jessie's words would come back to her, how some people were trees and some were thistledown. They brought a curious comfort. For if the Katis of this world were trees who would grow strong rooted to the soil of this place, just as her ancestors had been for generations, then so it might be her own destiny to move on – to escape the drudgery of the life she knew lay in store for her just as soon as her fourteenth birthday was reached.

But there was no sign of the winds of Fate that her Great-aunt Jessie had spoken of when the eve of her fourteenth birthday came around. She lay in bed in her attic room at the top of the house in Amity Place that night and wept into her pillow at the thought of what lay ahead.

The fourth of March 1891 dawned not bright and clear as an early spring morning should have been, but dull and overcast, with a promise of rain in the air. Yes, she thought, as she stood at her bedroom window and looked out over the rooftops of the city, destiny had caught up with her all right. There was to be no escaping it. That was the day she took her place in the adult world and was put to work in earnest; it was the day her hair was put up, her skirts lengthened, and childhood was put behind her forever.

She was set to work as an under-parlourmaid for the Ashtons themselves in Lancaster House. 'And you should think yourself lucky, young lady,' her aunt had been quick to point out. 'Madam could just as easily have said she didn't need any more of the family on the payroll.'

And so she should have been grateful, she knew that. For a start she could have been given a post in the kitchens and that would have meant rising at five every morning to clean out, black-lead, then light the closed range, before washing down the stone flags of the kitchen and the back stairs. And that was before the day's work had even begun.

Yes, she should have been grateful, but as her hands grew red and sore with the endless cleaning, and her back began to ache with all the fetching and carrying of coal for the upstairs fires, she could not help thinking of her two friends Kati and Amy who, at the same time she had entered service in the Ashton household, had been sent away to finishing school in Boston. There they would learn all the arts and graces expected of young ladies of their station, in preparation, no doubt, for the English princes or lords that awaited them one fine day. She only had to think of the names Henk Smitt and Billy Boyle now and tears of anger and frustration would rush unbidden to her eyes. Nothing in this world, she determined, would make her remain a servant for the rest of her life, or marry one. That was the one certainty in her life that she clung on to and would never let go.

With Kati and Amy gone she wished she could share her feelings with Shona, for she knew that would please her aunt and uncle more than anything. But whilst Mhairi had grown tall and lithesome with the passing years, and her reddish-brown hair had grown thick and abundant down to her waist, so her cousin had remained short and thick-set, with her bright red locks hanging sparse and lank around a face which seemed ever more freckle-filled as time went by. And Shona wanted nothing more than to be in service. She did not understand when Mhairi spoke of a life outside their small closed world of Amity Place, for Shona rarely ventured beyond Washington Square, and could think of nothing better than working her way up to the position of housekeeper to a family like the Ashtons, such as her mother had achieved.

It was a year almost to the day after Mhairi entered

116

service that Shona left to achieve her heart's desire. She obtained a post as kitchen maid in Father Docherty's household over on the corner of Fifth Avenue and 116th Street. She was to receive ten dollars a week and her keep, and could not wait to try on her new uniform of dark blue print dress and white apron and cap on the morning of her departure for her new position.

'You look lovely, Shona,' Mhairi said kindly, as her cousin coaxed the last stray hair into the confines of her bun net. 'Father Docherty's a nice man. I'm sure you'll be very happy there.'

'Thank you, Mhairi. I'm sure you're right. And Seamus will be just down the block at Doctor Munro's.' Her twin brother was leaving the same day to join the household of Father Docherty's physician. 'I know what they say about "followers", but they know Seamus is my brother and I'm sure they won't mind him visiting now and again, when he gets some time off.'

'I'm sure they won't.' Mhairi found it hard to keep the bitterness from her voice. Why did employers have to refer to the maid-servants' young men by the degrading name of 'followers'? Were they not to be allowed to have 'beaus' or 'young men' like their own daughters?

She kissed her cousin impulsively on both cheeks, as Shona stood on the step, bag in hand, ready to set out on the longish walk to her new home. '*Beannachd leat, a Shona*,' she said. 'I'll miss you . . .'

Then she stopped and could say no more as the memories crowded in on her. It was the first time she had spoken a word of Gaelic since leaving Skye.

Book Two

THE WOMAN I AM

The woman I am
Hides deep in me
Beneath the woman
I seem to be.
She hides away
From the stranger's eye –
She is not known to passers-by.
She goes her way,
The woman I seem,
But the woman I am
Withdraws to dream.
The woman I seem
Goes carelessly –
When love goes by
Does not seem to see.
But the woman I am
Knows sudden fear . . .
And hides more deeply
When love draws near.
For love might look closely
Perhaps . . . and see
Her beneath the woman I seem to be!

The Woman I Am

Who can say when childhood ends and womanhood begins? I can only tell you that for me it was not that grey dismal day in March of 1891, when they made me put up my hair and lengthen my skirts, and don the uniform of the under class, to wait on table and carry the coals upstairs to the fine drawing-room of Lancaster House. But that *was* the day when the tiny flame of rebellion in me flickered brighter in the fresher air of the upstairs quarters of that household, and kept on flickering until the morning exactly four years later when it flared with such an intense heat that it scorched my very soul.

That the heat of that fire that glowed within me was to scorch others I cared for has been one of the great sadnesses of my life. But I was still a child then, an impulsive child who could still remember the wind blowing free through her hair on a hillside in late Spring. A time when the air was vibrant with the sights and sounds of approaching summer, and I could lie and watch a seagull soar and swoop above the blue ocean. And my heart would follow that bird, and down the years I would know that yearning still. In my narrow attic bed, at the rising of the moon I would know it, and I would hear the fading echo of a song, and smell again the wild brier rose that, down by the linn, hung in profusion over the swirling foam of the waters that rushed ever seawards towards the great Atlantic Ocean. And my very heart would break.

Freedom to me was the cry of my soul – no more, no

less. I could not accept that men and women who had endured so much in the Old World could cross that great ocean to place themselves once more in a class lower than their fellow human beings. That could never be right. They came to secure liberty for their bodies and their souls.

It did not occur to me then that that freedom must often be bought at a price. Or perhaps it did . . .

Today, over fifty years later, at the back of my wardrobe, there still hangs a grey nankeen jacket, and in the pocket, still folded since the day they were put there, are five faded dollar bills.

Chapter Eight

To a young girl eager to explore the wide world outside the confines of her own home, life in service became more unbearable as time went on. Mhairi was allowed only one day off a month, so she saw little of her cousins during her first few years in the grown-up world, and of Fiona she saw least of all. The older girl rarely called back to visit what remained of her family in Lancaster House, for the confrontations with her mother, Belle, had become too painful for both mother and child. Belle Rafferty was convinced that her elder daughter was leading a life of shame and Fiona did little to ease her mind in that regard, other than claim that, 'Dirty minds produce dirty thoughts', which incensed the older woman even more.

'You'd do well to avoid that besom next time she flounces in in her fine feathers,' her aunt warned Mhairi, after Fiona's last visit early in February of 1895. 'Her with her airs and graces, and expensive fripperies! There's a name for the likes of that young madam and I'll not soil my tongue by repeating it here!' She looked across at Mhairi, who stood with the afternoon tea tray in her hands, ready to take up to Mrs Ashton waiting in the drawing-room. 'Did you hear me, Mhairi?'

Her niece nodded solemnly. 'Yes, Auntie Belle, I heard.'

But in her heart Mhairi knew that nothing lightened her life more than her eldest cousin's fleeting visits home. Not only had Mhairi felt a closeness to her eldest cousin that she felt for no one, except perhaps her Uncle Finbar, but Fiona brought an excitement and promise of freedom that was totally missing from her own life. What if she had not come by her fine clothes through working in service? What harm was there in that? Mhairi was not completely clear in her own mind exactly how her cousin had come by them, but one thing was for sure, they were far better than she herself could ever afford.

It was not until one bright sunny morning, on the fourth of March that year – the day of Mhairi's eighteenth birthday – that her cousin reappeared in Amity Place. She arrived downstairs at a little after ten. Avoiding the kitchen area, in case she ran into her mother, Fiona made straight for the back staircase that led up to the servants' bedrooms at the top of the house.

Even though it was her day off, Mhairi had still had to get up and attend to the fires and breakfasts, and, having dispensed with those chores, she was just finishing a thorough wash at the marble-topped stand when the knock came to her bedroom door.

'Who's there?' Dressed only in her shift, she grabbed for a towel to modestly wrap around her.

'It's me!'

Mhairi threw open the door. Her eyes shone. She would know that voice anywhere.

'I bet you didn't expect to see me today!' her cousin laughed, as she entered the small attic room. She was carrying a large brown paper parcel which she set down with a sigh of relief on the edge of Mhairi's bed.

'How did you know I'd be in my room?'

Fiona picked up Mhairi's much humbler, nankeen jacket from the bed and examined it casually, before tossing it back down on the patchwork quilt. 'You said you hoped to get the day off on your birthday, so I took the chance.' Fiona picked up the parcel and tossed it into her arms.

'Try that on!'

'What is it?' Mhairi looked in curiosity and mounting anticipation at the parcel.

'Open it and you'll find out.'

Inside was one of the prettiest gowns Mhairi had ever seen. Made of striped green taffeta, it was similar to Fiona's own outfit, with deep flounces at the neck and on the bustle.

'It's high time you had something decent to wear,' Fiona said, smiling at the obvious delight on the other's face.

'But, I couldn't – I couldn't possibly!'

'Of course you could. It's not new, you know. I've worn it more than once myself. But with your hair colour . . . Well, I thought it would suit you much better than me. Try it on!'

'Oh, I couldn't possibly!' But she laid down the towel all the same.

'Mother of God, have you no corselet even!'

Mhairi glanced down at her untrammelled bosom and stomach. Her Auntie Belle had never mentioned any change in her underclothing when she had entered service, and it was not something that she had given much thought to herself.

'Well, it's about time you did! Good God, Mhairi McLeod, how do you expect a frock like that to look like anything with an uncorseted body inside of it!'

Mhairi's lower jaw jutted defiantly as she bent to pull up the new gown over her hips. 'Fancy underpinnings like whale-bone stays cost money, and that's not something I've got exactly a great deal of at the moment!'

Fiona reached across to help the bodice of the gown over her cousin's shoulders. 'Well, now, that's something we'll have to do something about, isn't it?'

Mhairi heard the remark but let it pass for she was too preoccupied with the sight that met her eyes in the mirror above her washstand. No longer was she the awkward young adolescent; a poised and remarkably adult-looking young woman looked back at her. 'I – I'm beautiful!' she exclaimed, too thrilled to be modest.

Her cousin's blue eyes narrowed critically, then she nodded back appreciatively. 'Yes, you certainly are – if you do say so yourself! Fancy a stroll to give your fine feathers an airing?'

Mhairi did not need to be asked a second time. And never did she enjoy walking out so much. Now, attired in her new gown, she felt the equal of any of the fine ladies who alighted from their carriages on to the sidewalks of Fifth Avenue to lunch at their favourite restaurant, or simply to take the air as they window-shopped at all the best stores. For the first time in her life she felt that she too could be taken for a lady as they left Washington Square behind and strolled on up Fifth Avenue towards Madison Square. This was the area where all the money lived, and as they passed the fine brownstone houses with their carved façades, she tried hard not to look at the gleaming brass letterboxes and nameplates, for her hands still bore the traces of the polish with which she had rubbed at the Ashtons' that very morning.

And so on up Canal Street towards Broadway they went, passing the broad-fronted houses of the bourgeoisie, and Barnum's Museum, and past the brand new Olympia Theater. The block-long palace of entertainment, with its concert and music halls, and theatre, and with its enticing display of playbills, advertising the latest shows had been a Mecca for Mhairi on her all too rare days off. She made to stop to admire the colourful notices, but Fiona hurried her on. 'We've no time for that now!'

Mhairi looked at her in surprise. Why was time suddenly so pressing? Were they headed somewhere special? If her cousin had yet another birthday surprise up her sleeve she was keeping very quiet about it.

When they reached Madison Square, it was Fiona herself who paused outside Hoyt's Theater and took a step back to admire the framed posters that decorated its imposing façade. Mhairi was only too happy to join her,

126

and together they gazed up at the bevy of attractive young women advertising the forthcoming shows.

'Have you ever thought it could be your picture up there?' Fiona's voice asked from behind her shoulder. 'You can sing every bit as well as most of them – and look far better than most into the bargain.'

Mhairi gave a derisive laugh. That was the stuff dreams were made of. 'You're kidding! They would never consider the likes of me.'

'That's just where you're wrong!'

Mhairi turned to face her. 'Whatever do you mean?'

'Why do you think I brought you out all dressed up to the nines today? Just to have the pleasure of walking with you up and down the street? Lord, Mhairi McLeod, I have better things to do with my time, I can assure you of that! . . . No, young lady, you are going in there – and you're going to prove me right!'

She linked her arm in Mhairi's. 'There's someone in there who could mean all the difference between you wearing dresses like that one for the rest of your life, or ending up with nothing better than the likes of that grey nankeen thing you left back home!'

'Who on earth do you mean?'

Fiona beamed. 'None other than Good-time Charlie Hoyt himself!'

'You've got to be kidding!' Everyone knew that apart from Augustin Daly, who now had other fish to fry in London right now, Charles Hoyt was the biggest theatre impresario in New York. He was Broadway's golden boy, who had written and produced a string of musical comedy hits as long as your arm. His latest, *Trip to Chinatown*, had just closed after a run of almost two years – a record for any show in the United States. To be actually going to meet the great man in person! She could only shake her head and repeat herself, 'You've got to be kidding!'

'I am not!' They stood facing each other in the middle of

the sidewalk and Fiona burst out laughing. 'Lord, you should see your face!' She tightened her grip on her cousin's arm and began propelling her towards the door. 'Look, there's no point in standing out here making a spectacle of ourselves – that's the type of thing people pay to see inside!'

And, to Mhairi's amazement, a minute later she found herself inside the foyer with its plush flock wallpaper and heavy gilt decoration. Lining the walls on either side of them were large coloured posters of Charles Hoyt's latest lovelies, many of whom, she knew, had gone on to even greater fame and fortune as some of Charles Dana Gibson's already legendary Gibson Girls.

Mhairi's eyes were wide with wonder as she followed her cousin through the great swing doors into the auditorium itself. And the sight that met her eyes made her want to turn and run. About a hundred other young women were clustered around the stage, on which one was singing, accompanied by an elderly man at the piano. The lines of seats stretched out before them, all empty save for two figures in the middle of the front row. Fiona took hold of her arm and propelled her in the direction of the crowd.

As they drew level with the two men in the front row, she whispered, 'That's Charles Hoyt, with the supercilious expression and the cigar. And the other, I presume, is Dick Stael, his musical director. They're casting for their next show this morning. And I have it on good authority that they're looking for a new batch of fresh talent for this one!'

Mhairi stared at her. 'You don't honestly think I'd stand a chance?' Fear and excitement mounted in her.

But Fiona was completely at ease. 'I most certainly do, otherwise I wouldn't be wasting my time. So calm down and enjoy it. He can't kill you!' She grinned. 'Eat you alive maybe, but not kill you!' Her face softened. 'I would've told you before, but the idea only came to me last week — and, anyway, if you *had* known about it, you'd probably have chickened out.'

That was perfectly true. In fact, half of her wanted to turn and run right now. She glanced back towards the stage. A plump girl was beginning 'After the Ball', the hit song from the record-breaking *Trip to Chinatown*. She got no further than the fourth line, when the great man waved her away with a shout of, 'Next!'

They stood together looking and listening to several more, and Mhairi had to admit Fiona had a point. She *was* better looking and *could* sing a darned sight better than any of them. Not that she had done much singing recently. In fact, apart from church, the family had never really sung together since Fiona had left home. Somehow neither Belle nor Finbar had had the heart to have the occasional sing-songs around the fireside they had enjoyed every so often back home in Manchester. She clutched her cousin's arm as nerves tightened in her stomach. 'All right, I will! I'll give it a go! Heaven knows, I can't be much worse than most of them!'

It was almost an hour later when she took to the stage to gaze down into the cynical eyes of the good-looking man with the cigar. Charles Hoyt was in his thirties, immaculately dressed, down to the very latest ascot tie, and his face was adorned with the most luxurious handlebar moustache that Mhairi had ever seen. He also had that air of world-weariness so typical of his breed. His eyes narrowed somewhat about his pince-nez as she moved nearer the front of the stage. He cast a look at the man beside him, and silently they concurred. At least this one looked a cut above the common herd. 'What's it going to be, honey?'

'I — I don't rightly know . . .' Anxiety enveloped her. She had never sung in front of a real professional before. 'What would you like me to sing?'

Charles Hoyt raised his eyes heavenwards and sighed. 'Anything you like, girlie,' he called back, a little too patiently. 'Ed there knows 'em all, right back to "Greensleeves"!'

The man at the piano was smiling encouragingly at her as she moved closer to him. 'Well, then, young lady, what'll it be?' Ed Parker reached for his album of latest tunes, for all the girls wanted to be right up to date.

Mhairi's mind raced. 'Do you know "The Cottage by the Sea"?' she asked tentatively.

'I beg your pardon, Miss?'

' "The Cottage by the Sea",' Mhairi repeated, a little louder this time.

The pianist pushed his cap back and scratched his head. 'Afraid that's a new one on me . . . How does it go?'

And so, with an apprehensive glance at Charles Hoyt and the other man listening down below, she took a deep breath and began to sing:

> 'Childhood's days now pass before me,
> forms and scenes of long ago;
> Like a dream they hover o'er me,
> Calm and bright as evening's glow;
> Days that know no shade of sorrow,
> When my young heart, pure and free,
> Joyful hailed each coming morrow,
> In the cottage by the sea . . .'

She paused at the end of the first verse, conscious of how small her voice sounded without an accompaniment, and how lonely she felt standing there in the centre of the almost empty stage.

'Well now that was real pretty,' Charlie Hoyt's voice called up from below.

'It – it's a song that always meant a great deal to me,' Mhairi began, before he could say more. 'It reminds me of my own childhoo . . .' She got no further before the impresario interrupted.

'For a Mothers' Union convention, it would go down real well, sweetheart. But this is the New York stage. Or didn't anybody tell you? What else you got up your sleeve – "Twinkle Twinkle Little Star"?'

She stared down at him as the colour rose to her cheeks. He was turning to his companion and laughing now. Laughing. They both were. They could see right through her. They knew she had no right to be there – pretending to be something she wasn't. Her mind flew back across the years as that same feeling she had felt as a young child in the Lowells' kitchen swept over her. Old Lizzie, the cook, had seen right through her then, just as they had now. Tears of frustration and rage sprang to her eyes. Was there to be no escape? 'Damn you!' she cried. 'Damn you all! I'm as good as any of you, any day!'

Then, picking up her skirts she fled from the stage, her boots clattering down the wooden steps.

'Hey, hold on a minute there!' Dick Stael, the musical director, rose to his feet.

Mhairi made to rush past Fiona, heading straight for the door, but her cousin grabbed her arm. 'Don't be an idiot! They're calling after you!'

She attempted to shrug off her cousin's grasp, but Fiona had her held fast. 'Don't be an idiot!' she hissed. 'If you run out now, then that's it. Is that what you are, Mhairi McLeod – a quitter?' She had sung beautifully up there on that stage, they would have to be deaf not to realize that.

Mhairi wiped a hand across the tear-streaked skin of her cheeks as Charlie Hoyt himself came striding down the aisle towards her, with Dick Stael in his wake.

'Well now, young lady, it isn't every day a young woman – I can hardly say "lady" – swears at me from my own stage.'

Mhairi gazed into the face looking back at her own. He

131

had a faintly amused, but distinctly supercilious smile on his lips. 'You had no right laughing at me like that!'

'Right?' Charles Hoyt mimicked in amusement. 'Since when do I need to ask permission to smile in my own theatre?'

'If I am no lady for swearing, then you are certainly no gentleman for making me!' Mhairi retorted, amazed at her new-found confidence. If she was to be rejected by a man like this, then she would walk out of here with her head held high.

Charles Hoyt's grin grew broader as he looked round at his musical director. 'Spunk!' he declared. 'Wouldn't you agree there, Dick? The kid's got spunk!'

He took hold of Mhairi's arm and gently began to lead her towards the door. 'Some call it spirit, my dear,' he began quietly. 'But me, I prefer to call it spunk. It's that rare quality that all would like, but few possess.' He could have added that rarely had he heard a voice of such purity, but that would have been superfluous in the face of that other quality that singled out the gold from the dross in this profession. 'Yes, you've got spunk all right and we just might be able to use you – provided you behave yourself, that is!'

Mhairi turned to Fiona who was straining her ears to hear what was being said.

'Give her a card, Joe!' Charles Hoyt said, letting go Mhairi's arm to give her bustle a playful pat. 'We'll give her a go!'

A white-coated young man came towards her brandishing a small piece of cardboard which he thrust into her hand.

'Upstairs at twelve o'clock. Mr Hoyt's office,' he muttered.

Mhairi stared down at the card. It had the number 9 scrawled on it. She looked across at Fiona. The other's eyes were shining.

'Honey, it looks like you could be in a job!'

'You do that young lady and you know where you'll end up!' Belle Rafferty's voice rose in anger as she faced her niece across the kitchen table. 'Why the whole world knows it's nothing but trollops go flaunting themselves on the stage like that. Who put you up to this anyway? Was it Fiona?' She could smell her elder daughter's hand in this.

Mhairi rallied defensively on her cousin's behalf. 'And what if it was? Whoever it was, I can't see that's anybody's business but mine. At least it means I can earn decent money, wear nice clothes, and not spend my life skivvying for other people in future!'

'Well, would you harken at that lip!' Her aunt turned to her husband, who was silently observing the confrontation from the depths of the pantry next door. 'Skivvying for other people, is it? Did you hear that, Finbar? That's all we are now – skivvies!'

She pushed up her sleeves with the same combative gesture she had used so many times back in Manchester before tackling a pile of dirty washing, then her forefinger wagged in her niece's face. 'There's bad blood in your veins, Mhairi McLeod. Bad blood that considers the likes of us not good enough. It had to come out sometime and, by God, it's coming out now.'

Her face hardened, as she continued darkly, 'The Good Book tells us the sins of the fathers will be visited on future generations and that's what we're seeing now. The dirty devil who defiled my sister Mary Anne has done you no favours, for it's his wicked blood, with all its airs and graces, that runs in your veins.'

'Now, Belle, that's enough. I think you've said enough,' Finbar Rafferty cut in, seeing the stricken look on his niece's face. 'There's no call to bring the lass's father into it.'

But his plea went unheeded as his wife's anger at the

133

news of Mhairi's new job fermented with the hurt that had been festering beneath the surface about her daughter Fiona. 'Brought you up in a God-fearing home we have, and this is how you repay us! You give up a decent, respectable post to prostitute yourself on the stage. A whore, that's what you'll be, young lady, a common whore!'

Mhairi's lips twitched as she stared back at her aunt out of a face drained of all colour. This was the last thing she had expected when she all but flew home on wings of happiness, with the contract clasped in her hand this afternoon. Good God, it was a place in the chorus she had been offered, not a contract to walk the streets!

'Well, if it's a whore I'm to be, then that's that, isn't it? You won't be wanting such a creature under your decent, respectable roof!'

With that she turned abruptly and made for the door to the back stairs, only to be caught by the arm by her Auntie Belle.

'And where do you think you're going?'

Mhairi attempted to wrench herself free. 'Away!' she found herself shouting. 'Away from this house. Away from you with your narrow prejudices and spiteful tongue. You're jealous, that's all. You're jealous of the fact that I've got out. That I've escaped this – this prison to which you're still chained. All your life you've spent slaving for others, so they can lead a life that you'll never be any part of – so they can live in sunshine, while you remain in shadow!'

Her aunt dropped her hold of her arm and took a step back as if stung, and Mhairi made a despairing gesture with her hands at the hurt and bewilderment on the older woman's face. 'Dear God, Auntie Belle, can't you see? Even the fact that the servants have to spend their lives below ground in dark, dank places like this, while *they* live in the fresh air and daylight upstairs, is proof enough how we're regarded by them.'

They had been joined in the kitchen by Mr Buss, the butler now, who had been attracted by the raised voices. All three of them stared at her in silence as she continued. 'Look at you all! Just look at you! Content to live in a world of "Yes, madam, this and no, madam, that. Yes sir, no sir, three bags full, sir!" It's pathetic – do you hear me? Pathetic! And I tell you this, it's not for me. Oh no, it's not for me! I'm getting out of this dungeon right now before I suffocate. I'm going to breathe fresh air – above ground! I'm going places, Auntie Belle. I'm going places in this life and neither you nor anybody else is going to stop me!' Her Auntie Jessie's words were ringing in her head: 'You are thistledown, Mhairi. Fly on the wind, lassie. Fly on the wind . . .'

With a strangled sob, she turned and ran from them, her booted feet clattering noisily up the stone steps of the back stairs, towards her bedroom in the attic.

Once there she threw herself down on the bed, where she lay flushed and panting, her mind in turmoil.

But the pounding in her heart lessened, and her breathing calmed as the resolve in her took shape and hardened. And she knew she must carry on with her dream. She had known ever since she was a small child in Ancoats, that she could not flower in such a life as lived by her Auntie Belle. On Skye they had been poor, but they had been free. In a life of servitude she would wither and die as surely as the sun rose every morning above the rooftops of Washington Square and set way out of sight behind the new houses that were going up on the West Side.

She reached into her pocket for the piece of paper on which her precious contract was written. Through misty eyes she reread the words, her gaze lingering on the black ink flourish that was Charles Hoyt's signature. He had faith in her. She must have faith in herself.

There was a tap at her door. She struggled to sit up on

the crumpled quilt. 'Come in,' she ventured, a trifle apprehensively.

Her Uncle Finbar entered the room. His face beneath the freckles was pale and he shifted uneasily from one foot to the other, before walking over to the end of the bed where her grey nankeen jacket lay in a crumpled heap. As she watched, he slipped something into one of the pockets. She made to reach out and investigate, but he held up his hand. 'No, don't. Wait till I've gone.'

They looked at one another and this time she did get off the bed to run to his arms. 'Oh, Uncle Finbar, I'm not really so wicked. Honestly, I'm not.'

Her uncle took her by the shoulders. They were now the same height and he looked directly into her eyes. 'I know that, Mhairi love. And your Auntie Belle knows that, if only she wouldn't let her hurt over Fiona get in the way. She doesn't mean half the things she says these days, you know. She's not been herself lately, that's all . . .' He shook his head, his face colouring. He couldn't bring himself to confide further about what was a woman's complaint. 'It's her age,' he said wearily. 'She'll come round when she's feeling better. I know she will . . . Take that job, Mhairi. Get out of this place, girl. You were right in what you said down there just now, only not one of us who heard it would have the courage ourselves to admit it.'

'But you have,' she said softly. 'You have the courage.'

Her uncle gave a wry smile. 'Aye, I have. Maybe now and again I'm not quite the daft galoot your Auntie Belle would like to make out.'

She hugged him to her once more. 'You're not a daft galoot, Uncle Finbar, and never could be to me. You're the finest friend anyone could ever have.'

They looked at one another, both remembering that day now so long ago when she had denied all knowledge of him on the platform at Manchester station. 'We've come a long way together, Mhairi love.'

'Yes, Uncle Finbar, we have.'

He forced a smile to his lips. Now they had all gone; Mhairi was the last; Fiona, Shona and Seamus – all of them gone. 'I've loved you like one of my own, so I have.'

'I know that.'

He took her hands in his. There was so much he wanted to say. 'It's a big world out there, Mhairi love . . .' He shook his head. Whoever said the Irish had the gift of the gab? He would have given anything to put his feelings into words. The sadness in his smile came from the heart. 'Just promise your Auntie's daft old galoot this – promise me you'll always remember we loved you, and will go on loving you . . .'

His voice cracked and tailed off, and Mhairi hugged him to her once more. 'I promise, Uncle Finbar,' she vowed softly. 'Believe me, I promise.'

When he had gone she looked inside the pocket of the jacket and found five carefully folded, green dollar bills. Probably all the money he had managed to save for himself from his wages since God knows when. Her first impulse was to return them, but she decided against it, for that would surely have hurt his pride more than anything. Instead, she replaced them in the pocket of her grey nankeen jacket, determined never to use them unless she found herself positively starving to death in the world outside.

There was very little to pack in the way of clothes or possessions, as she pulled out from beneath her bed the small cardboard case her aunt and uncle had bought her years ago for her weekends spent with the van der Doncks. She had one set of underwear for best and one for working, and the same went for outer clothing. She glanced down at the beautiful creation she was still dressed in, that Fiona had presented her with only a few short hours ago. Once the case was packed, her grey nankeen jacket was carefully laid on top before she closed the lid. Never would she wear such a thing again, but neither could she part with it.

She did not return to the kitchen to bid goodbye to those within, for she could not bear the thought of another such scene with her aunt. And as far as the Ashtons themselves were concerned, they were away for the week in Lowell, and she had no doubt Mr Buss, the butler, would take great pleasure in recounting the scene he had witnessed this afternoon. It would certainly give her employer, Adeline Ashton, something to tittle-tattle about over the coffee-cups for some time to come. That the rich loved to chatter over the tea and coffee-cups about their servants' inadequacies, she was well aware. 'Love and scandal are the best sweeteners of tea!' Fiona had once declared, and she was certainly supplying them with plenty of the latter.

Well, they could gossip to their hearts' content now, she thought, as she climbed the stone steps that led up from the basement into the fresh air and sunlight of a lovely spring day. It would no longer affect her. Nothing about Lancaster House could affect her any more; she would be as far away from them as possible, as far away as her voice and looks could carry her.

She had arranged with Fiona that she would go straight from home to her cousin's apartment on Thirty-third Street, and it took her almost an hour to find the place. It was on the third floor of a building that had seen better days, but had not quite lost the mark of respectability about it.

Outer appearances, however, could be deceptive, as she was very soon to find out. Once inside, the interior of the three-roomed apartment was like nothing she had encountered before.

Fiona opened the door herself and showed her through to the drawing-room. At first it was difficult to make out very much at all, for the windows were heavily shaded with plush red drapes, and the heavy flock wallpaper and carpets were also in shades of a deep blood red. Large oriental rugs and cushions were strewn about the floor, as if the occupants spent as much time relaxing there as on the heavy gilt chairs. But it was the wall-hangings and paintings which sent the blood rushing to her cheeks as she caught sight of them for the first time.

' "Erotic" is the word, so I'm told,' Fiona informed her, in a tight voice that betrayed little emotion.

Mhairi turned away, her face still flushed. She was totally at a loss for words.

Her cousin walked to the drinks cabinet and poured two sherries from a cut-glass decanter. She handed one to Mhairi with a tight smile and took a sip of her own. 'So now you know, don't you!'

Did she? Mhairi took a deep breath and drank half the drink in one gulp. 'You – you entertain people here?' she ventured.

Fiona laughed. Entertain! She liked that. But her laughter had a bitter edge, and her eyes had a hardness to them, as did the lines of her face. 'I let them use my body,' she corrected, so there could be no mistake. 'And in return Lincoln buys my clothes, sees to my worldly needs, and takes the money.'

'Lincoln?'

'Lincoln Currie his name is. He's what they call on Wall Street a property speculator and financier.' She gave a grim smile. 'He even advises such illustrious people as the Vanderbilts and the Astors what to do with their spare cash . . . Yes, Lincoln is very good when it comes to money, especially other people's.'

Mhairi had sat down by now and was looking at her cousin in a mixture of horror and fascination. In the half-light of the room, with her jacket removed, Fiona looked older and thinner than she could ever remember. 'Don't – don't you mind this kind of life?' she whispered.

'Mind?' Fiona refilled both their glasses. 'I guess the

question really is, do I mind it more than the alternative – scrubbing floors for the likes of the Ashtons or waiting at table?'

She hesitated, then gave a weary shake of the head, 'And then the answer is still Yes. Yes, I darned well do mind it, but I would have minded the other a darned sight more.'

She lifted her glass to Mhairi. 'Here's to you, kid, and your new life on the stage. If I'd been born with half a voice, then, by God, I'd have used *that* to get me out. But as it was . . .' Her voice trailed off as she gazed down at the golden-brown liquid in the glass. 'Well, I use what I have, as long as there are those dumb enough to want to pay for it.' She gave a bitter smile. 'And they say England is the only place where social snobbery still exists! I tell you, Mhairi, in this town, if Cinderella gets to go to the ball, it's to do the washing up!'

Mhairi looked down at her hands. What she was hearing obviously cut deep, although her cousin was attempting to make light of it. 'You – you never met anyone you fell in love with . . . that you wanted to marry?'

Fiona shrugged. 'I was in love once. Marco Bonetti, his name was, but he was killed several years ago. Never get mixed up with an Italian. Their family's honour will always get between them and their common sense.'

Mhairi nodded. 'I knew an Italian boy once . . .' she began, but was cut short.

'Maybe it was just as well really. If he'd never made it big in The Family, as they call it, and had never been killed, I'd have ended up being just another housewife on the wrong side of town.' Her cousin's lips twisted at the edges in a parody of a smile. 'You know what they say: Love begins when you sink in his arms, and ends with your arms in his sink!'

Mhairi looked down at her glass. Despite her bravado,

she could sense that her cousin would have been only too happy to have ended up with her arms in Marco Bonetti's sink.

'Here's to Broadway's newest rising star!' Fiona announced brightly, changing the mood completely. 'Here's to Mhairi Cloud!'

Mhairi's eyes widened. She had almost forgotten she had been given a new name. 'About all this, Fiona, I – I just don't know how to thank you. It – it's like a dream to me . . .'

'Then make that dream come true,' her cousin said with a vehemence that surprised her. 'It's too late for me. Not that I had the talent to begin with. But you're just starting out on life, Mhairi. Grasp it with both hands, and never let go.'

She downed the remainder of her drink and studied the empty glass in her hands. 'I haven't exactly made a great success of my life, as my mother no doubt tells you often enough. And I haven't managed to do a lot of good either. But this was something I felt I *could* do. When I read last week that Charlie Hoyt was looking for fresh young talent for his next show, I would have been mad not to have persuaded you to apply.'

She paused, as if searching for the right words, 'It's not all one-sided, you know, Mhairi. You helped me more than you'll ever know at a time in my life when I needed someone badly.'

Mhairi knew she was referring to the time of her baby's death on the ship. She lowered her eyes as the painful memories came flooding back.

'No one can ever know what something like that does to you – watching your child die. Something died in me that day that can never be brought to life again.' Her mouth twisted, as she turned the empty glass between her fingers and saw again her child's coffin being claimed by the restless waves. 'He never had a chance, poor little bastard. Rejected by his own father – just like you were.'

A faraway look came to her eyes, 'Yes, maybe that's why I felt so close to you then. You had been rejected too.' She looked across at Mhairi sitting silently nursing her drink. 'You have no idea who he is – your father – do you?'

Mhairi shook her head.

'Then find out. Find out and rub the bastard's nose in it!' Fiona said with a passion. 'Make a success here in New York, then go back to Scotland and find him. Find him and tell him just what a skunk he is. Tell him that, for all the poor little bastards in this world, who, like my Bobby, get thrown on the rubbish heap of this life before they have even drawn breath!'

There were tears in both their eyes as they looked at one another across the few yards of carpet.

'It's funny,' Fiona said, wiping them away with the back of her hand. 'I've never cried since leaving that ship all those years ago. I can't cry for myself, you see, not after losing Bobby. It's as if nothing else can ever hurt me after that.'

She walked to the mantelpiece and took down a small velvet-lined box which she walked over with and laid in Mhairi's lap. 'One of my more cultured clients took me to a play the other week,' she said. 'Shakespeare's *King Lear*. And to tell you the truth I couldn't make much of it, but there were a couple of lines in it that stayed in my head.' She gazed down at the box in Mhairi's hands. 'I went straight out and had that made for your birthday. That was your real birthday present, Mhairi love. The rest is just the icing on the cake.'

Mhairi opened it and extracted a silver bangle, which appeared to have a message engraved around it. She held it up to the light and read:

I grow, I prosper;
Now, gods, stand up for bastards!

142

'Do that, Mhairi,' she heard Fiona say. 'Go out there into that world. Grow and prosper, and pay them back. Pay them back, all those sons of bitches, for it is not the children they sired who deserve that name. It is those men themselves who walk out on their responsibilities who are the real bastards of this world. Find your father and pay him back. Pay him back for you, and Bobby and me . . .' Her voice broke as she looked imploringly at her cousin. 'Will you do that, Mhairi? Will you do that for us?'

Mhairi slipped the silver circle around her wrist and looked up to meet her cousin's eyes. The face that looked back into her own was no longer recognizable as the fresh-faced young woman who had met her that day at Manchester station. The youth and beauty that had bloomed for an instant in that barren Ancoats soil had long since fled. Just as her own would. There was nothing so certain. An involuntary shudder ran through her.

Chapter Nine

Mhairi's first few weeks of rehearsals were much harder work than she had ever imagined, with practice often going on well into the evening if Dick Stael, their musical director, was not satisfied with the progress they were making.

About a third of the company were new to New York, and most of them, like Mhairi herself, relied on the experience of older members of the chorus line, such as Sally Sutton, to ease their way into the demands of the 'big-time' stage. Sally was an easy-going, buxom blonde, five years older than Mhairi, and she lost no time in taking the younger girl under her wing. Ever ready with a spare hat pin, or a quip for any occasion, she seemed intrigued by Mhairi's habit of popping into church on the way to rehearsals. 'I don't go in for religion much myself,' she confessed. 'All that kneeling bags my stockings. But say one for me, anyway, next time you're there.' Even old-timers liked to hedge their bets.

Several of the others had come fresh from successes in out-of-town shows and were convinced they were about to take the big city by storm. Mhairi envied them their confidence, although even the most hardbitten amongst them quaked when they came under the cynical eye of their new employer. Charles Hoyt was not given to mincing his words, but he was also a man with a devilish sense of humour; the trick was to know when he was serious and when he was only leg-pulling. It was an almost impossible task, especially for the likes of Mhairi, who took everything about her new career extremely seriously.

They were informed Mr Hoyt would be having a few words with them each morning before rehearsal began, and to Mhairi's surprise it was in front of her that the great man paused as they all lined up on stage to greet him on the first day, and she was even more amazed when he actually remembered her new name.

'Well now, Miss Cloud, before Dick here gets started with you, there are a couple of small items that I'd like to clear up. The first thing is, I take it, at your age you haven't got a problem with strong liquor?'

Mhairi flushed and glanced around her. Why did he have to ask such a question in so loud a voice? 'I most certainly do not!'

'Now, there's no need to get uppity. I have to check up, that's all. You know what they say:

> Little nips of whisky, little drops of gin,
> Makes a lady wonder, where on earth she's bin!'

'In other words, too much of a good thing is simply wonderful!' Sally Sutton added with a grin.

'That'll be quite enough from you, young lady!' their employer said sharply. 'I'm merely warning Miss Cloud here that certain habits will not be tolerated in this company. I'll have no vices in my girls. Pure as the driven snow they must be, or they're no good to me. And that brings me to the second point, Miss Cloud: I will need your certificate of purity before your career as one of my girls proceeds any further.'

'My what?'

'Your certificate of purity, girl. Something wrong with your hearing – as well as your dress sense?'

Mhairi glanced down in embarrassment at the ubiquitous green frock that she was wearing yet again, then turned helplessly to Sally, who sprang to her defence immediately.

'Oh Mr Hoyt, surely that won't be necessary? Why, Mhairi here is so pure she won't even read the begats in the Old Testament!'

But Charles Hoyt's handsome face showed no trace of a smile, nor did he even let on he had heard the interruption, as he continued to peer over his pince-nez and fixed Mhairi with his well-known stare. 'All young ladies in my employ must have one, Miss Cloud. As I said, pure as the driven snow they must be when they enter my employ. The fact that some – and I won't mention names – in this town hire young ladies more of the driven slush variety is neither here nor there. It's my own reputation I'm concerned about. If there's one thing I've learned in my twenty years in this business, it's that plain girls are virtuous for one reason only – lack of opportunity to be otherwise. Given that I hire only the best-lookers in town, the dangers are obvious.'

He took a step forwards and dropped his voice to a more confidential tone. 'There are big names – yes, star-billing they've got – in the likes of the Olympia Theater, that have been on more laps in this town than a napkin . . . No – let's not mince words – have been in more beds than a warming pan!'

He shook his head at the very idea. 'That's not my style, Miss Cloud, not my style at all. I like my girls pure – and that means they must be seen to be pure. You just make sure you have that piece of paper here for my inspection by this time tomorrow.'

And with that he passed down the line, to muffled titters by some in the row behind and the aghast stares of others.

Mhairi's cheeks were still aflame several minutes later when he finally left the stage to allow the practice to proceed.

Where could she go for such a thing? And the embarrassment! She worried about it for the rest of the day, before finally choosing a doctor at random from the many gleaming brass plates around Madison Square. He turned out to be a young man little older than herself and she was convinced her shame was complete as she submitted herself to the required examination, then paid the ten dollars fee.

The next morning she waited with bated breath for her employer to reach her place in the line-up, and sure enough it was the first thing he asked. 'Well, Miss Cloud, you have that certificate of purity by now, I take it?'

Why did he have to speak so loud? He stood back, thumbs hooked into the armholes of his waistcoat, with just the faintest hint of a superior smile on his lips, as her complexion heightened once more.

Mhairi cleared her throat. 'Mr Hoyt,' she began, as the company fell to a hush around them. 'I feel what you asked for yesterday was quite uncalled for, but since you were so ungentlemanly as to demand such a thing, I have it here for you.'

She produced the piece of paper, with the doctor's signature, and handed it to him with a flourish. She would show him her pride was still intact, along with everything else.

Her employer made great play of examining the certificate carefully through his pince-nez before passing it on, with a puzzled expression, to Dick Stael at his side. He shook his head. 'My dear girl, how do you expect this to possibly satisfy our exacting standards?'

Mhairi looked blank. The wind taken out of her sails. She looked first at one and then the other. 'Whatever do you mean? It states quite clearly I am *virgo intacta*!'

'My dear young lady, what possible good is this thing? It was dated yesterday!'

And so the great man retrieved the piece of paper from

his musical director, to screw it up and toss it carelessly over his shoulder, before passing on down the line with a grin as big as a Cheshire cat's across his bewhiskered face.

Mhairi stared at it lying there in a crumpled ball – the thing she had suffered agonies to obtain. She was speechless with fury and humiliation, as the titters of the other girls grew to a crescendo in her ears.

'Don't worry, kid,' Ed Parker consoled her, after their boss had departed. 'The bigger you are in his estimation, the harder he likes to see you fall. It's all part of Charlie's idea of fun. He must really like you to put you through that!'

'Well, if that's really liking me – Lord help me if he hated me!' she fumed, still smarting at the thought of that needless examination the night before.

She was absolutely determined, however, not to let her annoyance show. She would stand on her dignity if it was the last thing she did. So much so that the thought of appearing another morning in the dress he had made such fun of was impossible to contemplate. She made a special visit to Fiona that evening to borrow a fetching pink muslin creation, with leg of mutton sleeves. It maybe wasn't the height of fashion, but it was most becoming, and the flared skirt was well-suited for the high kicks demanded by Dick Stael at rehearsals. In fact her only reservation was that the unusually low neckline showed rather more of her cleavage than she was used to.

She felt well pleased with herself, however, as she stood, chin held defiantly high, in the middle of the stage next morning waiting for the great man's appearance.

True to form, after a few passing comments to some of the other girls, it was once again in front of Mhairi that he stopped. Very deliberately he looked her up and down, even taking the pince-nez off his nose to peer at closer range at the extremely low-cut bodice, above which the swelling skin of her breasts was flushed a bright pink with nervous perspiration.

'My God, what have we here?' he exclaimed. 'Why that's quite a dress you *almost* have on there, Miss Cloud!'

He turned to Sally Sutton, standing next to Mhairi in the line. 'Did *you* know pink muslin was making a comeback, Sal? Maybe we should inform Mr *Joseph*, and some of the other couturiers. I'm sure they'd be real interested to know.'

He gave a pitying shake of the head towards Dick Stael. 'Why, if I'd known we had someone with as great a sense of humour on the premises as this, I do declare I'd have written the whole comedy around her!'

'Easy, kid, easy!' Ed Parker said, putting a restraining hand on Mhairi's arm as her employer moved on down the line. 'Remember what I said – the guy thinks a lot of you!'

But it was several days after that before she came to realize the truth behind the pianist's words. Incredibly Charles Hoyt did think a great deal of her talent – and her beauty – so much so that he called in the well-known commercial artist and photographer Charles Dana Gibson himself to do her portrait.

This was an honour rarely bestowed on a mere member of the chorus line and it provoked quite a reaction amongst the rest of the girls. Some whom she was particularly friendly with, although envious, were glad for her sake, but others lost no time in insinuating she must have earned the special favour by her activities off-stage rather than on. This was a smear she found infuriating but impossible to refute.

'You could always go for another certificate of purity and post it up backstage!' Sally suggested helpfully.

An anguished wail put paid to that idea.

Within days of being told of her boss's decision, a special fitting was arranged with the show's corsetière and wardrobe mistress to ensure that her figure came up to the exacting standards of the ideal Gibson Girl, with the full bosom, handspan waist and ample hips.

When the time came for the session to take place, Mhairi barely recognized herself in the full-length mirror. Just who was she, this other woman who gazed back at her from beneath that picture hat? She could search all day and find little to remind her of the waif who had made that long, lonely train journey from the Highlands of Scotland to Manchester, and had then travelled thousands of miles across the sea to reach this place that now claimed her as its own. But the strange thing was, she felt no different inside. It was as if this was simply another part she was being asked to play, and when she shed the fancy clothes, so she shed the character that they all now knew as Mhairi Cloud.

The gown had been hand-picked by Charles Hoyt himself and it was the most beautiful creation she had ever seen.

'Virgin white, Miss Cloud – most appropriate, wouldn't you say?' her employer declared, with a twinkle in his eye, as he surveyed the finished product for the first time.

It was of pure white taffeta and sat off the shoulders to reveal the pale, creamy skin of her upper arms and breasts, and was tightly pinched in at the waist with a sash of cherry-red velvet. A large picture hat decorated with a matching red velvet ribbon, and hand-sewn red roses, adorned her carefully coiffured hair, and around her long neck hung a red feather boa.

'I do declare I have never seen a finer advertisement for this country's young womanhood!' Charlie declared magnanimously.

And so great a success was the resulting photograph that it was sold to the *New York Globe*, where it was given a full-page spread. Even the more serious-minded *Herald* printed it. Postcards were made of it by the thousand, and within a very short time, her likeness was out-selling all other Gibson Girls in the range.

In fact, her success as a Gibson girl began to assume such

proportions in such a short space of time that it was almost eclipsing her budding stage career, and her position in the chorus was becoming something of an absurdity. It was no longer the established stars of the show who were receiving all the publicity, or having their name chanted by the Stage-door Johnnies. Everyone wanted to wine and dine the young woman whose ravishing face and form were now the talk of the town, and even Charles Hoyt himself was taken by surprise at the growing popularity of his new creation.

When she had first left Lancaster House, Fiona had assisted her in obtaining the lease on a two-roomed apartment on Thirty-third Street, only one block along from her own, but, as her success as one of the nation's favourite pin-up girls grew, Mhairi reluctantly exchanged it for a larger one on Fifth Avenue itself. Image, she was learning, was all; but thankfully she still had someone like her cousin to keep her feet on the ground. The well-heeled young men who were queuing up to wine and dine her cut little ice with Fiona, and, indeed, many had been frequent visitors in the past to her own apartment, where the money they paid out for the pleasure of her body bore little relation to what they were prepared to spend on her younger cousin, for no more than a peck on the cheek.

And neither was she ever asked to dine in the illustrious watering-holes that were becoming so familiar to her cousin.

Now it was nothing new for Miss Mhairi Cloud to be lunching at the Hoffman House, with its 25,000 dollars' worth of Bouguereau gambolling nymphs, cut-glass chandeliers, and ornate pilasters, or to be taken to Delmonico's for a meal of terrapin and oyster salad washed down with champagne.

And for many of her admirers, mere lunch was not enough and the meal would be followed by a trip in a University Club hansom to Dunlap's exclusive hat shop, on Fifth Avenue, or Joseph's, high society's favourite couturier, to choose a hat or gown in the latest fashion.

It was all head-turning, giddying stuff, but to her intimates such as Sally and Fiona, she would simply joke about her success as happening to 'that other woman Mhairi Cloud', for this helped add a perspective to a life in which it seemed as if suddenly all doors were opening, and all things were possible.

Charlie Hoyt had generously allowed her to keep the outfit in which she had posed so successfully for Charles Dana Gibson, but now there was no question of her ever having to wear the same dress two days running. Every single day she was attired in the height of fashion, and was thrilled to be the first in the company to sport the latest 'rainy-daysy' skirt that cleared the ground by a scandalous six inches!

As her world grew, she found herself meeting people from all walks of life. But, despite the senators, the big-shot lawyers, and bright young financiers from Wall Street, her particular favourite among her escorts was a stout, white-haired old soldier by the name of Honeycomb who declared at their first introduction, 'Sweet by name, and sweet by nature, my dear! William J. Honeycomb's the name. Colonel, US Army . . . Retired now, I'm sorry to say, by virtue of certain fatuous opinions held by those dimwitted pen-pushers in our War Department who judge a man's usefulness in this life not by his experience, or his ability, but by the number of years that have passed since he was weaned!'

She felt safe with old Willie Honeycomb. Unlike so many of the younger men, he demanded nothing of her except the delight of having her on his arm.

Since leaving the Army he had turned into something of a Bohemian, with his velveteen jackets, Scotch caps and corduroy trousers, and his love and knowledge of the arts was something he particularly enjoyed imparting to his beautiful young companion. He was now renting an apartment in Washington Square. The area around Mhairi's old home was gaining quite a reputation as an artists' colony, and she had read with interest the series of articles in *Godey's Magazine* on the prominent women painters and writers who were making it their home. The Colonel was able to keep her informed of all the latest gossip about these exotic creatures, many of whom he had come to regard as his personal friends, and it pleased her to know there were other women in the city who were also making their mark by virtue of their own talents.

She read with relish the copies of their books that Willie turned up with, as well as the numerous others he recommended. She had always been an avid reader, but, under his fatherly tutelage, her literary horizons broadened so much she soon felt able to hold her own in almost any company. Her favourite book was George du Maurier's *Trilby* and she would joke with the Colonel about him being her own personal Svengali. The old man would beam and nod sagely. 'You could be right there, my dear. You could be right.' And it was then she knew he was getting as much out of their relationship as she was. It was a good feeling.

Willie Honeycomb also introduced her to one of the city's favourite Bohemian establishments: Maria's, a basement restaurant-cum-nightclub in MacDougal Street. There the resident singer was a character by the name of Mickey Finn, who had given his name to a quite intoxicating concoction, after a few glasses of which the customers were only too willing to break into song, or give entertaining monologues of their own poetry and prose.

With the Colonel's active encouragement, Mhairi found herself blossoming in such an environment that mixed the best cultural happenings of the day with sparkling repartee, and they became frequent visitors to the cellar. And it was in Maria's that she suffered the ignominy of getting drunk in public for the first time – although he gallantly assured her he was the only one to notice it. Willie himself was a teetotaller of long standing, and had been quite unaware of the amount his young partner was drinking – until the moment they came to leave. He could only look on in amazement as she got up from her chair, to slide gracefully back down under the table.

Although she was totally oblivious to everything and everyone by then, he was quick to point out to her the error of her ways when he called to take her out to lunch the following day. 'Next time just knock yourself over the head with a hammer, my dear,' he advised, when she complained of her well-deserved headache. 'If you hit yourself hard enough, you'll achieve instant oblivion and get the same results as from a whole gallon of champagne, or half a dozen Mickey Finns – with much less wear and tear on the liver into the bargain!'

Yes, she knew with the old soldier around, her feet would be kept firmly on the ground. 'Those that fly the highest have the furthest to fall,' he would say, with a shake of his head, whenever her youthful ambitions threatened to get out of hand, and she would immediately come down to earth with a gentle thud. Willie Honeycomb was her anchor, her safe haven, in a world that with each passing day threatened more and more to sweep her off her feet.

As her success as a Gibson Girl continued to grow throughout the late spring and early summer, it became more and more obvious that it was Mhairi and not the official stars of the show the public was clamouring to see. So much so that Charles Hoyt took the decision to build up her part by taking her out of the chorus and writing in two solo singing spots. And, perhaps most exciting of all, he added her name to the billboards.

The news of her promotion in the star stakes came one

month into the show, and that morning proved memorable for another reason: through the post she received a gilt-edged invitation to an extra special luncheon date. She was to dine with none other than George Washington Vanderbilt himself. She could barely contain her excitement, for to cross the threshold of either a Vanderbilt or an Astor was to make that all-important breakthrough into the highest echelons of society itself.

She had met George Vanderbilt at a party at Charles Dana Gibson's house, shortly after her first full-page Gibson Girl picture had appeared in the newspapers, but she had not really taken seriously the millionaire's rather off-hand remark about having her round for lunch sometime.

When the coveted invitation did finally arrive, she deliberately did not mention it to the other girls, for there was enough bitching backstage already. But she determined to make the most of it, and decided to wear her original white Gibson Girl outfit for the occasion, considering it to be the most flattering she possessed.

She was relieved to hear that Charles Hoyt had also received an invitation and on the day in question he ordered a cab to pick them up from the theatre, after morning rehearsal, to take them over to the Vanderbilt mansion.

When the cab drew up right outside the large brownstone house that was 640 Fifth Avenue, there was already a line of carriages disembarking a succession of well-dressed passengers on to the sidewalk outside its ornate façade. And, as the hansom rattled off over the cobbles, Mhairi linked her arm into that of her employer as nerves tightened in her stomach. She could hardly believe she was about to enter the home of a real live Vanderbilt as a guest, and not merely as a below-stairs maid.

They stood on the sidewalk for a moment or two gazing up at the huge bay windows, with their classic columns and elaborate wrought-iron work, then paused before the enormous bronze entrance doors, depicting the Wonders of Heaven from the Old Testament.

'They were originally cast for an Italian Prince, and they're called the Gates of Paradise,' her employer informed her knowledgeably. 'And believe me they're well named. This place is quite something inside!' As a celebrity of long standing himself, he was well acquainted with the interiors of the homes of almost all New York's top families, but this one was something special.

Mhairi was soon to find out how true his comment was as they followed the butler into a marble-floored vestibule which was even larger than the Ashtons' great hall itself. The walls too were of polished marble and surmounted by a mosaic frieze.

'Look up!' Charles prompted, pointing with his cane to the ceiling, and, as she raised her eyes she gave a gasp of wonder. The roof was of stained glass, through which the midday sun was shining and reflecting off a huge vase of green malachite, almost nine feet in height, which had pride of place in the middle of the floor. 'It's one of a pair,' Charles said knowingly. 'The other is owned by the Tsar of All the Russias and stands in the Winter Palace at St Petersburg.'

'Where else . . .' Mhairi murmured, her gaze falling on the two lifesize figures of Fame which hung suspended on either side of it. Never had she been in such an incredible place.

After being divested of her hat, wrap, and parasol, and Charles of his top hat and cane by a liveried footman, they continued on through the great hall, the ceiling of which rose the whole four storeys to the roof of the house, with balconies tiered on all sides in the style of an Italian palace. Huge multicoloured marble columns rose to the roof, overpowering the breathtaking array of treasures and works of art that were displayed all around them.

Several other rooms appeared to open off this central atrium, and they were ushered towards one identified by Charles as the drawing-room. The butler led the way through a velvet-draped archway and announced their names to the assembled company, most of whom stood around in small knots, too deep in their own conversations to hear anything going on elsewhere.

'Heavens, half New York's here by the looks of it!' Mhairi exclaimed, her eyes widening at the size and composition of the crowd before them. Already she could spot at least one Astor, and a Stuyvesant or two.

'Only the half that matters!' Charles added, with a worldly smile. His eyes too scanned the faces, then he spotted their host. He raised his hand at a youngish man, in his early thirties, who excused himself from the party he was with and came striding across the floor towards them.

'Charles, how good you could come!' George Vanderbilt shook hands warmly with the impresario before turning to Mhairi. 'And you don't have to remind me who this is . . . It wouldn't be Charles if he didn't have the most beautiful young lady in town on his arm! How are you, my dear?'

Mhairi affected a modest smile as the millionaire took her hand and raised it to his lips. She was becoming quite inured to such comments about her looks, but she was pleased for her employer's sake.

Charles Hoyt beamed. But despite his pride in the young woman at his side, he had other things on his mind. These lunchtime gatherings of the cream of their city's society were too good an opportunity to pass up for sounding out possible investors in his forthcoming shows. His eyes continued to scan the faces around them as their host complimented Mhairi on her gown. Wasn't that Pierre Lorillard, the tobacco magnate, over there talking to Hilary Herbert, the Secretary of the Navy? The politician wouldn't be much good, but Lorillard was a definite possibility. He'd been trying to catch up with him for months. 'George, there's someone here I simply must have a word with. Be a good man and find someone interesting to keep this young lady amused till I get back.'

George Vanderbilt looked a trifle discomfited and glanced around him. Trust Charlie! But before he could come up with a suggestion, it was Mhairi herself who solved the problem with a gasp of recognition.

'Why Mr Vanderbilt, I'm sure I know that young woman over there!' There was something about the tilt of her head that was disconcertingly familiar. She continued to stare as she indicated with her fan in the direction of a plumply pretty, dark-haired young woman in a gown of emerald green velvet. She was half-turned from them and was in rapt conversation with a tall, well-built young man, with a strong jaw and a shock of dark unkempt hair that flopped unfashionably over one eye. And he was dressed in, of all things, a kilt. Mhairi stared at the fine figure in the velvet dress jacket, her eyes travelling down to the well-muscled calves beneath the tartan of the kilt. It was the first time she had seen a real-life example of her country's national dress since leaving Scotland, and her heart beat faster.

George Vanderbilt looked round, his eyes following the pointing fan. 'You mean Miss van der Donck?'

'Then it *is* Kati!' Mhairi could barely contain her excitement. 'Oh, please, I've got to meet her again. Do call her over!'

Her host left to obey her request with an amused smile as Mhairi craned her neck to obtain a better view of her childhood friend.

She could hardly wait for her host to deliver the message, but in such illustrious company decorum had to prevail, and she stood her ground with some impatience, as the three of them made their way across the floor

158

towards her. She could not fail to notice that her old friend showed no trace of a limp. Obviously enduring the horror of that awful leg iron as a child had paid dividends.

Kati van der Donck's brown eyes widened as she approached, escorted on either side by the two men. 'Why, as I live and die – it *is* you!' She stopped just far enough away to avoid Mhairi's waiting hug as she shook her head in amazement. 'Mama said the other day that she was sure that new Gibson Girl they were all talking about was you, but I just didn't believe it.'

'Well, it is me,' Mhairi assured her, clasping her hands together in frustration. She was longing to envelop her friend in the bear hug to end all hugs, but there was something about Kati's demeanour that told her that would not be in order.

Kati shook her head as she regarded Mhairi with a faintly amused air. Her lips pursed then broke into a sweet smile. 'Who would've thought it, little Mhairi McLeod, a star!'

'I – I've just been lucky, I guess,' Mhairi said quickly, anxious that her friend did not think she had got too big for her boots. 'You know the right face at the right time – that sort of thing . . .' She was floundering about for something to say to cover her nervousness, when the young man in the kilt spoke.

'Would someone care to introduce us, please?'

At that, their host excused himself. 'Kati, my dear, would you mind doing the honours? I see Alva and her intended have just arrived, and she will kill me if I'm not there to welcome them!'

He excused himself with a bow to each of the young women, and the young man, and made for the door, where a middle-aged, stoutish woman stood looking around, with a rather nervous looking male companion at her side.

'That's the famous Alva Vanderbilt,' Kati informed the

young man at her side, attentively brushing an invisible piece of lint from the arm of his immaculate jacket. 'Apart from Mrs Astor, she's probably this town's most famous hostess. But things are a bit tacky at the moment socially. She's recently divorced Willie K. Vanderbilt and has already got another husband lined up.' Her eyes darted back to the door. 'That's him presumably.'

Her voice dropped, as she lifted her fan to cover her mouth in a confidential gesture. 'And I have heard she also has a husband lined up for her daughter Consuelo – a countryman of yours, the Duke of Marlborough, no less! And do you know, I have it on good authority that the Marlboroughs are demanding a dowry of two and a half million dollars in William Kissam Vanderbilt's Battle Creek Railway Company stock, plus an allowance made to the young couple of a hundred thousand dollars a year for life!' Kati's eyes widened at the thought. 'All in all, they say the deal amounts to some fifteen million dollars!' The figure was breathed in an awed voice.

The young man by her side showed no surprise. 'Six million pounds is about right.'

Kati's brows rose. 'Why, you've heard too!'

'Sunny is one of my oldest friends.'

'Sunny?'

'Charles – the ninth Duke.'

'I should have known!' Kati declared, as she clutched her companion's arm that bit tighter. 'Ralph knows everyone who is anyone in the English aristocracy . . . But, of course, that's only natural, being a part of it himself!'

'Correction, my dear . . . I'm Scottish, remember.' He extended his right hand towards Mhairi. 'I'm Ralph MacLachlan, by name. Gentleman by occupation . . .' He grinned. 'In other words, I live by robbing the poor.'

'Ralph, really!' Kati exclaimed.

Mhairi gave a quiet smile and raised one eyebrow as she

looked at him quizzically. 'With a good Scottish name like MacLachlan I'd find that hard to believe . . . Unless you're one of those terrible absentee landlords that are the curse of that lovely land.'

The young man looked at her curiously, but reluctantly refrained from pursuing the matter further, as Kati intervened: 'Mhairi, this is Lord Ralph MacLachlan – not Robin Hood in reverse, despite what he claims . . . And Ralph, dear, this is Miss Mhairi . . .' She paused, her brow puckering, 'What is it you're calling yourself now?'

'Cloud,' Mhairi answered. 'Mhairi Cloud.'

'Of course – Miss Mhairi *Cloud*.'

'Cloud – what a perfect name for such a heavenly being!' Ralph MacLachlan had a lazy, laconic voice that bore little trace of the Scottish pedigree he claimed, and an easy smile that tilted to the right, sending the fashionably luxurious moustache askew, and causing his grey eyes to wrinkle at the corners. He bent from a height of well over six feet, to raise Mhairi's hand to his lips and kept it there for much longer than was necessary.

She found herself having to extract her fingers from his, as she gave Kati a conciliatory smile. The last thing she wanted was for her old friend to think she was trying to monopolize her partner. 'It's so marvellous to see you again, Kati dear,' she said, deliberately turning aside from the young man. 'It must be what – all of four years?'

Kati smiled benignly as she turned to the young man. 'Mhairi and I haven't seen each other since she went into service as a mere child of fourteen. What was your title again, Mhairi dear –under-kitchen maid, wasn't it?'

'Under-parlour maid, actually,' Mhairi said quietly. Why was she doing this? She could feel the smile on her lips become more fixed as the hurt welled within her.

'Yes, it's certainly changed days,' Kati continued. 'And I couldn't be happier for you!' She leaned across and kissed Mhairi lightly on the cheek, her lips barely skimming the surface of the skin as she continued, 'Now you will excuse us if we dash – there are so many people to get round at a luncheon like this, and I do so want Ralph to meet as many as possible before they call us through for the meal.'

Mhairi watched them go, disappearing back into the crowd, Kati's fingers clutching tightly at the young man's left sleeve. She felt a cold emptiness within her, and a sense of humiliation, although no real insult had been given. She forced a smile to her lips as she walked across and pretended to admire one of the many fine oil paintings that adorned the walls. What on earth was there to feel so upset about? After all, Kati had been perfectly friendly, hadn't she?

Chapter Ten

The new show, *Sunshine Girls*, was going from strength to strength and playing to packed houses every night. The talk was that it might even break the previous American record for a run held by *Trip to Chinatown*. But throughout it all, Mhairi was determined not to let herself be swept away by the many glamorous invitations that were coming her way. 'Old friends, like old shoes, are the most comfortable,' she told the Colonel, when he mentioned he might well call by to take her out to supper after the performance one particularly sultry evening in early July.

At just after ten o'clock, a knock at her dressing-room door made her look round. Surely it couldn't be him already? The curtain had only just come down, she was hot and sticky, and had barely had time to catch her breath. She sighed, then called, 'Come in!' in a less than enthusiastic voice.

The bell-boy entered carrying a card and a single red rose. 'There's a gentleman outside and he asked me to deliver this, ma'am.'

Mhairi took the card and the flower, with a murmur of thanks, and read the scrawling handwriting:

> Go, lovely rose!
> That now she knows,
> When I resemble her to thee,
> How sweet and fair she seems to me . . .
>
> > Her devoted servant,
> > Ralph MacLachlan.

Her brow furrowed at the name for a moment, then, 'Ah . . .' She gave a quizzical smile.

'He's waiting outside, ma'am. Will there be an answer?'

'Tell His Lordship to come in.'

And a moment later he was there, his tall frame crowding the small dressing-room. This time there was no kilt; he was immaculately turned out in a bespoke evening suit, but his head of dark, curling hair quite patently lacked the obligatory application of Macassar oil regarded as so necessary for the well-groomed man. He ran a hand through the wayward locks and then extended it towards her.

She stood up and accepted it with a polite smile. 'Lord MacLachlan, how unexpected! And what a charming verse. You're quite a poet!'

He had a roguish grin and used it to effect. 'I have to admit, ma'am, the words may not be entirely mine, but the sentiment . . . Well, I'll save your blushes on that for the moment.'

His eyes were smiling directly into hers, and, feeling her cheeks begin to flush, she broke his gaze and craned her neck to see behind him. 'Is Kati with you?'

Ralph MacLachlan looked surprised. 'No, should she be?'

His rejoinder unsettled her, but she deflected the question with another. 'May I – may I offer you a drink?' She glanced round at the cluttered top of her dressing-table. She should have something left somewhere.

'I came to ask you that question . . . We're going out on the town. Just the two of us. Unless you have a prior engagement?'

'Wouldn't Kati object?'

He smiled that quirky smile once more. 'Probably. But I'm not asking her, I'm asking you. You *will* come?'

Mhairi took the flower over and placed it in the ewer on her washstand to give herself time to think. There was not only Kati to consider – she had never let the Colonel down before. 'I really don't think so,' she said finally. 'I have already arranged to meet an old friend tonight.'

'Cancel it.'

'I beg your pardon?'

'Cancel it,' he repeated, more firmly this time. 'You're coming out with me. You must, I return to London tomorrow. The *St Louis* sails at ten.'

There was something challenging in his tone of voice that took her aback and she turned to face him. 'I – I don't think I can do that . . .'

'You can and you must. You know that as well as I do.'

Did she? She gazed in growing curiosity into the eyes that bore down into her own. They were grey, and fringed with long curling lashes like a girl's, but that was the only feminine thing she could discern about him. There was a definite arrogance about his bearing and attitude that she found difficult to cope with. Were the British aristocracy always so sure of themselves?

'You walk in here and demand I cancel a prior engagement simply to go out with you! Just who do you think you are?' she demanded. But her tone was more amused than anything else.

'I am the man who has fallen in love with you, as no one else will ever love you.'

Mhairi let out a peal of laughter, but it died on her lips as she saw the expression in his eyes. 'Heavens, I do believe you could be serious!'

'I have never been more serious.'

She sat down on her chair, feeling for all the world as if the breath had been knocked out of her, when there was a familiar knock and voice at the door: 'Mhairi honey, it's me . . .'

She got up looking quite flustered, as if she had been caught in some dreadful act. 'Oh Willie – how lovely to see you!' Never had her old friend been more welcome. She

165

made a dash for the door and all but hauled the Colonel into the centre of the room, causing its other occupant to have to stand aside.

'Willie, this is Lord Ralph MacLachlan,' she began. 'He — he tells me he is returning to Britain tomorrow.'

She got no further, for the young man in question thrust out his hand at the newcomer and stated firmly, 'How do you do, sir. I'm honoured to make your acquaintance. I just called by to invite Miss Cloud here out to supper — since it's my last evening in New York.'

The Colonel's eyes moved from one to the other. 'Well now, young Lord . . . Honeycomb's my name. Colonel William J. Honeycomb, US Army, retired . . . but we won't go into that.'

His eyes twinkled beneath the shaggy white brows. 'Take her out you say? Well, I think that's a first-class idea. It's only right and proper that a young lady like Mhairi here should share a table tonight with a fine young man like yourself, rather than an old fogey like me!'

'Oh, but of course we would insist on you joining us!' Ralph MacLachlan put in, well aware of the risk he was taking.

'Wouldn't dream of it, young man! No, you young things go on out and enjoy yourselves.'

He turned to Mhairi, 'Only you, young lady, remember that hammer I warned you about!'

Ralph MacLachlan looked perplexed as Mhairi stifled a laugh. 'I had a slight accident some time ago,' she said enigmatically, 'and the good Colonel here has been afraid for my safety ever since.' She had no doubt at all that it was an opportune warning, for she could almost hear the champagne corks popping already.

She stayed behind a moment or two to take her leave of her old friend as her new, younger companion went out to hail a cab. 'You're sure you won't join us, Willie dear?'

The Colonel's head shook emphatically. 'Wouldn't

dream of it. He seems a fine young man. Just you remember, though, if he spins you a line — flattery is like a good cigar, you get the best out of it as long as you don't inhale!'

She hugged him to her; his whiskers prickling her cheek. Trust Willie to be always on the lookout for her welfare. 'Don't you worry,' she assured him. 'I wasn't brought up by an Irishman for nothing! I can recognize blarney a mile off — even coming from a so-called Scot like the good Lord there!'

To her surprise, Ralph MacLachlan had chosen none of the famous hotels or restaurants for their supper, but had settled on a small, exclusive establishment called Benno's, a few doors down from Dunlap's, her favourite hat shop.

It was the first time she had been there and she glanced approvingly at the walnut and brass furnishings, and the discreet lighting as they were escorted to their seats. They were led to a booth for two reserved in both their names and Mhairi could not resist a smile as she handed the waiter her wrap and took a seat. 'You were very sure I would come.'

He grinned. 'And I was proved right, wasn't I?'

'You really are an unbearable man!'

His grin grew broader. 'Some things, Miss Cloud, are out of our hands. As something of a gambler myself, I know that Fate has been playing the cards since that first moment we met. It may sound crazy to you, but ever since we were introduced yesterday I have had the strangest feeling of destiny closing in on me. There was no way you could have refused to accompany me here tonight . . . You do believe in destiny, don't you?'

Mhairi took a deep breath as Willie Honeycomb's warnings rang in her head. But she was given a moment's grace as the waiter handed them the menu. She watched her new companion closely as he scrutinized what was on offer. He certainly looked quite sane, if a little too cock-sure of himself.

After a moment or two he politely passed the leather-bound cards across for her inspection, but she waved them away. 'I'll leave it entirely up to you.' As her Auntie Belle used to say, hunger was a good sauce, and she had gone without too often to be fussy about her food now.

Cream of celery soup was ordered, to be followed by water souchet of flounders, fricandeau of veal with spinach, then fresh fruit salad to follow. 'And we'll have coffee to finish,' her companion added, 'and one bottle of champagne now, and two on ice for later.'

When the waiter had departed, Ralph MacLachlan's attention turned to her once more. 'You were about to tell me that you believed in destiny.'

'Was I?' She gave an amused smile. It was going to be no easy matter holding her own with this particular young man. But, despite that, she had to concede he might well have a point. She looked thoughtful. 'Do I believe in destiny? I find that a very difficult one to answer, although, to be perfectly honest with you, both my mother and my great-aunt on Skye would have agreed wholeheartedly with the idea. They believed all things to be preordained.'

His eyes widened. 'On Skye? You're not a full-blown American, then?'

'No,' she confessed. 'I'm as Scottish as you are. Although, like your good self, I may not sound it now. But I was certainly born in Scotland. On the Isle of Skye to be exact.'

'Mmm . . . a West Highlander.'

'You're not, I take it.'

He shook his head. 'No, I'm from the east coast. A beautiful part of the country in its way, but not so haunting as Skye.'

He said the right thing, for her eyes softened as her thoughts returned to that most beloved of places. 'We call it *Eilean a' Cheo* in the Gaelic,' she told him. 'The Island of

Mist. And its children are known as the Children of the Mist.' She toyed with the stem of her champagne glass as her voice dropped, 'No, I am no New Yorker, Lord MacLachlan, except by adoption. I am Mhairi McLeod, from Skye – a Child of the Mist.'

A silence fell between them as he sat looking at her curiously in the soft light of the candles on the table before them. This was not at all what he had expected to hear, but it only served to intrigue him even more. 'So you're a Gael,' he murmured. 'Do you know what they say about your people, Mhairi?' It was the first time he had used her name.

She shook her head.

'They say the Gael is a creature of extremes, his sadness is despair, his joy is rapture . . .'

He reached across and took her hand. 'Is that how it is for you, Mhairi McLeod? Is that how your life will be – either despair or rapture?'

She looked up and met his eyes, and a most peculiar feeling swept over her. 'We shall just have to wait and see about that, won't we?' she said quietly.

She leaned back in her chair and regarded him thoughtfully, determined to break the spell the evening was weaving. Her tone was matter of fact. 'You don't sound much like a Scot.'

He gave a wry smile. 'That's what comes of being sent off to school south of the border. A top hat, a caned bottom, and an English accent – that's what Eton did for me . . . Oh, and the ability to keep a stiff upper lip at all times.'

She gave a wry smile. 'That's probably what gives Englishmen their reputation as the world's worst lovers.'

'So you've heard!' he exclaimed in mock despair. 'The rest of the world have love lives, while the English have hot-water bottles! And it's perfectly true, believe me. Why even today, some still consider the waltz to be thoroughly indecent!' He grinned across at her as he pushed back his chair. 'Do you fancy being thoroughly indecent with me, Miss McLeod?'

He rose from his seat and held out his hand and she took it, a trifle apprehensively, and they joined the other couples on the dance-floor.

It was the first time he had held her in his arms, but she had no need to worry, for their steps synchronized in perfect rhythm to the swelling strings of the quartet on the dais in the corner of the room; it seemed as if they had been dancing together all of their lives. Close to, he smelt of oil of sandalwood and tobacco smoke, with just a hint of fine malt whisky. It was a disturbingly masculine smell that played havoc with her senses despite her resolve to remain as cool as possible.

The musicians ended their spot with 'After the Ball', the most popular song from Charlie Hoyt's hit musical, *Trip to Chinatown*. It was one of her favourites and she said so, as the strains of the familiar melody filled the air. And, to her embarrassment, he sang it to her in an attractive tenor voice as they whirled their way around the floor:

'After the ball is over, after the break of morn,
After the dancers are leaving, after the stars are gone;
Many a heart is aching, if you could read them all,
Many the hopes that have vanished, after the ball . . .'

'Our hopes won't vanish after tonight, Mhairi,' he whispered, as his arm tightened around her waist. 'I can promise you that.'

Her heart was beating much too fast as the final bars filled the air. But Willie Honeycomb's warnings still rang in her ears. She mustn't get too carried away, she told herself. For all she knew he shot lines like this to every female he met. And anyway, he was going back tomorrow. The great liner, the *St Louis*, was already out

170

there in the harbour waiting to weigh anchor and set sail for London. It would be crazy to let herself get swept off her feet by someone like him. But she gripped his hand even more tightly as they made their way back to the table.

The meal was delicious, and as they lingered over their coffee he told her of his home in Scotland, on the rugged headland, jutting out into the turbulent grey waters of the North Sea. Craig David Castle stood amid a forest of towering Scots Firs, and was as fine a fortress as was to be found anywhere in that far country that had given birth to them both. 'I want to show it to you one day, Mhairi,' he said, taking her hand in his. 'There are bluebells there by the multitude, and golden daffodils, and the air blows straight from heaven, pure and sweet.' And his eyes took on a faraway look as he said softly, 'I could go on, but we tend to become bores talking of what we love the best.'

'It sounds a beautiful place.'

'It is,' he insisted. 'And one day you shall see it for yourself.'

He sounded so positive that immediately her guard went up. 'If I want to, that is.'

'You will.'

She smiled into her glass. She knew when she had met her match. 'Tell me about your family.'

'Ah, my family . . .' And so he told her of his father, Hugh, the Earl of Inverbervie, and of his mother, Anne, the Countess. He was one of two sons, he said. His elder brother, David, who would inherit the title, was, at twenty-nine, seven years older than himself.

'David's done quite a bit of travelling, so I expect he wasn't too put out not to be making this trip to the States. He's been to India three times — and that's twice more than me!' And he went on to entertain her with tales of their trips out East, where as guests of the Viceroy, they had made the acquaintance of a maharajah or two, done a bit of elephant hunting, and tried their hands at pig-sticking for good measure.

At the mention of pig-sticking, Mhairi shuddered, but he knew she would shudder a good deal more if he confided to her the visits to the exotic *demi-monde* of Indian brothels, that David had taken great delight in introducing him to, and of the women they had met there.

But all that was not for the ears of his partner. 'I didn't fancy the idea of pig-sticking myself either, to tell the truth. But my brother is game for anything. You'll like him, I know you will. As long as he goes easy on the *water of life.*'

'Ah, yes . . .' She had known many a man back on Skye who had also been a bit too fond of the whisky.

But her companion was tiring of talking of himself. 'Tell me about that family you left behind, Mhairi – or did you bring them with you?'

She gave an uncertain smile and stirred the sugar in her coffee cup. Just how much should she tell? Her life had been so far removed from his own. And so she told him part, but by no means all that had happened over the past eighteen years of her life. The fact that she had not spoken to her aunt and uncle since she left home, she deliberately kept to herself, for that was still an open wound in her heart. Nor did she tell him of being sent from her home in Scotland to join them in England, before making the journey across the sea to America. The memory of those sunless, joyless days remained an indelible scar on her childhood, and this was no time to be reopening old wounds. Instead she concentrated on her life on Skye, and she could see he was listening with interest, and seemed well acquainted with many of the places she mentioned. 'Have you ever been to the West Highlands, or to Skye yourself?' she asked.

'Oh yes, quite often. My parents have friends on the island and we have gone quite regularly to visit them. But, to tell you the truth, we don't get back to Scotland nearly often enough. My mother's English, you see, and much prefers the life down south, so we spend most of the year in London. We make sure we get back to Scotland for the shooting, though, and have done — well, ever since my brother and I were strong enough to hold a gun.'

Mhairi felt herself tense and her expression changed to one of concern as he went on to tell her of the record number of grouse he had bagged in one shoot, and of the tracking and shooting of his first deer at the age of fourteen.

'Yes, although I enjoy living in London, it's marvellous having a place like Scotland to escape to. It's a beautiful land, and there are just no people up there. It's quite incredible . . .' And his eyes shone at the memory of those golden days walking the heather-clad hills, with the dogs at his side, as the beaters went on ahead scaring the birds into flight, and he did not notice the hardening of her eyes as they remained fixed on his face.

'There is a very good reason for our country being bereft of its people, and, as one of those aristocratic landlords yourself, you should know that better than anyone,' she broke in, when she could keep quiet no longer. 'Scotland *is* a beautiful land, but it is a mutilated beauty. The Highlands have become a virtual wilderness, due to the likes of you and your kind — the absentee landlords whose only interest is in the sport, and the profit that can be made at the expense of the people.' Her face was quite flushed now and she poured herself another drink and drank it down greedily as she fought to control her emotions.

He was quite taken aback by her unexpected outburst and was on the verge of saying so, but there was something about the set of her mouth as she replaced her empty glass on the table that made him keep his peace. She was a strange creature indeed, for her mood could change like the wind, and a look had come into her eyes that spoke of things that burned deep in her soul, the like of which he knew he could not comprehend, for they came from backgrounds as far apart as fire and water.

A silence fell between them, and as Mhairi looked across at the young aristocrat she felt a curious mixture of emotions. Fond though she was certainly growing of him, his comments on their shared homeland had triggered a reaction in her that had taken her by surprise almost as much as it had him. His remark on the land bereft of its people had brought memories back that were still as vivid today as they had been then, all those years ago.

A chill had come to her bones and she had recalled her mother's words, as they walked the hills of her childhood, for it was then, when they were alone with just the cry of the seagulls for company, that Mary Anne McLeod had told her small daughter of the tragedy that was their inheritance.

'Never forget, child. Those who have laid claim to this land have no place for its people.' And she had taken Mhairi's hand and, from the hill above their village, she had pointed to the places where homes had once stood. 'Whole communities there were once. And homes that rang with the laughter of children are now crumbling ruins . . .' Then her mother's voice had faltered and she could say no more. There were things in this life that went too deep for words. But the child at her side had felt it and remembered.

Mhairi's eyes found those of the young man sitting opposite her, and she shook her head in confusion. He was both hurt and puzzled, she could see that, but she could find no words to comfort him, and she wished with all her heart they had not got on to the subject of her homeland. Up till then she could almost forget that his class had been the one responsible for most of her country's troubles. And she felt a sense almost of shame within her, for how could she find herself so attracted to such a being, the likes of whom her own people still held in such contempt?

'What is it, Mhairi?' he said at last. 'What have I done to upset you like this?' Things could not have been going better a moment or two before.

She sighed and fought to keep the bitterness from her voice as she did her best to explain the pain within her. Then she told him, as her mother had told her, of the aristocratic landlords who had thrown the people off their land to make way for the more profitable sheep. 'Dragged like dogs from their homes, they were. Even for the old and dying there was no pity, for they like the others had their homes set fire to over them, and they were cast out to perish, or flee the land that they loved – a land that had been theirs since time immemorial. The Highland Clearances were a blot on the face of humanity,' she said quietly. 'A stain on the soil of my country that will remain as long as there are Scottish people on the face of this earth to remember.'

She looked at him across the table, her eyes dark and serious in the soft candlelight, as the wounds that had bled in her mother's heart bled still in her own. 'If God created the land for His people, what right have rich lords like the Duke of Sutherland and his ilk to take it from them?'

The young man listening on the other side of the table had no answer. 'I – I have only heard tell of the atrocities that happened in the past, Mhairi. I know no more than the average man about such things.' But even he had heard tell of the atrocities that had been committed by the inhabitant of Dunrobin Castle, in that far northern county, and he felt shame for his class as he reached out and touched her arm, 'I can only try to understand, for I see it still means a great deal to you.'

He was trying. He really was trying to understand.

'I'm sorry,' she said finally. 'It doesn't often affect me like this . . . It must be the champagne.' And it was true, often weeks could go by these days and she barely gave her old homeland a second thought. 'I didn't mean to offend you — to blame it all on you.' She gave an embarrassed smile. 'I'm sure it wasn't *quite* all your fault!'

But he was not in the least offended. On the contrary, the spell she was weaving around him grew stronger with each passing minute, and the youthful debutantes of his world back home paled into an insignificance so complete as to disappear entirely from his mind as his eyes met hers. 'You are a strange and wonderful being, Mhairi McLeod,' he said softly. 'A strange and wonderful being, the like of whom I had never hoped to meet.'

Inwardly he cursed the fact that he was leaving for England the next day, yet his father was relying on him to travel home when he said he would. So many hopes had been riding on this trip, and it had been his own idea that they chose him and not his brother David to make it.

The task of securing the investments in the growing American railroad and Carnegie steelworks stock that they all prayed would guarantee the future of the estate was something that had to be accomplished by the best man for the job. And he had no doubt that he was that man. He loved his brother, they all did, but David's mercurial personality and often erratic behaviour of late was not best suited for the type of informed decisions that this trip demanded, and he had had little trouble persuading his father of that fact.

Since leaving London, he had been determined to make this mission a success. The castle and surrounding estate were proving more expensive to keep up than his family's dwindling funds could cope with, and without a real infusion of fresh capital, the outcome was bleak indeed. The land had been in the hands of the Earls of Inverbervie since the twelfth century when his ancestor had been granted the title by a grateful King David I, for aiding in his rescue when his ship had run aground on the treacherous rocks beneath the great headland that had afterwards been named Craig David in his honour.

He just prayed that the stock he had purchased would merit the spending of most of their dwindling capital on it. Almost one hundred thousand pounds' worth of bonds lay in the hotel safe, back at the Waldorf, ready to be collected by him on his departure for England tomorrow. Although a gambler at heart, he had taken the best advice available on Wall Street before parting with the money, and now all he could do was to hope that it would produce the miraculous turn-around in their fortunes so desperately required.

But now, at the last minute, there was a hitch, and she was sitting right next to him. 'It's funny,' he said quietly, 'but I almost didn't go to that luncheon at the Vanderbilt place. To tell the truth, I was afraid that Katrina – Miss van der Donck – was becoming rather too serious in her feelings towards me.'

Mhairi toyed with the handle of her coffee-cup. It was painful for her to think of her old friend now. They had been so close once – as close as sisters, but it had not been the Kati of her childhood she had encountered at George Vanderbilt's home. In her own eyes, Kati had still been Kati, but as far as her old friend was concerned, she knew she was nothing more than a rival – another woman against whom her own beauty and charm must be pitted. 'Have you known each other long?' She was genuinely curious to know.

'If you can count nine months as long. She came over to Europe with her mother last autumn.' He took a sip of his wine and gave a mirthless grin. 'We call it the "tiara trail" back home: rich American Mommas hunting a title for their darling daughters, and obtaining it by the weight of Daddy's wallet.' He paused and nodded thoughtfully to himself, 'Yes, I would say the standing of the title – or the size of the tiara, if you will – is in direct proportion to the weight of Daddy's wallet.'

'That's disgusting. Love gives itself; it can't be bought.'

Her companion raised a sceptical eyebrow that suggested naïvety in the extreme on her part. 'What's so disgusting about it, if both parties get what they want out of the deal? Heaven knows, it's been going on since we came out of the cave. As long as men have had the brains to barter, then women have been traded for either beads or money – depending on the state of civilization. Believe me, there's nothing particularly new about the bartered bride, Mhairi.'

'If that's the case then I can see why Kati van der Donck didn't quite measure up,' she found herself saying. 'Seeing as how your friend, the Duke of Marlborough, is marrying into the Vanderbilt millions.'

She instantly regretted the remark, but he didn't appear in the least put out.

'If I really believed I could ever love Katrina van der Donck, I'd be only too delighted to do her the favour of taking her off her mother's hands,' he said, refilling both their glasses. 'And I'll be honest with you, Mhairi, I'm well aware she's in love with me, and has been ever since we met at a house party back in England last autumn. When she suggested corresponding, it would have seemed bad manners to refuse. Then when I came instead of David to do the business over here . . . well there was simply no way I could avoid calling on her.'

'I understand. There's really no need to explain.'

'But there is,' he insisted. 'You're jealous, I can tell!'

She stiffened immediately, but the outraged retort died on her lips as his face broke into a grin. 'You really are insufferable, you know that?'

'Yes, yes I do,' he confirmed in mock seriousness. 'But I have to be honest with you. Marriage is a serious business. My parents can testify to that.'

Her brows rose. 'They're not happy?'

'Oh, the first part of their marriage was extremely happy – then they got back from the ceremony!'

She returned his grin and his hand reached across the table and found hers. 'I didn't believe it, you know,' he confessed. 'All that stuff that the poets write about love. Utter drivel I thought it was . . .'

A shiver ran through her as she waited for him to go on.

'You can feel it too, I know you can. You don't have to say anything, your eyes are saying it all . . .'

She gave a gasp that was half a laugh, half an exclamation at his quite outrageous conceit, as the colour suffused her cheeks. She glanced across at the clock on the wall opposite. It was already well past midnight, they were the only couple left, and the waiters were hovering in the background waiting to go home. She extracted her fingers from his to raise her glass. 'Let's drink to the future,' she said softly. 'Let's drink to the future, whatever it may be . . .'

They spoke little on their way back to her apartment in the hansom after leaving the restaurant. Mhairi could sense something was on his mind, but she had no way of knowing for sure that he was fighting with his conscience on whether or not to delay his voyage home the next day.

All evening the decision had been looming larger in his mind. But perhaps, he told himself, he had known what the answer was to be as soon as he had laid eyes on her in the Vanderbilt drawing-room. It was quite a different matter, however, saying the words out loud on the sidewalk in front of her apartment. He rested his hands on her shoulders at the open door of the hansom cab. 'I will call for you at midday tomorrow.' There it was out, and the devil take the hindmost!

She looked up at him as her breath caught in her throat. 'But you can't, your ship sails at ten!'

'Then it can sail without me!'

Then, casting decorum aside, he hugged her to him, swinging her off her feet, beneath the amused gaze of the waiting cab driver.

'Do you really mean that?' He would do that for her? She held her breath, but already knew the answer. Nothing on earth could prevent him from cancelling his berth on the *St Louis* the following day.

When he climbed back into the cab, she watched and waved until it had completely disappeared from view.

Careless as to who might see, she did an impromptu dance on the stone flags of the sidewalk. He wasn't leaving! He was staying an extra week, all because of her! Suddenly the world was a beautiful place, and she loved it and everyone in it with a passion – just as she knew he must surely love her.

She climbed the stairs to her apartment in a delirious daze of too much champagne and too much emotion.

'After the ball is over, after the break of morn . . .' Her voice rang out in the empty stairwell as she slowly mounted the steps, trailing her feather boa behind her.

'After the dancers are leaving, after the stars are gone . . .'

She hiccuped once, then twice, as she paused to look out through one of the windows at the dawn breaking just above the rooftops of the city. She would be seeing him today – in less than eight hours. She could hardly wait.

Chapter Eleven

For the rest of the following week, Mhairi's world revolved around the young Scotsman who had arrived so suddenly into her life. He would be there to collect her from rehearsals each morning to take her to lunch, and be in his seat in the front of the stalls every night, ready to rush round to her dressing-room the moment the performance ended. And every day a single red rose would be delivered to that same dressing-room, along with a loving message in the now familiar scrawl.

Their romance had become common knowledge, with photographs of them appearing in such illustrious newspapers as the *Herald*. And the *New York World* went so far as to do a full-page spread on their romance, likening it to that of another of the city's favourite daughters, Jennie Jerome, who, a generation earlier, had married Lord Randolph Churchill, the second son of the then Duke of Marlborough. If concern was being expressed in certain financial circles about the amount of American dollars being exchanged for coronets, as far as the general public was concerned, the love lives of the British aristocracy were a never-ending source of fascination.

Mhairi was even congratulated by Charles Hoyt himself on her choice of beau. 'A good piece of casting there, Miss Cloud. Great publicity for the show. There's nothing better than a British aristocrat to get those newspaper boys scribbling. Except maybe a Russian Grand Duke, that is. You haven't got one of them up your sleeve for when this one departs, have you?'

She had refuted the idea in no uncertain terms. The very idea of walking out with someone else after Ralph had gone was unthinkable to her.

After Ralph had gone . . . The very words horrified her. How on earth was she to survive? She had grown so used to him being there. Her initial healthy scepticism about his protestations of love at first sight had changed into an amazed but delighted acceptance that he really did appear to be as enamoured with her as he made out. And it was only in her very darkest moments that she questioned exactly who it was he was in love with – her image, or the real Mhairi McLeod who remained locked inside the glamorous exterior. That there was a difference she had no doubt.

Thankfully, however, there was only one Ralph MacLachlan, and she was certain that the man she had grown to know – and, dare she admit it, to love? – was as honourable and decent a suitor as even the Colonel could have dreamt up. It seemed a cruel irony of Fate that no sooner should he come into her life than he should be destined to disappear again.

She confided her misery to Sally in the other's dressing-room, just prior to the last performance of *Sunshine Girls* before he was due to sail the following day. 'I honestly mean it, Sal. I don't believe I'll be able to go out there every night and go on singing and dancing as if I haven't a care in the world, knowing he's on the other side of the Atlantic.'

Sally Sutton paused in the rouging of her cheeks and sighed. She too had once been eighteen, and could remember the pangs of her first real romance, but she was an old enough hand at the love-game to know that sympathy was not what was required right now. 'Of course you'll be able to continue. You're a professional. You know what they say about the show having to go on and all that. And it's true. Your own heart may be breaking but the public must never know. They come here to get away from their own troubles for a few precious hours, not to have to endure ours as well.'

Then, seeing her words were having little effect, her brow furrowed, 'As a matter of interest, has he mentioned anything about you going over there – to meet his folks or anything like that?'

'Well, no, not exactly.'

'Not exactly – what's that supposed to mean? Either he has or he hasn't.'

Mhairi began to pace the floor. Her satin dancing-slipper tangled in a torn stocking and she bent down to pick it up and stuff it behind a cushion of the *chaise longue*, along with all the others that had been discarded rather than mended. Sally was rouging her lips now and looking at her quizzically in the mirror. Mhairi sighed. How could she possibly explain how it was between her and Ralph? It was accepted, that was all: when the time was right, he would send for her. It was not something that could be hurried. His family had other things on their minds right now. He had to choose his moment.

Her silence said all there was to say, and Sally's voice was more sympathetic now. 'Of course there is a way you can follow him over there perfectly legitimately.'

'What do you mean?'

Sally blotted her lip-rouge on the back of her hand and rubbed at the resulting stain. 'You could always transfer to the English stage.'

'What – leave Charlie?' The very idea was abhorrent to her. She owed everything to Charles Hoyt.

Sally shrugged and turned back to her mirror. 'It's only a suggestion. Plenty do it. I'm told American girls are all the rage over there – both on the stage and off. Especially with the Prince of Wales!'

'That fat old man!' Mhairi made a face, then fell silent. Her friend was only trying to be helpful. But something inside her balked at the thought of chasing any man across the Atlantic. If Ralph wanted her with him, then he would send for her just as soon as was humanly possible. And when he did . . . Well, she could see them now – all those newspaper headlines: Lord and Lady Ralph MacLachlan . . . Her heart turned over at the thought.

There was a sharp rap on the door and a young male voice shouted, 'Fifteen minutes, Miss Sutton!' The count-down to curtain-up had begun.

'I'd better go,' Mhairi said, glancing at the clock on the wall for verification. 'But thanks for listening.'

'My pleasure!'

The passageway outside was already crowded with chorus girls and the sweet, cloying scent of their powder and assorted perfumes mingled with the nervous per-spiration always in abundance at a time like this. There was no other smell quite like it, and perhaps that was just as well, Mhairi thought wryly as she squeezed her way past and hurried down the passage to her own room for the last-minute preparations. It would be a relief just to sit down by herself for a moment or two and compose her thoughts. She had not been able to concentrate on anything today, knowing that tonight would be their last evening together before his ship sailed.

But to her astonishment, she was not alone when she closed the dressing-room door behind her, and she gasped out loud with fright as a figure, half-hidden by the silk changing-screen, rose to greet her.

'Kati!' She stared in amazement at her old friend.

Kati van der Donck's face was pale in the bright lights of the room; her small mouth seemed even more pinched than usual, and her hands were clasped nervously in front of her as she said quickly, 'I hope you don't mind. The bell-boy let me in. I told him we were old friends.'

'And so we are!' Mhairi said warmly. She made a tentative move towards her childhood friend, but then

Kati took a half-step back, and Mhairi felt that familiar pang as she aborted all thoughts of a warm embrace.

'Would you care for a drink?' she asked, feigning a lightheartedness she did not feel, as she pointed to the champagne that was now always on ice, awaiting Ralph's arrival after the show. 'I'm afraid I'm due on stage in ten minutes, so it'll have to be a quick one.'

'No – I won't, thanks.' Her visitor was visibly nervous and unclasped her hands to fiddle with the fringes of her wrap as she struggled for the best way to phrase what she had on her mind. She had almost not come at all, but reading in the newspapers that his ship was sailing the next day gave her no choice. The air had to be cleared before it was too late. She raised her chin. 'What I have to say will only take a couple of minutes. It's about Ralph!' The final sentence was blurted out, her face colouring as she looked Mhairi straight in the eye.

Mhairi's pulse quickened. 'Really? You *do* surprise me.' She could feel herself stiffen and she deliberately turned her back to sit down at her mirror. In the bright glare of the spotlights her own face had assumed a drawn expression as she reached for her powder bowl to take the shine from her nose and cheeks.

'What you're doing is criminal!'

'Whatever do you mean?' Their eyes locked in the glass.

'Stealing him from me like that. You had no right. No right at all. And you of all people. How could you do it, Mhairi? We used to be friends.' Kati's voice was plaintive as it all came pouring out. This wasn't the way she had planned it, but seeing her rival again like this brought it to a head. There was no way she could remain calm and collected. 'Did our friendship really mean so little to you?'

Mhairi looked away, unable to bear the hurt in the other's eyes, and began to dab fresh powder on her brow. What could she say in return? Could she ask why, once she had donned the uniform of the under-class and gone to work for Adeline Ashton, her invitations to the van der Doncks had suddenly ceased? Oh sure, Kati herself had gone off to finishing school in Boston, but not one invitation in the past four years? That had hurt, really hurt.

'He can never marry you, you know.' Her visitor hesitated, wondering how best to phrase it. But there was no tactful way. 'Aristocrats just don't marry servants – especially in England. Breeding counts for something over there. And in their eyes that's what you'll always be – a menial. The fact that you're an actress now won't mean a thing. Quite the contrary – decent young ladies just don't go on the stage, everyone knows that.'

Then, disconcerted to be talking to the back of her old friend's head, Kati swept round to the side of Mhairi's chair, and her voice rose as she continued, 'You did it deliberately, didn't you? You deliberately went out of your way to trap him because you knew we were about to be engaged. You couldn't bear it . . .' Her voice quavered and trailed off, then, determined not to break down, she took another breath and her eyes filled with accusation as she continued, 'You've always been jealous of me, haven't you, Mhairi? Ever since we were children, you've resented the fact that I came from a good family and you didn't!'

The word 'good' in relation to her family was just too much for Mhairi, who pushed back her chair and stood up. 'That is quite the most ridiculous thing I have ever heard!'

'No it isn't. It's the truth and we both know it. But it won't work, you know – your little ruse – it won't work! He'll never marry you. His family won't hear of it. And, anyway, Mama has already begun negotiations.'

'Negotiations?'

'About my dowry – with the Earl and Countess.' She pulled herself up to her full five feet, three inches. 'I'm worth quite a bit in my own right now, you know. Or at least I will be soon. Both my father and Grandma Cate left me a substantial sum, which I'm due to inherit at the age of twenty-one, or on marriage, whichever comes soonest.'

'And you really believe Ralph MacLachlan would marry you for your money?' Mhairi looked at her incredulously. 'Poor you, Kati, that's all I can say. If you really believe Ralph is that kind of a man, then that just goes to show how little you know him!'

'And it just goes to show how little you know of what's going on over there in England right now!' Kati retorted. 'Why it said in the newspapers only last week that almost one hundred and sixty-two million dollars has gone out of this country this year alone, in the form of American brides' dowries – straight into the coffers of the English aristocracy!'

'Ralph's Scottish.'

'It's the same thing in tartan!' Kati declared impatiently. 'And if you think he only came over here for the good of his health, or to dabble in Wall Street, then you're even more naïve than I imagined! At least I'm not fool enough to believe that. Why they're pouring over by the boatload, all those impoverished aristocrats, and he's no different from the rest!'

There were three loud raps on the door. 'Five minutes, Miss Cloud!'

'Thank you, Tom!' Mhairi called, as she reached for her gloves. She pointedly avoided the other's irate face as she pulled the long, white satin sheaths up over her elbows, then worked the material smoothly over her fingers, so there were no wrinkles. Kati's words were hitting home, but she was determined not to let it show.

She was aware of her visitor watching her in growing frustration as she deliberately ignored her in favour of going about her preparations for the show. For the first act, she was wearing a ballgown of ivory Chantilly lace, covered with tiny, pink satin tea-roses. She was aware she had never looked better and the knowledge gave her a confidence she knew she would otherwise have lacked, as Kati's words chipped away at her veneer of sophisticated nonchalance.

She began to hum to herself as she turned back to the mirror to adjust one of the flowers behind her left ear, and her memory returned to that scene in Grandma Cate's apartment all those years ago. Looking at her now, could Kati still really believe she would ever be satisfied with a Henk Smitt or Billy Boyle?

But her visitor had had enough of being ignored. 'You think you're so beautiful, don't you? And so clever – stealing him from me like this! You and your fancy clothes – none of it's genuine. Your whole life is a sham. That's what it is – a sham! But your type always get . . .'

'Kati, please . . . !' Mhairi turned and looked at her old friend. Kati's lower lip was quivering in a mixture of indignation and frustration, just as it had always done all those years ago in childhood when she stood in danger of not getting her own way. She would break down in tears any minute now – it always happened. But the knowledge brought Mhairi no comfort, in fact the whole messy situation was almost as upsetting for her as it so obviously was for her friend. She held out her gloved hand in a conciliatory gesture. 'Look there's no use us shouting at one another like spoilt children. It's quite ridiculous you coming in here and shouting at me like this . . .'

She got no further as, ignoring the proffered hand, Kati began to fumble with the embroidered chatelaine that hung from her belt. 'All right, you asked for it! I wasn't going to show you this, seeing as it's none of your business. But here it is. Let's see who's being ridiculous now!' She extracted an envelope from the bag and handed it across with a flourish.

Mhairi looked down at the object thrust into her hands

and was on the point of handing it back unopened, when Kati insisted, 'Go on – read it, if you dare!'

Mhairi opened it up and took out the letter within. It was dated over three months previously, and written in black ink on gold-crested notepaper. The sight of the familiar scrawling handwriting made her heart turn over.

> Craig David Castle,
> Inverbervie, Kincardineshire,
> Scotland.
>
> Thursday, 4th April, 1895.

My dearest Kati,
I sail on Tuesday. Only a few short weeks and we shall be together again. Oh, how I long to see you. Then I will believe that Spring is really here, and the sunshine will have returned to my life.

My family send their united love to you and yours – and no one more than
Your devoted,

Ralph.

Mhairi's fingers tensed as she read, then reread the words on the page. He had lied to her. He had lied when he said they were no more than friends. This was not the letter of a friend. She replaced it in the envelope and handed it back with a deliberately lighthearted air. If this was meant to be the *coup de grâce* then it had quite the reverse effect. If Kati was insisting on playing dirty, then so be it. She would not pull any punches either.

'I really don't see that this is proof of anything,' she said brightly, picking up her scent bottle to aim a spray of *Muguet des Bois* behind her ears. 'It really was a bit premature of you to imagine that that tiara already had your name on it, Kati dear. It really doesn't do to count your chickens before they're hatched – otherwise you stand in real danger of ending up with egg all over your face.'

The sweet scent of lily-of-the-valley hung in the air between them as she picked up her parasol from the *chaise longue*. 'Now you really must excuse me, I have an audience waiting.'

She began to walk towards the door and her gaze fell on the glass vase holding the red roses from Ralph. Today's accompanying card still lay beside it. She picked it up and tossed it on to the top of her dressing-table, beneath Kati's gaze. 'Oddly enough I got a note myself today. Are you acquainted with the works of Robert Burns? They do say he wrote the finest love poetry in the English language . . . Not that he would have been very flattered by that, being a Scot like the writer of this!'

> My love is like a red, red rose
> That's newly sprung in June,
> Oh, my love is like a melody
> That's sweetly played in tune . . .
> I love you.
>
> Ralph

She turned once as she got to the door, just in time to see the card fall to the floor. Kati had her back turned to her, but their eyes met once more in the illuminated glass above the dressing-table. On Kati van der Donck's face was a look that mixed despair at what she had just read with hatred for her old friend in equal measure. Whatever there had been between them in childhood was there no more. They were two women in love with one man. The gulf was unbridgeable, but there was real sadness in her heart as Mhairi called, 'Close the door behind you on your way out, won't you, Kati dear?'

She did not wait for the reply.

And suddenly she was back in the colourful behind-the-scenes chaos of the show. But the nightly hubbub barely impinged on her as she pushed her way through the jostling crowd of stagehands and showgirls.

'Good luck, Miss Cloud!'

'Break a leg, Mhairi!'

The usual good wishes rang in her ears as she made her way up to the wings of the stage. This was the moment when her pulse should begin to race and the excitement well within her, ready to bubble over in that glorious moment when she took her first step on the boards for yet another performance. But for once there was no tingle in her veins, and no smile on her lips as she waited for the familiar bars of the melody that announced her entrance. And as she strolled out into the footlights' glare, she could not remember ever feeling so unhappy in this most enchanted of places.

She caught Ralph's eye several times during the show and just longed for it to be over, so they could be together and he could put her mind at rest over the Kati incident. Was there even the slightest possibility that he too had come over in search of more than Wall Street's bonds to take back to his family seat? The very question was abhorrent to her, and she dismissed it immediately, only for it to creep back and lie lurking in a corner of her consciousness as she went through the familiar song and dance routines of the show.

When she finally came off-stage for the last time, and the final cheers were dying to an echo in her ears, there appeared to be an even greater crowd than usual around her dressing-room door. Normally she would have been only too happy to spend a few minutes signing autographs and chatting to her admirers, many of whom she knew would have spent the best part of a week's wages to see her; but not tonight. Tonight all she wanted to do was to be with Ralph and reassure herself that the love he professed was indeed for her alone.

She caught hold of one of the production staff, before

entering the narrow passageway that led to the dressing-rooms. 'Get rid of them, please, Jerry,' she begged, intimating with her head the milling excited crowd outside her door. 'Tell them I don't feel too well tonight. Tell them anything, only get rid of them.'

The young man looked at her in concern. 'Shall I call for the doctor, Miss Cloud?'

She shook her head. 'No, thanks all the same. Just get rid of them.'

She waited in the wings until he had done just that, then she rushed through the empty passage to the sanctuary of her room.

The white card that had come with the roses was still lying where it had dropped from Kati's fingers, and she picked it up and replaced it beside the flowers, allowing herself a strained smile as she did so. It had been silly to allow the confrontation with her old friend to upset her as much as it had done. What if he had once believed himself to be in love with her – that certainly wasn't the case now, and the other stuff Kati had come out with . . . well, that was merely sour grapes.

'May I come in?'

She whirled round in anticipation at the familiar voice, only to have the smile die on her lips almost immediately, for he was not alone. A beautiful, raven-haired young woman of about her own age, with large eyes and a soulful expression, stood by his side. She was clad in a gown that could only have come straight from Paris and around her slim throat was a black velvet band studded with diamonds.

Ralph sensed her dismay right away, and attempted a conciliatory smile. 'Mhairi, there's someone here who's dying to meet you. So much so, she insisted I bring her round here this evening right after the show.'

He took the dark-haired young woman by the elbow and brought her forward into the room. 'Consuelo, my dear – as if you didn't already know – this is Miss Mhairi Cloud . . . Mhairi, allow me to introduce Miss Consuelo Vanderbilt.'

Mhairi extended her hand to be shaken and forced a smile to her lips. So this was the much talked about daughter of the celebrated, and now divorced, William Kissam Vanderbilts. If America had its own royalty, then this was surely it. 'How very nice to meet you, Miss Vanderbilt. I've heard so much about you.'

'Really?' The other's brows rose in surprise.

'Oh yes, I understand you're to marry a good friend of Ralph's here – the Duke of Marlborough, isn't it?'

Ralph let out a groan as Consuelo's expression changed to one of consternation, and Mhairi looked from one to the other in confusion.

'I – I haven't put my foot in it, have I?'

'Both feet would be nearer the mark,' Ralph sighed. 'But no matter, I'm sure Consuelo is quite used to it by now.'

Consuelo, for her part, chose to ignore the matter entirely as she smiled politely at Mhairi and said in a soft, whispery voice, 'What I really came round for was to ask you if you'd care to attend my coming-out ball, at our Newport house, on August 28th. My mother's arranging it right now and absolutely everyone will be there.'

'Including Sunny Marlborough,' Ralph put in mischievously.

'Including Sunny,' Consuelo confirmed wearily. 'And I know they would all simply love to hear you sing.'

Mhairi's delighted smile faded on her lips. So she was to sing for her supper, was she? The gilt on the gingerbread was tarnishing by the minute. 'I – I'll have to consult my diary,' she began, determined to stand on her dignity, but was interrupted by Ralph.

'Oh go on, Mhairi. Be a sport. I've practically promised Consuelo you would.'

'In that case it looks like it's already settled, doesn't it?' she said lightly. 'I will be glad to come, Miss Vanderbilt.'

'Consuelo, please,' the other said, extending her gloved hand once more. 'I'm so pleased. I'm sure no one else this season will have such a coup!'

Mhairi watched, fighting hard to keep the bright smile on her lips as her visitor then kissed Ralph on both cheeks. 'And thank you so much, Ralphie. I won't forget it, you know.'

She swept out almost as unexpectedly as she had arrived, leaving only a cloud of expensive French perfume to remind them of her presence.

Mhairi glanced across at Ralph, who was looking well pleased with himself. 'So I'm quite a coup, am I?'

'You most certainly are,' he confirmed, not noticing the irony in her voice. 'There will be no one to touch you as a "turn" down in Newport this season.'

Mhairi stared at him. 'A "turn" — so that's what I am, is it — a "turn"?'

'Oh, come on, Mhairi, you know what I mean!' He rushed across to take her in his arms. 'It's only a turn of phrase!' He grinned. 'No pun intended!'

She shrugged herself free from his embrace. Suddenly, what with Kati and everything, this whole evening was turning into something of a nightmare. But she had to keep control of herself. 'I — I'm sorry,' she began. 'I'm just a bit overwrought, I guess. This being your last night and all that . . .'

'I know, I know.' He put his arm around her shoulders once more. 'Believe me, it's just as hard for me.'

'Let's just get out of here,' she said softly. 'Let's get as far away from the theatre as possible.' Right now all she wanted was to be appreciated for herself — Mhairi McLeod — not for that other woman, that cardboard image of the exotic creature they called Mhairi Cloud, that seemed to be plastered up everywhere she looked these days. That was another woman entirely, and it had nothing to do with the real her. On their last night together she had to be loved and wanted for herself. That was the most important thing of all.

For sentimental reasons, they had decided to spend their last evening together at Benno's, and for the first hour it seemed that their final night would be everything she had dreamt of it being. There were very few diners and the restaurant had a quiet, intimate air that lent itself perfectly to both their moods. At eleven o'clock, however, the whole atmosphere changed abruptly when a party arrived to celebrate a birthday.

They both groaned inwardly, then Ralph reached across and touched her hand. 'Do you want to go?'

She nodded, and adjusted the feather boa around her neck as he signalled for the bill.

They had no trouble hailing a cab and he instructed the driver to head for Central Park. The moon was high in the sky as they entered the wrought-iron gates and, once inside, he gave instructions for it to wait whilst they took a walk in the moonlight.

A slight breeze was blowing and although it was not cold she shivered. He put his arm around her shoulders and hugged her to him, his lips nuzzling her hair, as he said softly, 'I can't believe it's real, you know. Meeting you like this – it's the most wonderful thing that has ever happened to me.'

They had stopped beneath the spreading branches of a giant sycamore. Now was the moment. She had put it off all evening, but this was her last chance to ask him. She gently extricated herself from his embrace. 'I – I had a visitor tonight,' she began hesitantly. Then it all came rushing out – everything Kati had said, even the contents of his letter.

He listened in silence, then raised her face to his, with the index finger of his right hand. 'Do you really believe all that?' he asked softly. 'Do you really believe I came over here to ask Kati van der Donck, or any other heiress, to marry me?'

She shrugged miserably. 'I don't know what to believe any more.'

'Then I will have to do something to convince you, won't I?'

He took both her hands in his and lifted them to his lips. 'When I told you it was only you I loved, I meant it, Mhairi,' he said softly. 'I knew from the first moment I saw you that you were the only woman for me.'

He let go her hands and reached inside his pocket to extract a small heart-shaped box. She watched, hardly daring to breathe, as he opened it.

Inside, in a bed of velvet, sat the most beautiful ring she had ever seen. It was a giant pearl surrounded by diamonds and his fingers seemed to shake slightly as he lifted it out and took her right hand in his. 'It has been in my family for generations. And I want you to have it.'

She held her breath as he slipped it on to the third finger of her right hand. Her *right* hand. She stared down at it, in a mixture of elation and confusion. Didn't he *know*? Didn't he realize it was the wrong hand he was putting it on?

'Well, do you like it, my love?'

She gazed down at it, then up at him. 'It – it's the most beautiful ring I have ever seen,' she answered truthfully. 'I shall wear it always.'

His hands reached out and cupped her cheeks, lifting her face to his as his mouth found hers. 'I love you, Mhairi McLeod. I will always love you,' he vowed. His breath was warm on the cool skin of her cheeks.

It was not until an hour later, when she was in bed alone that night that the thought came. And a chill ran through her. How on earth did he happen to bring that ring all the way to America with him?

She lifted her right hand and gazed at it in the

moonlight from her open window. The explanation was not long in dawning, and it hurt, but then so did so much that was worth having in this life. And they had shared so much together, she and Kati van der Donck. Perhaps there was a divine providence in the fact that they were united once more in their love for one man. It was not a destiny she would have chosen, but then who amongst us was ever at liberty to choose their own destiny?

Chapter Twelve

Of present fame think little, and of future less;
the praises that we receive after we are buried,
like the flowers that are strewed over our grave,
may be gratifying to the living, but they are
nothing to the dead; the dead are gone,
either to a place where they hear them not,
or where, if they do, they will despise them.

Mhairi closed the Commonplace Book she had been given by Fiona and mused on the words she read. They seemed to have been written especially for her. They put everything in perspective, somehow. It was so easy to be dazzled by the adulation to which she was now being subjected, but how much of it was really genuine? Who was to say that next year, next month, next week even, Joe Public would not turn his eyes to the next attractive young woman waiting in the wings? Yes, fame like beauty itself was a transitory thing, given on loan and then so often snatched away again, so that at the end of one's life there was nothing left of that other woman whose success in life and love was founded on the whim of a fickle public who could not see past the pretty face and fine feathers. How much better, she thought, to end one's life truly loved by those around you, like her grandfather, Long Rob, and her own mother, Mary Anne, had done. And her heart would ache for those who had gone and were not with her now to share these moments with her. But what exactly they would have made of it all she could not think, for her life in the theatre was as far removed from that on the Isle of Skye as it was possible to be.

Fiona's Commonplace Book was placed by her bedside – something to be dipped into before she fell asleep each night – something to keep her feet well and truly anchored to the ground as the remainder of the summer of 1895 passed in a colourful haze of applauding audiences, gay parties, and letters to and from Ralph.

Sunshine Girls continued to play to packed houses and the show was booked up for weeks in advance. 'And most of it's down to you, sweetheart,' Charles Hoyt told her. Then, as she laughed and shook her head, he insisted, 'They're not stupid, you know – you can't fool the people, not for long at any rate. They know talent when they see it. And, by God, they are seeing it in this show!'

And so, as Mhairi's prestige as a musical comedy star continued to grow, so did her popularity as a Gibson Girl. At Charlie Hoyt's special request, Charles Dana Gibson took a whole new series of pictures of her dressed in her now famous gowns, feather boas and picture hats. 'Good for the show, honey, and good for you, too!' Mhairi could not argue for she knew her employer was the consummate showman. 'He could make my old granny into a star – and she's been dead these forty years!' Dick Stael told her, and she did not doubt it. In Charles Hoyt's hands she was on the way up all right, the only trouble was for how long?

But as the summer wore on, it seemed more and more that she had little to worry about in that regard. A general public who had had little to celebrate over the past two years, with the country undergoing an economic depression, suddenly found that life could still offer something to sing about. While banks went out of business, railroad companies went bankrupt, and businesses went bust, on the New York stage at least life had never seemed more worth living. Charles Hoyt rubbed his hands and declared his philosophy had been proved correct: during a depression, the people flock to the theatre to be taken out of their misery. 'When you give them what they want, they will find the money to pay for it!' he told Mhairi.

Yes, Charlie knew better than anyone that there had never been a better time to discover a new star, and he glowed with pride as Mhairi began to sparkle brighter than almost any other in his galaxy. It seemed that the public could not get enough of her. To her initial embarrassment, then amusement, young girls imitated her dress and hairstyles, and her famous feather boa became an essential for the well-dressed young lady on an evening out; and their young men carried her postcard likenesses next to their hearts. Even the *New York Herald* paid its own personal tribute with a headline: 'Mhairi Cloud Brings A Silver Lining To Broadway'.

She cut out the headline and placed it inside her Commonplace Book. It would be something to look back on when her grandchildren gazed at her in scepticism when she told them of how she had once had all New York at her feet. Their disbelief at that piece of yellowing newsprint would be a confirmation of those other words in that book that she never failed to cast her eyes over when the applause ran a serious risk of going to her head.

But even the thought of grandchildren brought a stab of pain these days, for with Ralph on the other side of the Atlantic, marriage and children seemed as far away as the moon. The public's interest, however, in her long-distance love affair with the second son of the Earl of Inverbervie seemed as keen as ever. Columns of newsprint each week were devoted to the ups and downs of the romances of the Broadway stars, and if one half of a much-publicized duo happened to be an aristocrat, so much the better.

Suddenly the country seemed besotted by the British aristocracy, and the deeper the nation's financial crisis grew, the more intrigued they became. Earlier in the year the United States' gold reserves had reached rock bottom and had had to be underwritten by the millionaire financier J. P. Morgan, and this had infuriated many patriots. Exactly what was happening to the country that it had to be bailed out by a private banker? Other millionaires became the focus of intense interest, especially to those American nationalists who took exception to the nation's richest and most distinguished families apparently bartering their daughters with good American dollars to impoverished aristocrats on the other side of the Atlantic. This was no time to be bolstering another nation's coffers with American money when their own banks were starved of funds.

As the year wore on, so the amount of newsprint devoted to the subject multiplied. Likely participants in the 'tiara trail' became the subject of much speculation, and none more so that summer than Broadway's favourite, Miss Mhairi Cloud, and high society's darling daughter, Miss Consuelo Vanderbilt.

Those same newspapers speculated that Lord Ralph MacLachlan might take the opportunity to accompany his old friend the Duke of Marlborough to the much-publicized coming-out ball on 28 August, at Marble House, Newport, presently being arranged by Alva Vanderbilt for her daughter Consuelo. Could it be that the two young aristocrats would announce a double engagement that night, and the nation's two most eligible young women would be whisked off across the Atlantic to join all the others? It was no secret that Mhairi had been asked to sing at the function, and that only served to fuel the fires of speculation.

At the theatre everyone was gossiping about the likelihood of such an event, and as Mhairi continued to read the vast amounts of newsprint devoted to the subject, the idea began to become more and more of a reality in her own mind. It would be so typical of Ralph wanting to surprise her like that; after all, wasn't he responsible for her invitation to the ball in the first place?

The nearer she got to the end of August, the more excited she became, and the only person she felt really confident about confiding in was Fiona.

But it was during one of her regular visits to her cousin's apartment one afternoon in late July that something occurred that put all thoughts of the forthcoming ball out of her mind, and reminded her that there had been another dimension to her life that she had given little thought to of late.

'Good heavens, what brings you two over here?' Mhairi entered Fiona's drawing-room to stare in surprise at her two younger cousins, Seamus and Shona, who sat side by side on the plush sofa. It was the first time she had set eyes on either of them in months. Both sixteen-year-olds sat straight-backed and awkward, their hands clasped in their laps, their well-worn boots shining in the dull light from the window.

The faces of all three were anxious and drawn, and an awkward silence filled the air. For both of the twins to have requested time off work to visit their elder sister was quite unheard of, and by the expression on each of their faces this was no ordinary social call. Mhairi looked anxiously at Fiona who stood nursing a sherry by the window. Two crystal glasses containing the same golden-brown liquid sat untouched on the small sidetable in front of the twins. 'What's happened?'

'Mam's sick,' Fiona said quietly, then gazed back out at the traffic, as if unable or unwilling to say more.

'How sick?' Mhairi looked at the twins.

'Dr Munro says it's only a matter of time,' Seamus answered huskily. 'Maybe weeks.' His normally cheerful freckled face looked tired and drawn, and he nervously fingered the cap in his hands. 'We felt you should both know.'

Mhairi and Fiona looked at one another. Neither had been back to Amity Place since Mhairi's sudden departure for the stage, although Fiona had made one or two visits to her brother and sister, and she had made sure they had her address and kept her informed of her parents' wellbeing.

'Do you know what's wrong exactly?' Mhairi remained standing in the middle of the floor, looking from one to the other in turn.

At that Shona began to sob quietly to herself and Seamus put his arm around his sister's shoulder. 'Dr Munro says it's a woman's complaint,' he said, his face colouring. 'At any rate, she's got a fair-sized tumour and they say at the hospital there's nothing they can do.'

'But tumours don't just materialize out of the blue like that!'

'And neither did this one,' Fiona broke in bitterly. 'It seems she's been bleeding heavily for the best part of a year, but we've all been too concerned with our own lives to notice.'

'Oh God.' Mhairi made for the nearest chair and sat down.

All four looked at one another, then all eyes turned on Mhairi, and she knew they were waiting for her reaction. Her success outside the family had obviously endowed her with a certain respect within it. It was an open secret that she had placed enough money at Finbar and Belle's disposal so they need never work again, and it was equally well known by all the family that not one penny of it had been touched. They might not have much in worldly goods, but they still had their pride, and Mhairi respected that more than anyone.

She was also aware that ever since they were children the twins had held her in some kind of awe, but now she felt that even Fiona was looking to her for guidance. 'She must have the best treatment,' she found herself saying. 'If there's anything money can buy that will help, then she must have it . . . Where is she now, anyway?'

'She's at home,' Shona said thickly, dabbing her eyes with her brother's handkerchief. 'But there's nothing that your money can buy, Mhairi, that will help her now. Only God can do that.'

And so they went round there, all four of them; an unlikely quartet that made the cab driver look at them curiously as they got out on the sidewalk in front of the Ashton house in Amity Place. 'Aren't you what's-her-name?' he asked Mhairi, as she reached inside her purse for the fare.

She forced a tight smile to her lips as she handed over the money. 'Yes, I'm what's-her-name,' she confirmed, but she had never felt less like a star as she followed her cousins down the stone stairs and in through the tradesmen's entrance of the house that was still home to her aunt and uncle.

'It was good of you all to come,' Finbar said as he led them to the room where his wife lay. 'I prayed to God that you would.'

His hair was greyer and sparser than Mhairi remembered and his clothes had a dishevelled look to them; a collar-stud was missing on one side of his neck and the wing of the collar stuck out at a rakish angle. That was something her aunt would never have allowed.

Mhairi felt the sting of tears in her eyes as they followed her uncle in single file through the back passages of the house that had been their first home in the New World. Stale cooking smells from lunch hung in the air and they could hear the rattle of dishes being washed in the scullery as they passed. Mhairi was aware of the curious gaze of the kitchen maids following them and she deliberately avoided all eyes. There was an incongruity about her finery down here in the basements, and she felt almost ashamed of her fashionable gown and wide-brimmed picture hat as they were shown into the small room, with its half-window looking out into the dim light of the back-yard.

Belle Rafferty was lying in a single iron bedstead that had been brought down into a small room partitioned off the butler's pantry. As her condition had worsened over the past few weeks, the long flight of stairs up to the attic she shared with Finbar had become just too much. And now she could not get out of bed at all.

The room was dark and had a peculiar smell to it; the smell of death was in the air. Mhairi had experienced it too often in the past, with her mother, her grandfather, and little Bobby, not to recognize it now. But she barely recognized the face that looked up into her own from the depths of the white pillow. The skin that covered her aunt's features looked shrunken and translucent and her eyes looked dully out from within hollow sockets.

Fiona knelt by her mother's side and Shona sat on the foot of the bed, leaving Seamus and Mhairi to stand at the edge of the mattress, looking fearfully at the pale face on the pillow before them.

'You came, bairns . . .' It was the first time she had called them that in years.

'I think it would be better if you each had a couple of minutes with your mother alone,' Finbar's voice said from the doorway. 'We don't want to tire her.'

So Seamus, Shona and Mhairi left Fiona alone with her mother, and retired to stand silently in the dank gloom of the back passage, until it was their turn to say their goodbye, for not one of them had any doubt that was what it would be.

Seamus put his arm around his sister's shoulders; he was only sixteen but was trying so hard to be a man. His boots were shining and he had slicked down his unruly mop of red hair with a liberal helping of Macassar oil which accentuated the smallness of his head. Mhairi felt her heart go out to him. He had always been the quiet one in the family, and probably the one who was now feeling his mother's pain the most. Belle Rafferty had never been one who found it easy to show her feelings, but there had never been any doubt of her love for her only son.

It was agreed that Seamus would go in last, so when Fiona came out and disappeared down the passage in search of her father, it was Mhairi who stood with Seamus while Shona went in. She wanted desperately to say something – anything that might ease his suffering, but no words would come, so they stood silently, lost in their own thoughts, until a few minutes later a distraught Shona came out to join them.

Mhairi removed her hat and thrust it into her cousin's hands, along with her parasol, as if they somehow contaminated the moment. 'Hold these for me, please.' Her heart was pounding as she entered the room once more to stand by the bed.

Belle Rafferty looked up and lifted her hand from the bedcover. 'Thank you for coming, Mhairi *aroon*,' she said faintly. 'Thank you for coming.'

Her eyes had a faraway look, and they were looking past Mhairi's shoulder towards that dull, grey light of the window; but it was another light she was seeing; a light as pure and clear as ever had been on God's earth. 'She's waiting for me, bairn. Your mother, Mary Anne, is waiting with the others.'

Mhairi nodded, unable to speak. But she knew it was the truth. She could feel them all here now: her mother, her grandfather Long Rob, her Auntie Jessie . . .

And she knew somewhere out there above the tall buildings and hustle and bustle of the city it would be circling – the white bird that would guide her aunt to the Gaelic heaven of *Tir-nan-Og*. And she knew that this was the last time she would ever see or speak to her Auntie Belle.

A great love welled in her heart for this worn-out woman who had taken her into her own home and loved her as a daughter. 'I want to thank you, Auntie Belle,' she said huskily. 'I want to thank you for taking me in like you did, although, God knows, there was no room . . .'

Her aunt's voice was barely audible as her eyes turned from the window to her niece's distraught face. 'There's no need to thank me, bairn,' she said softly. 'Where there's room in the heart, there is always room in the home.'

Belle Rafferty's eyes were moist, and still had that faraway look as they turned back to the grey city light of the window, and she said softly, 'Sing to me, bairn. Sing to me of Skye . . .'

Tears blurred Mhairi's vision and choked her throat as her aunt's head turned slowly on the pillow to implore her. And Mhairi knew she was the last link that remained with the dying woman's home. None of her own children had ever set foot in Scotland, and none could know the pull of the island that had once been home.

Her aunt opened her mouth once more but no words came. Only her eyes were speaking.

Mhairi's own voice cracked and broke as she attempted a song of their island:

'Far away from Love and Youth, I'm yearning,
Isle of Skye, *mo chridhe*, far away . . .'

and she could sing no more. The tears streamed from her eyes as she gazed into the face of death. She shook her head. 'I can't, Auntie Belle. Forgive me, I just can't . . .'

She fell to her knees by the bed. Never would she be asked to sing for a more beloved audience, and she could not utter another word. Sobs racked her body as she laid her head on the quilt. Her aunt reached out and touched her hair.

'*Tha mo latha giorid, Mhairi mo chridhe, tha mo feasgar fada . . .*'

They buried her on 5 August and Father Docherty said the prayers over the grave, just as he had done a decade before over the tiny coffin of Belle Rafferty's first grandchild. And Mhairi's heart went out to the husband her aunt had left behind as Finbar scooped a handful of earth from the soil to scatter on her coffin, now deep in the earth of their American homeland.

He looked much older than his years. His whole being seemed faded somehow. A lifetime spent below stairs had given the familiar freckled face an unhealthy pallor, and the red hair had long since faded to grey, and barely covered his scalp. But the few strands that remained he had painstakingly oiled that morning, and slicked down in honour of the wife he had come to lay to rest. Theirs had been an unlikely match, but he had truly loved the woman with whom he had spent all the years of his adult life.

Mhairi had taken his arm as they left the graveside, with his other three children, to return to the waiting cab, and she had felt a deep and protective love for this man she had first denied all those years ago on the platform of Manchester station. She made a silent vow that she would make sure he wanted for nothing of the world's material goods in the future. No amount of money could ever make up for what he had lost this day, but if she could make his life a little easier through her earnings, then she would certainly do that. She would do her very best to persuade him to use at least some of that money she had put at their disposal in their neighbourhood branch of the Chase Manhattan. It was little enough for the lifetime of love he had given her.

It was only with difficulty in the following days that she turned her thoughts back to the stage and her impending appearance at the Vanderbilt ball. And she was relieved that no newspaper man had attended her aunt's funeral or intruded on that very personal part of her life. There were some things that one did not share with the public at large, despite their insatiable appetite for the details of her private life.

Although they had failed to discover the death of her aunt, the press, however, appeared in force at her frequent appointments with Mr Joseph, her dressmaker, and there was much speculation as to who would have the most exotic creation, herself or Consuelo Vanderbilt, on the night that the whole town was talking about. Five one-hour fittings it took to get the gown exactly right, and finally it was ready, all twenty-five yards of it.

Fiona came round from her own apartment to help her dress, and could not disguise her envy, or her pride in the young woman she regarded as her closest sister. And at the end of an hour of primping and preening, interspersed with many sighs and groans, Mhairi at last stood in front of her mirror, a vision in crimson satin, with a wide-brimmed white straw picture hat bedecked with red roses. 'You look beautiful,' her cousin told her. 'You'll be the envy of every female there and will send every male wild!'

But Mhairi was not interested in sending every male wild. There was only one man she was interested in and her heart was in her mouth at the thought of perhaps seeing him again before the night was out. She could barely contain her nerves as she waved Fiona goodbye at the door of her apartment and set off for the Vanderbilt mansion in Newport.

If she had had any doubts that this was to be the greatest social occasion of the year, they were dispelled as soon as she came in sight of Marble House. The gentlemen of the press were all there, lounging around the entrance to the drive, and several cries of recognition went up as her carriage rattled past and carried on up to the main door.

Once inside, it was obvious that anyone who was

anyone was there. The guest list of five hundred read like a Who's Who of high society. But, incredibly, they all seemed as interested in her as she was in them. It was impossible to ignore the head-turning stares, and whispers that went on as she walked in through the magnificent front doors and took stock of her surroundings. A footman in breeches and a powdered wig relieved her of her wrap as her eyes widened in amazement at the scene before her.

In an effort to outdo anything previously organized by her arch-rival Mrs Astor, Alva Vanderbilt had transformed the whole of the first floor of the house into a flower-filled park. Everywhere fresh bouquets and garlands of flowers of every hue blossomed in their thousands, their dazzling colours and perfumes giddying the senses as soon as one stepped over the threshold.

The centrepiece of the extravaganza was the bronze fountain in the middle of the great hall, which formed part of a tropical water tableau, with blue and white hyacinths mingling with lotus blossoms in the pool beneath.

As she neared the cascading water Mhairi noticed the immaculate figure of George Washington Vanderbilt, at whose home she had met Ralph. He was leaning, with a rather bored look on his face, against the bronze lip of the pool, smoking a cigarette. He recognized Mhairi immediately, and, proving that chivalry was far from dead, he picked a sprig of white hyacinth from the blue water and dried it with his handkerchief, before presenting it to her with a deep bow. 'A hyacinth to feed thy soul, my dear.'

'I beg your pardon?'

'If of thy mortal goods thou art bereft,
And from thy slender store two loaves alone are left,
Sell one, and with the dole
Buy hyacinths to feed thy soul.'

He broke into a wry smile. 'A Persian ode, of which I am particularly fond . . . Not that I shall ever be bereft of mortal goods – or down to my last two loaves, come to that, but the sentiment is a worthy one, wouldn't you agree?'

Mhairi sniffed the perfumed bloom in her hand and smiled. 'I think it's a perfectly lovely sentiment, George.'

The millionaire offered his arm, as Mhairi tucked the sprig of hyacinth into her waistband. 'Have you been presented to my niece yet? Consuelo and her illustrious Mama are receiving their guests in the Pink Room. Allow me . . .'

And so Mhairi ascended the magnificent staircase on the arm of one Vanderbilt, to be received by two others, in a room which appeared to be fashioned entirely of Nubian marble. And the colour of the stone was an almost perfect match for Consuelo's face, as she stood, tense and unsmiling, next to the well-upholstered figure of her mother, and received her guests. The young woman at the centre of the country's speculation was wearing a gown of white satin trimmed with lace, and after the initial pleasantries, Mhairi complimented her on it.

This time Consuelo managed a smile. 'It belonged to my grandmother,' she confided, in her little girl voice. 'She wore it at all the best balls back in her hometown of Mobile before the Civil War.'

'Was that the American Civil War or the British, my dear, I can't quite recall?' her Uncle George enquired.

Consuelo raised her eyes heavenwards. 'I don't know how you put up with him, I swear I don't!' Then, lowering her voice, she added, 'By the way, Miss Cloud, is it true what we read in the papers that your *real* beau is Lord MacLachlan?'

Mhairi felt herself colour. Was this some kind of a cue for her to admit her love for Ralph, so Consuelo could spring the surprise of the night on her? 'Lord MacLachlan and I are very good friends.'

'Everyone in this town is just "very good friends" with someone until the moment they walk down the aisle,' George Vanderbilt opined. 'But at least it gives the gossip columnists something to speculate about!'

The queue of people behind them waiting to be received was building up, so, presenting his elbow for Mhairi to rest her hand upon, they moved on, after a few words to Consuelo's mother.

As they walked back through the hall, Mhairi's eyes were wide with wonder at the swarms of humming-birds that hung suspended from the ceiling, their beaks stealing the nectar from the garlands of flowers so artfully that one almost believed they were real. Floral bowers of sweet-smelling hollyhocks and old-fashioned roses abounded in such profusion that, much to her embarrassment, she began to sneeze, and did not stop until George had escorted her outside.

'That's all I need – a bout of hay fever!' she groaned, as she found herself on the lawn overlooking the ocean, where rows of exquisitely decorated tables had been laid out.

George led her to one and solicitously poured her a drink of fresh lemon ice-water, which she sipped gratefully as she dabbed at her twitching nose. She had little time to enjoy the fresh air or the drink, however, for she was immediately spotted by an official who hurriedly removed her from her companion, and rushed her through to the other side of the house to meet the orchestra.

'They've been looking for you for ages, Miss Cloud,' she was told. 'They were beginning to think you hadn't turned up!'

If she had had any thoughts she was there as a guest rather than an entertainer, they were immediately dispelled as she was introduced to Mullally's Casino Orchestra. They had been hired, along with a Hungarian band, to entertain the guests, and had been anxiously awaiting her arrival.

'Why didn't you report as soon as you arrived?' she was asked. 'Didn't you know the entertainment always has to check in?' To the public at large she might be a star, but to hard-bitten professionals like these, she was simply part of 'the Entertainment'.

'Have you any idea what you want to sing?' the bandleader enquired.

Mhairi looked at him, then turned to glance behind her at the milling throng that was the cream of their country's high society. This was their big night – everyone was happy here except herself, for she still lived merely on hope – the hope that *he* might somehow be here. Oh how she envied Consuelo, for she had everything in life her heart desired: looks, wealth, and the love of one of England's greatest aristocrats whom she surely loved every bit as much as she herself loved Ralph.

'Well, Miss Cloud, what's it gonna be?'

Mhairi's brow furrowed. She had thought of singing one of the popular songs from the show, but something inside her made her change her mind. There was something far more appropriate that had just come to her notice. It epitomized exactly how she viewed herself in the midst of all these evening-suited millionaires and their dazzling, bejewelled wives. The Vanderbilt's Marble House here on Newport's millionaires' row was nothing but a gilded cage, into which tonight she had been invited to perform the duty of song thrush. In their eyes she was merely the canary who was to sing for her supper. Well, if that's how they viewed her, then that's what they would get. 'Something that's appropriate for "the Entertainment" I think, don't you?'

The bandleader looked puzzled.

Her resolve grew as an ironic smile lifted one corner of her lips. The only trouble was – the vast majority of them were probably far too stupid to realize she was blowing a very glamorous, but quite unmistakable raspberry in their direction. 'Do you, by any chance, know "A Bird In A Gilded Cage"?'

'Do you mean that new song that's just come out?'

'That's the one.' It had not even been officially published yet, but it was already going the rounds amongst the professionals, and there couldn't be a band in town that hadn't given it a run through.

'Are you sure you really want to sing that?'

She ignored the dubious tone to his voice. 'Of course. I think it would be a perfect choice.'

The bandleader shrugged. Who was he to argue with the guest star of the evening? He strolled over to check with the rest of the band. They too expressed some surprise, but at least half felt competent enough to give it a try. 'We're game if you are.'

When finally the moment came, a hush fell over the guests who crowded into the ballroom. Mhairi could feel her heart racing. At least one half of the newspapers' prophesies looked set to come true. She had already seen Sunny, the Duke of Marlborough, to whom everyone believed Consuelo's engagement would be announced later that evening, and a chance remark by Consuelo herself had raised her own hopes of Ralph's arrival.

'I wouldn't rush off too soon after your song, if I were you, Miss Cloud. I understand there's a certain gentleman arriving later who may well want a word with you.' Consuelo had said no more as she was hurried off by her mother to meet yet another party of late arrivals, and Mhairi did not have the courage to seek her out to find out more.

It had to be him. It just had to be. She was pinning all her hopes on it.

The whole ballroom fell silent as her name was announced, and then broke into a spontaneous round of applause as, with a nervous smile, she walked up on to the stage that had been erected at the end of the ballroom.

Her face was flushed as she gazed down on the eagerly waiting audience. 'Ladies and gentlemen, it's a great pleasure for me to be here tonight, and I would like once more to wish Consuelo every happiness at this her coming-out ball. The song I would like to sing for you is brand new and I am sure will prove to be one of the most popular of the coming years.'

And with that, Mullally's orchestra struck up and Mhairi's clear voice began to fill the air:

'The ballroom was filled with fashion's throng,
It shone with a thousand lights,
And there was a woman who passed along
The fairest of all sights.
A girl to her lover then softly sighed,
"There's riches at her command."
"But she married for wealth, not for love," he cried.
"Tho' she lives in a mansion grand,
She's only a bird in a gilded cage,
A beautiful sight to see.
You may think she's happy and free from care,
She's not, tho' she seems to be.
'Tis sad when you think of her wasted life,
For youth cannot mate with age,
And her beauty was sold for an old man's gold,
She's a bird in a gilded cage . . ." '

As the last resonance of the last note died on her lips a hush descended as the words sank in. And the hush grew longer and longer.

Mhairi stood awkwardly in the middle of the dais gazing down at the faces that stared back up at her. Instead of the spontaneous burst of applause she expected, there was a look akin to horror on almost every countenance. What

215

on earth had happened to make them react like this? Surely they couldn't all have seen through her gentle dig in their direction for treating her merely as 'the Entertainer'?

Almost every other person present could have answered that question, and it had nothing to do with Mhairi herself. As far as they were concerned, those words they had just had sung to them had been specially written for the girl in whose honour the ball was being held. As intimates of Consuelo's social circle, there was hardly a guest who was not privy to the uncomfortable knowledge that Charles Richard John Spencer Churchill, ninth Duke of Marlborough, was not the love of Consuelo Vanderbilt's young life. They, unlike Mhairi, knew of a fine young American called Winthrop Rutherford whom Consuelo loved with all her young heart, but whose ring she would now never wear, for he did not possess either a fancy title or such a gilded cage as the wonderful Blenheim Palace that now awaited her.

Mhairi was not aware of how long she stood there as the silence continued to deafen her ears. But eventually she felt the touch of George Vanderbilt's hand on her arm, as he led her gently from the stage.

Consuelo's mother, Alva, was standing less than ten feet away from the foot of the dais and her voice seemed to echo round the silent hall as she fixed Mhairi with a frozen stare and then turned to her brother-in-law. 'I hope, George dear, you are in the process of escorting that young lady to her carriage.'

George Vanderbilt made no reply as they ran the gauntlet of a whole row of scandalized Vanderbilts and their guests.

'What did I do wrong?' Mhairi asked in a dazed voice, as he led her away from the numbed crowd, and out into the fresh air of the terrace.

'Wrong?' Her companion gave a dry laugh. 'My dear,

you just told them in there a few home truths, that's all. And maybe, for the sake of our country, as well as young Consuelo, bless her heart, it was as well that you did!'

She looked at him, uncomprehending. It was as if he were talking in some strange code. She had not meant to offend. Surely they knew that? It was quite a harmless jibe, after all – and surely the majority of them did not give a damn whether she had been offended by the type of invitation she had received or not. 'I don't understand . . .'

George Vanderbilt gave a world-weary smile. 'Then maybe that's just as well.' His gaze fell on an approaching figure. 'Oh, by the way, did Consuelo mention there was someone here who wanted to have a word with you before you left?'

The words jerked her back to reality. 'Why yes, yes, she did!'

'Well, I think this is him now.'

She whirled round in the direction of his gaze. All thoughts of her audience's reaction flew from her head. Let it be him! Oh please God, let it be him!

A portly middle-aged man was coming towards them, his ruddy face beaming, and his hand outstretched.

'Mhairi dear, this here is Mr Augustin Daly. He has expressed a special desire to make your acquaintance.'

Mhairi felt her hand being shaken and was aware of the admiration in the eyes that looked into her own, as the bottom fell out of her world. This couldn't be him! This couldn't be the man who was to be her surprise of the evening! They couldn't all have got it so wrong – every one of those newspapers who were so sure he was to be here!

'My dear, are you feeling all right?' George Vanderbilt looked in concern at her pale face and vacantly staring eyes.

'I think it was the reception in there,' she heard Augustin Daly say. 'It was vintage brass monkey, if you ask me.'

She allowed herself to be led to a nearby chair. 'Mr Daly — I'm so sorry,' she began. 'I guess I must have felt rather faint.'

The only theatre owner in New York to rival Charles Hoyt held up a hand to stem her apologies and smiled sympathetically. 'No need to explain, young lady. You've obviously got spunk to choose that particular ditty, tonight of all nights.' He chuckled to himself. 'They had it coming to them, mind. There are a darned sight too many good American girls being bought for old men's gold — and young men's come to that — over there in England. Wouldn't you agree, George?'

But George Vanderbilt had other things on his mind. 'If you'll excuse me, I'll leave you good people to chat, now that Mhairi's feeling better.'

He took his leave, with a kiss on the cheek to Mhairi and a shake of Augustin Daly's hand. He had business to attend to now that the festivities had obviously been brought to an untimely end. He had just employed Frederick Law Olmsted, the country's foremost architect, to build him a house near Biltmore, North Carolina, that would outclass any home owned by any other Vanderbilt — including the one they were in right now. And who knows, it might even rival that celebrated gilded cage, Blenheim Palace itself!

Mhairi watched him go, still in some confusion. What on earth did Augustin Daly want with her?

'I expect you're wondering why I asked to see you, Miss Cloud,' the impresario said, and seeing her nod, he smiled and continued. 'The fact is I'm only interested in the best — and, despite your reception tonight, as far as the American stage goes right now, you *are* the best!'

Mhairi gazed at him, her face now flushed beneath the glow of the Chinese lanterns swaying above their heads in the breeze. 'That's very kind of you to say so.'

'Kindness doesn't come into it, my dear. I'm not a

charitable institution, I'm a businessman. I hear Charlie Hoyt has just announced you're to take over the lead with your name above the title, is that right?'

Mhairi made no reply. He had intimated that would be the case, but there was nothing on paper yet.

'And he's paying you around six hundred dollars, am I right?'

She nodded, too confused to be coy.

'Then I'll double it. I'll pay you twelve hundred a week, with a dress allowance thrown in!'

'Twelve hundred a week!' Was she hearing properly? That was riches beyond her wildest dreams. She thought of her Uncle Finbar, and the twins and Fiona. What couldn't they do with some of that? Then reluctantly she shook her head. 'I'm sorry, Mr Daly, but I couldn't leave Charlie. I really couldn't. He gave me my first big break. I owe everything to him.'

Augustin Daly's smile faded somewhat, but he admired loyalty in an employee. 'Admirable sentiments, Miss Cloud. Admirable sentiments indeed. It's a great pity, though, for you are just what my new London theatre needs.'

'Your new London theatre?' Her ears pricked up immediately. There wasn't a single person who hadn't read of the new Daly's Theatre in London's Leicester Square. It had opened two years previously, in June 1893, with *The Taming of the Shrew*, but sensing British audiences did not appreciate their Shakespeare classics being done by Americans, her new companion had very wisely resorted to a series of musical comedies which had gone down very well indeed.

'Yes, I've got an excellent producer over there called George Edwardes, who has just produced a little beauty of a show for me called *A Gaiety Girl*, but, quite frankly, Miss Cloud, I have just come up with the best idea yet.'

He reached inside his jacket and extracted a folded copy

of a front page from that morning's *New York World*, emblazoned with the headlines: 'The Belle of New York looks set for record-breaking run in *Sunshine Girls*!'

She had not seen it herself, but guessed it referred to her taking over the lead in the show.

'They're referring to you, my dear,' he said, as he refolded the paper and replaced it in his pocket. 'The Belle of New York — it would make one helluva title for a new show!'

'Really?'

'Yes, I can see it now — "Mhairi Cloud *is* The Belle of New York"!' His eyes shone as he waved an arm in the air at an imaginary illuminated sign above his theatre door. 'You'll be the toast of London, Miss Cloud. There'll be no one to touch you. And it'll be written specially for you — every song will be tailored to suit you and you alone!'

He took her hand in his. 'So what do you say, my dear? Does that sound like a good deal to you? Can you imagine yourself living over there in England as the toast of good old London town?'

He glanced back over his shoulder towards the other guests just beginning to recover from their shock in the ballroom beyond. 'If you ask me, it might be a sensible move. I reckon you've managed to offend every one of the famous Four Hundred in there tonight, and it would be better all round if you left town of your own accord, before they get the chance to run you out!'

She turned and looked round herself at the eyes of society still staring at her from the lighted ballroom. To offend a Vanderbilt, no matter how unintentionally, was to offend against the whole of New York society. Her sin would not be forgiven in a hurry.

Then she glanced down at the ring that still adorned the third finger of her right hand, and slowly began to nod her head. 'Yes, Mr Daly,' she answered softly. 'You could very well be right.'

Chapter Thirteen

Daly's Theatre, London
Monday, 19 November 1895

'Letter for you, Miss Cloud!'

Mhairi turned from her dressing-stool and accepted the envelope from the bell-boy, her eyes lighting up at the sight of an American stamp. It was Fiona's writing – even better! She had not heard from her cousin since arriving in London the previous month.

Impatiently she ripped it open. It contained a single sheet of paper, and a smaller envelope. Puzzled, she extracted the single sheet and began to read:

2nd October, 1895

My dear Mhairi,

My apologies for not being in touch before, but things have not been the same here in New York since you left. The twins are well, but Dad does not seem able to get over Mother's death, despite the generous financial help I know you provided for him before you left. He continues to live and work at Lancaster House, but for how much longer I cannot say. I called round to see him the other day and he handed me a letter which he found amongst Mother's things. Since it concerns you, we both feel you should know about it. When you have read it, remember to take a look at the bracelet, will you?

We all send our love,

Fiona.

Intrigued, Mhairi pulled out the other envelope and her eyes fell on the old British penny black stamp. It was addressed to her Auntie Belle in Manchester, and both the ink and paper had faded to a dull shade of beige. She was aware of her heart quickening as she slid the letter out and unfolded it. Her eyes fell first on the neatly scribed signature, Mary Anne. Dear God, it was from her mother!

It was dated 8 March 1877, and was written from her grandfather's home on Skye. Mhairi's fingers gripped the cheap scrap of notepaper as she held it beneath the light of her make-up mirror and read on:

Dearest Belle,

I am writing you myself before any one else does to let you know I was recently delivered of a live female child I have named Mhairi Anna McLeod. She is a beautiful baby and, despite what the wagging tongues may say, I can feel no shame when I look at her. I have made no claim on her father for I know he and I can never be one in the eyes of Our Lord. His name is Gregor McGregor, and he is the only surviving son of McGregor of Dalriada. I have spoken his name to no one, and nor shall I, for I fear what the brothers might do if they were to learn his identity. I tell you, dear sister, for I feel should anything ever happen to me, the facts should not die with me. I would prefer that the child does not learn the truth. What good could it do her? Her inheritance can only ever be the blood that runs in her veins, and I pray that it will flow true and strong, for, God knows, she will need that strength. It is a heavy cross she has to bear.

Pray for her, Belle dear, and for your sister,

Mary Anne.

Mhairi's eyes returned to the top of the page and she reread the words written there in that neat angular script. 'Holy Mary and Joseph . . .' It was there in that faded brown ink for herself and all the world to see: Gregor McGregor, the only surviving son of McGregor of Dalriada . . . Her father.

She slumped against the back of the chair and let out a sigh that was more of a groan. 'Dalriada . . .' she said the word aloud, then again, over and over, like an incantation. 'Dalriada . . . Dalriada . . . Dalriada . . .'

She shook her head as emotion took over. Was that not the very place she had loved from afar all those years ago? And now it all made sense. All those walks with her mother to gaze across the glen at its turrets gleaming above the dark green of the pines. It was her father's home. And the grandfather's she had never known. It had been the home of the McGregors for as far back as anyone on the island could remember.

She stared with unseeing eyes at the wall opposite, and instead of the old posters of past shows, her eyes beheld such a scene of mist and beauty as she had never known in her life since. Gleaming white walls and battlements, and turrets that pointed straight to heaven. And a flag flew from the highest of them when the Laird was at home; a flag with a lion and a crown, and the words 'Srioghal Mo Dhream' in Gaelic: Royal is my race.

'Royal is my race,' she repeated. The motto of the Clan McGregor. Her mother had told her that, and the words had stirred her heart even then. Yes, it was all falling into place. Mary Anne McLeod had wanted her daughter to know of the inheritance that would never be hers. She had wanted her to know, but could never tell her in so many words.

Carefully Mhairi folded the letter and replaced it in the envelope in which it had lain unseen for over eighteen years. 'Royal is my race,' she repeated softly once more to herself. 'I am no longer Mhairi McLeod of Ballintuim, but Mhairi McGregor of Dalriada.' Her heart swelled with pride, until she reached across to lay the precious envelope on her dressing-table top, and her eyes lighted on the silver bracelet on her wrist. 'No,' she said aloud. She was not Mhairi McGregor of Dalriada. 'I am a right royal bastard – he has seen to that!'

And suddenly she hated the man for whom the flag flew above those enchanted turrets, for he had cheated her. He had cheated her – his own child – of her birthright. Of the right to acknowledge the origins of the very blood that ran in her veins. Could any man be guilty of a greater sin?

'Five minutes, Miss Cloud!'

223

The call brought her back to reality. The reality of starring in what was predicted would be one of the biggest hit shows to reach the London stage in years.

The Belle of New York was opening tonight, right here in Daly's Theatre, Cranbourne Street, Leicester Square. And she would be on stage in five minutes. Her heart pounded as she stood up and adjusted the picture hat on top of her carefully coiffured curls. 'Please let it be a success,' she prayed aloud. 'For Augustin, who put up the money. For George Edwardes, the producer. And for me . . . !'

Yes, most of all for herself. And suddenly it was more important than ever. They were all out there tonight – everyone who was anyone in London society. Even the Prince and Princess of Wales. But more important than the heir to the British throne and his wife, perhaps HE was there: Gregor McGregor, Laird of Dalriada, for didn't the Scottish aristocracy spend more time in the English capital than in their own one of Edinburgh?

And for the first time since her arrival in London, it was not Ralph MacLachlan who was uppermost in her mind as she closed the dressing-room door behind her and made her way into the wings, ready for the band to break into the familiar bars of the song she had been rehearsing to perfection for the past few weeks.

And then it was all happening. She was on stage, and tonight was better than any rehearsal. First-night nerves had been given an especially sharp edge by the news of her father, and seemed to add an extra impetus to heighten her performance. And the cast around her responded as never before. The songs were sung with more verve, and the dances danced with more vigour, and the people cheered till the whole theatre resounded to the sound of yet another success for Augustin Daly and his American-led cast.

The great man himself was in the audience, seated alongside the stout, indolent figure of his British producer

George Edwardes. He was here to bask in the glory of what he was convinced would be one of the most memorable first nights ever seen on the London stage, and it looked like he was being proved right.

At the end of the performance, the American impresario's eyes gleamed as he gazed upon his new star, standing arms outstretched receiving the adulation of the English audience, then he half-turned in his seat to gaze up at the box of honour. There sat the portly, bearded figure of Albert Edward, Prince of Wales, next to his beautiful Danish wife, Alexandra.

'He's standing!' Augustin Daly could not suppress his excitement as he clutched his producer's arm. 'Old Bertie's rising to applaud her!'

Both men gazed up as the heir to the British throne rose to his feet to applaud the slim figure of the young woman in the centre of the stage down below. Then the audience followed suit, and all eighteen hundred people were on their feet.

'Thank you! Thank you!' Mhairi's eyes glowed as she curtsied once more to the royal box, then rose to blow yet more kisses to the audience. She threw her arms wide as if to embrace them to her. Even the rest of the cast behind her were joining in the applause. She turned to thank them in turn, before gazing once more on the scene before her. The plush décor, in shades of red, burnished gold, silver and bronze seemed to merge into one gigantic rainbow as her eyes brimmed.

Behind the circle fronts and boxes carved as boatloads of sea-nymphs and cherubs, the people stood and cheered. The cream of high society was on its feet paying homage to theatreland's brightest new star, their tiaras and family jewels sparkling beneath the glittering chandeliers.

Mhairi blinked her eyes to clear her vision, but she could see nothing except that spectacular rainbow; each of the bubbles blown by the cavorting nymphs and cherubs was a coloured electric light bulb, so the whole auditorium was a dazzling blaze of every hue.

Her eyes gazed up at the huge domed ceiling, with its immense winged figures of Fame, and her heart turned over. She had seen just such figures once before, on that fateful day in the Vanderbilt house . . .

They were bringing down the curtain for the last time, and she wiped her eyes in a final desperate attempt to search the applauding throng below her. They were all here – all those who made Queen Victoria's London the most exciting city in the world. But were THEY – the two people who really mattered? She knew she would not recognize her father, Gregor McGregor, even if he were to be standing in front of her, but she would recognize Ralph all right, and her eyes continued to scan the sea of faces until the velvet drapes swished their way into place before her.

With the echoes of the final curtain call still ringing in her ears, she was swept backstage in the centre of a cast drunk on the applause and excitement of the moment. She was aware of being kissed by an ecstatic Augustin Daly and hugged by his jubilant producer George Edwardes.

Then the cry went up: 'The Prince of Wales is on his way!'

Hastily they lined themselves into some sort of order as the future King of England came to offer his personal congratulations.

The air was thick with the smell of greasepaint, Macassar hair-oil, assorted perfumes, and tobacco smoke. She could feel her face flush, and a sweat break out on her skin beneath the elaborate gown, as the excitement of the moment and the nauseating proximity of her perspiring fellow artists took its toll. She prayed she would not faint as she took a deep breath of the fetid air and attempted to calm her pounding heart as the royal party came into view.

'Ah, Miss Cloud . . .'

Mhairi found herself gazing into the protuberant, watery eyes of Albert Edward, the fifty-four-year-old heir to the British throne. So this was the face that had launched a thousand biscuit tins! Close to, it was impossible to see what the likes of the legendary Lillie Langtry saw in him. He might well have bedded almost all the beauties of the day for two generations past, but for a man not long past his prime, he had not worn well. A life dedicated to wining, dining, and womanizing had left its mark on his figure which was several stones overweight; what was left of his hair was sparse and grey, and beneath the close-cropped grey beard, his complexion had an unhealthy ruddiness to it.

The future king transferred the large Havana to his left hand and extended his right. His palm had a damp, clammy feel to it as fingers encircled hers, and his eyes rested admiringly on the flushed swell of her breasts, above the low-cut gown, before moving up to meet her own curious gaze. 'Another welcome American export to our shores! May I congratulate you on a fine performance, Miss Cloud.' To her surprise, his voice had a faint, guttural, quite distinctly Germanic accent.

She sank into a deep curtsey. 'Thank you, Your Royal Highness. I am delighted to be here.' She continued to gaze into his eyes as his hand held on to hers; they were moist and red-veined, and his breath wafted the un-mistakable odour of Cuban tobacco towards her as she rose to her feet.

Next his wife, the beautiful Princess Alexandra was introduced, and Mhairi marvelled at the violet eyes that met her own, and at the long, elegant neck adorned with the multiple rows of pearls, worn to cover an operation scar, but now adopted by ladies everywhere as the height of fashion. How could anyone so frequently betray such beauty? 'So enjoyable, Miss Cloud,' she murmured in her attractive, Scandinavian accent.

'Thank you so much, Your . . .'

But the sentence was never finished, for the Princess was already moving on, her gloved hand outstretched towards the next in line.

'She's almost stone-deaf,' she heard George Edwardes whisper in her ear. 'That's why she won't stop to chat.'

But although his wife had moved on, the Prince himself turned back to personally introduce two extremely attractive dark-haired women in early middle age, who had been guests along with several others in the royal box. They were Daisy, Countess of Warwick, and Jennie, Lady Randolph Churchill, and the latter, a New Yorker by birth, was only too happy to stop to chat to her old hometown's most successful export.

'I'm moving house shortly, my dear, from my present home in Grosvenor Square to 35A Great Cumberland Place – I do hope I shall have the pleasure of your company there before long.'

She tapped her chin thoughtfully with her closed fan. 'No, on second thoughts, why should we wait so long? I'll get an invitation in the post as soon as possible. I'm sure lots of my friends would love to meet you . . . You will come, won't you?'

'I would be delighted.'

Lady Churchill had lustrous brown eyes, beneath heavy dark brows, and a beautiful head of raven hair done up in the fashion favoured by the Princess of Wales. Without doubt she was one of the most stunning beauties on the social scene and was well aware of it. 'Have you been over here long?' she enquired, in her attractive American accent.

'Not long enough, ma'm!'

Jennie Churchill laughed. 'And Amen to that! I swear I've yet to meet a fellow American who doesn't love it over here! I hope we shall see plenty more of you, my dear, both on the stage and off.' And after divesting herself of another dazzling smile in Mhairi's direction, she moved on to add her congratulations to the others in the line-up.

Mhairi gazed after the royal party as it made its exit, as George Edwardes commented in her ear, 'It's not many men who get away with parading their mistresses in public, is it?'

Mhairi's brows rose. 'You mean the Countess and Lady Churchill are . . . ?'

But she got no further, as her producer continued confidentially, 'Of course, it's one of the first times Lady C.'s been seen out since her husband died. Syphilis they say it was. Mad as a coot he went. Shocking thing a death like that at his age. And him such a promising politician at one time.'

His voice dropped even further. 'They thought she'd marry her long-time lover Count Kinsky when her old man died, but it seems his family back in Austria wouldn't hear of it. She's a commoner, you see – an American by birth, just like yourself.'

Mhairi tensed as Kati van der Donck's words rang in her head. 'You mean that type of snobbery still goes on?'

'Good God, yes! If there's anything the European aristocracy cares passionately about when it comes to marrying their offspring or buying a racehorse, it's good breeding. You can have the most noble soul on this earth, but it doesn't make one whit of a difference if your standing in *Debrett's* or in the *Almanack de Gotha* doesn't measure up! In fact, the only time they're prepared to make an exception to that rule is when they're really hard up, like the Churchills – or Marlboroughs, whatever you want to call them.' He nodded towards the departing group. 'Lady Churchill there was Jennie Jerome, the daughter of an American millionaire before her marriage, and everyone knows about her young nephew, the present Duke, and that Vanderbilt gal.'

'You mean Consuelo.'

'That's her. You know her, then?'

Mhairi nodded, her face expressionless. 'We've met once or twice.'

'Hey, you two! It's time we were off. The party's getting underway!' Augustin Daly's voice interrupted from a few yards away.

Mhairi's eyes desperately searched the faces still milling around backstage. Where *was* he? She had been here in London for over three weeks and there was still no word or sign from Ralph. Her last letter from him had been almost six weeks ago now – over two weeks before she was due to set sail. In it he had been his usual self, declaring his love and asking her to be sure to let him know just as soon as she had her exact sailing times, so he could make preparations for her arrival. She had done that immediately she had booked the passage, but she had heard nothing since. Her misery was made all the more unbearable by reading in the newspapers of the eighteen-year-old Consuelo Vanderbilt's wedding to the Duke of Marlborough, in St Thomas's Episcopal Church, New York, on 6 November.

Somehow, despite her embarrassing *faux pas* at the coming-out ball in Newport, because they were the same age, and Ralph had first introduced them, she had always felt an affinity with Consuelo, and in her dreams, she had even imagined attending the Vanderbilt–Marlborough wedding on his arm. But instead she had been left to read of it alone in her dressing-room here in London, and England's capital city seemed a much less welcoming place without him. The disappointment and emptiness she had felt reading of the marriage had been almost unbearable, but she had convinced herself that although he might well have been unavoidably out of town over the past few weeks on family business, he would have made the effort to be here tonight of all nights.

The first-night party was held at the Savoy. 'Where

else?' Augustin Daly had declared, for wasn't Mr Richard D'Oyly Carte's new hotel the best in town? In César Ritz, it had the best manager money could buy, and in Auguste Escoffier, it had the best chef. And whilst other high-class hotels still made do with gas lighting, the Savoy was entirely lit by electricity and boasted seventy marble bathrooms. In fact, Mhairi had been informed, rumour had it that when D'Oyly Carte asked the builder to install the required seventy bathrooms, the astonished trades- man immediately inquired if he expected his guests to be amphibious.

But the nearest any of the company from Augustin Daly's theatre, or their invited guests, came to swimming was when an exuberant pair of male actors threatened to toss Mhairi into the fountain that stood in the courtyard of the hotel, sending sprays of sparkling water up to the flower-bedecked balconies above.

The mood of the entire company was one of elation, and the hotel had risen to the occasion with a culinary triumph of its own: the centrepiece of the meal laid out on damask-covered tables was a huge bell carved out of ice, and inlaid with a selection of exotic tropical fruits.

The main course, created specially for the star of the show, was *Zéphyr du poularde Mhairi, Belle de New York*. Its composition of delicate slices of chicken breasts on *pâté de foie gras*, served with fresh asparagus salad, would normally have been devoured with relish, but as the evening wore on and there was still no sign of Ralph, Mhairi found her appetite had disappeared along with her high spirits, and she could only pick half-heartedly at the food on offer.

When, just after midnight, George Edwardes escorted her home in his private brougham, with Turner his personal coachman aloft on the box, she found herself only half-listening to the fatherly advice he was intent on giving her.

'I advise all my female stars to lunch exclusively at Romano's, my dear. It's most important you get seen in only the best places, and there's no need to worry about the expense, I've arranged for you to be allowed a special tariff there.' Romano, the dapper little Italian with the fine crop of greying hair and fractured English, who had given the famous Strand restaurant its name, was a personal friend. He could rely on him to take good care both of his stars from Daly's, and also of his crop of beauties from the Gaiety Theatre, of whom he was justly proud.

His companion in the carriage merely murmured, 'Of course, George darling,' in the appropriate places, for her mind was on other things. Well-meaning though her producer was, she was tired of all this image-building, and longed for a real confidante to whom she could confess her disappointment over Ralph. If only Fiona or Sally were here, for both her cousin and her former colleague possessed exactly the right brand of common sense to jolly her out of the depression she felt herself to be sliding into.

The instant success of the show with the public and the critics alike did little to lighten her mood, and over the next few weeks she read with growing indifference the newspaper reports of the scenes that were being enacted outside the theatre each evening.

Those not fortunate enough to have already booked were forced to join in the regular mêlée that began at least two hours before the curtain was due to go up. There on the pavement, hundreds of well-dressed citizens could be seen gathering outside the ticket office, until the doors were finally opened and the surge began. Well-bred ladies, not used to having to fight their way into any-where, wailed in anguish as their elaborate coiffures became dishevelled, and umbrellas got trodden underfoot in the undignified scramble to secure a seat for the show all London was talking about.

The main entrance of the theatre opened into a large

hall in which stood an enormous cast-iron American stove, and within the radius of its cheering warmth became *the* place to be noticed. Here nightly the cream of *Burke's Peerage, Baronetage and Landed Gentry* gathered to see and be seen by their peers. The fact that the Prince and Princess of Wales had graced the show with their presence on the first night made it something that no one who aspired to be within their social circle could afford to ignore.

Other stars of the London stage made frequent visits backstage to offer their congratulations, and Mhairi was particularly interested to meet those who had recently returned from her native New York. Such a pair was Ellaline Terris and her husband Seymour Hicks. And with the dainty, flaxen-haired actress and her husband Mhairi discussed the animosity against England that was rife in the States at the moment, and the pair talked with great sadness of the closure of all British shows over there.

George Edwardes had himself sent a recent Gaiety Theatre hit, *The Shop Girl*, across the Atlantic, with Seymour playing the male lead; Ellaline had also been appearing in New York, in a comedy by W. S. Gilbert, and both shows had been boycotted and forced to close by a public incensed over Great Britain's argument with America over territory on the Venezuelan border. 'To think such a thing could happen over a silly South American border dispute! It's such a pity,' Ellaline sighed. 'We did so love it over there, although the press were absolutely rotten to Seymour.'

Mhairi nodded sympathetically, but diplomatically kept her peace. Before she came over, she herself had seen the headlines in *Variety* which read: '*Comedians beware! Stealmore Tricks is in town. Padlock your gags! Lock up your jokes!*' Ellaline's youthful husband had been branded a thief of other people's material, and that, above all else, was regarded as a cardinal sin amongst actors on either side of the Atlantic.

But New York's loss was London's gain, for, with so many of their top stars back in town, the city positively buzzed with excitement. Throughout the first few weeks of the run, the cast of *The Belle*, as it was known to everyone, suppered in a different restaurant every night. Romano's, the Carlton Grill, the Savoy Grill – all became familiar haunts, and famous faces that Mhairi had only ever seen on billboards or in magazines became firm friends.

But amidst all the excitement of new people and places there was a darkness at the heart of things, for there was still no word from Ralph. None of her letters had received an answer, and, surprisingly, at none of the well-heeled gatherings she had been invited to had he appeared. She was convinced she had been introduced to almost every member of the British aristocracy, from the Prince of Wales down, and at none of the fine houses was he to be found. It seemed as if he had simply disappeared off the face of the earth.

To live with her disappointment was not easy, but she was trying desperately to put him to the back of her mind and divert her attention to other things when an invitation she had been only half-expecting arrived. Her spirits rose as she read it, for she had warmed to the writer at their first meeting. It was written on card that still had a thin black line next to the gilt edging.

50 Grosvenor Square

Dear Miss Cloud,

I am having a small At Home on Wednesday afternoon for a few close friends, and would be delighted if you would care to join us. Any time around three o'clock will be perfect.

Kindest regards . . .

The name Jennie was scrawled in black ink above the printed official title of Lady Randolph Churchill.

. Mhairi could not resist a wry smile as she stuck it, along with the many others she received, into the bevelled edge of the make-up mirror, in her dressing-room. It seemed ironic that her success behind the footlights in London should have become the key that was unlocking the doors of the highest echelons of society for her so soon after her terrible *faux pas* at the Vanderbilt ball, in Newport, had so firmly closed them in New York.

She chose her clothes with care when Wednesday came, settling on an amber velvet suit, trimmed with matching fox fur. Around her neck, in place of the ubiquitous feather boa, she threw the skin of a white Arctic fox that set off her pale complexion and dark auburn hair to perfection.

The drawing-room of the exquisitely decorated house in Grosvenor Square was already full when she arrived at three o'clock precisely, and she was greeted warmly by her hostess who lost no time in making introductions. Jennie Churchill, not completely out of mourning, was dressed in a gown of deep mauve taffeta, trimmed with black velvet, and had her thick dark locks anchored on top of her head with a black velvet bow. For a woman already in her forties, she could still turn heads in any room.

Taking Mhairi by the elbow, she shepherded her across the floor in the direction of the tall, willowy figure of Millie, Duchess of Sutherland. Inwardly Mhairi balked at the name. For their part in the Highland Clearances, the Sutherlands bore a family name that would surely remain reviled amongst her people as long as there was a Scottish nation.

The other two women in the group were Jennie's younger sister, Lady Leonie Leslie, and Mrs Patrick Campbell, the celebrated actress. She had already been informed by George Edwardes that Leonie Leslie was the long-time mistress of Queen Victoria's third son, Arthur, Duke of Connaught, and was also a close personal friend of the Prince's wife, the former Princess Margaret Louise of Prussia. And as she listened to the American chat animatedly about them both, Mhairi could not help wondering if the Princess did not mind that her husband's heart, and often, presumably, his body, lay elsewhere. Sex it seemed, particularly with someone else's husband or wife, seemed to be the main preoccupation of the upper class in Victoria's England, and she thought back wryly to Ralph's joke about the rest of the world having love lives, while the English had hot-water bottles. Just who was fooling who?

The conversation sparkled only slightly less than the jewels that adorned the necks, ears and wrists of those present. Indeed the diamond necklace that graced the throat of Millicent Sutherland had once formed part of the *collier de la reine* of none other than Marie Antoinette of France. 'It was actually designed for the King's mistress, Madame du Barry,' the Duchess informed Mhairi, after she had complimented her on it. 'For some reason Louis decided to present it to his wife on the birth of their first child. Silly man! He might have known Marie Antoinette was no fool and, knowing full well it was originally intended for his mistress, she quite rightly refused it.' She took another sip of sherry and smiled. 'Luckily for me, it was then split up and sold, and that's how the necklace came to be in our family.'

'Not that the poor thing would have had much use for it, anyway,' Mrs Pat Campbell added. 'I can't imagine anything less useful than a necklace once you've had your head chopped off!'

'Stella, really!'

But the actress was in no mood to be silenced. She delighted in the wicked remark whenever possible, and within seconds she had everyone either scandalized or laughing at her seemingly inexhaustible store of theatre gossip.

As the country's most celebrated female lead, she had opened on 21 September at the Lyceum in *Romeo and Juliet*, to her usual avalanche of critical acclaim. But like everyone else in the theatre at the moment, even her own production took second place to the latest gossip on the downfall of poor Oscar Wilde.

'Stupid man,' she sighed. 'Now, if only he'd stuck to affairs with the opposite sex instead of bedding that silly young man Alfred Douglas, he would have found that life could be a lot more fun, and certainly a lot safer. At least you don't get thrown into jail for that yet!' She flashed a wicked glance around the assembled company. 'I fear there would be an awful lot of people serving penal servitude alongside poor dear Oscar if that were the case!'

The conversation then moved on to Paris and it transpired that Jennie had spent the early part of the summer in her apartment on the Avenue Kléber, and she delighted them all in telling of her exploits in pedalling through the Bois de Boulogne on a bicycle, something quite unheard of for middle-aged ladies still in mourning.

'I do hope you were suitably attired, darling,' her sister said, with a laconic smile.

'Of course, Leonie dear. I wore the most fashionable pair of black bloomers money could buy!'

Here in Europe, Mhairi was aware she was listening to Old Money talk, and there was an aplomb, an unself-conscious arrogance about it, that could only come with the complete conviction that the Bible had got it wrong; there could be no question of the meek inheriting the earth whilst the English aristocracy were around, for they already had it well and truly bought and accounted for. It was not a comfortable feeling.

After several more minutes engaged in chatting to her hostess and the animated trio, Mhairi became gradually aware of being watched by a slight, auburn-haired girl of around her own age who was standing by the window.

She was soberly dressed, in a gown of slate-grey, and that she was eavesdropping on the conversation there was no doubt. Eventually the young woman was spotted by Jennie who thoughtfully led her across to meet London's brightest new star, whilst the others wandered off to chat to various old friends.

'Miss Cloud, I'd like you to meet a young Scottish friend of mine who I know is looking forward to seeing your show herself before long: Lady Euphemia Hastings . . .'

She took the young woman by the elbow. 'Effie, dear, this, as you must already know, is none other than Miss Mhairi Cloud —the Belle of New York herself!'

The two young women shook hands politely. They were almost the same height and colouring, with Mhairi's hair being only slightly darker, but a great deal more luxuriant than the other's, and whilst her own eyes were of a hazel hue, Effie Hastings's were a much darker brown with no trace of green. Her face fell short of being conventionally pretty due to the size and shape of her nose, which verged on the patrician, but her expression was pleasant and her manner genuinely interested as she confided to Mhairi, 'I'm so very pleased to meet you like this, Miss Cloud. I'm afraid I couldn't make it to the first night of your show last week, I – I've only just come out of mourning. But I'm hoping to catch it before I travel up north for Christmas.' She gave a wistful smile. 'It'll be a year this week since my husband was killed, and one gets quite out of touch, you know.'

Mhairi gave a sympathetic smile. She seemed more like a child than a widowed woman. 'I'll make sure you get tickets, if you leave me your address.'

'Would you?' The young woman's eyes sparkled. 'That would be so kind!'

There was something fetchingly unaffected about her, and Mhairi felt herself warming to her new companion. 'It'll be my pleasure.'

'It must be so exciting, the life you lead . . .'

She had just the faintest trace of a Scottish accent, and remembering their hostess's introduction, Mhairi queried, 'Lady Churchill said you were originally from Scotland – which part would that be?'

Effie Hastings laughed. 'Oh, about as far removed from your own hometown of New York as it's possible to get! I'm from the island of Skye in the Western Highlands.'

Mhairi drew in her breath. 'Skye, you say?'

Her new companion nodded. 'That's right – but it's not the famous Dunvegan Castle, if that's what you're thinking. Our family seat is on the west of the island too, but much further south. Overlooking Loch Scavaig, to be exact. You won't know it of course, being American, even few Scottish people do.'

'Try me.'

'It's called Dalriada.'

Chapter Fourteen

'Dalriada!'

'Why yes . . . Do you know it?' Effie Hastings looked puzzled. Surely news of her family home couldn't have travelled all the way to New York?

Mhairi was aware of gaping at her new acquaintance. Just who was this young woman? 'I – I believe I may have read something somewhere . . .' she began as her mind raced. 'But I seem to recall Dalriada belonged to the McGregor family.'

'Yes, that's right,' her companion confirmed. 'My name was Euphemia McGregor before I married Jack.'

'And your father is?'

'Gregor McGregor.'

Mhairi felt her knees buckle. 'Do you mind if we sit down?' she heard herself say. 'It must be the heat in here . . .'

Effie Hastings looked concerned as she glanced towards the blazing fire in the ornate Adam fireplace. 'It is a trifle stuffy. Here, let me . . .' She took Mhairi's arm and led her gently to a nearby sofa, where they sat down side by side. 'Are you sure you're going to be all right? You wouldn't like me to fetch you a drink of cold water or something?'

'No . . . no, thank you. Honestly, I'll be fine.'

Her companion looked relieved. 'I must admit to being rather a hot-house plant myself. In fact it was always rather a joke at home. Skye is rather prone to quite chilling Atlantic mists and I'd just have to set foot outside the door and I'd come down with some awful cold or something, while my father could roam the hills for days on end and not get a sniffle.'

Mhairi could feel herself breaking out in a cold sweat as she stared at the young woman. Her father . . . She was talking about *their* father. This young woman sitting next to her making small talk was her half-sister. The knowledge made her head spin as the palms of her hands grew clammy and her mouth dried so that her voice was a mere croak. 'Is – is your father here in London with you?'

Effie Hastings shook her head and her eyes clouded. 'Oh no, Pa's rarely left home for the past year,' she confided. 'He had a heart attack last Christmas, just after my husband was killed in a hunting accident.'

'How awful for you!'

'Yes, it was at the time, but one gets over things – or tries to . . . To be honest I think Pa took Jack's death much worse than I did. It certainly contributed to his heart attack, Dr Cromar was convinced of that.'

Dr Cromar . . . Dr Cromar . . . It was years since Mhairi had heard that name. Not since her grandfather had died. But Effie Hastings was continuing her reflections, totally unaware of the effect her words were having on the young woman sitting next to her.

'I'm an only child, you see, Miss Cloud. My mother died when I was young, so there was only my father and me throughout most of my childhood.' Her voice dropped. 'We are very close, and it meant a lot to him to see me safely married. "A good man to take care of you after I've gone" was what he used to say about Jack. It seemed unbelievable to him that his son-in-law should go before he did.'

Mhairi listened, her eyes never leaving the other's face. She took it all in: the candid brown eyes, now troubled as she talked of her father, and the proud, slightly Roman nose that looked so out of place above the still childish mouth, with the rows of small, even, white teeth. Had

241

Gregor McGregor bequeathed her that nose? Involuntarily Mhairi touched her own much shorter, straighter one. She had inherited Mary Anne's, there was no doubt about that. But what of the other McGregor traits? Suddenly she felt an overwhelming envy for the young woman beside her who had grown up with her inheritance, who had walked the corridors of Dalriada and grown to know the portraits of their McGregor forebears that must most certainly hang on those ancient stone walls. 'He – he must love you very much – your father.' The catch in her voice almost betrayed the emotion behind the words.

Effie Hastings agreed wholeheartedly. 'Oh yes, yes he does. Almost too much. There's just us left, you see. Just the two of us. The last of the line he calls us, and he so longs for a grandson to inherit the castle.'

'How old are you, Lady Hastings?' The question was totally out of order, but she had to know.

Effie Hastings looked surprised, but answered honestly nevertheless. 'I'm eighteen. I was born on mid-summer's day 1877.'

Mhairi drew in her breath. So Euphemia Hastings was not Gregor McGregor's eldest child. She – Mhairi McLeod – was. And but for a single scrap of paper they called a marriage certificate, Dalriada could have been hers. The old Colonel, Willie Honeycomb, had once told her that the tragedy of life is not what we suffer, but more often what we miss, and now those words were coming so painfully true. All her life, ever since her mother had shown her those blinding white turrets piercing the blue heavens above the pine trees, she had yearned for that place. Dalriada was etched on her soul. And it could have been hers. It *should* have been hers . . .

'Miss Cloud – ah, there you are!' It was Jennie Churchill's voice, and its owner appeared from behind Mhairi's back to interrupt her musing. 'Would you mind very much, Effie dear, but there are several new arrivals just dying to meet our celebrated actress here!'

'Not at all!' Effie Hastings assured her, but the disappointment was obvious on her face as she rose to shake Mhairi's hand. 'It's been a great pleasure to meet you, Miss Cloud, and do remember those tickets ... I'd be so grateful.'

'As if I could forget.' Mhairi gave a bitter-sweet smile as she shook hands, and left her new acquaintance standing by the sofa to follow her hostess to the other side of the room. Euphemia Hastings would never know the irony behind those words, just as she would never know that the celebrated actress she so admired was none other than her own half-sister.

'Will you be going to Skye for Hogmanay?' Jennie Churchill asked, as soon as they were out of earshot.

Mhairi froze. No one here knew she was from the island. 'I – I don't understand.'

Jennie looked surprised. 'The Hogmanay house-party at Dalriada, of course. It's quite an event: lots of tartan and whisky, and Highland reels. You know the sort of thing. They didn't have it last year because of Jack's death, but I've told Effie she should certainly hold it this year. She'll be out of mourning by then and the company will do both her and her father the world of good.' The American's dark brows rose quizzically. 'I'm surprised she hasn't invited you, but it's probably my fault for stealing you away before she had the chance, poor thing.'

Throwing propriety to the wind, Mhairi took hold of her hostess's arm, causing her to pause before they reached the group waiting to be introduced. 'Lady Churchill ... could you let her know – Lady Hastings ...' She was stumbling over her words as she struggled to express herself. 'If you get the chance, and it doesn't sound too presumptuous ... Could you let her know I'd be delighted to attend?'

'Why, of course, my dear, I'd be only too pleased.'
Jennie Churchill bestowed one of her dazzling smiles on
the young woman at her side. 'And I'd start rehearsing
those Scottish songs right now, if I were you, for the
McGregor is sure to ask you to sing. You won't have met
him yet, will you?'

'No . . . No, we've never met.'

And no sooner had she uttered the words than she
knew it was not the truth. She had met the McGregor all
right. She had met him one cold November night at the
graveside of her mother, and he had carried her in his
arms back up the hill to her grandfather's cottage.

And suddenly her fine gown fell away, and the elegant
drawing-room with its chattering throng, and she was
that child again. That child who had heard the voice of the
wind in the pines as she had run barefoot to her dead
mother's side, so she would not be lonely in that loneliest
of places by the cold Western sea.

And she relived that scene again in bed that night, and
almost every night for the next week until the letter came
in reply to the two complimentary tickets for the show she
had despatched in the name of Lady Euphemia Hastings,
care of Lady Randolph Churchill, at 50 Grosvenor Square.

And Jennie Churchill had done her bit. In a childish
hand the invitation was there to: 'join my family and
friends at Dalriada Castle, Isle of Skye, on 31st December,
1895, for the Hogmanay celebrations, and feel welcome to
remain at your pleasure over the next few days.'

Mhairi received the letter in her dressing-room just
before curtain-up on a bitterly cold night in mid-
December. Despite the fire that burned in the grate to the
right of her dressing-table, she had been shivering with
cold until she opened the envelope and read the words
within. Now her whole body was bathed in sweat and her
heart palpitated beneath the tight bodice of her gown. Not
only would she be returning to the home of her childhood

and her beloved island, but she would be entering her father's home for the first time. 'Dalriada . . .' The very name was music to her soul.

That night, after returning to the small Regency terraced house she rented not far from the theatre, she sat and wrote her first letter to Fiona since she received the truth of her paternity:

My dear Cousin,
How I have longed to write you since receiving your letter containing the news of my birth, but somehow I found it impossible to put on paper what I had still not come to terms with in my own heart. So the McGregor of Dalriada is my father. So be it. Perhaps in my heart I always knew, for why else would that enchanted place have remained so dear to my heart?
Incredibly I am to meet him in two short weeks. The invitation came from his daughter Euphemia, whom I have met by pure chance here in London. My heart is so full at the thought of returning to my beloved island that I can barely think straight at the moment. Are the uncles still alive? To my shame, I confess to not knowing, for it is many years since I saw a letter from them. How I will cope with so much emotion I cannot yet imagine. But fear not that I will succumb to the seductions of the McGregor household and forget the fact that he shamed my mother and denied me, his own child. I still wear the bracelet and it will be on my wrist as the clock strikes the end of this fateful year.
How are you all? How is dearest Uncle Finbar? And the twins, how are they? How I long to see you all again. London is wonderful, but it is not home . . .

Her pen paused above the line as her brow furrowed. But where *was* home? Was it still New York, where she had grown to young womanhood, or was it still *Eilean a' Cheo*, her misty island?

It was a cruel December that year, with snow lying in dirty, frozen piles by the roadside and water freezing in the pipes. It was the coldest Mhairi could remember since that dreadful winter of 1888 back in New York when she was involved in that sub-zero train ride with Kati that almost ended in disaster. Her mind often returned to her old friend these days, for she had almost convinced herself that the unthinkable had happened: Ralph had returned to America to make Kati van der Donck his wife.

With no real information to go on, it was almost the only explanation she could come up with for his total disappearance from her life. It was either that or he had been the victim of some terrible illness or accident. At any rate, she had now been in England for over two months and there was still no word from him and, despite her resolve to get on with her life, her heart ached more with each passing day.

At first she tried to tell herself she was being stupid pining for a man she had only known for one heady, wonderful week, but it had been the happiest seven days of her life, and try as she might she could not get him out of her mind.

As one of the biggest stars appearing on the London stage that season she was not short of invitations from the opposite sex, for flowers arrived by the armful at her dressing-room door each night, and invitations to dine piled up behind the French ormolu clock on her mantelpiece at home, and so many were stuck around her dressing-room make-up mirror that she could hardly see to apply her greasepaint. She even accepted a few, and had become especially friendly with a good-looking young man by the name of George Cornwallis-West. At twenty-one he was near enough her own age to be lots of fun, and with his sister, Daisy, married to Prince Hans Heinrich of Pless, George was brother-in-law to one of the richest and most well-connected men in Europe.

To her astonishment, he also informed her that his beautiful, high-spirited mother, Patsy, had once had a passionate love affair with the Prince of Wales, who also happened to be his godfather. Mhairi had listened fascinated as he confided to her the secrets of the private dining-room reserved for Albert Edward in Kettner's Hotel, in Soho, where, as well as a comfortable sofa, there was a secret panel button which when pressed brought down a disappearing bed on which the heir to the throne could round off the evening with the lady of his choice.

'And Uncle Bertie's particularly fond of actresses,' George informed her. 'So you'll no doubt be asked to give a personal Royal Command performance before long. It'll do your career no end of good . . . Look what it did for Lillie Langtry!'

'If you mean on that disappearing bed, then tell your dear godfather that he can forget it!' she had retorted indignantly. 'It would be the price of him if one of his titled concubines pressed that darned button while he was still between the sheets!'

George had looked askance. 'My dear Mhairi, you mean you would turn down the future King of England?'

'George, dear, if that fat old man were to pay me a million dollars, I wouldn't let him lay a single podgy finger on me!'

'Good God, I do believe you mean it!'

'And you would be right!'

'Well, if you'd turn down our future king, what hope is there for us lesser mortals?' He had looked pained, then added, 'Unless your affections are already engaged elsewhere?'

Mhairi had given an enigmatic smile, but deliberately avoided any mention of Ralph. Then she had hated herself for her cowardice. There wasn't a thing going on in British high society that George West did not know about, so if anyone could give her news of Ralph MacLachlan it would be him. But her lips had remained sealed nevertheless. If it was really all over between them, then she wanted to hear it from Ralph's own lips, not from another's.

But as December drew to a close, even thoughts of the absent Ralph faded into the background as the time drew near for her departure for Skye. The show was to close for two weeks over the Christmas period, while George Edwardes presented what he described as his *Festive Frolics*. That gave her plenty of time to make her preparations for the long journey north. Hogmanay, the last night of the old year, was due to fall on a Tuesday, so, not wishing to appear presumptuous by arriving too early, she arranged her timetable to arrive at Dalriada on the afternoon of Tuesday, the 31st, just a few hours before the festivities were due to begin.

Christmas Day itself was spent at the Park Square home of her producer George Edwardes and his wife Julia. Under any other circumstances it would have been a day to remember, for it seemed that half the stars of the London stage were there to join in the fun, but for Mhairi all Christmas Day meant was one day nearer Skye.

When she finally set off for the journey north she found herself almost wishing she had never asked Jennie Churchill to arrange the invitation. She was about to open a door on the past that she might well find herself wishing she had kept shut. And, as the train clattered its way over the tracks, through the frozen wastes of English countryside, before at last crossing the border into Scotland, she began to wonder just *who* exactly was returning to Skye – Mhairi Cloud, the celebrated actress, or Mhairi McLeod, the native Child of the Mist. And, once there, would she be able to keep up the pretence of being a born and bred American?

These thoughts were still troubling her when, tired in body and flagging in spirits, she at last stepped on to the Mallaig ferry for the sea crossing to Skye.

She had stayed the night in a seafront hotel close to the harbour of the small West coast fishing port at the end of the 'Road to the Isles', and had heard with some trepidation the talk of heavy snowstorms over the island, as she sat sipping a toddy made from finest malt whisky, honey, and hot water in the cosy sitting-room that doubled as a public bar. To be surrounded by the warmth of Scottish voices once more brought a joy that almost overwhelmed her as she listened to the villagers chatting amongst themselves about the small everyday things that were no longer part of her own life of privilege in England's capital city, now so far away.

'I'm going home,' she whispered aloud in the silence of her room, as later on she snuggled down beneath the blankets of the comfortable double bed and watched the flames of the fire in the grate shadow dance on the wall opposite. 'I'm going home, and I'm almost there . . .'

'By the looks o' it, it'll no' be so bad,' she was informed by Kirsty, the young girl who served her breakfast. 'The sky's clearing to the West, and they say the boats will have no bother getting away.' Mhairi glanced out of the window by the side of her table, as the maid laid out the plate and piping hot, golden brown kippers and home-baked buttered bannocks. Even the elements were in her favour. How could it be any other way? What could stop her now? Home . . . Her heart sang at the word. She was going home at last.

She had deliberately chosen the much longer sea crossing from Mallaig round the southern tip of the island and on up its western coast, than the more usual one from Kyleakin to Portree and then overland to Dalriada. The latter, she imagined, would be the route used by all the other guests and she had no wish to find herself part of an upper-crust boat party. The return to her old home meant far too much to spend it in the company of a group of people whom she neither knew very well nor particularly liked.

The ferry captain was an old West Highlander by the name of MacDonald, who had piloted his craft around these waters for over fifty years. Mhairi had passed the time of day with him just after the boat left the mainland

and he had guided his charge past the dangerous rock so close to the harbour entrance. To her embarrassment, tears sprang to her eyes at the first sound of his voice. In the soft, sing-song lilt, it was for all the world her grandfather speaking. And as she looked across at him in his dark blue jersey, with his bonnet pulled down over blue eyes that could see to the very horizon and beyond, it was Long Rob McLeod himself standing there beside her, his callused, capable hands gripping the ship's wheel. Yes, these were her people, and a great feeling of love welled within her for each and every one.

Memories of people and places long forgotten came rushing back as she stood by the rail over the next hour and let the craft ferry her across the sea towards her destination. They were all here guiding her over the last long miles: Long Rob, her grandfather, her Auntie Jessie, and most of all her mother, Mary Anne. Mary Anne, whose death had been the beginning of the end of her life on Skye, whose death had caused her to leave her own land and its people.

She could remember nothing of the crossing she had made in the opposite direction as a small child, so it was as if she was seeing her old home for the first time from the deck of a ship, as it headed westwards to round the Point of Sleat.

She was not the best of sailors, and it was not a comfortable crossing, for the strong wind tossed the creamy foam of the waves into what appeared to be giant snowflakes that were carried up on to the deck, and the music of the breaking swell rose in harmony with the raised voices of the seabirds as they left their perches on the sheer cliff faces on the distant islands to dip and soar, then glide on the eddying current of air above the turbulent waters. But her physical discomfort was lost in the elation she felt as she gazed about her, determined not to miss a moment of this pilgrimage she had waited so long to make.

In the distance, above the Sound of Sleat hung a garland of freezing fog, and beyond the heaving waste of grey waters, five miles to the south-west, rose the islands of Eigg, Rhum and Canna, their features indistinguishable in the wraiths of silver-grey vapour that hung in the air, promising further snow before the day was out; their very names music to the soul.

Soon they had rounded the southernmost tip of Skye itself and were heading up its western shore, crossing the wide mouth of Loch Eishort and continuing on through the grey waters towards the entrance of its northerly neighbour Loch Scavaig, the Loch of Shadows. Her home loch. Her heart pounded so much she felt she would suffocate as she clung, half frozen, to the rail, determined not to miss a single second of the sight she had waited so long to see.

The entrance to the great sea-loch was wide, though half blocked by the island of Soay, with its sheer rock face looming above them in the freezing mist. Buffeted by the wind, with the white horses on the crests of the waves racing ahead of them, the small craft ploughed on into the deep, narrow fiord beneath the glowering heights of Gars Bheinn and Sgurr Alasdair, and the other peaks of the Black Cuillin, those dark beloved mountains so dear to her heart.

She joined old Captain MacDonald on the bridge as their craft continued into the very centre – the dark, brooding heart of the Black Cuillin – to ask the question that had been haunting her ever since she stepped on board. 'Will we be able to see Ballintuim as we pass?'

She held her breath as the old seaman scratched a day's growth of beard and narrowed his eyes landward. 'It lies beyond yon crag just ahead of us. If the mist lifts we should catch sight of it just before we land you at Scavaig. It's not much of a place these days, you know.' He sighed. 'No, it's not much of a place. Most have either died or emigrated.

But then that's the story of the Highlands these days, isn't it?'

He was not expecting an answer, and she gave none as her eyes joined his, looking ahead through the ethereal blanket of grey mist that wrapped the coastline, lifting just enough now and then to give a tantalizing glimpse of what she had waited so long and come so far to see.

'There it is!' the old man said, and her heart leapt as his right index finger pointed in the direction of the cluster of grey single-storey dwellings clinging to the rocky fore-shore around the old kirk. Her mother was buried in the shadow of its walls, and her grandfather, Long Rob, and her Auntie Jessie. Her heart ached for those that had gone, never to return, and her eyes peered through the icy mist to catch sight of the row of straggling cottages that wound up the hill. At the very top there stood her grandfather's. She peered with all her might to catch just the tiniest glimpse of it, but a dripping shroud of freezing vapour hid it from her view.

Before long the rattle of the anchor chain racing through the hawse holes told her that the time was approaching to get ready to transfer to the broad-bottomed ferryboat, with its blue-jerseyed oarsmen, already manoeuvring alongside, their voices calling in Gaelic to Captain MacDonald, who answered them in the same tongue. They were now at anchor under the lea of Gars Bheinn, the southernmost peak of the Cuillin range.

She took her leave of the old sailor who had guided her to her destination, and strong arms helped her down into the much smaller craft for the last few hundred yards of her journey, and the salt water soaked her boots and the bottom of her skirts as she half-jumped, and half-slid into the rowing-boat. But by now she was oblivious to all but the fact she was almost home, and a peculiar thrill ran through her as she gazed upon the towering hills, the grey rocks, and the mysterious waters of the loch, with its islands appearing, then disappearing in the shifting mist. It was as if she was embarking on the unknown. There was an almost cathedral atmosphere about the place that filled her with a sense of both awe and desolation. Never could there be a place so different from New York.

She was the only passenger to disembark from the ferry into the rowing-boat. It was manned only by a white-haired old man and a rosy-cheeked youth, with corn-coloured hair and blue eyes, who smiled at her and said something in Gaelic that to her shame she could no longer understand, as he helped her into the swaying craft.

As she watched them man the oars, their muscles flexing beneath the coarse ribbing of their blue jerseys, she thought of her uncles, Long Rob's four sons, who had also rowed these waters and must surely know her two companions, for they were less than two miles from Ballintuim.

Within minutes they had reached their destination, and it was hard to contain her excitement as they manoeuvred their small craft alongside the small pier.

After being helped up the slippery wooden steps of the jetty, then having her case hauled up behind her, she rewarded the young boy with a florin as he took his leave on the end of the old wooden pier that jutted like an accusing finger into the turbulent waters of the loch.

Around her was a scene like none she could ever have imagined, and her sense of isolation and loneliness was almost overpowering. The silence was awe-inspiring, and seemed to be composed of a thousand whispers as the elements claimed this spot on the edge of the world for its own.

Her eyes moved out to the waters of the loch, where drifting wraiths of mist moved tremulously onwards towards the great ocean beyond, weaving the dark waters and the mountains surrounding them into a weft of such sheer beauty as she had never before encountered.

Strange murmurings surrounded her, as the waves lapped the ancient wooden boards beneath her feet. Murmurings of times and people long gone, but whose spirits still remained a living part of this place. And the murmurings grew louder in her ears, whisperings in the very depths of her soul: *'Tir nam Beann s'nan gleann' s'nan ghaisgach'* they were repeating in her native tongue. And, incredibly, she was understanding, for the words were making sense in her heart, and not her head. 'The land of hills, and glens, and heroes,' she whispered. That was what their ancient bards had called it. The land of hills, and glens, and heroes was welcoming her home.

Her teeth chattered uncontrollably, but not from cold, as she stood with her case at her feet, in the middle of the rotting timbers, and watched the rowing-boat disappear into the mist. In the distance, she could see the much greater bulk of the Mallaig ferry turn around and head out into the waters of the grey Atlantic to continue its journey northwards round the island.

Then to her astonishment, through the turmoil of her thoughts, she heard a cry. She turned and peered through the freezing fog. A pony and trap was waiting to take her the last mile of her journey to Dalriada. Relief flooded through her at the sight of another human being.

'How did you know I would be here?' she asked the driver as he helped her on to the running-board, then loaded her case up behind them, before setting off along the rough road that led to the castle gates.

'I had my orders to watch for the ferry arriving,' he replied. ''Tis the last to get here you'll be.'

The familiar accent sent shivers of sheer joy through her as Mhairi glanced across at him. He had to be at least eighty years old, his hair was snow white beneath the tweed bonnet, and his stooped shoulders were wrapped in a tartan plaid that had seen better days. 'Are – are there many guests staying?'

'Aye, there is that. About fifty at the last count, the cook tells me.'

Mhairi fell silent. It was as if this visit to the castle with all its undoubted jollity and festive fun had become an unwanted intrusion into her own very private homecoming. She longed to creep away to some quiet place, to savour this moment, this very special moment. All her life, ever since that day her Uncle Ian put her on that train for England, she had yearned to return home; her love affair with Skye had remained a very private, very personal part of her being; it was not a time to be sharing it with a horde of strangers, and most of them English strangers at that. The chances were she would not know a soul there except the young woman who had issued the invitation, her half-sister Effie. She craved to know more of what she had let herself in for. 'The McGregor – is he keeping well? I understand he's been ill.'

'Aye he has that. And what's more he's had the black dog on his back for long enough into the bargain.'

'You mean he's depressed?'

But Donal MacCrimmon, the driver, had said enough on that score. 'You'll be looking forward to the dancing, I've no doubt – a young thing like you.'

Mhairi smiled to herself. Here there was no question of her being Mhairi Cloud, the so-called star. Here she was just another 'young thing'. It was a good feeling.

It took a mile of rattling over rough roads before it loomed into sight. Dalriada. Her breath caught in her throat, then was emitted slowly to form a jet of pure white vapour that clouded her sight for a moment before dispersing in the icy air.

There were four castles on the western seaboard of Skye: Dunvegan, the fortress still inhabited by the McLeods; the ancient ruin of Dunscaith on the road from Ord to Tokavaig where the brave Cuchullin had gone to learn the arts of war from the feared Sgathach the Terrible, the warrior Queen of Skye; Duntulm, the ancestral home of the MacDonalds; and Dalriada, the home of the McGregor — her father. Only the first and the last were still inhabited.

And there it stood, more magnificent than she had ever remembered it, soaring out of the mist like some great, proud creature from the depths of the sea-loch that moaned and lapped at the foot of its towering cliffs, while behind it the dark, glowering peaks of the Black Cuillin hovered, ever watchful, in the background.

To live in such a place was to have one's finger on the pulse of time. Generations of her forebears had lived there, and those ancient walls had witnessed within them the recurring cycle of hopes and fears, joys and sorrows. Men and women of her own blood had lived there, whole generations living and dying, while in the wide world outside nations rose and were overthrown, new lands such as her own beloved America were discovered and settled, and all the time those walls had stood in silent witness, shrouded in the mist that was as much a part of life here as the very air you breathed.

Most of the castle was obscured by a wreath of tall pines that stood guard around its ancient walls, and she commented on the fact to the old man at her side.

'Aye, and so it should be,' he confirmed. 'Would you not be knowing that "*Ard-coille*" is the old war cry of the McGregors, and that the Scots pine is their clan mascot?'

'*Ard-coille*,' Mhairi repeated, trying hard to remember her long-lost Gaelic.

'The tall forest, it would be in the English,' the old man said. ''Tis to my mind a prouder thing than yon juniper tree that the McLeods of Dunvegan make do with.'

He cast her a glance. 'Would you be kin to the McGregor, then, or is this just a social visit you're making to the island like so many of that lot already enjoying themselves in there?'

Mhairi warmed to the old man. Highlanders tugged the forelock to no one. 'Oh, it's purely a social visit, I'm afraid . . . I – I'm American, you see.'

It was her first lie since she set foot in her old home. How many more would she tell before this day was through?

Chapter Fifteen

Above the massive oak door to Dalriada the head of a crowned lion was carved into the ancient stone, with the words, 'Srioghal Mo Dhream' – Royal Is My Race – above it. Mhairi glanced up at it as she pulled the heavy rope that would ring the bell within. Nerves tightened her stomach. No one who entered these portals could be left in any doubt that the McGregors stemmed from an ancient and proud line. And the fact that she knew she was one of them only heightened the mixture of fear and excitement she felt as the sound of the latch being opened on the other side brought her moving backwards in apprehension on the stone step.

The door was opened by an elderly man in full Highland dress. The butler, Hamish Mhor, stood well over six feet in height and had a head of silver hair, a beard to match, and an expression that was little short of ferocious. His voice, however, was as gentle as his body was strong. 'A hundred thousand welcomes,' he said first in Gaelic then in English, before lifting her case as if it weighed no more than a puff of thistledown.

'Is it far you've been coming from?' he asked politely, as he carried her luggage across the polished floorboards of the great hall, with its gleaming display of ancient armoury.

'I've travelled up from London,' Mhairi replied as her eyes tried to take in everything at once. The vaulted ceiling of the hall reached up a full two storeys in height, and was supported by enormous blackened timbers, which she imagined could only have come from the majestic trees of the tall forest that surrounded the castle. They, like the building, seemed to have been here since the beginning of time.

A huge fire of crackling logs burned in a cavernous grate, in front of which two enormous Irish wolfhounds yawned and stretched on a bearskin rug; they took no notice of her as she passed. Above the fireplace, the antlered head of a Monarch of the Glen hung, and the heads of lesser stags, and a variety of other hunting trophies hung alongside it. On the panelled wall opposite was a row of portraits in oil: generations of McGregors. Her people. She longed to pause and let her eyes linger on their faces: proud, noble countenances that had gazed out on the comings and goings of this great house down the ages.

The sound of laughter came from behind a half-closed door as they passed. 'They've been taking high tea in the drawing-room,' Hamish Mhor commented as they moved on towards the staircase, and her eyes darted back to the room in question. How many people were in there? Another peal of laughter rang out, followed by a chorus of male guffaws, and she felt strangely resentful that she should be sharing this moment — her homecoming to the house of her ancestors — with a party of aristocratic revellers. But that was stupid. She was a mere guest here herself.

On up the broad winding staircase they went, past the first floor, with yet more portraits of kilted Highlanders, and their beautiful fair-skinned women, hung on the wall space between the closed doors; then on up to the second, where this time the pictures were delicate watercolours of local scenes. Perhaps they had run out of ancestors by this time, Mhairi mused as her guide came to a stop outside what was to be her bedroom door.

The butler opened it and allowed her to enter first. It

was a large room overlooking the sea, and was furnished in shades of red and green – McGregor colours. A mixture of peat and logs glowed brightly in the grate, and in front of the brass fender sat an enamel hip bath, with clean white towels airing over a rack alongside it.

'There'll be a lassie up to see to the hot water in five minutes,' she was informed. 'And she'll be bringing you up a tray with a bite to eat. If there's anything else you'll be wanting, you'll only have to ask.'

'I'm sure everything will be fine,' Mhairi assured him, her spirits lifting at the thought of a hot cup of tea and the chance to relax in the warm water before the festivities began. She looked at the clock on the mantelpiece. It had just gone six o'clock.

Hamish Mhor caught her glance. 'The evening proper begins at eight,' he said. 'They'll all be gathering in the big hall for the fun to start about then.'

'And Lady Hastings and her father?' Would she be meeting them beforehand? Her heart raced at the thought.

'The Lady Euphemia will not be back from Portree till later on this evening. She's gone to meet the Kyleakin boat.'

'And her father?' she pressed.

''Och, 'tis a mind of his own the McGregor has.'

'Oh.' There seemed no more to be said.

Hamish Mhor took his leave, and the room seemed empty without him. She gazed around her, still not quite able to believe she was actually here in Dalriada.

There were two tall windows framed by deep red velvet drapes, both overlooking the sea, and the bedroom walls were covered in a heavily patterned paper in shades of green and gold. Two small oil paintings of the Cuillin mountains hung on the wall between the windows. But the picture that had her heading straight to it for a better look was hanging above the mantelpiece. A young woman of about her own age gazed down at her and for all the world she could have been looking at her twin sister. That the sitter was of noble birth there was no doubt, but she was dressed simply in a plain white, high-waisted gown reminiscent of those popular during the early years of the century. She was sitting on a hillside Mhairi immediately recognized as Craig Mhor, the small mountain that lay between Ballintuim and Auchindoir. She had trod that weary path too often as a small child, to and from Mr McPherson's schoolroom, not to recognize it now. At the young woman's slippered feet sat two Irish wolfhounds: the ancestors of those that basked in the warmth of the fire down below, perhaps? They were obviously a family that remained loyal to that and those they loved. Mhairi's eyes narrowed as they searched the painted likeness of the young woman. Who was she? One of her own grandmothers, perhaps? It was a strange feeling.

Her eyes strayed to a faded sampler hanging to the side of the fireplace. Beautifully done in a variety of intricate embroidery stitches, the words *With God Nothing Shall Be Impossible: Luke 1:37* were picked out in strands of coloured silk. Beneath the text was the name Malvina McGregor. Mhairi's eyes strayed back to the portrait. Was that her? Was that beautiful young woman Malvina McGregor? And her thoughts pondered on the words.

She walked to the window and gazed out over the snow-covered lawns of Dalriada to the grey waters of Loch Scavaig that flowed into the great Atlantic Ocean beyond.

She was wrong. Malvina McGregor, whoever she was, was wrong. Some things were impossible in this life, even with God on your side. Reclaiming her inheritance for one. And as she stood there she knew she would give up everything to change places with her half-sister. All her success, all the adulation that had been heaped upon her was as naught when it came to what had been denied her by the man whose home this was – the man they called the McGregor. She wanted Dalriada as she had wanted nothing in her life before. Every stone of the place was embedded in her heart. The life-blood that had flowed in the people who had inhabited this house was her own blood, and it pulsated through her veins with a passion that she had felt for nothing and no one before.

A tap at the door made her look round. 'Come in.'

It was opened by a young, fresh-faced girl of about fourteen. She carried a wooden tea-tray which she set down on a small writing-desk by the side of the fire. 'Some refreshments, if you please, ma'm.'

Mhairi looked gratefully at the teapot, and the plate piled high with a variety of sandwiches and plain teacakes. 'That's very kind of you.'

The girl bobbed a curtsey. 'And when would you be wanting your hot water, ma'am?'

'Oh, just give me long enough to enjoy my tea . . . Say, twenty minutes. Would that suit?'

'Yes, ma'm.' The girl bobbed again and began to back out of the room, as if she had been serving royalty.

'Before you go . . . What's your name?' Mhairi asked.

'McLeod, ma'm. Fiona McLeod.'

'Thank you, Fiona.'

'You're more than welcome, ma'm.' Mhairi was rewarded with a genuine smile as the young woman disappeared from sight.

Fiona McLeod . . . But then half the island was called McLeod. Mhairi stared at the closed door. Was that what she would have been doing if her mother hadn't died; if she'd never been sent to join her Auntie Belle in Manchester, then left these shores for the New World? Would she have been a skivvy in what should have been her own home? She shuddered at the thought.

It took her all of an hour to have her meal and then wash herself down in the tub in front of the fire. The girl had returned, as promised, with two large cans of hot water and one of cold, and Mhairi had enjoyed the luxury of soaking away all the grime of the two-day journey, then drying herself before the blazing fire. And she began to feel almost human again as she changed into clean underwear, before donning her evening finery.

She had brought with her the white dress that Charles Hoyt had bought for her first Gibson Girl portrait, believing it to be not only the luckiest she possessed, but also the prettiest. And before leaving London she had scoured the English capital for a tartan sash to wear over it. She had eventually found a small shop in the Tottenham Court Road that sold such things and had had to make a decision as the doughty Scotsman behind the counter asked, 'And what would be the tartan you're entitled to wear, ma'm?'

They were all there arrayed on his wall, every tartan under the sun; Cameron, Campbell, MacDonald . . . All the great Scottish clans were represented. But only two mattered, and her eyes were drawn to the blue of the McLeod of McLeod, and then to the red and green of the McGregor.

'Would you be having anyone on your father's side with Scottish blood?' the shopkeeper asked. 'For if you have, then his clan would take precedence.' Then when she remained silent, he added quickly, 'Of course, your mother's will do . . .'

'No,' she broke in, before he could go any further. 'There's no need for that. I'll have my father's. I'll have the McGregor.'

And there it was, lying on the bed, as she stood within the walls of the McGregor's own home.

She bent to pick it up and slipped it over her head, then turned to look at herself in the full-length mirror on the wardrobe door. Tears sprang to her eyes and she blinked them back in irritation. Now was not the time to be getting sentimental, for she felt no love and never would towards that man she had yet to meet. The silver bracelet on her wrist would see to that.

Through the closed door she could already hear the sound of revelry downstairs, and the strains of an accordion and fiddle band reached her ears. They were tuning up, and as she pulled her long evening gloves on, they broke into the jaunty 'My Love She's But A Lassie Yet', a song she hadn't heard since her grandfather sang it to her as he dandled her on his knee. This was to be an evening to tug at the heartstrings and no mistake.

After a last glance in the mirror, she picked up her fan and made for the door, but determined not to join them downstairs quite yet. More exciting than the fun they all seemed to be having was the old castle itself. Now would be as good a time as any to see some more of it, before she too became caught up in the festivities down below.

Gripping tight to the polished wood of the banister so her satin shoes would not slip on the oak treads, she descended one flight of stairs and paused on the first-floor landing. On the way up one of the doors had been ajar and she had glimpsed what appeared to be a music room, for she was sure she had seen a grand piano before she swept past in the wake of Hamish Mhor. It had been the third from the top of the stairs, if she remembered rightly.

Cautiously she turned the knob and pushed it open. It creaked on its hinges, as if it did not get too much use these days. Then her breath caught in her throat, for she had entered a room of spectacular beauty. Even in the subdued lighting that came from the two oil lamps on either side of the mantelpiece, she could see that this was no ordinary music room. As in her bedroom, a fire had been lit in the grate beneath the huge marble fireplace, and its flames added an ethereal glow as she closed the door quietly behind her and walked into the middle of the floor to gaze in awe around her.

The ceiling was painted in scenes from the Ossian

legends. And as she gazed upwards she could recognize each and every one. Yes, all her favourite heroes of Gaeldom were there: Fingal the bold, and the beautiful Malvina; Cuchullin and his love Blathmaid, whose wooing was so sweet that the fragrance came into flowers, and the birds of the air broke into song. And the voice of Cuchullin became the music of the world. And Mhairi remembered how, as a small child, she had cried when her mother told of how a rival king, Curoi, had carried the lovely Blathmaid away, and left her lover Cuchullin bound and shorn of his yellow locks. But he had regained his strength and freedom to rescue his love, and his return was symbolized today by Spring, the returning breath of life. And Blathmaid's spirit was to be found in the warmth and the blossom of summer, that reminded us of the awakening world, while the spirit of the dreaded Curoi was in the wild wind of autumn, and the fierce and silent time we knew as winter, that turned all things cold and bare, and froze the very heart of the northern world to stone.

It seemed from the very day she was born her mother had told her those beloved tales of the ancient people of these Scottish Highlands and islands till they were engraved in her heart. There were some, she knew, who would pity the Highlanders, for they would see only the poverty of their existence, and in worldly wealth it was true, their lives were hard and bare. But in their soul they had a treasure greater than any king's ransom. That treasure was enshrined in their music and song, in their stories and legends, that each generation passed on to the next. It was an inheritance beyond price.

'The Health of the Body, the Thoughts of the Mind, and the Feelings of the Soul,' her mother had told her. 'To the Gael these are the greatest treasures on God's earth. You are part of a race that dreams dreams, Mhairi *aroon*. Your race is one of poetry, of song, and of visions. You are part of an ancient people that even today, as its seed is scattered to all four corners of the globe, still has the power to move the hearts of men . . .'

And she felt her mother was with her now as she moved across to the grand piano and lifted the lid. Her fingers slid across the ivory keys. There had been no money for luxuries such as music lessons when she was a child, but moments stolen at the Bechstein in the Ashfords' drawing-room, when they were safely away in Lowell, had taught her that she could pick out a tune by ear as well as any trained pianist.

The temptation was too great, and soon her lips were adding voice to the old tune that her fingers were bringing to life:

> 'Ye banks and braes o' bonnie Doon,
> How can ye bloom sae fresh and fair?
> How can ye chant, ye little birds,
> And I sae weary, fu' o' care?
> Ye'll break my heart, ye warbling birds,
> That warbles on the flow'ry thorn,
> Ye mind me o' departed joys,
> Departed never to return . . .'

'And what little bird might this be warbling in my music room?'

The sound of the male voice behind her brought Mhairi whirling round on the piano stool. Colour rushed to her cheeks as she stared at the man just inside the doorway. He was at least six feet tall in height, although he stooped slightly over the horn-handled walking stick clasped in his left hand. His face was strong and he had the high cheekbones of his race. His high, broad forehead was crowned by a full head of dark reddish-brown hair, shot through with silver at the temples, and his eyebrows, sidewhiskers and beard were a pure silver-grey. Beneath his brows, his eyes, even at a distance of some feet, were dark and penetrating. He was angularly rather than powerfully built, and his spare figure was clad in the tartan of his clan. To the shoulder of his green velvet jacket a tartan plaid was pinned; a tartan plaid that bore the same red and green hue as the one she wore in the sash over her own shoulder.

'You must be the McGregor.'

She got up from the stool and, instead of moving forward to offer her hand, she found herself backing away towards the window as a feeling akin to panic enveloped her.

'That would be a fair assumption, since apart from my daughter I am the only one at this gathering entitled to wear this particular tartan.'

Mhairi's fingers stole to the sash across her breast as her eyes locked with his and the blood in her veins quickened. 'Meaning I am not?'

Gregor McGregor smiled politely. He had no wish to offend a guest who quite obviously was not acquainted with the Highland tradition. 'My dear young lady, I have no idea who you are, or where you have come from. I only know I heard my piano being played and came to investigate.' He had only the faintest hint of a Highland lilt in what otherwise would be taken for an upper-class English accent.

He walked further into the room till he was standing barely an arm's length from her. 'But in answer to your question, I would say it is a fair comment. I myself made out the guest list with my daughter and there was no other of our clan named on it.'

He made an impatient gesture with his hand. 'Anyway, you're an American by the sound of it, and will not be aware of our Highland ways. And you can sing, I'll say that for you.' Then realization dawned in his eyes. 'You must be that American actress Effie said she'd invited!' He looked at her curiously, as if not acquainted with the species. 'Are you?'

'I am.'

'Then I was right!' He smiled and for the first time Mhairi could see what must have attracted her mother all those years ago. His whole face seemed to light up; the dark eyes creased at the corners and lost their suspicion, and his features lost their gaunt, strained look. 'And where about are you from?' He raised a hand. 'Don't tell me – New York! All Americans are from New York!'

'Actually I'm from Skye.' What in heaven's name had made her say that? Was there a perverse streak to her nature? Perspiration bathed her armpits as she took a deep breath to calm her beating heart and inwardly cursed the demon within her that had caused the truth to be told.

'I beg your pardon?'

'I said I'm from Skye.' Her voice sounded distant and foreign to her ears. But if the truth must out, then she would hold nothing back; there might not be another chance. But God only knew how he would take it. She took a deep breath in an attempt to keep her voice calm. 'I was born right here – about two miles over the hill to be exact.'

Gregor McGregor's smile faded, and his heavy brows knitted. 'I don't quite follow.'

She had gone too far to turn back now. 'It's quite simple really. I was born Mhairi McLeod eighteen years and nine months ago in the village of Ballintuim.'

'McLeod . . .'

She could almost see his mind working behind the furrowed brow. 'My mother's name was Mary Anne McLeod.'

There was a long silence. Too long. The McGregor's knuckles whitened as he gripped the horn handle of his walking stick. His eyes were transfixed on the face of the young woman in front of him. 'And your father's?' The question was asked in a hoarse whisper.

'My father's name is Gregor McGregor. And mine would be McGregor too, if he had had the common decency to marry my mother.'

'Holy Jesus!' Gregor McGregor took a step back as if physically struck. Had he just walked into some kind of nightmare? 'Just who in God's name are you?'

He seemed to crumple before her very eyes. And as his face paled, Mhairi's courage grew. 'I just told you. I'm your daughter. Your *elder* daughter.'

The man before her let out a grunt like a wounded animal, before making his way to the nearest chair to sit down heavily. He sat for several seconds, quite motionless. Then a thin film of perspiration appeared on his brow and bathed his upper lip beneath the moustache as he gripped the wooden arms of the chair and stared across at her.

His silence unnerved her. It was not the reaction she had expected and her nervousness grew, but she was determined not to let it show. 'We've met before, you know,' she continued. 'At my mother's grave. Don't you remember, you carried me home, all the way up the road to my grandfather's cottage?' Her voice was sweetness itself.

Gregor McGregor shook his head. 'No, no . . . Stop it, damn you. Stop it!' This was too much. Much too much. What was she doing to him? What had he done to be punished like this, tonight of all nights? This evening was meant to be special. He had promised Effie. She deserved some happiness after a year of mourning. 'What do you want of me?' he said at last.

Mhairi stared down at him and shook her head. She had only set eyes on him once before as a small child, and yet his face was already so familiar. It was as if she had known it all her life. 'What do you want to give?' she asked softly.

Could he not see? What she wanted, money could never buy. You could not buy back your birthright. It had to be given, and given freely, with love, or it was worthless. And a great sadness overwhelmed her, for this man had no intention of ever granting her that. She could see that by the look akin to horror etched on his face.

He gazed up at her through eyes that mirrored confusion and near panic. If this had to happen, why hadn't it happened when he had had the strength to deal with the situation? He was sure if he were to stand up his legs would go from him. But he could not sit here forever. Effie would come looking for him soon. She must never know. His beloved daughter must know none of this. This was to be her big night. Never had there been so much time taken over a guest list. 'Is it money you're after?'

The words hit Mhairi like a slap in the face, and she had to fight to keep the anger from her voice. 'I want no money from you. All I ask is honesty. Honesty that admits the truth for the first time in your life. We both know you are my father . . . I am your daughter, Gregor McGregor, and no amount of money can buy back that fact.'

She gazed around her at the fine furnishings and priceless family treasures that stretched back generations. Even that piano she had been playing was worth more than her grandfather could have earned in a lifetime of toil. 'You are a wealthy man, Lord McGregor. A very wealthy man. But money is not everything.' Her voice fell to little more than a whisper as their eyes met and held. 'No man on God's earth is rich enough to buy back his past.'

She was staring down at him and he looked away unable to bear the truth in her eyes. 'Look at me!' she commanded. 'Look at me, Gregor McGregor. For God's sake, look at me – recognize your own child!'

He shook his head. 'I have only one child.' His voice was thick with emotion. He took out a large red handkerchief from the pocket of his velvet jacket and blew his nose, then mopped his brow. He felt drained. Physically ill. The doctor had told him he would be taking a risk joining in the festivities this evening. He had made the effort for Effie. Only for Effie. Never had he expected anything like this. He shook his head once more, as if to negate what had just occurred.

Mhairi continued to look down at him as a curious mixture of emotions raged through her. She wanted to feel resentment, anger even, at this man who had shamed her mother and denied her own existence. But she could feel only pity. Whatever he had once been, he was no more. True, he was not an old man in years, but she knew she was looking at a shell of whoever had once been the man they called the McGregor. Effie had told her he had been ill, and looking at him now, she did not doubt it. She felt almost ashamed of her confession. 'You really love her, don't you – my half-sister?'

'I love my daughter more than anything in this life.'

She felt herself physically wince. Why did those words have the power to hurt so much? She half-turned from him and stared into the fire.

'I beg you – whoever you are – to say nothing of this . . .' He searched for the right words. 'Effie, you see, she is little more than a child . . . She knows nothing of life . . .'

'Your daughter is a widowed woman,' Mhairi broke in impatiently, turning back to him. 'What you mean is, you know exactly who I am, just as you know I am telling the truth, and you cannot bear the thought of her finding out her sainted father is not such a saint after all.'

'Have it your way.' His voice was weary, and there was pleading in his eyes as they found hers. 'Just don't tell her. I beg you, don't tell her. Not tonight of all nights.'

'And what's so special about tonight?'

But before the question could be answered there was a knock at the door, and Hamish Mhor's voice said, 'Your Lordship, is it in there you are?'

271

They both turned as the butler came into the room. Hamish Mhor's shaggy brows rose in surprise at the sight of the young American woman with his employer. 'They're all gathered downstairs, your Lordship. Lady Effie's getting impatient. She is waiting for you to say a few words so the dancing can begin.'

Gregor McGregor got slowly to his feet, leaning heavily on his stick, as the butler's voice said, 'I'll leave you to escort the young lady downstairs, then.'

Mhairi and the McGregor looked at one another as Hamish Mhor's kilted figure disappeared out of the door. 'We'd better do as he says,' she said quietly. 'After all, this is Effie's big night, isn't it?'

The man she knew to be her father nodded. For the meantime at least, there was nothing more to be said. And so, on the arm of the McGregor himself, Mhairi slowly descended the wide sweep of the main staircase into the great banqueting hall of Dalriada.

At first the crowd appeared to be a sea of indistinguishable faces, as all the men were in full Highland dress and the women in white gowns and tartan sashes, but to Mhairi's surprise she managed to pick out a few she actually recognized. Over by the fireplace stood the quite unmistakable figure of Jennie Churchill, next to none other than Mhairi's own occasional beau, George Cornwallis-West, and just beyond them was the tall, elegant figure of Millie, Duchess of Sutherland. Perhaps this evening was not going to be quite such an ordeal after all.

The band that had been playing in the corner by the fire ceased their reel at the sight of the Laird on his way down, and broke into 'Hail To The Chief'. And the chatter and laughter of the gathered guests melted away as all eyes began to turn towards the staircase. Then, to the surprise of everyone present, the young woman on the arm of their host halted in mid-step and clutched at the banister for support.

'Are you all right?' Gregor McGregor asked.

Mhairi opened her mouth but no words would come. She was looking straight into the amazed eyes of Ralph MacLachlan.

Chapter Sixteen

Mhairi stared at the tall figure in the full Highland dress, with the shock of unruly dark hair. He was standing only a few feet from the foot of the stairs, in the middle of a small group that contained Effie Hastings herself. That he was equally astonished to see Mhairi there was no doubt for his face had paled to the colour of the wax candles that burned in the bronze candelabra on either side of the staircase.

Mhairi's first inclination was to turn and flee back upstairs. The thought of meeting him after so long and in front of all these people was too much to bear. But the McGregor had her by the elbow. 'Are you feeling all right?' His concern was grudgingly given, but he had no wish to appear ungallant in front of his other guests.

'Yes, yes . . . I'm fine.' Then she felt herself being propelled by his hand on her arm down the remainder of the stairs. They were heading straight for the group that contained Ralph, and the panic within her grew with every step.

'Why, Pa . . . We were wondering what on earth had become of you!' Effie rushed forwards to embrace her father, kissing him on both cheeks, before slipping her arm into his as the group opened up to welcome the new arrivals in their midst.

As Mhairi stood on the sidelines, Gregor McGregor hooked his walking stick over his arm and extended his right hand towards Ralph MacLachlan, as he clasped him on the shoulder with his left. 'So you've arrived at last, young man! I doubt if there's anyone else Effie here would have insisted on going all the way to Portree to meet in this weather!' He shot a conciliatory smile in the direction of the others in the group. 'No offence intended to the rest of you good people. Rather, it underlines my daughter's affection for this young rogue here!'

'Pa – please!' Effie broke in, before he could embarrass her further.

But Ralph MacLachlan had not even heard the remark. His eyes were still fixed on the young woman standing a mere arm's length away.

Effie followed the direction of his gaze with a puzzled frown. 'Why, Miss Cloud – you must forgive me . . . I see you have already become acquainted with my father, but you won't have met Lord MacLachlan yet.' She turned to Ralph. 'Ralph, dear, this is our American guest, the actress Miss Mhairi Cloud . . . Miss Cloud, this is a very old friend of the family, Lord Ralph MacLachlan.'

As she was speaking, Mhairi was slipping off her glove, and as she extended her right hand, the young man in question made no attempt to shake it, but raised it to be kissed. They were the only two people in the room to recognize the ring that glittered on the third finger of her right hand as it was pressed to his lips.

The other names in the group went right over Mhairi's head as Effie performed her hostess's duty by introducing them each in turn. More than half had come from south of the border, and all the men were attired in full Highland dress, but she doubted if even half could claim Scottish blood. Mhairi deliberately avoided Ralph's eyes throughout the introductions, but was acutely aware of his on her as she murmured the correct things to each person in turn.

Then Effie spoke. 'Pa, I think it's time you said a few words, so the fun can begin.' She laid a concerned hand on his arm. 'Would you prefer me to come with you?'

Gregor McGregor nodded. 'Aye, that I would.'

Effie threw a 'would you excuse me' look in Ralph's direction and, gently leading her father by the arm, she disappeared with him into the body of the hall, in the direction of the podium erected for the band.

Mhairi felt a hand grip her elbow from behind. She did not have to turn to know whose it was. 'Head for the door on the left,' she heard his voice say in her ear.

Her eyes darted in the direction ordered, and she could make out a small door just beneath the stairs. It was only a few yards away, but could she reach it without being noticed? To her relief, he went first, edging his way towards the back of the group, before disappearing inside the door and closing it behind him.

Mhairi caught the eye of a young woman she had met at Jennie Churchill's; the two exchanged smiles. Dear God, how could she possibly sneak out without anyone noticing? She went up on tiptoe and craned her neck in the direction of Effie and her father. They had almost reached the other side of the hall and would be climbing on to the podium any minute now, when thankfully all eyes would be on them.

Taking her courage in both hands, she began to back her way through the knot of guests still blocking the foot of the stairs, murmuring her apologies as she did so, and cursing the wide skirts of her ballgown for the disruption she was causing.

After pausing for a second or two at the back of the group until she was sure everyone's attention was on Effie and her father who were now climbing on to the make-do stage, she turned and made for the door. Within a few seconds she had edged it open and slipped inside.

She found herself in the darkness of a back passage and the chill hit her immediately. She shivered with cold and apprehension as she peered into the gloom.

'Over here!'

Lifting her skirts, she hurried in the direction of the

voice and found herself in an ante-room surrounded by guns and all manner of hunting equipment. There was an overpowering smell of gun oil and polished metal. Then his figure loomed out of the darkness towards her, his hand reaching out, 'Mhairi . . .'

She backed away. 'No – don't touch me!'

He gazed at her in the strange half-light that came from a lantern outside the narrow window. Her words cut him to the quick, but he could understand. It was no more than he expected. 'I don't blame you,' he whispered hoarsely. 'I don't blame you at all.'

She stood looking up at him through the darkness. Her teeth began to chatter, whether from nerves or cold she could not say. Then gradually her eyes became accustomed to the dark, and her heart turned over at the expression on his face. That he loved her still there could be no doubt. She longed to run into his arms, but pride held her back. She had not been the one to break her word. 'Why, Ralph, why?' was all she could say.

He made to touch her again, but seeing her flinch, he gave a helpless shrug. 'If I had dreamt in my wildest dreams that I would meet you again like this I would have . . .'

'Had your excuses at the ready?' she broke in.

He fell silent. He deserved her bitterness. For months now he had been striving to forget her, to put her out of his mind forever. He had even returned to Scotland before her show opened in London to make sure there could be no chance of running into her by accident. It was the coward's way out, no one knew that better than he, but it was the only way. Had he seen her again he could not have gone through with it. And nothing on earth could have brought him to write and tell her it was all over. But all over it had to be. 'We have to talk, Mhairi,' he said huskily. 'But not here.' He too shivered as he glanced around him. 'It's too cold, and we will be missed if we stay much longer.' He paused . . . Dare he ask? He could feel the excitement stir within him. He took a deep breath. This was no time to be faint-hearted. 'What room are you in?'

Her heart quickened its beat as her eyes met his. She knew exactly what he was saying. The very air around them was alive as they stood looking at one another in the dim light of the gun room. What he longed for, she longed for too, with every breath in her body, but it could not be. She had to retain some vestige of dignity until this whole mess had been sorted out. Until he had explained himself. Surely he owed her that? 'No, Ralph, please . . . Leave me some pride . . .'

He watched with a sinking heart as she turned from him to head back towards the door. What she had wanted from him right now was what he could not give: a heartfelt apology for the hurt he had already caused her, and a reassurance of his love – a promise that she, and only she, would be the one he ultimately chose to spend his life with. Instead of that he had ended up insulting her.

She paused at the door to turn and face him. 'Apologies can be made just as easily in the warmth of the hall as anywhere else, you know. Or were you perhaps hoping for rather more than a statement of acceptance on my part?'

'Mhairi – no! For God's sake . . . !' Her words, so sweetly said, had the impact she intended. He reached out an arm towards her, but she was already opening the door back to the hall.

'When you are ready to be the man I first took you for, you will find me only too ready to be a woman. But until then, please don't imagine I have the morals of those of your own class, whose love lives owe more to alley-cats than the so-called ladies they profess to be!'

Then she was gone, and the door clicked back into place behind her. He stared at it for a long time before moving. It was no more than he deserved.

Whether they were missed or not, she could not tell, for the band had already started up and the assembled guests were forming themselves into the necessary groups for an eightsome reel when they returned separately to the hall. And, to her dismay, it was in the direction of Effie that Ralph headed, to offer his arm for the coming dance. Obviously no apologies were to be forthcoming yet-awhile, at least.

After what had just passed between them, she had never felt less like dancing, and she deliberately hung back until all the sets had been formed. Then, seated on a chair at the side of the hall, she watched as the guests threw themselves energetically into the most favourite of Scotland's reels.

Tonight was only the second time she had seen Ralph in his national dress. The muted reds, greens, and black of the MacLachlan tartan set off his dark colouring to perfection, and, despite her upset and the sense of betrayal she felt, she could not take her eyes off his kilted figure as he whirled his partner around the floor.

They were dancing in the same set as Jennie Churchill and George Cornwallis-West, and Mhairi felt even more of a wallflower as the whirling couples passed within a few feet of where she was sitting.

'They make a fine pair, don't you think?' The voice belonged to Millie Sutherland, who had appeared at her elbow with a glass of whisky punch in each hand. With her reddish-gold hair swept up above the long, elegant neck, around which the celebrated Marie Antoinette diamonds gleamed, the Duchess was a stunning sight. She handed one of the glasses to Mhairi who accepted it with a grateful smile.

'You mean Effie and Lord MacLachlan? . . . Yes, yes, they certainly do.'

'It would do the McGregor no end of good if she were to accept Ralph.'

279

'Accept him?'

Millie missed both Mhairi's question and her astonished look, as she concentrated on the young couple in question. Her own husband, Cromartie, the fourth Duke, was fifteen years older, and having married him on her seventeenth birthday, the young Duchess had missed out on real romance herself. But nothing gave her greater pleasure than observing it blossom in others. 'Yes,' she continued confidentially, 'to be honest with you, it would make the McGregor even happier than her marriage to Jack Hastings did – Ralph being one of their own, so to speak. Scottish I mean – and the son of his best friend.'

She paused long enough to take a sip of the punch, then continued, 'And as Countess of Inverbervie, the dear girl would be only a day's journey from her old home here on Skye. That would be a wonderful relief for her father, with his heart condition.'

Millie's words confirmed the fear that had been forming in Mhairi's mind since the second she caught sight of Ralph at the foot of the staircase. But surely Millie Sutherland had it wrong? 'The Countess of Inverbervie? But hasn't Ralph an elder brother?'

Millie's hazel eyes widened, then her voice dropped to a more confidential tone. 'You haven't heard about David, then?'

'Well, no . . .' What on earth was there to know about Ralph's elder brother?

'It's the most frightful blow for the whole family. And him so young . . . Although Prince Eddie was only in his twenties too, and Jennie's husband only in his forties.'

Mhairi looked askance. Was she telling her that Ralph's elder brother, like the Prince of Wales's eldest son, and Lord Randolph Churchill, had died of *syphilis*? Panic gripped her. What exactly would that mean to the family? That Ralph would now inherit the title was beyond doubt, and that meant all the financial problems that went with it.

Hamish Mhor was passing with a silver tray containing more glasses of punch, and Mhairi downed her drink in one and reached for another, as did Millie Sutherland. She fortified herself with another gulp of the potent brew. 'When – when did he die?'

Millie's brow furrowed above the immaculately arched eyebrows. 'Die? Dear me, he's not gone yet. But they do say, it's just a matter of time. Weeks at the most.'

Mhairi took another sip of punch, and as the warming brew found its way to her stomach, she attempted to lessen her fears. 'Perhaps Effie won't care to marry again so soon. There's no real need, after all, for didn't her husband leave her a very wealthy woman?' She was grasping at straws and had not the faintest idea what Jack Hastings had left.

Her companion acceded the point on Effie's wealth, and as the wife of the country's richest Duke herself, she knew a thing or two about the subject of money. 'That's certainly true. I doubt if there are many better-off young women than Effie in the whole of Scotland, to tell the truth – taking her Dalriada inheritance into consideration too, of course. But she'd be the first to admit that money isn't everything, as I'm sure you'll agree.'

Her eyes fell once more on the fine figure of Ralph MacLachlan as he whirled round in the centre of the eight dancers. 'And you have to admit he is rather a catch,' she added wistfully. She thought of her own much older husband and sighed. 'To find a man these days who has both a respected title, good looks, and youth on his side – well that's something indeed.'

'But he has no money.'

Millie Sutherland looked round sharply. 'Money only matters to those who haven't got it . . . Outsiders, I mean. Amongst ourselves no one gives a hoot if one side is a bit short. In this country it's breeding that counts, Miss Cloud, nothing else.'

281

So that was her put in her place. Kati had been right, it was breeding that counted. But then she had always known that to be the case. She could feel the atmosphere between her and her companion cool immediately, and she could have bitten her tongue. She had had no intention of appearing to slight Ralph because of his dire financial state; she had been merely searching desperately for a reason for Effie to reject him. In an attempt to retrieve the situation, she made one or two ill-fated attempts at small talk, then gave up. 'If you'll excuse me . . .'

She fled to the other side of the hall, taking sanctuary behind the enormous Christmas tree that dominated the opposite corner of the fireplace to the band. She could feel her cheeks still flushed with the embarrassment of being put in her place by the Duchess. Not that she blamed her. That stupid comment had made her sound like a common gold-digger.

'Well, there you are!' The dance had ended and George Cornwallis-West's cheerful face appeared from the crowd. It brought a smile in return. 'I bet you thought I'd deserted you by asking Jennie for the first dance, but I really had little choice . . .'

'You don't have to explain,' Mhairi assured him, as she linked her arm in his. 'Lady Churchill is the most beautiful woman in the room – even if she *is* old enough to be your mother!'

'Meeiow! But the second most beautiful I'd certainly go along with. Shall we dance?'

And so they took to the floor, just as Ralph MacLachlan came striding across in their direction.

Mhairi was acutely aware of him standing staring at her from the side of the floor as she waltzed round the hall in George's arms. And she was glad that next to him her partner was without doubt the best-looking man in the room.

'What are your plans for tomorrow?' George asked, and she had to jolt herself back to reality to consider his question.

'I – I haven't really given it much thought.'

'May I lodge my interest in the pleasure of your company when you do?' he asked, squeezing her hand that bit tighter.

As she was swept round in Ralph's direction once more, to her dismay she saw he had been joined by Effie. They were laughing together and a pang of jealousy shot through her. Millie was right, they *did* make an attractive couple. 'I'd be delighted, George dear,' she lied. '*When* I do.' At the moment she preferred to keep her options open. Hope took a long time dying, when it was all that had kept you going over the past few months.

They served supper at ten and everyone was grateful for the pause in the dancing, as they gathered, red-faced and perspiring, like greedy chattering children around the long trestle tables that had been set up on the far side of the hall. All the traditional Scottish foods were there, but Mhairi's appetite would only run to a small piece of the moist Black Bun that always accompanied the Hogmanay festivities.

As she ate it and sipped a glass of the fine malt whisky that the McGregor had supplied for his guests, she found herself cornered by a group of young London debutante friends of Effie, and their partners. All were keen to hear the latest theatre gossip from her, and, as she tried in vain to sound half as amusing as the likes of Mrs Patrick Campbell, her eyes darted continually in the direction of Effie and Ralph.

Effie and Ralph . . . How often had she heard their names run together tonight. Effie and Ralph . . . Ralph and Effie . . . It was becoming an accepted partnership, and the very sound of it tore at her heart.

She had remained standing in front of the table

carrying the whisky and Black Bun, and was halfway through her second drink when she caught sight of him striding across the floor in her direction. In his hands he held two empty glasses. He was coming to refill their drinks before the storytelling and songs began.

She half-turned towards the table, to avoid his eyes as he bore down on her. For the few seconds it took for him to cross the floor, she hardly dared breathe. His hand touched the bare skin of the back of her shoulder as he murmured, 'Excuse me, Miss Cloud,' and leaned across to place his empty glasses on the table in front of her.

She jumped involuntarily and half-turned. His face was only inches from hers; so close she could feel the warmth of his breath on her face. As he bent forward, the silver clan badge pinning the plaid to his shoulder accidentally jabbed into her bare skin and she let out a small yelp of pain.

'Good God, what have I done!' He looked in horror and concern at the scratch already oozing blood on the pale skin. 'Here let me . . .'

He pulled out a clean white handkerchief and dabbed at the wound, and when at last he lifted the linen square, they both gazed down at the spots of red blood on the white cloth.

'Rowan berries . . .' Mhairi murmured, her thoughts flying back through the years to when as a small child she had likened her mother's blood on the pillow to the red berries of the Rowan tree.

'Pardon?'

'Rowan berries,' she repeated softly. 'Those tiny spots of red blood. That's what they remind me of . . .' She could explain further, but had no wish to.

He was looking at her curiously. 'Did you know the Rowan tree was the emblem of my clan?'

She shook her head. She had had no idea. Her eyes rested on the badge that had caused the wound, but the lighting was not good enough to read the inscription.

'It says "Brave and Faithful",' he said, avoiding her eyes. 'It's the motto of the MacLachlans.'

'Brave and faithful,' she repeated, as her lips broke into an ironic smile. 'How appropriate, Lord MacLachlan. I'm sure you have both of those virtues in abundance.' Her hazel eyes remained fixed on his so he was forced to look away. 'Wouldn't you agree?'

'Ralph, dear . . . We haven't run out of whisky, have we?' Effie's voice brought them both back to reality. 'I wouldn't have to be dying of thirst, would I?'

She smiled gaily at Mhairi. 'Why, Miss Cloud – the very person I was looking for! Would you be a perfect dear and begin the *ceilidh* for us?'

This time Mhairi was prepared, for Jennie Churchill had warned her that almost everyone had to participate in the songs and stories that led up to the welcoming in of the New Year at twelve o'clock. 'I'd be delighted.'

The *ceilidh* was begun in rousing fashion a few minutes later by the band playing a verse of 'McGregor's Gathering', as bands had done since time immemorial in Dalriada at Hogmanay. Then Hamish MacCrimmon announced that they were especially honoured that year to have with them a special guest all the way from New York. There was a round of applause, accompanied by a few cheers and whistles, as Mhairi climbed on to the podium beside the band. There could be no doubt about the song she would sing.

'My Lords, Ladies and Gentlemen, I have been asked by our hostess to begin the *ceilidh* for you tonight with a Scottish song . . . Scotland has many beautiful airs, but this one especially is very dear to my heart:

'Oh, Rowan tree, Oh, Rowan tree, thou'lt aye be dear to me,
Entwined thou art wi' mony ties o' hame and infancy.
Thy leaves were aye the first o' spring, thy flowers the summer's
     pride,
There wasna sic a bonnie tree in a' the countryside . . .'

285

Her eyes met Ralph's and remained there for the duration of the song. She poured her heart into every word and was aware of the hush that had descended throughout the hall as she captured the audience and held it in the palm of her hand. She had never sung with more feeling, and the applause that followed meant that there was no question of her being allowed to leave the stage. They were all cheering and clapping, except him. He was standing to one side pensively sipping his drink as those around him yelled their approval, and called out requests for their own favourites to be sung.

Before she was allowed to leave the stage, she had to provide them with her renditions of 'The Skye Boat Song' and Burns's own, 'My Love is Like a Red, Red Rose'.

As she began to sing the latter, she saw Ralph turn away, and knew it was more than he could bear. He had written those very words to her last summer back in New York, and she knew exactly what was going through his head. In his behaviour since, he had been neither 'Brave' nor 'Faithful', and had made a mockery of every letter he had ever sent her, and of the motto of his clan.

The festivities continued until a few minutes before twelve, when the band left the stage to a lone piper. Calum MacCrimmon had performed this duty every Hogmanay for the past forty years, the only exception being the previous year, when Effie's husband's fatal accident had put paid to any thoughts of celebrations. He made an impressive figure, in full Highland regalia, and with the golden eagle feather in his bonnet held in place by the white cockade that symbolized his family's old allegiance to the Jacobite cause.

All eyes in the hall gravitated between him and the grandfather clock that Hamish Mhor had carried on to the podium earlier in the evening. And as its minute hand reached the fateful hour of twelve, its chimes were totally drowned out by the cheer that went up from the assembled company, as the lone piper broke into 'Auld Lang Syne'.

All round the hall the guests crossed arms and joined hands in one huge circle as they sang Robert Burns's words that had been sung at such gatherings for over a hundred years. Then the hugging and kissing began.

It did not surprise Mhairi that Gregor McGregor pointedly ignored her, but it hurt nevertheless. She had had no wish to hurt him, and in confessing the truth she had ended up hurting herself even more. She knew he believed that to acknowledge her was to somehow deny his love for Effie, and that was a conviction that would never change. No amount of wishing could make it otherwise.

But there were plenty of others who did wish to embrace her and wish her 'A Very Happy New Year'. And it seemed as if half the hall had done so before Ralph came across.

He made no attempt to touch her as, 'Happy New Year, Mhairi,' he said softly.

'Will it be?' she asked.

He had no answer.

Chapter Seventeen

The party went on until almost three o'clock in the morning, and there were still some stragglers unwilling to bring the festivities to an end when, exhausted and slightly the worse for drink, Mhairi bid them a very good night and eventually climbed the stairs to her room.

Anticipating the late end to the day, the maid had built up a good fire in the grate, and it was still burning brightly when she closed the bedroom door behind her and kicked off her shoes.

In her stockinged feet she padded across the carpet to place two more logs on the fire from the wicker basket that sat alongside the fender. Within minutes the sparks were flying, and as the wood hissed and crackled and fresh flames danced up the chimney, she squatted down beside it and held her hands to its cheering warmth. And as she gazed into the fire's red heart, she remembered the nights she had spent as a small child in her grandfather's kitchen, where tired eyes stared into the red glow of the peat-flame and watched a dream go by, or later at her Auntie Jessie's fireside, after they had told her she would have to leave Skye. They said you could see the future in those leaping flames and she had tried with all her might to read what would happen to her in the unknown world outside her island.

And now, in this much grander house, as she rose with a sigh to cast off her party finery and don the expensive lawn nightdress she had bought specially for the trip, she reflected on how much had happened in her life since then. It would have taken a much bigger fireplace than her Auntie Jessie possessed to read the half of it in its flames.

Once attired in her nightgown, she sat down on the stool in front of the dressing-table and began to brush out her hair. If ever there was a time for seeing into the future it was now. Here they were in the opening hours of a brand new year, but the close of the old had brought her no satisfaction. The old year of 1895 had brought her happiness beyond her wildest dreams. But it had also brought her great sadness. Sadness at the death of her Auntie Belle, and sadness at the death of her first real love affair. For it was dead, wasn't it? Her romance with Ralph – it *was* over? She frowned into the glass and her brush strokes slowed as she tried to make sense of what was happening to her.

One thing was for sure, she would remember this day for the rest of her life, for it was the day she had met the two men who she knew would, in their very different ways, mean more to her than any others: her father, Gregor McGregor, and the man she loved, Ralph MacLachlan. And how ironic it was that the woman who now stood between her and her rightful place in both their hearts was Effie Hastings, née McGregor, her own half-sister.

But try as she might she could not hate her. In a curious way she felt almost protective towards her. She obviously loved their father, and who could blame her for loving Ralph?

She found she had no need to keep the candles burning when she finally slipped between the sheets of the great four-poster bed, for the firelight lit the whole room with its warm amber glow. She lay back on the pillows and watched the shadows dancing on the wall and ceiling as drowsiness overtook her. That she would dream of *him* tonight she had no doubt, for she had dreamt of him almost every night since they met. But tonight was special, she could almost feel his breath still, warm on her face, and smell that special scent that was his alone.

Then she was in his arms, and as he covered her face with his kisses all the hurt melted into the night. 'Ralph . . . Ralph . . .' She murmured his name over and over as his face swam before her, and she was borne away, deeper and deeper, into the comforting oblivion of sleep.

'Mhairi . . .'

'Mmmm . . .'

'It's me . . .' Then the squeak of the door, and the lock clicking back into place, pierced that warm, black cocoon of sleep, and she struggled to open her eyes and sit up on the pillow.

The fire in the grate was now little more than glowing embers, but it still cast enough light to see the dressing-gowned figure of Ralph just inside the doorway. His hair was tousled, as if he too had just been roused from sleep, and he was looking at her with a wildness in his eyes that made her catch her breath as she whispered hoarsely, 'Am – am I still dreaming?'

'You're not dreaming, Mhairi my love.'

'You – you shouldn't be here. You shouldn't have come.' She gripped the sheet to her breast as both excitement and fear welled within her. She wanted to be angry, to stand on her dignity, but the words would not come; all she could do was to lie there and shake her head as she continued to gaze at him as if he were some sort of apparition.

'I had to come, Mhairi.' He moved swiftly and silently to the side of the bed and sat down on the quilt. He could see she was nervous and sought to allay her fears. He had not come here to ravish her, merely to be with her, to try to explain. 'Forgive me. I just couldn't lie there any longer and go through this . . . this . . .' he searched for the right word to describe the misery he felt inside. 'This hell.'

She pulled herself up on the pillow and looked at him a long time without speaking, then slowly she shook her head. 'Oh Ralph . . .' He was like a small boy unable to cope with the consequences of his own actions. 'Can't you see? Whatever hell you're going through right now has been brought about by yourself. It is not of my making.'

'You don't know what you're saying . . . Things happened, Mhairi. Terrible things, since I last saw you. Life is no longer as simple as it was last summer.'

'Millie told me about your brother. I'm so sorry. Really I am.'

He gave a bitter smile. 'Not half as sorry as I am . . . Poor, stupid Davey, he has learned too late that the sweetest rose can have the sharpest thorn. They give him no more than three months – and my father perhaps less, for this will kill him, we have no doubt of that.'

'And then you will be the Earl of Inverbervie.'

He sighed. 'Aye. I will be the Earl of Inverbervie.'

He got up from the bed and walked over to the fire, where he stood staring down into the flames. 'And, if there was any justice in this world, then you would be my Countess.'

'But I have no money – at least not enough. Not enough to save Craig David. Only Effie has enough to do that.'

'You make it sound so sordid.'

'And isn't it?'

'Mhairi . . . Mhairi . . .' He made a despairing gesture with his hands. 'This is the real world. We are not children now. We have responsibilities to others than ourselves.'

She got out of bed to join him by the fire, and her face was pale in its glow as she tried to understand. 'But I thought those stocks – all those railroad and steel bonds and things you bought on Wall Street – I thought they were to save Craig David.'

He gave a hollow laugh. 'So did we. And so they might have.'

'Might have?'

'They're gone, Mhairi – all gone. At least the bulk of everything I bought has. Gambled by Davey in one last mad spree after his illness was diagnosed.'

Then, seeing the horror on her face, he added quickly, 'Oh, he didn't mean it to happen. He genuinely believed he would be doing us a favour. At least doubling their worth overnight . . . He really believed he could do it. He always regarded himself as a whizz at the tables, you see, and with that amount in his pocket, he believed he could take on the best in the world and win. It's like that, you know – syphilis. Before it's all over, you go mad in stages – say and do crazy things – and in between you can be quite lucid.'

He made a mirthless attempt at a smile. 'Right now he's positively suicidal at what's happened. He can't believe he could be so stupid. But it's too late – some damned little Frenchman is back home in Paris right now rubbing his hands to the tune of almost a hundred thousand pounds. *Our* one hundred thousand pounds.'

He knelt down on one knee and poked disconsolately at the fire, then carefully placed a fresh log in the middle. Mhairi watched him in silence as he blew fresh life into the sputtering flames with the bellows.

'It means a lot to you, doesn't it – saving Craig David.' She knelt down beside him, and placed a hand on his arm.

'It's more than our home, it's eight hundred years of our family's history. Eight hundred years . . . Imagine it, Mhairi. For eight hundred years MacLachlans have lived in that place. They have been born there, raised their children there, and died there. Am I the one to bring that proud history to an end? Am I the one to sell my family's birthright?'

Once, not so long ago, she would not have understood. To put a pile of stones – a mere home – before someone you loved would have seemed incomprehensible to her.

But not now. Not after knowing Dalriada. 'No, my love,' she said softly. 'No, you are not the one.' And her eyes had tears in them as she reached across and touched him.

Then she was in his arms, and he was kissing the salt from her cheeks, his lips moving over the soft skin of her face and down the slope of her neck, as her fingers tangled in the dark, curling hair, and her body yielded to his.

He carried her to the bed, lying her down gently on the soft quilt. She watched in silence as he cast off his dressing-gown. He was naked beneath it and his body was firm and white in the firelight. His eyes glowed with an intensity she could hardly bear as he moved forwards, then slid on to the quilt beside her. His fingers undid the pearl buttons of her nightgown and it slipped from her shoulders and she could feel the mat of dark curling hair of his chest against the soft skin of her breasts.

Then he was kissing her as she had never been kissed, and, as their bodies melded, she no longer cared about tomorrow, next week, or next year . . . Tonight he was hers. And hers alone.

The following morning brought clear sunshine and a bright blue sky that sent shafts of pale sunlight in through the windows at the front of the house as Mhairi sat up in bed and called a tentative 'Come in' in reply to the tap on her door.

'It's only me, ma'm, with your hot water.' The young maid, Fiona McLeod, entered carrying the tall copper can, and laid it down with a sigh on the marble top of the washstand. She turned and curtsied to the figure of Mhairi in the bed. 'And a very Guid New Year to you, ma'm.'

'Thank you, Fiona,' Mhairi said, sitting up on the pillows. 'And the same to you. Did you spend it here at Dalriada?'

'Oh yes, ma'm. We never get off for Hogmanay. They

need all the help they can get for their gatherings . . . If I get the chance, though, I'll take a walk over to see my ain folk after the breakfast things have been put by. But if the Master or Mistress needs me, then I hope to get a chance at the weekend, if . . .' She broke off, with an embarrassed flush of her cheeks.

'If we have all gone by then?' Mhairi finished the sentence for her with a sympathetic smile. 'And have you far to go to get home?'

'Oh no, ma'am. Just over the hill to Ballintuim.'

'Ballintuim?' Mhairi sat upright in the bed. 'You're from Ballintuim?' Why should she be so shocked, the village was less than two miles away, after all? And didn't she say last night her name was McLeod? Mhairi's mouth was dry as she asked tentatively, 'Are there many families by the name of McLeod still in Ballintuim?'

The girl looked at her curiously. 'Just my Da's . . . though my Uncle Ian still bides in the village.'

Mhairi caught her breath. 'And your Da's name is?'

'Dougal,' the girl replied. 'But why would you be wanting to know that?'

'Oh, I – I knew someone from the village once by the name of McLeod. But it was a long time ago, and I'm sure you wouldn't know of her.'

The girl nodded. So many people had left for the mainland, or Portree, over the past few years that it was little more than a ghost village now. 'Will that be all, ma'm?'

'Yes, Fiona, that will be all.'

When she had gone Mhairi collapsed back on the pillows and let out a sigh. So that young rosy-cheeked creature that served to her needs was her own flesh and blood – her Uncle Dougal's girl. She thought of her grandfather's youngest son, with his sandy-coloured hair and ready smile. Dougal was always the one ready with the joke, the one to pull her Uncle Ian's leg whenever the opportunity arose, which was quite often. But her kindest thoughts were of her Uncle Ian. Ian of the serious look, and the firm belief in God that brooked no defiance, and gave no countenance to the devil's brew – the whisky – that the likes of Hamish, Neil and young Dougal set such store by. And her eyes softened as she remembered the Ian of Glasgow station who had bent down and kissed her, and told her to remember them – to remember Skye.

And now there were just the two of them left: Ian and Dougal, her grandfather's eldest and youngest sons. A great longing came over her to see them again, to see once more the old house, with its well-scrubbed table around which they all used to sit to be attended by her mother, Mary Anne, before the blood as bright as Rowan berries became a flood and her young body could take no more . . . And that was when it all fell apart.

Then suddenly tears formed in her eyes, and she was weeping. Weeping for all those she had lost in the eighteen years of her own young life: her mother, Mary Anne; her grandfather, Long Rob; her Auntie Jessie, and her Auntie Belle. She had loved them, each and every one. They had been whole once – a united family, the McLeods of Ballintuim, but now all that remained were Ian and Dougal. Surely she could not leave this place without seeing them once more?

She dressed slowly, taking time and care over her toilet, for this morning, the first day of the new year, she was a woman. Last night, in that very bed in her father's house, she had left girlhood behind. And she felt no shame. It was right that it should have been him, for she knew she would never love another man as she loved Ralph MacLachlan.

He had been both gentle and strong as they came together on the soft quilt. He had sworn his love from the very depths of his being and she had heard him and believed every word. And, most important of all, he had left her with hope. If there was a way on this earth to find the money to save Craig David without marrying Effie, then he would find it; he had promised her that. He would find it, and they could be together forever – man and wife in the eyes of the world, as they already were in their own hearts.

Breakfast was a leisurely affair, with guests coming and going at will, helping themselves to the ample fare spread out on the damask covered tabletops of the breakfast-room. The smell wafted through the hall, now strangely silent after the revels of the night: kippers covered in melting golden butter, mounds of bacon still crispy and sizzling on the silver, heated platters, and eggs with yolks the colour of the summer sun were all laid out to tempt palates still jaded from too much of the *water of life* the evening before.

Mhairi did not know whether to be relieved or disappointed that Ralph failed to appear throughout the half-hour she was there. And despite the temptations on offer, she could only summon the appetite to nibble at a piece of buttered toast and sip a cup of fine Assam tea as she listened to the others make their plans for the day. In her own mind, she had already decided. She would set off straight after breakfast to make the long walk to Ballintuim.

She gathered from Millie Sutherland that some of the men had made an early start and had already set off for the hills with their guns. None expected to bag anything, but the winter sunshine had been too great a lure. 'And besides,' Millie added, wiping the toast crumbs from her lap, 'after all the over-indulgence last night, the exercise will do them the world of good.'

She leaned nearer to Mhairi, over her cup of tea, and confided that the exodus to the hills would not go down too well in certain quarters. 'Poor Effie, she will be quite distraught that Ralph has taken off with his gun and a dog before she's even out of bed! She'll simply have to learn, poor dear, that after dogs and horses, women come a very poor third in most men's lives!'

Mhairi smiled quietly to herself, and felt relieved that it was the hills that had claimed him this morning, not her half-sister. 'I was thinking of taking some exercise myself,' she added. 'So once Effie gets up, I would tell her not to worry if I'm not back for lunch.'

Millie Sutherland raised her eyebrows. 'Of course, dear.' These actresses were a funny breed. Nothing on earth would entice her to leave a warm fireside for the rigours of the great outdoors on a day like this.

It was around ten-thirty when Mhairi, warmly wrapped in her best fox furs, set off for the long walk over the hill to Ballintuim. And to her surprise she had no bother finding the path, although she had never walked the whole of the road as a child. Whenever her mother had taken her by the hand to gaze upon the white turrets of Dalriada, they had gone no further than the top of the hill. To come down the other side would have been to risk being sighted from the windows of the castle itself.

She could hear the guns going off in the distance, and wondered which shots were Ralph's, as she left the well-manicured grounds of Dalriada behind to head over the hill that would take her to her native village.

The path was much steeper than she remembered it, and on the Dalriada side it skirted the edge of the cliffs to a dangerous degree that had her picking her way very carefully indeed over the icy ground. The fall over the edge to the rocks beneath was all of two hundred feet.

It took almost half an hour to make the climb to the top and her heart leapt as she stood by the huge boulder they called McGregor's *Clach* and looked around her. The hill was not one but two really, for the road to Dalriada that meandered along the edge of the cliffs was separated from the much gentler slope of Craig Mhor by a long gulley, down which a stream rushed towards the waters of Loch Scavaig to the west.

She raised her hand to shield her eyes from the brightness of the winter sun as she gazed in the direction of the small village of Auchindoir. And there it was – just as she remembered – the old schoolhouse. Was Mr McPherson, the dominie, still in residence? He had been old when Mhairi knew him. A thin spiral of smoke rose heavenwards from the chimney and she longed to set off in its direction to find the answer to her question. But that would have to wait for another day. Today she had a much more important visit to make.

It took her another ten minutes to reach the point in the road where Ballintuim came into view. And when it happened she had to pause and compose herself, for the lump that had been in her throat ever since catching sight of Auchindoir had transformed itself to the hot sting of tears in her eyes as she gazed on the small cluster of grey stone dwellings that had once been her home.

There was the church by the foreshore, where they had laid her mother and grandfather to rest. And beyond it was the cottage of her great aunt, Jessie McLeod. More cottages straggled up the hill, and the one that sat at the very top, with its two tiny windows looking seawards, was her grandfather's, Long Rob's.

She found herself almost running down the last half-mile of her journey, so keen was she to get home. For that's what it would be, she told herself. She was going home.

She chose not to go into the village itself, but took the path that led back up the hill, in an easterly direction, towards her grandfather's cottage. It was obviously still inhabited for smoke was coming from the chimney.

She passed four other cottages on the way, but only one of them showed any sign of habitation. Tufts of grass and tall weeds sprouted from the derelict chimney stacks of the other two. Their doors stood ajar, their windows broken and open to the elements, and hens pecked and scratched around the sterile, hard-packed earth of what had once been their kitchen floors. She hurried on by, her high buttoned boots slipping on the icy stones that had served as a road for generations past.

But as she came within a few yards of her destination, her steps slowed. What on earth was she to say once she got there? Would she make herself known as her Uncle Dougal's long-lost niece, Mhairi? And if so, surely word would get back to Dalriada, for his daughter Fiona would never keep such news to herself.

As she stood wondering on the next step to take, a young girl of about nine emerged from the front door. Her light, reddish-brown hair was done in two thick plaits which hung down over a home-knitted Fair Isle cardigan. On her feet were a pair of boy's boots at least two sizes too big by the look of them. 'Are you lost?' the child asked the well-dressed stranger in Gaelic, then when there was no response from Mhairi, she repeated the question again in English.

'Why, yes. I do believe I am,' Mhairi replied, relieved to have the decision of what to say taken from her. 'I'm looking for a family named McPherson, but I may have the wrong village.'

'There's nae McPherson in Ballintuim,' the child replied. 'But I'll ask my Mam.'

Then, before Mhairi could say anything to stop her, she had disappeared inside the cottage, to emerge a few seconds later with a woman at her side. The child's mother was around thirty, with a pleasant, but weather-worn face that creased into a concerned smile, as she stood drying her hands on the front of her apron. She looked curiously at Mhairi. 'Jean here says you're looking for a family named McPherson.'

Mhairi nodded, acutely aware of her own expensive

furs, and finest worsted coat, as she looked at the drab, homemade garments that clad the other woman. 'Well, yes . . .'

'It's to the wrong village you've come, I'm sorry to say,' the young woman said. 'It's the old dominie from Auchindoir you'll be after.' She indicated with her head in the direction of the other village. 'It's just o'er yon hill there.'

'He's still teaching, then?'

'God love ye, no!' the woman laughed. 'He's been retired for eight or nine years past . . . Let me think now, my wee sister, Jean-Belle had just turned twelve, and it was her last year at school when he retired.'

Jean-Belle. Jean-Belle . . . the name rang bells in Mhairi's head, as Moira McLeod, née Morrison, continued, 'You'll be from the big house, nae doubt. American too by the sound o' it, so it's no surprising you're lost. Would you care to come in for a cup o' tea before you carry on o'er the hill?'

Mhairi's eyes lit up, then clouded as nerves got the better of her. Desperate as she was to see the inside of her grandfather's cottage, it could cause too many embarrassing questions to be asked. Somehow to land on these decent folk, all dressed up in her finery like this, was not how she wanted it. If she were to visit, she would do them the common courtesy of informing them beforehand. She would give them time to prepare. Dignity meant a lot, when it was all you had.

'Thank you, no . . . I'd better be pressing on.'

The young girl at her mother's side looked disappointed, as she chewed at the end of her plait. And Mhairi knew just how she felt. It was not every day someone so exotic landed on your doorstep in a place like Ballintuim. Impulsively she unwound one of the red fox furs from her neck and thrust it into the hands of the child. 'Here, you have this,' she said, as the mother looked on in astonishment. 'It's far too hot for all these poor dead creatures I've come out attired in today!' She cast a glance towards the sun still climbing in the heavens. 'It *is* a lovely day, isn't it?'

The two on the doorstep could make no reply, so astounded were they at the gesture. They could only look on in wonder as Mhairi turned on her heel and hurried off down the hill in the direction of the village.

'Da . . . Da! Look what that wifie's given me!' The child's exulted cry reached Mhairi's ears as she retraced her steps down the hill. And she smiled to herself. She could buy a hundred such furs and never feel the pinch, but she knew that that child would never have a more treasured gift.

She deliberately by-passed the church, and the grave-yard where her mother, grandfather, and Auntie Jessie lay. Somehow she could not bring herself to go in. Another day perhaps, before she made the long journey back down south, but not today. Today her nerves were too on edge. Ever since reaching the village she had had a feeling of destiny closing in on her. Perhaps it was simply the emotion of being back in the place of her birth . . . But whatever it was, she knew she could not take much more of it in one day.

She was now within sight of her Auntie Jessie's cottage and noticed that there were great gaps in the thatch just above the front door, which looked as if it had not seen a coat of paint in years. And as she neared the low, stone building, she could hear the sound of singing from within. She walked closer. It was a man's voice, crucifying that most lovely of Scotland's songs, 'Loch Lomond'. Whoever it was, he was drunk, roaring drunk.

She began to turn on her heel when the door opened and a tall, stooped figure emerged. His clothes were filthy and dishevelled and his trousers tied up with string. It was impossible to tell his age for his gaunt features were almost obscured by greying matted hair on his face and chin. The man peered at her through bleary eyes. 'Whaddya want?'

Mhairi stood open-mouthed in the middle of the path as he began to lurch towards her.

'I said whaddya want round here?'

'Nothing,' Mhairi gasped, as he took hold of her sleeve. His breath stank of whisky and bad teeth.

'Then bugger off! Bugger off, d'ya hear!' He let go her sleeve to stagger back and bring her into focus. 'You're from the big house,' he said, almost spitting the words at her. 'You're one o' they hoity-toity buggers who like to wander down to see how the peasants live!'

'No!' Mhairi said, aghast. 'No, really I'm not!'

But the man was no longer listening, he was staggering back in the direction of the hovel that had once been his Aunt Jessie McLeod's neat cottage.

Mhairi stood motionless in the middle of the frozen path. Pity and horror in equal measure flooded through her. Her voice was choked with emotion as, 'Uncle Ian . . .' she called after him. 'Uncle Ian . . .'

But Long Rob McLeod's eldest son was not listening. He had something far better to do with his time, as he lifted the Johnny Walker bottle from the kitchen table and pressed it once more to his lips.

Chapter Eighteen

Tears streaked the cold skin of her cheeks as Mhairi ran, half-stumbling on the icy ground, away from the village that had been her home. The sight of the drunken oaf that had once been her Uncle Ian had shocked her to the core. What had happened in these intervening years to turn a fine man such as he had been into that revolting creature? To begin to guess was beyond her.

But, despite her disgust, she felt a great love and pity for this place and its people. They were the forgotten ones. While up at the big house the McGregor and his like were making merry, the real people of this place were still living out their lives in abject poverty. And often for so many the only recourse for their loneliness, or personal problems, was the bottle. The *water of life*, they called whisky in the Gaelic, but to so many she knew it brought only misery and premature death. And it hurt her to think that her Uncle Ian was already well down that road of no return.

Yes, despite her dreams over the years, there had been nothing romantic about her homecoming. Nothing romantic at all. But, as she made her way towards the path that would take her back to Dalriada, she made a vow that she would return. Someday she would come back. She did not know how or when, but someday, somehow, she would return and bring dignity and decency back to Ballintuim. She would give her people back their pride. It was the least she could do.

By the time she reached the path above the cliff face the sun had gone in and a fresh wind was blowing. There was a distinct nip in the air, and it felt as if the temperature had dropped several degrees; the ground was harder and more slippery underfoot as she made her way, head down against the wind, in the direction of the castle.

Below her to her left, the turbulent waters of Loch Scavaig thrashed against the rocks at the foot of the cliffs, and the cry of the gulls rekindled memories of long ago, and she wondered on the strange twist of Fate that had brought her back here on this, the first day of the new year.

She tried to avoid looking down at the grey waters of the loch, and concentrated on keeping her footing on the frozen puddles that had formed overnight in the hollows of the rough ground. By the looks of it, few people had trod this route over recent years, for the path was rough and overgrown in places, and had she not remembered it from old, she was sure she would have wandered off on the wrong track by now.

She had almost reached the very top, to begin the long descent into Dalriada, when she spotted a figure making its way towards her from the direction of the castle. At first it was impossible to tell who it was, and it was not until the young woman was within a few yards that Mhairi made out the pale face of Effie Hastings inside the thick, fur-trimmed hood of the cloak.

Mhairi's face broke into a smile of welcome, but the eyes that stared back at her were as cold as the ice underfoot.

'So you've come back!' Effie's lips were thin as she spoke the words, and it was more of an accusation than a statement of fact. 'You have returned to make a fool of me in front of all the others!'

'A fool of you? I don't understand.'

'Oh yes, you do!' Effie was less than ten feet from her now and Mhairi could see she had been weeping, for her eyes were bloodshot, the lids red and swollen from recent tears. 'You have the gall to come here and accept my father's hospitality, and you repay us by stealing from me the one man I care about more than any other. You come here and seduce Ralph!'

Mhairi stared at her, hardly able to believe her ears. 'S-seduce Ralph!'

'You didn't think I would find out, did you? You thought you could keep it your nice little secret until you got back to London, but it hasn't quite worked out like that, has it, Miss Cloud?'

'Hasn't it?' Mhairi asked, perplexed.

'You obviously didn't bargain on Ralph doing the honourable thing in telling me.'

'He told you!' Mhairi gasped. This was beyond belief.

Effie shook her head in irritation; technicalities did not matter. 'He told my father. Pa thought that this morning would be the best time to have a chat with him about . . . Well, about Ralph's intentions, since he had made no mention of them on his arrival last night.'

Her voice took on a plaintive air, and her words came out jerkily. She was still out of breath from the long walk up the hill in search of this woman – this destroyer of her happiness. 'It was perfectly in order for him to enquire. Perfectly. Everyone knew – absolutely everyone. All our friends took it for granted that the engagement would be announced over the New Year celebrations here. In fact they were surprised when Ralph didn't do it on Hogmanay. That was his intention, I know it was. We couldn't imagine what had happened to delay things . . . Pa was only doing his duty in trying to clarify the matter.' She could have added that she herself had wept with disappointment on her father's shoulder before finally retiring to bed in the early hours of the morning. Gregor McGregor had had little choice but promise to clear the air with his prospective son-in-law first thing next day.

'And Ralph?' Mhairi enquired.

Effie prodded at the frozen ground with the point of her umbrella. She could just imagine the scene when her father confronted Ralph after breakfast this morning, before he had gone out on the shoot. Gregor McGregor was still seething with rage almost two hours later as he recounted the outcome to his daughter over a steadying glass of whisky in his study. 'Ralph told him there could be no question of an engagement. Not now. Not ever.' Effie's voice was bitter, her face white and pinched, despite the red, swollen eyes, and her mouth twisted as she thrashed at the ground with her umbrella in a gesture of both anger and despair. 'He wasn't going to tell. He tried to cover up for you. But in the end Pa got it out of him . . . Your seduction of him under *our* own roof!'

Mhairi stood her ground. 'My what!' This had to be some sort of distortion of what had actually taken place. But she was both shocked and exhilarated by the revelation nevertheless. Could it be that he really did intend to make her his wife, not Effie? Hope surged through her. 'You mean Ralph told your father he was in love with me, not you,' she said quietly. She had to fight to keep her voice steady.

Effie made no reply, but came back with a question of her own. 'Has he told you? Has he told you he loves you?'

Mhairi's first inclination was to lie to spare the other's feelings – but why should she? Had not Ralph himself admitted the truth? To speak anything but the truth herself now would be to make a mockery of his own confession of their love for each other. 'Yes,' she replied quietly. 'Yes, he has.'

Although she had been half-expecting that answer it brought a cry of 'No!' from Effie. Then her eyes narrowed. 'You can say that – but why should I believe you? Tell me why I should believe the likes of you – someone who spends her life acting out lies on the stage!'

'I am no liar, Lady Hastings,' Mhairi replied icily. 'I am

the woman Ralph MacLachlan loves — and there's nothing either you or your father can do to change that fact.'

And those words proved too much for Effie. This actress she had invited into her home was nothing more than a common slut — a gold-digger who had repaid their kindness and hospitality by stealing her future husband from her. She could see it in her face, in the way she stood there with that smug, half-smile on her lips. 'Prove it!' she demanded. 'Prove it if you can!'

And still Mhairi stood there, a picture of serenity, while her insides churned. She longed to yell her happiness to the world, but, despite the excitement running through her, her heart went out to the young woman who stood before her with that look of sheer misery on her face. She knew just what Effie was going through, for she too had been down that road over Ralph MacLachlan, not so long ago.

But Effie did not want her sympathy. All she wanted was the young man she had set her heart on, and Mhairi's continued silence was the confirmation she needed so badly. 'You can't, can you? You can't prove a thing!'

Then, extracting her hand from the muff at her waist, Mhairi slowly began to remove her glove and, under Effie's curious gaze, she held out her hand. The pearl and diamond ring on her third finger glinted in the pale winter sun. 'He gave me this,' she said softly. 'Is that proof enough for you?'

Effie let out a strangled gasp. It was a ring she had seen so many times in the past on the hand of his grandmother before the old lady had died. She had even been allowed to try it on herself as a child on one of their many family visits to Craig David. It was a ring that should be on her own finger — not the hand of that — that actress! Her lips were white. 'You have no right to that ring, no right at all. Give it to me! You have no right to that!'

Tossing aside her umbrella, she made a lunge towards Mhairi in an effort to tear the offending piece of jewellery from her finger. All she cared about was to get hold of it. 'It's mine – not yours – mine!' She pulled at Mhairi's right arm, bringing her almost toppling on top of her. The two staggered backwards as if in some crazy dance.

'Stop it! For heaven's sake, stop it!' Mhairi tried in vain to wrench herself free from the younger woman's grasp. This was quite ridiculous. Effie was acting like a spoilt child. Grown-up people did not fight. What if someone were to see them? If there were differences to be settled then this was certainly not the way to do it.

But Effie would not let go. She was hanging on to Mhairi like an enraged terrier and pulling with all her might on her hand. Reason had gone flying on the wind that gusted on them from the grey Atlantic less than a mile away. 'Give it to me! Give it to me!' she kept repeating. 'It's mine! Give it to me!'

Mhairi found herself weakening under the other's determined assault, and she knew the long walk to Ballintuim must have tired her more than she realized, but there was no way she could allow Ralph's ring to be taken from her. 'Please,' she gasped. 'Please, let go . . .'

They were locked in their grotesque dance on the clifftop for several seconds, before Mhairi finally succeeded in wrenching herself free.

They stood panting and glaring at one another on the grassy verge at the very edge of the path.

'Please . . .' Mhairi begged once more. 'Don't make it any worse. Don't let's be stupid about this.'

'You came up here to steal him from me!' Tears were blurring her vision now as Effie spat the words across the few feet of path, determined to vent all her rage and pent-up emotion on her rival. How could she have stood there like that, adding insult to injury? She had not even had the good grace to apologize, but had merely stood there flaunting that ring in her face – that ring that should have been hers, should be on her finger right now.

Mhairi bent down to retrieve her muff that had been torn from its cord at her belt in the struggle, then yelled out in pain as Effie gave a sharp tug at her hair. 'You little . . . !' She jerked upwards and aimed a blow in Effie's direction which missed by a yard. Then Effie came back at her, her hands clawing at Mhairi's carefully arranged coiffure. Hairpins went flying as the curls were tugged at from all angles, and Mhairi's cries of pain grew louder by the second.

Then, as Effie's left hand clutched a long lock of hair, her right aimed a blow which caught Mhairi at the side of the cheek and sent her staggering backwards. It stung and brought tears to her eyes. This was too much, she had to defend herself. One arm went up to ward off the other blows that began raining down, as her other arm tried in vain to hold back her aggressor, who was now shoving at her like a petulant child as she lashed out with both fists clenched.

Mhairi was aware of pushing at Effie's shoulder in return, then when this did nothing to lessen the attack, she thrust her fist into her assailant's face. She must have caught her nose, for the action brought a sharp yelp of pain, and Effie went staggering backwards, her high-heeled boots losing their grip on the grass verge at the edge of the path.

'You bitch!' Effie protested, as she fought to regain her balance and in so doing staggered backwards another few feet. She pressed her hand to her smarting nose, and her eyes were swimming with the sudden rush of tears caused by the blow.

'Look out!' Mhairi made a grab towards her in a desperate attempt to pull her back from the edge, but she succeeded only in clutching at the tips of the fingers of Effie's left hand as the younger woman fell heavily sideways on to the very rim of the cliff.

The frozen grass sent Effie's booted feet sliding over the

edge to disappear out of sight, but she was saved from following them by Mhairi throwing herself to the ground beside her and clutching at the voluminous material of her cloak. 'Help me,' Effie gasped. 'Help me . . . please . . .'

Mhairi continued to clutch frantically at Effie to prevent her from sliding further, but could not get hold of her body. All she could grasp at was the garment in which she was wrapped. Her knuckles were white as her fingers clung on to the fine worsted material of the cloak, but the sheer body weight of her half-sister caused the smooth cloth to slip through her fingers, and she could feel her nails snag and break as she tried in vain to keep her grip. She could feel the energy drain from her own body as she tried frantically to keep hold, but finally she knew it was impossible to hang on any longer without being dragged over the edge herself.

She let out a low moan that seemed to come from the very depths of her being, and at that moment they both knew it was hopeless. 'I'm sorry, Effie . . . I'm so sorry . . .'

For a few horrifying seconds that seemed to last forever, Mhairi found herself looking helplessly into Effie's terror-stricken eyes as the younger woman opened her mouth to say something, but no words came. And, gradually and irretrievably, the last few inches of material slipped through Mhairi's fingers, and the body of her half-sister slowly disappeared from sight over the edge of the cliff.

Exhausted and half-dazed with shock, Mhairi crawled forwards as far as she dared to watch in horror as her half-sister's hands clawed in vain at the air, as she plunged downwards towards the grey waters of the loch and the rocks beneath. Her black cloak billowed out behind her, as her shriek of despair echoed on the eddying wind.

For several seconds Mhairi lay there on the frozen grass, unable to move. She was panting and covered in a cold sweat. It had all happened so fast. She closed her eyes. Maybe when she opened them again the nightmare would be over and she could continue her journey back to Dalriada.

But when she opened them, the nightmare was not over, and as she scrambled to her feet, she realized that the screams that were still ringing in her ears were not those of her half-sister. They were coming from a different direction entirely.

Confused, she turned to find herself looking into the aghast face of Fiona McLeod, as the maid came running along the path from the direction of Dalriada.

'You killed her! I saw it with my own eyes – you killed the Mistress!' The young girl was red-faced and gasping for breath, as she stopped within a few yards of Mhairi's dishevelled figure. 'Oh Mother of God, is this not a terrible thing!'

Still too shaken to think straight, Mhairi stood there speechless, barely able to comprehend what she was hearing. She was trembling violently and staring vacantly at the newcomer.

'I canna believe it,' the maid was saying. 'I canna believe it. But with my own eyes I saw it!' Then she began to back away from Mhairi's trembling figure, as if she too was under threat.

She had left the castle only minutes after her Mistress, to pay a fleeting visit to her parents in Ballintuim, and she had stumbled upon the scene being played out on the clifftop. She had seen her Mistress and the American actress wrestling, and then the push that had sent Effie Hastings plunging to her death. 'You're a murderess,' she cried, half-hysterical now, as she continued to back down the path. 'You murdered my Mistress! You killed Lady Effie!'

Then she turned on her heels and began to run back in the direction of the castle, her booted feet slithering and sliding over the frozen path.

Mhairi remained rooted to the spot. The trembling had

enveloped her whole body which was shaking violently now, and her teeth were chattering noisily as she gazed after the retreating figure. The wind had got up and was howling and whistling about her ears. The very elements were screaming at her – accusing her. She had killed Effie. For a second a panic gripped her and she almost believed it herself. But it wasn't true. What the girl had said just wasn't true. Then the fear set in, for who would believe her? Certainly not their father. Certainly not the McGregor.

Then a thought took her – what if Effie had not perished? What if, by some miracle, she had survived the fall? Frantically she looked around her. There was a small promontory about twenty yards to her left. She began to run on leaden legs in its direction.

Once there, she threw herself down on the frozen ground and looked as far over the edge as she dared. What she saw brought a gasp to her throat and the tears to her eyes. Effie's body was lying beneath the black cloak, spreadeagled on a rock around which the waves were crashing, sending showers of spray over the prostrate figure. And as Mhairi lay there the waves grew stronger and the spray heavier, until great breakers were crashing over the rock. Then the body, still wrapped in its black shroud, was lifted and tossed by the icy waters like some piece of flotsam. Mhairi watched through her tears as her half-sister's head bobbed on the waves for a few seconds, before disappearing forever beneath the grey waters of the loch.

'I'm sorry, Effie,' she cried. 'I'm so very very sorry . . .'

Just what she was apologizing for she was not quite sure. But, as she pulled herself wearily to her feet to begin the long, lonely trek back to Dalriada, she knew, till the day she died, she would feel not only sorrow and pain for what had just occurred here this day, but also guilt. For wasn't it her love for Ralph that had brought Effie running up to this clifftop in the first place? Wasn't her happiness in some way responsible for her half-sister's death? Suddenly her whole world was tainted, and the elation she had felt those few short minutes ago at the knowledge of Ralph's love for her had been washed away by the tears that continued to stream from her eyes as she trudged the last weary mile back to the castle.

She covered the final few hundred yards half-running, half-dragging her feet. All her instincts made her want to run as far away from this place as possible, to put that awful accident out of her mind, but that she could not do. She had to go back there and face the consequences. She had to face her father.

The castle was strangely quiet on her return: there was no sign of the female guests, and she could still hear the distant echo of the guns. She felt a wave of relief that the men were still out on the hills. She had no wish to run into Ralph at a time like this.

Fiona, the maid, must have reached the castle a good few minutes before her, and Mhairi expected to be met at the door by the distraught figure of the McGregor, but there was no sign of him as she ran the last few yards up the drive. Perhaps the McLeod girl had not found her Master yet. Whatever the consequences, however, Mhairi resolved to take her courage in both hands and tell him herself of the terrible accident that had just occurred.

The kilted figure of Hamish Mhor was standing with the dogs by the fire in the main hall when she entered, and she felt her legs would barely support her as she went over to ask him the way to the Master's study. 'Is he there?' she queried anxiously, after being directed to the appropriate room on the first floor.

The butler looked curiously at her and she knew she must look a sight, with her head of loose, tangled hair and dirt-streaked clothes. 'Aye, he's there,' he replied. 'But I'd better warn ye, the Laird's no in the best o' moods the day.

I understand he had words wi' Lord McLachlan before the young man took to the hills this morning and the black dog's been on his back ever since.'

Mhairi's courage almost failed her as she murmured her thanks and set off up the main staircase. God only knew what his reaction would be. She felt sick with fear and so physically tired she could barely drag one foot past the other.

The door to the Laird's study was ajar and she could just make out the sound of voices within, as, taking her courage in both hands, she pushed it open even further and looked in.

A female cry greeted the action. 'It's her, Master, it's her!'

Gregor McGregor was standing by the window, his face the colour of parchment, his eyes staring from across the room, as the young girl began to sob at the sight of Mhairi.

'It's her . . . It's her . . . I saw it with my ain eyes!'

'Hush your wailing, girl!' Gregor McGregor walked forwards a few feet, his eyes still on Mhairi. 'Get to your room,' he ordered the weeping girl. 'And say nothing of this, you understand. Nothing. Say no word to man or beast of what you have seen this day.'

The young girl looked at him, uncomprehending, for a moment, then, giving Mhairi a wide berth, she fled from the room.

Father and daughter stood looking at one another. She could see he was fighting to control himself and her heart went out to him. Finally Gregor McGregor spoke. 'So you have done it, have you? You have finally wreaked your revenge on this house – on me.' His voice was thick with emotion and there were tears in his eyes.

'No!' Mhairi protested. 'No – believe me! You have to believe me! That young girl, Fiona – she has it all wrong! I tried to save Effie, not kill her!'

The man before her grimaced, and the lips in his ashen

face twisted bitterly. 'Spare me that. Have the decency to spare me that.'

'But it's true,' Mhairi continued, desperate for him to hear her out. 'Believe me, it's true!' She had an almost uncontrollable urge to fling herself at his feet, to beg his forgiveness for a sin she knew she had not committed. 'Effie came looking for me . . .' She shook her head, as she tried to make sense of it herself. 'At least I presume she came looking for me. Anyway, we met on the clifftop. She began accusing me of stealing Ralph from her, and then she began hitting out at me. I tried to protect myself, and she lost her balance and fell. I tried to save her – believe me I tried to save her . . . I didn't kill her. Please believe me, I didn't kill her!' The last sentence was almost shouted at him in her desperation to be believed.

Gregor McGregor continued to stare at her, his eyes glistening with tears as yet unshed. His face was expressionless, save for a nerve which twitched at the side of his right eye. His own mother had lost her life on that very clifftop, and now it had claimed the only other person he had loved as much.

His silence unnerved her. She had not expected this. Shouting perhaps – violence even – but not this . . . 'I know I have no evidence to prove my innocence,' Mhairi said faintly. 'And you have only my word.' Her face was drawn and tears hovered behind the surface of her eyes, but she was determined not to break down in front of him. If he could hold himself together, then so could she. 'I am at your mercy.'

The McGregor was silent for a long time, then sighed, 'Aye, you are at my mercy.'

As she watched, he turned abruptly away from her to face the fire, and gazed down at it. When he finally spoke, his voice had a bitter edge. 'It is over nineteen years since I too committed a sin, Mhairi McLeod – if sin it was – against your mother. I could have married her, but chose

315

not to. Instead I married a woman – Effie's mother – who made a fine wife and brought with her a lineage as long and as proud as the McGregors, and the wherewithal to ensure that Dalriada would stand for another thousand years.'

He paused, turning back to face her, and his voice had a catch in it as he continued, 'Some would say that in denying my own flesh and blood I committed a sin that was grave indeed, and perhaps you have suffered for that sin. But the revenge you have wreaked on me this day goes far deeper than any ill I have done you. You have taken from me the one thing dearer to me than life itself. You have taken my daughter.'

The tears that had been threatening since she arrived back at the castle ran hot and bitter down Mhairi's cheeks as she shook her head and pleaded with him to listen, to believe her. 'But *I* am your daughter too. You know that, so why can't you accept it? Effie was my half-sister – my own flesh and blood. I beg you to believe me, I didn't kill her. She lost her temper and lashed out at me, and slipped. I tried – as God is my witness – I tried to save her!'

But the McGregor was looking past her, his eyes fixed on some unknown object in the far corner of the room. 'I want you to leave here,' he said quietly. 'I want you to pack your bags and go now. Hamish will drive you to Portree, where you will get the boat to the mainland, and no word will be said of your part in the death of my daughter.' His fingers trembled on the handle of his stick. It was the first and last favour he would ever do her. To do less would be to bring shame beyond redemption on his name – the McGregor name – and that was unthinkable. For should he accuse this young woman, as sure as there was a God in heaven, she would fight back, and would acquaint the whole world with the follies of his youth.

'But the maid?' Had he forgotten the maid?

'The McLeod girl will say nothing, you can be sure of

that. Her father's land and cottage are feued to the Dalriada estate.'

So he would buy her silence.

They stood looking at one another across the few yards of carpet. After eighteen years of searching she had found her father. And now this.

She knew it was useless to argue. His mind was made up. Whether he really believed her to be guilty or not, she could not tell. But one thing was certain, he wanted her out of his life.

'I will instruct Hamish to have the carriage ready in fifteen minutes. It would please me if you said nothing to anyone before you left. I will make your excuses to the company, should it be necessary.'

He knew only too well that the moment she had gone and news of the fall became common knowledge his composure would be at an end. A man could only take so much in one lifetime. And in a strange way he had been waiting for this moment all his life. They were an accursed tribe, the McGregors. Never a generation passed without tears enough being shed to fill Loch Scavaig itself. But that his punishment should be meted out by his own flesh and blood . . .

He shook his head as he gazed at the distraught face of the young woman in front of him. 'God help us all,' were his last words to her.

He turned back to the fire, and she stared at him for several seconds, as if to imprint the image of him on her mind. Then, silently, her lips formed the words that had taken on a whole new meaning for her:

> I grow, I prosper,
> Now, gods, stand up for bastards.

And she knew from now on there would be no one but herself. No one else would ever stand up for her in this life. But then it had always been like that.

Book Three

HOPE DEFERRED

I looked for that which is not, nor can be,
But hope deferred made my heart sick in truth:
But years must pass before a hope in youth
Is resigned utterly.

I watched and waited with a steadfast will:
But though the object seemed to flee away
That I so longed for, ever day by day
I watched and waited still.

Sometimes I said: This thing shall be no more,
My expectation wearies and shall cease;
I will resign it now and be at peace;
Yet never gave it o'er.

Sometimes I said: It is an empty name
I long for; to a name why should I give
The peace of all the days I have to live?
– Yet gave it all the same.

Alas, thou foolish one! alike unfit
For healthy joy and salutary pain:
Thou knowest the chase useless and again
Turnest to follow it.

Christina Rossetti

If there was one thing that visit to Skye, for the Hogmanay of 1895, taught me it was that you may go back to the place of your birth, but you cannot go back to your childhood. I found no happy memories there during those fateful few days I spent on my beloved island, and, with one all-important exception, I lost far more than I gained. I found and lost my father; I lost my half-sister Effie; and I lost the man I loved.

Yes, I lost Ralph. And I think I knew I had lost him that moment Effie's terrified eyes met mine and her body slipped from my grasp to disappear forever into the grey waters of the loch.

Ralph had not returned from the hills when Hamish Mhor told me the carriage to take me to Portree was waiting at the door. Neither did he contact me once I returned to London. And oh, how I waited and watched for the post. Far more desperately than I had waited for any letter over the previous few months. For I knew by then that he had truly loved me. I had Effie's word for it, after all.

Effie . . . How that very name brings sadness to my soul, even after all these years.

I could understand the reaction of Gregor McGregor, our father, for from the very moment he had learned the truth of our relationship from my lips, he had feared that somehow I had come like an avenging angel to blight his happiness and that of his beloved child. I shall never know if he really believed me responsible for her death, but I accept fully that he had no choice other than to send me away. What I could not accept, however, was that Ralph must have believed me guilty. There could have been no other explanation for his failure to get in touch.

That knowledge cut deep – far deeper than any wound before or since. And it proved most painful of all one bright spring morning in early October, 1896 – just over nine months later. For that was the morning I gave birth to our son.

Yes, Robert Ralph MacLachlan McLeod was what I gained from those fateful few days on my island, and he was as bonnie an heir as any father could wish for. But, like his mother, he had been born a bastard. And as I lay in that bed and cradled him in my arms, I vowed that if the gods would not stand up for him, then as long as there was a breath left in my body, his mother surely would.

And now as I look back on those days, I wonder if Balzac was right when he said that the women who lose their lovers are the women who love, and those who keep them are the women who possess the art of love. If that is true, then I am guilty. I am guilty of loving too much.

Chapter Nineteen

It had been a scorching hot day in England's capital city, and there was a carnival atmosphere about the crowds that thronged the main thoroughfares of the West End. They had been there all day, streaming across Westminster Bridge, and congregating on the pavements outside Parliament as Mr Asquith, the Prime Minister, read to a hushed House of Commons the terms of the ultimatum just delivered to Germany: war would be declared unless there was a satisfactory answer by midnight – eleven P.M. London time – to His Majesty's Government's request that the Kaiser recall his troops from Belgium. A solemn cheer had risen from the packed benches as he uttered the fateful words 'by midnight, Berlin time', and there was an even greater cheer from the crowds massing outside in the sunshine as word of the decision reached them.

'We Want War!' the chant went up, to be echoed by the thousands who packed Whitehall and Horseguards Parade, causing chaos to the traffic around Westminster.

In Trafalgar Square Londoners cooled themselves with water from the fountains as they sang their patriotic songs and talked of what they would do to the Hun. Most were young people, the men in straw boaters and gaily striped blazers, the young women in bright summer dresses; all were determined to enjoy every minute of the crisis to the full.

As the evening shadows lengthened and the hour for the deadline approached, the numbers on the streets were swelled by the evening-suited theatre and restaurant crowd, and the excitement grew to fever pitch.

In the midst of the crowd that evening was a tall, dark-haired youth of not quite eighteen. His grey eyes shone with the sheer thrill of it all as he waved to the cars that passed with French tricolours and Union Jacks fluttering from their open windows. Other flags in the British and French colours abounded everywhere you cared to look, and as he passed through Bedford Square they were singing 'La Marseillaise'. He joined in lustily, as leaflets were thrust into his hand exhorting him to rally to the flag without delay. Those already in uniform were the recipients of much back-slapping and hand-shaking, and the young man took pains to assure every uniformed soldier, 'I'll soon be joining you, sir!'

Just before eleven, the mass of people began to move on up the Mall to the gates of Buckingham Palace itself. They would show King George just what they thought of his cousin Willy across the Channel in Berlin! And as the King and Queen appeared on the balcony they roared their approval with cries of 'Long Live the King!' and 'Down with the Kaiser!'

Then, as the fateful hour struck, it seemed as if the whole city was on the streets, as a great war cry of delight went up and echoed round the rooftops.

The young man with the grey eyes had no hat to wave but he cheered himself hoarse nevertheless, before running home to share the experience of the most exciting night of his life with his mother.

And in the elegant drawing-room of the Georgian terraced house, just off Bedford Square, the woman with the beautifully coiffured dark-auburn hair and hazel eyes listened impassively to what her son had to say. She was tired, for it had gone midnight; she had remained at her window waiting for his return for the past hour, and it had been with a heavy heart that she had watched the revellers pass on their way to congregate in front of the Palace. Their war chants had sent a shudder through her soul. And their excitement was now mirrored in the eyes of her own son, as she said quietly, 'Has it never occurred to you, they are out there cheering their own deaths?'

The young man sprawled on the window-seat gasped as he pulled himself up straight and glared across at his mother. 'But that is the most monstrous thing I have ever heard!'

Mhairi paused in the rearranging of the roses in the crystal bowl on her desk and turned to face him. When he had that look on his face he reminded her so much of that man, now long dead, who had sired her, but who had never been her father. There was the same angularity of feature, the same penetration of gaze; only the eyes were different; Gregor McGregor's were dark brown, while his grandson's were the same steel grey of his father, Ralph MacLachlan. Yes, two very different men had gone into the making of the young man that was her son, and, at moments like this, she could only try to understand the passions that were burning in his breast. It was not every day, after all, that your country declared war on another.

She sighed as she turned to face him. 'Oh, Rob, Rob . . . You're still only seventeen, after all – a mere schoolboy until this summer!'

Rob McLeod pushed a hand impatiently through his shock of dark hair and swung his long legs on to the carpet. In three strides he was by his mother's side. 'Leave those flowers alone, can't you, and listen to me! I'll be eighteen in a few weeks' time. I'll be old enough then! Old enough to fight for King and country!'

In his right hand he clutched the copy of *The Times* with its appeal for young unmarried men between the ages of eighteen and thirty to enlist. 'We're at war, Ma! Don't you understand? As from tonight we're at war!' The excitement in his voice was matched by that in his eyes as he adopted a more pleading tone. 'For goodness' sake – when even oldies like Uncle George are joining up, what would it say for us young ones if we all decided to stay at home and wait till we're called up?'

Mhairi sighed once more. She was becoming more tired by the minute, and she wished he hadn't brought her old friend George West into it. This past year had found her loyalties painfully divided. It seemed only yesterday that Jennie Churchill had scandalized society by marrying Mhairi's own one-time beau, George Cornwallis-West, who at twenty-five had been even younger than her son Winston. But that was all of fourteen years ago now and much murky water had passed under that particular matrimonial bridge. And in April of this year, within one hour of his divorce from Jennie being declared absolute, George had shocked society once more by marrying their mutual friend Stella, Mrs Patrick Campbell, at Kensington Registry Office.

If he was not the most constant of husbands, however, George West was certainly a good and faithful friend, and had been particularly so to the young Rob as he had grown from boyhood to young manhood over the past seventeen years. Mhairi's son now regarded his Uncle George, as he called him, as much a surrogate father as a family friend, and he believed passionately that he would be letting both himself and his uncle down if he did not rally to the colours at the first opportunity. His mother, however, had other ideas.

Mhairi had remained close friends with both Jennie and George over the years, having been a guest at their wedding in the first year of the new century. And in response to her friends' recommendations, and after much heart-searching, she had sent Rob to Harrow, the public school to which both George himself and Jennie's two sons Winston and Jack Churchill had gone. It had been a sound choice, for the school had done its job well, although, as she both listened to and looked at her son these days, she wondered what his namesake, her grandfather Long Rob McLeod would make of the young man who was his great-grandson. The old crofter would have found little to relate to in the young, upper-class Englishman his granddaughter had produced, and the knowledge saddened her. Despite her pride in her offspring, it was as if she had somehow sold out on his birthright. Who could tell now it was only Scottish blood that flowed in his veins? She had turned him into an Englishman. But had she had any choice?

So much had happened in her life since that day in the spring of 1896, when she had visited her doctor's Harley Street surgery to be told that she was not in fact suffering from recurring bouts of food-poisoning, but that she was expecting a baby.

The news had left her stunned. Not only had she neither heard from nor seen anything of Ralph since leaving Skye, but she was due to open in a new George Edwardes production, *My Girl*, at the Gaiety Theatre in the middle of July.

After her success at Daly's with *The Belle of New York*, it was to be another step up the glittering ladder of theatrical success to be asked to star at the Gaiety, for it was not only London's most beloved theatre, but the acknowledged favourite of King Edward himself.

A baby! Her whole career – her whole life – would be in ruins. It was quite one thing for ladies of the aristocracy to have affairs and get away with it, but for an unmarried woman in the public eye such as she was . . . Her whole being quailed at the prospect.

But that spring brought a lesson which she had never forgotten. If she had ever had any doubt that there was one law for the rich and one for the poor, then the truth of that old adage was certainly brought home to her then. She had balked at confiding in her producer, but George

Edwardes' production talents proved equally effective in real life as in the theatre. Almost instantly, a notice was issued to the press that his leading lady, Miss Mhairi Cloud, was suffering from nervous exhaustion and would be taking a few months off before rejoining his company in the Gaiety Theatre, at the eastern end of the Strand.

If there were knowing looks and whispers exchanged behind the scenes in theatreland, or over the coffee-cups of London society that spring and summer, she never saw or heard them, for she decided to return to America to have her child.

Robert Ralph MacLachlan McLeod was born on Monday, 5 October 1896, in a private clinic on Park Avenue, with Fiona by her side.

He was a beautiful baby, born with a head of thick dark hair and a pair of blue eyes that very soon turned to grey, just like his father's. And her heart wept that Ralph was not there to see him.

She returned to England, along with the baby and Fiona, in mid-October. Mhairi returned to her own home in Bloomsbury, but she arranged for Fiona and the baby to rent a house in nearby Gray's Inn Road. Only when sufficient time had elapsed for it to cause no comment, did she allow her 'widowed' cousin, Mrs McLeod, and her child to move into the third floor of her own home. That occurred on the day of Rob's third birthday, and it was one of the happiest days of her life.

For her part, Fiona had been only too delighted to give up her life of 'entertaining' gentlemen in New York, for the much more satisfying and respectable one of surrogate mother to Mhairi's child. And neither of them had been unaware of the poignancy of the situation as they had recrossed the Atlantic together, with little Rob in his cot beside them. Fiona's own child, little Bobby, had also been named after his grandfather, Long Rob, and Mhairi hoped in her heart that having another small boy to care for would go some way to filling the gap that she knew had been in her cousin's heart over the past ten years.

The only awkward part was what the child would call them, for in the eyes of the world their roles were reversed, but this was overcome by the infant himself, who settled on a lisping 'Fi' for Fiona, and 'Ma' for Mhairi, as soon as he began to talk.

That it was not Fiona but Mhairi herself who was his real mother was made clear to him before he went off to boarding school. It was a secret he took very well, for he loved both women who had lavished such love and devotion on him for so long. And to Mhairi's surprise, he did not ask about his father. That he wondered about him she had no doubt, but whether it was embarrassment for her sake, or simply indifference that caused him to remain silent on the subject she had no way of telling. But it was a gap in his knowledge that loomed larger in her mind as time went on.

Once Rob went off to school, Fiona remained living in her own two rooms on the third floor of the house and had become even more devoted to Mhairi and her son with the passing years. 'Fi' had been the perfect foil between her soft-hearted cousin and the headstrong, likeable young man that Rob had been growing into, for there had never been a moment when he could not twist his mother around his little finger.

And now, at seventeen, he towered over them both, and seemed to have an intellect to match the prowess at games that had produced a display cabinet full of sporting honours in the drawing-room of his mother's home. That he should have reacted as he had done to the talk of war surprised neither of them, for he was at an age that felt everything passionately, but, nevertheless, it affected Mhairi deeply. She had been passing through Trafalgar Square just two days previously and had paused in the rain to hear Keir Hardie, the Scots Labour politician, address an anti-war rally. What he had said made such sense to her that she had rushed home to tell Fiona all about it.

'In fact, while I was there a young woman pushed a leaflet into my hand about a meeting especially for women that's to be held on the fourth of August.'

She had searched in her jacket pocket and pulled it out. 'Here we are! It's called "What War Would Mean" and is to be addressed by a Mrs Fawcett of the National Union of Suffrage Societies!' She continued to stare at it thoughtfully, then said, 'I really think I should go!'

Fiona had laid her knitting in her lap and looked up. 'Do you think that's wise? I mean, you know you've been warned before by Mr Edwardes about getting involved in anything too political. He wasn't at all happy when you invited that Mrs Pankhurst and one of her daughters to that party.'

Fiona had meant well, but the memory of the argument Mhairi had had with her much-loved producer still rankled. She could not for the life of her believe that people would stop coming to see the show just because she approved of what the likes of the Pankhursts were doing to get women the vote. 'If standing up for my rights is being political, George dear, then political I shall jolly well be!' she had insisted.

But to her shame she had taken it no further. If she owed anyone a debt of honour in this life it was George Edwardes and to do anything to directly upset him was unthinkable. But that had not stopped her going to hear what Mrs Fawcett had to say, and what she had heard about the future for all of them if Britain declared war made it all the more unbearable to hear her son, only a few hours later, talk so passionately about joining up.

She sighed as she laid a restraining hand on Rob's arm, her eyes begging him to understand. 'Darling, far be it from me to make you look a coward in the eyes of Uncle

George or anyone, but you know what I want for you more than anything right now.'

'Oxford!' he snorted derisively. 'What's that but an extension of school! But that's what you want, isn't it, Ma? You want me to remain a child forever!'

'No, darling, that's not what I want. But neither do I want you to give up your chance of a place there to take part in a silly little skirmish in Europe that everyone knows will be over by Christmas.'

'Well, if it's to be over by Christmas as you claim, then that's all the more reason for me to sign up. Heaven knows, there might not be another war in my lifetime and look what I would have missed . . . What you would have prevented me from experiencing!'

Mhairi was beginning to lose patience. He was sounding just a little too much like Jennie's Winston, for her liking. All this *Boy's Own Paper* talk was quite ridiculous. She should never have allowed him to join that rabble out on the streets tonight. He would have been far better employed coming to that women's meeting with her. War was not a game and the quicker he realized it the better.

'Robert, you are not impressing me in the least with this sort of talk. I want to hear no more of it, until you're at least of an age when they would accept you, anyway.' That gave her two months' grace, and for all either of them knew this silly war could be over by then anyway. She glanced at the clock on the mantelpiece, and stifled a yawn. It was well past midnight. 'I think it's high time I turned in.'

But no matter how hard she tried to put the war to the back of her mind, it proved impossible to ignore it. It was as if the whole country had been gripped by some sort of fever.

Over the next few days the talk was all of enlisting, and doing one's bit for the homeland. Even Fiona had taken to knitting socks for the soldiers. There were notices everywhere exhorting young men to rush to the colours, and even old men, long past the age of call-up, were flocking to enlist in the volunteer reserves. It was impossible to ignore the posters printed in the national colours of red, white and blue that shouted at you from every hoarding: 'Your King and Country needs – YOU!'

Prices had risen sharply in the shops on the day war was declared and had gone on rising, and although Mhairi had no need to shop for food personally, she listened sympathetically to her cook, Mrs Chambers, talk of ordinary families she knew who could no longer afford basic foodstuffs. 'Near to starving some are down my sister's way in Catford – them whose husbands have been called up. Not a penny piece to their name they're left with. It's a national disgrace, if you ask me, ma'm, and that's the God's truth! But then nobody does ask the likes of us, do they?'

It seemed to Mhairi that this awful war which was in danger of turning the Western world upside down was somehow symbolic of the upheaval in her own life, and that of the Gaiety Theatre, over the past few months. An era was coming to an end, and it seemed as if the whole of the old world they had known and loved was in chaos. In fact, the death throes of her own small part of that world went back to before the war – to 1912, in fact. Yes, it was almost two years since dear George Edwardes, the Gaiety Theatre's legendary producer, and her own mentor since her arrival in London all those years ago, had had his first stroke.

The past two years had seen his condition deteriorate badly and when Mhairi visited him at home in London in the middle of September, she was shocked at what she found. His hair, which had been simply greying when she last saw him, had gone quite white, he was very weak and stooped, and his hand had a permanent shake to it. There was little to recognize of the big, bluff extrovert who had made her an even bigger star of the London stage than she had been of the American.

But he appreciated her coming, nevertheless, and they spent over an hour reminiscing on the trials and triumphs they had both shared in over the past nineteen years.

Mhairi had been with him in the sunset years of the old Gaiety Theatre at the end of the Nineties, when George's shows and the girls in them had carved out a place in the life of London as no others had done before or since. Yes, the Gaiety shows had glittered their way to success after success, and given the capital captivating melodies, laughter, and gorgeous girls such as it had never known.

And Mhairi had been with him when the old Gaiety closed its door for the last time, on 4 July 1903, and she had been with him once more at the opening of the new Gaiety Theatre, a few months later, on 26 October 1903. And as she sat there holding his hand and reminiscing, she reminded him of how it had rained all day, but it had made no difference to the box office. The general public were only too happy to queue in the wet to obtain tickets for the pit or the gallery to be part of the rebirth of their favourite theatre. The more expensive seats had long since been sold out, as King Edward had made it very clear that he would personally attend the first night with Queen Alexandra.

'And do you remember the note he sent you, George dear?' Mhairi asked, as she reached out and took his shaking hand.

And her old producer nodded his head and tears came to his eyes, as he recalled his King's handwritten letter:

I've loved the Gaiety, I love you, and I love the Girls. Am bringing Queen Alexandra to the first night.

'And he kept his promise, didn't he?' Mhairi said softly.

Then, the old man sat lost in his own thoughts of that memorable night, before he leant forward to pat her knee, and she was certain she could still detect that old twinkle in his eye as he whispered, 'That was the night the old blighter asked you to dine at Kettner's with him, wasn't it, my dear?'

Mhairi gave a knowing smile. 'It was indeed, George . . . And what a disappointment for him I wasn't hungry!'

But now dear fat Bertie had gone and his son George was on the throne, and those heady days they were already calling in France *La Belle Epoque* were at an end. And it had been a beautiful era: all those summers at Ascot, when the Sunday crowds would wait at Boulter's Lock, in Maidenhead, to catch a glimpse of her and the other Gaiety Girls in their gay summer dresses and picture hats being punted up the river by their straw-boatered admirers.

All those suppers in the Star and Garter at Richmond, where the waiters served champagne by the magnum in the large, bow-window dining-room, and a six-piece orchestra played the hits from her latest shows in the background, as the Chinese lanterns swayed gracefully in the breeze and she watched the moon rise, silvan and glowing, over the river.

It had been there that a young German count had asked for her slipper and returned it a few minutes later with a note saying: 'Dear Miss Cloud, Thank you so much for the loan of your slipper. That was the most wonderful champagne I ever tasted! Your devoted admirer, Alex, Graf von Heidenburg.' And two days later a box containing two dozen slippers, handmade in all the colours of the rainbow, from the royal shoemakers, H. & M. Rayne, was delivered to her dressing-room.

But perhaps saddest of all, there would be no more visits to her beloved Paris to stroll along the tree-lined quays of the Île Saint-Louis, after a visit to the theatre and a late meal, and then wander on down the narrow streets to say a prayer in the Jesuit Church at the Place Saint-Sulpice, before watching the dawn come up on the banks of the Seine. She could see it still in her mind's eye, the river as smooth as glass as the first rays of the sun broke through the drifting mist to lace the silver water with threads of gold.

Before returning to London, she would pack her bag with all the tastiest glacé and chocolate sweetmeats from Boissier's to bring home to Rob – an extra special tuck-box for his next term at Harrow.

Yes, those were the golden days all right, but they would be no more, for Europe – her beloved Europe – was at war with itself.

And as she returned home after her visit to her old producer, the words of Sir Edward Grey, the Foreign Secretary, kept repeating in her head. 'The lamps are going out all over Europe; we shall not see them lit again in our lifetime.' He had uttered them in the House of Commons on the eve of war, and after reading them in the newspaper the next day they had lived on in her head.

She felt drained of all energy as she took off her coat and made for the dining-room where she knew dinner would be waiting. It was as if she had expended all her own strength on her old friend, and it had been quite deliberate, for she had willed herself to somehow transmit some of the zest she herself still possessed into his weakened body. 'It's so sad,' she said to Fiona at the end of the meal. 'It's as though I'm watching part of me die with him. He knows the Gaiety closed this summer and he believes he will never live to see it open again.'

'Do *you*?' Fiona asked, over her coffee-cup.

Mhairi looked thoughtful. Did three successive flops really sound the death knell for so beloved an English institution? She shook her head. 'I can't really believe it's all over,' she sighed. 'For dear old George, yes, and maybe even for me . . . but not for the Gaiety.'

'What on earth do you mean, maybe for you?'

Mhairi glanced across at the empty chair where Rob usually sat. He was out for a meal this evening with his Uncle George and that spelt trouble. 'It's this dratted war,' she sighed. 'It's changing everything. I can't really believe any of us will be the same when it's all over. Rob tells me that George Cornwallis-West has rejoined the reserve battalion of his old regiment, and has volunteered for this new Royal Naval Division that Jennie's boy Winston has just inaugurated. He's First Lord of the Admiralty now, so I believe, and absolutely in his element.'

She toyed with her coffee spoon and sighed. 'It seems that all men are boys at heart. They all love dressing up and playing at soldiers. The trouble is, as children when someone shouted "Bang, bang, lie down, you're dead!" they still managed to get up again when the game was over. This time, now that they're fully grown, I think they're in for a shock!'

Fiona sipped her coffee and agreed. Her blue eyes, now faded behind a pair of metal-rimmed spectacles, wandered to the open window through which the last rays of evening sunshine were glinting. The still air of the room was fragrant with the scent of the old-fashioned roses that rambled up the front of the house and filled the ornamental silver bowl in the middle of the table in front of them. 'It seems so wrong somehow to talk of war and death on an evening like this. It seems terrible to think that as we speak, someone's loved ones are being killed out there already . . . That the Angel of Death is hovering over all of us.'

'That's just what I'm afraid of!' Mhairi said vehemently. 'I've lost far too many people I've loved in my life already to just sit by and let this happen now!'

Fiona reached for the coffee pot and poured herself another half-cup. She sipped it thoughtfully for a few seconds as her brows rose sceptically, 'My dear Mhairi, what on earth can you do about anything sitting here?'

'Not sitting here,' Mhairi said impatiently. 'That's just the point. I can't do a thing about anything sitting here – or strutting about the stage, come to that. But I can refuse to do any more shows until this dreadful state of affairs is over.'

Fiona gave her cousin a severe look. 'You know jolly well you can't. Even with the Gaiety closed for the time being, you're committed to do two more shows at least, either there or at Daly's, and that would take you well into the year after next, and, let's pray to God this awful war will be over long before that!'

Mhairi was silent. She had needed the break these past few months, and had been wise enough to choose to take it at the same time the Gaiety had seen an unprecedented run of three flops in a row. But Fiona was right, that didn't get away from the fact that she was contracted to star in at least two more shows for the Edwardes organization over the next two years.

She leaned forward over the table and helped herself to a second cup of coffee as her thoughts crystallized. She had never broken a contract in her life and couldn't start now. 'All right, so I have to do two more shows,' she sighed. 'But at the rate they are opening and closing in the West End at the moment, they are not exactly going to tie me up for years to come. Then I can retire and do something really useful with my life. It's not as if I need the money any more.'

Fiona gave a dry laugh. 'Mhairi Cloud give up the stage! That I'll believe when I see it!'

But Mhairi was already pushing back her chair. She had a lot of thinking to do. She felt as if, for the first time, by saying it out loud, she had come face to face with her future. And it was not to be on the stage. Momentous things were happening to the world right now, and not only the war in Europe. Women – half of mankind – were on the march and calling for others to join them. And suddenly her head was full of voices: Mrs Fawcett's, the woman from the Suffragette Society she had heard the other week, Mrs Pankhurst's and her daughters', Keir Hardie's and Ramsay MacDonald's, two Scots like herself who were going round the country firing the blood with their call for workers' rights. Yes, she had heard them all over the past few years and they had moved something within her that had lain dormant for a long time – too long. 'If you'll excuse me, Fi dear. I think I'll get a breath of fresh air before Rob gets back.'

Why she headed for St Paul's Cathedral she was not quite sure, except that it was one of her very favourite places on earth. It was a place where she could sit and find herself – find that inner peace others knew as God; a place where the cares of the world outside would slip from her shoulders and she could rise refreshed to face the future with renewed strength. Yes, the peace she found there was like nothing she had known since she used to slip into the old Church of the Messiah, on Broadway, on her way to work, back home in New York all those years ago.

As she took her place in a pew by the door, she lifted one of the Bibles from the bench beside her. She opened it at the page marked by the red silk ribbon. Someone had been reading from the Book of Revelation, and as her eyes fell on the printed page, she found herself whispering the words out loud:

'. . . and, lo, there was a great earthquake; and the sun became black as sackcloth of hair, and the moon became blood; and the stars of heaven fell unto the earth, even as a fig tree casteth her untimely figs, when she is shaken by a mighty wind. And the heaven departed as a scroll when it is rolled together; and every mountain and island were moved out of their places. And the kings of the earth, and the great men, and the rich men, and the chief captains, and the mighty men, and every bondman, and every free man, hid themselves in the dens and in the rocks of the mountains; and said to the mountains and rocks, Fall on us, and hide us from the face of him that sitteth on the throne, and from the wrath of the Lamb; for the great day of his wrath is come; and who shall be able to stand?'

There were tears in her eyes as she finished the passage and replaced the book on the seat beside her. It was as if God Himself had spoken.

Chapter Twenty

'But, Fi dear, of course you must go! There can be no question of you staying here if Finbar needs you!' Mhairi put her arm reassuringly around her cousin's shoulders and was quite insistent. 'You mustn't worry about us. Rob and I will be perfectly fine on our own . . . No, you must stay and look after him till he's well enough to travel, then you must bring him back here to stay with us!'

Fiona nodded slowly as her eyes brightened. 'Do you really think he'd come?' They both knew her father could be stubborn when he wanted. 'He's been over there the best part of thirty years now. It's his home. And Seamus and Shona are still there.'

'Good gracious, you talk as if New York is at the other end of the earth! He can always go back and pay them a visit, you know . . . When this dratted war is over.'

Fiona refolded Shona's letter and replaced it in its envelope. It shouldn't really have come as a shock that her father had been taken so ill, after all he wasn't exactly a young man any more. But it had to be serious for Shona to mention it. The Raffertys were never much of a family for letter writing and there was far more to be read between the lines in these two short pages than in the words actually written in her sister's awkward script.

'Anyway,' Mhairi said. 'It's as well you go now before this awful fighting makes the seas as dangerous a battle-ground as poor Belgium and France. And it shouldn't be any problem getting back from the States because America is not at war.'

Fiona sighed. Mhairi made it sound so eminently sensible. But it was a big decision, nevertheless. She had never been back to the States since she came over with Mhairi and the baby Rob. Eighteen years it was since she had last seen her father and the twins. The twins . . . 'It would be great to see them all again.'

Mhairi gave a wistful smile. What wouldn't she herself give to see her old home and family right now! Never a day passed but she thought of her Uncle Finbar and wondered how he was coping now he was retired and living on his own. He never was one who bothered too much about his own wellbeing. But she had done her best by him over the years. He had the rent paid on his small apartment overlooking Central Park, and a good allowance into the bargain. Taking Fiona's advice, she had resisted making him a lump sum payment for fear the Irish in him would take too good a liking for a wee drop of the hard stuff once he had retired and had time on his hands.

Shona had remained unmarried, and had long since been promoted to housekeeper to her beloved Father Docherty. If she missed having children of her own, this was compensated for by being a doting aunt to Seamus's twin girls, Shona and Sheena. It could have come as no shock to Seamus's pretty Dutch wife Elise that their two daughters had the same red hair and freckles as their father and aunt. Mhairi smiled. She could just imagine the pair of them, as she could still so vividly picture her first sight of the twins themselves that dismal day in Manchester when they had put out their tongues at her and she had burst into tears.

'We could do out my sitting-room as a bedroom for him,' Fiona murmured, her mind already racing on to when they actually had her father back here.

'We'll do no such thing! He'll have his own sitting-room, and bedroom, thank you very much!' Mhairi said in mock severity. 'Those two guest rooms on the third floor can be converted while you're in the States. And if Rob wants to fill the house with his old Harrovian chums in future, then they can jolly well all crowd into his room!' She rubbed her hands in glee at the sheer pleasure of anticipation. 'Oh, Fi, it'll be so wonderful having him here with us!'

'But he's got to get better first, remember,' her cousin cautioned.

'Well, the quicker you make arrangements to get over there and see to that, the better!'

And that was exactly what Fiona did the next day, while Mhairi was in Harrods mulling over the best present to buy a son who was simply dying for his eighteenth birthday to come so he could go off to war.

Fiona was due to sail for New York on Monday, 5 October, the day of Rob's eighteenth birthday, and so they brought the celebration meal at the Savoy forward specially so she could attend. It was decided Sunday lunch on the 4th would be as good a time as any to toast the young man who was now old enough to take the King's shilling.

The White Room in the Savoy was currently being used as the headquarters of the American Citizens' Committee, dealing with the thousands of Americans who had suddenly found themselves unhappy guests in a Europe at war, and Mhairi was delighted to run into several familiar faces as their small party made its way up to the dining-room.

'You'll probably find most of them on the boat with you tomorrow, Fi dear,' she commented. 'There seems to be still a grand exit from our shores going on at the moment. Silly people – if only they'd hang on a few weeks I'm sure they'll find it'll all have blown over before their ship even docks in New York!'

'I wouldn't be too sure of that, if I were you,' George Cornwallis-West remarked, as the tail-coated waiter led the way to their reserved table. 'This little skirmish, as you seem to regard it, could surprise quite a few before it's all over.'

Rob's eyes were bright as he listened. There was time for him yet.

Over lunch the talk was mainly of Stella Campbell, George's new wife, who was due to leave for New York herself that weekend; she was opening in Shaw's *Pygmalion* over there the following month. George had been given forty-eight hours' leave to see her off and had generously agreed to spend a couple of them celebrating Rob's birthday with him. He cut a fine figure in his Scots Guards officer's uniform, and Mhairi noted philosophically that almost every other male under middle age in the restaurant was also in the uniform of one or other of the armed forces.

As well as the champagne that was ordered to drink the young man's health, George ordered a bottle of his favourite hock, a glass of which he was downing with relish as the *Maître d'hôtel* arrived to offer his own good wishes and enquire if all was satisfactory with the meal. The hotelier's eyebrows rose just a fraction at the German label on the table before them, but diplomatically he made no comment.

Mhairi however noticed the look. 'I wouldn't worry, Mr Reeves-Smith,' she remarked sweetly. 'We know it's German, but dear George is simply interning it!'

George grinned, for even the Kaiser wasn't going to deprive him of his favourite tipple.

When the man had departed he reached into the pocket of his jacket and produced an envelope containing a letter he had received that very day from George Bernard Shaw. He knew Mhairi was a great fan of the Irish playwright. 'You might be interested in this, my dear,' he smiled. 'The old boy has written some copy he suggests we send to the Berlin newspapers about the way British soldiers are behaving over in Belgium, he reckons it will counter-balance the stuff our press is printing about the Hun. Just listen to this . . .'

His grin grew broader as he began to declaim in a sonorous voice: 'We kill the wounded; we poison wells; we toss babies on the points of our bayonets; we burn field hospitals full of German wounded; we chop off Belgian babies' heads in their mothers' arms, having previously put on the helmets of slain Uhlans; we make collections of breasts and eyes; we never venture into battle without driving crowds of women before us; we mock the Kaiser's grief for the death of the thirty-seventh and last of his six sons; our men shoot their officers who surrender with tears of joy to their kind captors; and the Tsar's mother is Sir Edward Grey's mistress!'

Rob's loud guffaw had heads turning at the next table, but Mhairi was not at all amused. 'I know it's meant as a joke,' she said, 'but it's sick all the same. This whole war is sick.'

'Well, if it's sick, then it's up to all of us to make it better isn't it?' Rob declared. 'Personally I feel ashamed of sitting here stuffing myself with good food whilst others are out there defending my freedom.' His eyes were challenging as they met his mother's across the table. 'Don't you?'

Mhairi could not hold his gaze and dropped hers to the fruit salad on the table before her. He had struck a chord that she knew would resound in her head long after this meal was over.

It was with a heavy heart that she kissed George goodbye on the steps of the Savoy as they took their leave of each other. Heaven only knew when they would see him again – or, God forbid, *if* they would see him again.

She looked on with sadness as he held out his right hand to Rob and clasped him on the shoulder with his left. 'Look after yourself, young man,' he said. 'And, who knows, the next time we meet there might be two of us in uniform!'

'I hope so, sir. I really do!'

The remainder of the day passed in a frenzy of last-minute packing, for Mhairi had insisted that Fiona take her largest cabin trunk with her, packed with all manner of goodies she felt might tempt an invalid's palate.

'For heaven's sake, it'll be a stuffed goose I'll be bringing back across the Atlantic with me, not Pa!' her cousin declared. But Mhairi merely smiled, and wished that she was going with her. Suddenly America seemed about the only sane place on this crazy planet. 'Just you look after him, won't you?' she begged for the umpteenth time. 'Make sure he gets better soon so you can bring him back with you to join us here in England.'

Rob went with her to Southampton docks to see the boat set sail for New York the following afternoon. The whole of the seafront area of the Channel city seemed to be full of American citizens cutting short their vacations to return home because of the war.

Dressed in her best two-piece suit and crushed velvet toque hat, Fiona looked quite lost and vulnerable amongst all the waving and shouting passengers who lined the rail to bid their last goodbyes to those left on shore. She had never been a large woman, but middle age had seen both the bloom of youth and its softly rounded contours drop away to leave a certain scrawniness about her features and physique that reminded Mhairi of her Auntie Belle. She had never thought of her aunt over the past years without a great feeling of sadness and of guilt. She knew all too well from her years on stage that if your foot slipped you could recover your balance, but if your tongue slipped you could never recover your words. And oh how she bitterly regretted some of those words that had slipped out that day she left Lancaster House behind forever. But all that was a long time ago now, and Belle Rafferty was long dead, along with so many others she had loved in this life. And, as she shaded her eyes from the autumn sun with her left hand, to get a better view of Fiona away up there at the ship's rail, she reached out and found her son's arm with the other. A fleeting smile was exchanged between them that said more than a thousand words.

They stood on the dockside waving their white hand-kerchiefs until the great Cunard liner was merely a speck in the distance, before they finally turned and made for their waiting car.

With Fiona gone Mhairi felt a great loneliness descend. It was the first time she had been without her cousin in eighteen years. 'We'll miss her,' she said to Rob, and her son put a comforting arm around her shoulders in reply.

Once back in London, they shared a taxi from the station and Mhairi instructed the driver to let them off in the centre of town. Rob had declared himself to have an important errand to attend to and Mhairi had his birthday present to collect from Harrods. She had been unable to take it home with her on her earlier visit for it required engraving with his initials, so she had promised it in time for his birthday tea. There would be just the two of them at home this time, and it was something she greatly looked forward to.

The taxi let them off in Brompton Road and she had said goodbye to Rob and was crossing the street towards Harrods' western corner when the sight of someone on the opposite pavement made her gasp and draw up sharply in the middle of the traffic. Horns sounded impatiently all around her but she could not move. It was HIM! It had to be him!

He was almost exactly opposite her. She would recognize that face anywhere. And he was in uniform. Her heart turned over at the sight of him. It was a Scottish regiment – the Black Watch, most probably, she thought, cursing her ignorance of the tartans of her own land; but the dark green and black checks of the kilt that swung from his hips looked vaguely familiar. He was marching away from her now, in the direction of Harrods' main door, with that same jaunty, almost swaggering gait – just as tall, just as well built. Just Ralph.

'Hey, love, make a move, would you? You're gonna get killed if you stand there much longer!' A policeman had appeared at her elbow, and she suddenly became aware of the cars still sounding their horns as they swerved around her. But still she remained rooted to the spot.

'I'm so sorry! . . . I – I just saw someone!'

'Must have been a bloody ghost by the looks of it!' the officer muttered as he watched her suddenly take off and begin to run in the direction of the disappearing figure in the kilt.

She slowed down as she rounded the corner and held her breath as he too stopped in front of Harrods' door. She saw him glance at his watch, then turn to gaze about him. Automatically she drew back and flattened herself against the wall, almost obscuring herself behind a sailor and his girlfriend who stood gazing at the colourful window display of the last collection of Paris fashions to arrive before the outbreak of hostilities.

In between the two of them she could still make out Ralph's figure, which was half-turned from her. She saw him raise his hand. Then she let out a gasp that was more of a groan as the object of his greeting appeared into view. It was a woman of about her own age; a woman with pertly pretty features and soft blonde hair that was plaited into two thick braids, one round each ear, above which a cheeky little hat with a feather sat, quite unlike the large picture hats she herself still favoured.

'Are you all right, lady?' The young sailor looked at her in some concern, but she was not even aware of the sound she had emitted.

'Yes, yes, I'm fine!' she insisted in some irritation, her eyes still on the two by the door.

He was bending to kiss her and she was laughing into his

face and telling him something. Then, arm in arm, they disappeared in through the main door of the store.

Mhairi felt for all the world as if she had been kicked in the stomach. It was the first time in almost nineteen years she had set eyes on him – and he was with another woman. His wife most probably. But what did she expect? Did she expect him to have lived like a monk for almost the last two decades?

She was trembling from head to foot as the young sailor and his girlfriend eventually moved off and left her leaning against the wall of the shop. Her reaction to what she had just seen had left her both confused and dismayed. Here she was, a mature woman, feeling like a lovesick schoolgirl. She took a deep breath to steady her breathing as she glanced around her. Thankfully, no one was taking the slightest notice of her. But what on earth was she going to do? She had come to collect Rob's birthday present – their son's birthday present! – and HE was in there with another woman.

For several minutes she remained there, uncertain whether to go in and risk running into them, or go on somewhere else and collect Rob's present later. She glanced at her watch and frowned. She didn't really want to put off too much time today of all days. No, she would take her courage in both hands and risk it.

She was sure all eyes were on her as, as nonchalantly as possible, she sauntered up to the main door and walked through. The ostrich feather in her hat caught in the peaked cap of a Merchant Navy officer a step ahead of her and she found herself apologizing profusely as he re-adjusted it and moved on.

The store was full of men in uniform with their wives or girlfriends on their arms, and it was difficult not to feel her own lack of an escort as she made her way up to the luggage department on the second floor.

The tail-coated sales assistant recognized her

immediately. 'Ah, madam, we have your order ready for you!'

She gave a strained smile as she waited by the counter, her eyes darting to all corners of the floor as prospective customers wandered in and out.

'Here we are! One gentleman's leather attaché case, one medium-sized matching leather suitcase, and one matching leather officer's cabin trunk. All with the initials: "R. R. MacL. McL." engraved in brass in the top right-hand corners, and the full name Robert Ralph MacLachlan McLeod embossed on the insides of each item.' The elderly man beamed at her. 'I would hazard a guess with a name like that the gentleman in question must be a Scotsman,' he said, handing her the account slip to sign.

'You would be right,' Mhairi murmured, as she scribbled her signature across the bottom line.

Behind the counter was a large plate-glass mirror which gave a full view of the rest of the department and the top of the stairs leading up from the floor below, and as she handed back the pen her eyes caught sight of that cocked hat perched so cheekily above the blonde hair just appearing into view, as its owner ascended the stairs.

She drew in her breath and stood transfixed as Ralph's dark head in the Black Watch officer's cap appeared just behind. Then they were both in the department, standing looking around them for a moment or two, before the woman said brightly, 'Oh look darling, those are just what we want!'

To her utter horror Mhairi realized she was pointing to Rob's birthday present, which was displayed for all to see on the counter beside her.

She was still standing with her back to the stairs as the woman came hurrying across, with Ralph in her wake. Should she turn and face him? Oh God, should she turn?

'I'm afraid these are already spoken for, madam,' she

heard the assistant address the woman, as she kept her face firmly averted.

'Goodness me, I can see that!' the woman said brightly. 'Just look at those initials!'

Mhairi glanced into the mirror in front of her and felt the blood drain from her face, for he was staring straight at her in the glass as if he too had seen a ghost.

'Your husband must be a true Scot,' the woman was saying to Mhairi, 'to have initials like those!'

Slowly she turned to face them both. 'Actually they're for my son,' she said quietly. 'He was eighteen yesterday.' She looked directly at Ralph as she spoke the words, and for the first time since the night they made love their eyes met and held.

'Your son?' His lips mouthed the words, but no sound came.

Mhairi smiled at the woman. 'And they are rather grand initials, aren't they?' Then her eyes moved to Ralph as she said softly, 'I named him after my grandfather Robert McLeod, but his middle initials are those of his father.'

She then turned with a bright smile to the assistant behind the counter. 'Mr Palmer, have them wrapped immediately, won't you? And arrange to have them sent round to my home straight away. I need them delivered by four at the latest.'

'Certainly, madam. It'll be a pleasure.'

She picked up her gloves from the counter and rewarded the elderly assistant with a charming smile, before bestowing one on the woman in the cheeky hat, and murmuring, 'Good-day to you all.'

Her legs had turned to lead, but she walked as casually as possible in the direction of the stairs. She did not turn to see, but she could feel his eyes on her every step of the way.

When she got home she was still in a state of shock as she took off her coat and handed it to Annie the maid. 'Is

Rob back yet, Annie?' she enquired, as she examined her face in the hallstand mirror.

'Yes, ma'am, young Mr Rob got back about ten minutes ago.'

She hoped he wasn't in the drawing-room as she made her way up to the first floor. All she wanted was to pour herself a stiff drink and to sit down and collect her chaotic thoughts. Ralph's face still swam before her. The years had been kind. His figure and features had filled out and broadened slightly with age, but it had led to a strengthening of his face and body that added a stature and maturity. There was no doubt about it, he had been a good-looking young man, and he was a devastatingly attractive older one who had had that same dizzying effect on her that he had had when they first met all those years ago in New York.

'Ma, is that you back?' Rob's voice met her as she approached the half-open door to the drawing-room.

Her heart sank. 'Yes, darling, it's me.'

He was stretched out on the sofa, one leg slung casually over a wooden arm. He straightened up as she entered the room and gave her one of his most charming smiles. 'You look tired.'

She immediately forced a smile to her lips. 'Do I?' she said lightly, making for the drinks' cabinet. 'It must be the heat. The sun is quite strong today – for October . . . Do you fancy a sherry?'

He raised his eyebrows. 'At this time? Are you sure you're feeling all right?'

'What is this?' she said sharply. 'The Spanish Inquisition? I just happened to feel like a drink, that's all, and I thought it only manners to offer you one.'

'I know! . . . God, I am stupid! I'm sorry to be so insensitive. I should have realized the effect it would have on you.'

Mhairi spun round to face him. 'Whatever do you mean?' She could feel her face begin to flush.

351

'Why, Fi's leaving, of course. What did you think I meant?' He was looking at her curiously now.

'Oh . . . Oh, yes of course . . .' She could feel the relief sweep over her. How stupid she was. How could he possibly have had any idea? He had never even asked about his father.

She poured them both a large sherry and handed Rob his with a smile. 'Let's drink to Fi!' she said brightly. 'Let's drink to a safe crossing and may she bring Uncle Finbar back safely with her before Christmas.' She raised her glass to touch his, then took a long sip of the golden liquid. 'Wouldn't that be wonderful if we could all spend Christmas together?'

Rob took a sip of his own drink but did not return her smile. Instead he looked down into his glass. 'Ma, there's something I have to tell you. It – it's about that errand I was on this afternoon. I didn't tell you where I was going, did I?'

She looked puzzled and shook her head, her mind still on that encounter in Harrods. 'Should you have?'

'I think so,' he began. 'In retrospect it would have been fairer to warn you.'

'Warn me of what?' She looked at him sharply, all thoughts of Ralph banished.

He ignored the question as he took a deep breath and looked her squarely in the eyes. 'When I left you this afternoon it was to go to 59 Buckingham Gate.'

'Buckingham Gate,' she repeated the address. It meant nothing to her. 'That's in the south-west of the city, isn't it? What on earth were you doing there?'

He reached inside his jacket pocket and handed her a buff-coloured sheet of paper. 'I was getting this.'

'What on earth is it?' she asked, taking it from him.

'It's my signing-on form. That address – 59 Buckingham Gate – is the recruiting office for the London Scottish Regiment. I enlisted this afternoon in the First Battalion.'

'Whaaat!' She let the paper drop from her fingers as if it were poison. 'You did *what*?'

'I enlisted . . . I'm sorry, Ma. Really I am.' Then immediately he had said it he corrected himself. 'No, damn it, I'm not sorry. I'm not sorry at all. I'm proud of what I did this afternoon. But I am sorry about the distress I know it will cause you.'

She stared at him, her eyes blurring. He had enlisted. Her son had enlisted in this bloody war. But he was still a boy – a mere boy. She shook her head as if to negate what she had just heard, as the tears spilled from her eyes to run freely down her cheeks.

He stood looking at her as she slipped to her knees on the carpet in front of him. She was sobbing now, great noisy sobs that seemed to rack her whole body. He had never seen her like this before.

'Please, Ma . . . Please, don't . . .' His own eyes were glistening now as he knelt down beside her and cradled her head on his chest. 'Please don't cry. I don't want you to cry. I want you to be proud of me . . . Be proud of me, Ma, please . . .'

Chapter Twenty-One

The news from America was not good as Mhairi had hoped; Finbar was suffering from an illness that sounded worryingly like TB, although the term was never used. He was being cared for at home with the help of a paid nurse, with Fiona in attendance to see to his other needs and keep his spirits up. She wrote Mhairi long letters from New York, telling her of how the invalid was progressing and of the changes that had taken place in their old hometown since the mid-1890s.

'I feel like a tourist,' Fiona wrote in late November, 'for now I have got over the journey and have settled in, when I am not keeping Pa company I am doing all those things I used to dream of back in England: I spoil myself by indulging in new hats and gloves and all manner of pretty but useless items from the likes of Wanamaker's, Macy's, and Lord and Taylor's, and the other day I went to a public rehearsal of the New York Symphony Concert at the Carnegie Hall. Oh, Mhairi, how you would have loved it! But how you would have loved even more to have been with me when I took a taxicab the length of Fifth Avenue to our old haunts around Washington Square. My, how things have changed! It seems the developers are everywhere, tearing down and putting up buildings at the speed of light, as if they feel they must rush headlong into the future with no thought of what might have been valuable in the past. Thankfully for Pa, Amity Place has not changed much and Lancaster House is still there, but the Ashtons have sold up and retired to Lowell. And can you guess who has bought it? Your old friend Kati van der Donck and her husband! She came to the door when she saw me standing on the pavement outside. Her husband is something on Wall Street — I forget his name. She was looking well, though much plumper. She says the house suits them admirably being so near her old family home where I believe her mother still lives with her brother Andy and his wife. She seemed pleased to see me and sent her regards . . .' Mhairi read, then reread the last sentence several times, and was surprised at how much it meant to her.

But then her spirits, which had lifted so much in the first part of the letter, sank as she read on, for what Fiona had to say there confirmed the doubts that were already forming in her own mind about her plans for the festive season which was now less than a month away. In Fiona's neat script she read: 'Unfortunately, they tell us there can be no question of us making it back to Britain in time for Christmas, for it would be too dangerous to move Pa in the middle of such a severe winter as this. But the doctor says come spring he should be well enough to undertake the sea crossing to England. I can hardly wait to get back to London, war or no war . . .'

So that was that. They would not be home for Christmas, and she would be destined to spend it alone. The chance of Rob getting leave so soon after enlisting was virtually non-existent.

She knew she had upset him greatly by breaking down as she had done when he returned with the news of his enlistment on the day of his eighteenth birthday, and she had resolved to remain strong when the day came one week later of his actual departure for Officer Training School. But she had wept all the same. He looked so young. He *was* so young. Too young — far too young — to be setting off to be trained to lead men often old enough to be his father to fight to the death . . .

His father . . . Oh how she had tried to put that chance encounter with Ralph in Harrods behind her, but it had remained with her. Not a single day or night had passed since then but she had not thought about him – had not wondered who the fair-haired woman in the cheeky hat was, and envied her with all her heart.

But he had been in uniform too. And was he too now over there somewhere in France like his son? It was a chilling thought that the two men she had loved most in this life were both at war, and not a minute of the day or night passed but their lives were at risk.

She had met Jennie Churchill in Fortnum and Mason during Christmas week and the American had been full of news of the war work her titled friends were now indulging in. Along with the list of friends and acquaintances whose names she had chronicled, she had mentioned that Millie Sutherland was now over in France working as a nurse at the Western Front. The news had had a peculiarly depressing effect on Mhairi. What on earth was she doing hanging around in London when she could be over there too doing her bit? Then reality crept in. She knew only too well why she was still here. She had a contract to fulfil. But the first thing she would do after Christmas would be to get those two shows over with as soon as possible, then perhaps she could look herself in the face in the mirror again.

And so Christmas 1914 came and went. On Christmas Eve a German aeroplane dropped a bomb on Dover and on Christmas Day itself another German plane had flown over Sheerness, but that was as near as the war came to her personally. Friends who had been on the south coast over the holiday told her they could hear the muffled sounds of the guns from across the Channel, if the wind was in the right direction. Yet still the fighting in the trenches went on. The first Christmas of the war which everyone said would be 'over by Christmas' had been and gone, and there was no sign of an end to it. One year had ended and another begun. She was not sad to see the back of the old. It had brought nothing but heartache to so many.

In the capital precautions were being taken against a possible aerial attack, and the lake in St James's Park had been drained to make it less recognizable to a German pilot. And although the newspapers attempted to keep up the country's morale with news of British successes on the war front, Mhairi knew it was not the whole story. Barely a week went by but she heard of someone's husband, son or brother being killed, and the casualty lists in *The Times* grew longer with each passing day. She could not bear to read them any longer after seeing the names of two of Rob's classmates at Harrow listed among the dead.

There was so much about this war that she found hard to cope with, particularly the reaction of some of her own sex who had taken to parading the streets handing out white feathers as marks of cowardice to those young men they happened upon who were not in uniform. Everywhere she looked there were posters depicting women waving to their khaki-clad men, under the caption: 'Women of Britain say "GO"!' Could there really be such mothers and wives, she wondered, who were actually keen to see their loved ones march off like lambs to the slaughter? And her own thoughts would turn once more to Rob, for there was never a moment in the day when she did not think of him.

But true to her promise to herself, just after Christmas she got in touch with George Edwardes' office and told them she was ready to return to work. And at the end of January she began rehearsals for *Tonight's the Night*, a new musical comedy at the Gaiety Theatre, which was due to reopen for business at the end of April. The news that the much-loved theatre was finally to open again she knew would do much to cheer up George, although her old boss was failing more with each passing day. She tried never to let more than a couple of weeks pass without paying him a visit, but now that he was living in Bournemouth it was not quite so convenient to pop round when the fancy took her.

She threw herself wholeheartedly into the production, however, after vetoing several of the songs suggested in the first run-through. Other stars of the London stage were not so scrupulous, however, and there were those such as Marie Lloyd who were making great capital and much money out of the patriotic fervour that was rife in the country. Some theatre managers were even stooping so low as to give out free front-row tickets to the matrons of convalescent homes for the wounded, so they could bring them along to be exhorted to get back to the Front as soon as possible. In fact, Annie, her maid, had told her of just such a night at the Chiswick Empire recently when they had even carried all the wounded on to the stage, to have a curtain rise behind them to reveal a spectacular reconstruction of a blazing Rheims Cathedral, with real flames spurting from a trapdoor on the stage, as, all round the wounded, strutted the saluting figure of Hetty King singing:

'We don't want to lose you but we think you ought to go,
For your King and your country both need you so.
We shall want you and miss you,
But with all our might and main,
We shall cheer you, thank you, kiss you,
When you come back again . . .'

But she had heard one quite different song recently that she knew they would never be singing on any music hall stage: it told the truth and was far more popular with the troops:

If you want the old battalion,
I know where they are, I know where they are,
If you want the old battalion,
I know where they are,
They're hanging on the old barbed wire.
I've seen 'em, I've seen 'em,
Hanging on the old barbed wire . . .

That song seemed to epitomize for her the real story about what was going on over there in the mud of Flanders; it symbolized the real war that the newspapers did not inform you of. And as such songs filtered back, and the injured were returned to their home shores, slowly but surely she became more and more convinced that this slaughter must end soon, or a whole generation of young men would surely perish.

But as winter turned to spring and the leaves of the plane trees around Bedford Square came into bud, her heart lifted, for, if there was no chance of seeing her beloved Rob in the near future, at least, she knew she would be seeing Fiona and her Uncle Finbar soon. They had decided to wait till after Easter, and sail for England at the beginning of May. Mhairi had made sure before Fiona left that she had enough money to pay for two first-class tickets on one of the great Cunard ocean liners, so Finbar could enjoy the luxury of crossing the Atlantic in far greater style than he had experienced going the other way.

They were due to set sail from New York on Saturday, 1 May, and it seemed a particularly good omen that she received a letter from Rob that very day from France. Knowing he was in good heart and still in one piece, and that she would be seeing Fiona and Finbar again in just over a week's time made her throw herself into her performances at the theatre with even more vigour. She even found there was a certain satisfaction at being back on the stage and performing to so many men in uniform. She knew most were on leave, before heading back to the Front, and it meant something to all the cast to make their last hours at home that bit special, and so a little bit of extra zest was added to the performances to make every night as memorable as possible.

As for Fiona and her father three thousand miles away in New York, the approach of that weekend was just as exciting. Never one for bothering much about his appearance, Finbar had even agreed to purchasing two brand new sets of clothes, and he was proudly attired in his 'going-away' outfit when Shona, Seamus and family came round to the apartment for dinner the night before they were due to sail.

'Well, who's a swell and no mistake!' Seamus declared at the sight of his father sitting proudly in his favourite armchair, his high collar as white and crisp as anyone had ever seen it, his necktie immaculately knotted just below his Adam's apple. 'Why, anyone would think you were headed somewhere special in that get-up!'

'I am!' his father replied, his eyes shining. 'I'm going home!'

Over the meal that followed there was much reminiscing about the voyage out almost thirty years previously, and recollections of their previous life in the Old Country. It was easy for Finbar and Fiona to remember England, but for Seamus and Shona Manchester was now little more than a dim and distant memory of grey skies and hours spent sitting on the front step of the Ancoats house listening to their cousin Mhairi tell them stories of her Isle of Skye.

'Yes, it'll be grand to see Mhairi again,' Finbar said, raising his sherry glass in a half-salute at the thought of his niece. 'And, who knows, I might even look up what's left of the Rafferty clan while I'm over there!'

Fiona and the twins exchanged looks, then Shona

reached and squeezed her father's hand. 'You do that, Pa. I'm sure they'll be delighted to see their long-lost relation – especially now he's a rich American!'

Finbar looked startled. He, like the others, was only too aware of the prospective boatloads of penniless Irish immigrants desperately seeking an American relative to latch on to. 'Aye, well maybe I'll wait a wee while before taking the train up to Manchester,' he mused. 'After all, they've got on fine without me for the past thirty years!'

It was the first time they had all been together as a family since their mother's funeral and there was so much catching up of news to do that it was after eleven o'clock before they could bring themselves to call it a night.

The moon was high in the sky, and there was a gentle breeze blowing from the direction of the river as they congregated on the sidewalk to say their last goodbyes. Across the way in Central Park several of the trees were already heavy with blossom, and the night air was resonant with the scents of springtime, as Seamus and his wife carried their sleeping daughters into the cab for the journey home.

Then, after the last round of hugs and kisses at the front door of the apartment block, Shona warned her father, 'See you don't miss that boat tomorrow now – for we'll all be there cheering like mad to see the back of you!'

Finbar grinned. 'Away home with the lot o' you – you've deprived a man of his sleep long enough!' But his heart glowed with love for his family. It had been a better tonic than any doctor could have prescribed to have them all around him like this.

First-class passengers were not due on board until ten o'clock the following morning, so it did not mean too much of an early rise, and, as promised, they were all there once more to see them off at Cunard pier 54.

'We sure wish we were all coming with you,' Shona said wistfully, as she kissed her father, then hugged her sister at the foot of the gangplank. Never one for being able to disguise her emotions, her eyes were wet as she brushed an imaginary speck of lint from the arm of Finbar's new jacket for the last time. 'And remember now to give Mhairi all our best wishes. Tell her it's high time she brought one of her shows over here!'

And so, after a final hug to his grandchildren, on the arm of his eldest daughter, Finbar turned to join the queue of passengers already boarding the ship.

His heart sang as he made his way up the main gangplank of the great ocean liner, with his first-class ticket clasped in his hand. This time he would be travelling alongside the likes of the Vanderbilts, the Astors, and all the other millionaires who took such luxury for granted. It was an amazing thought for a man who had never had two brass farthings to rub together for most of his working life.

He had to lean heavily on Fiona's arm for support, but his eyes took everything in. Above him the four enormous red and black funnels seemed to fill the blue sky. This was a ship to rival any in the world and no mistake. It ran to almost eight hundred feet from stem to stern, had nine decks, and her bridge was as high as Lancaster House – higher even, he decided, for by the looks of it it would run to a good six-storey building.

They told the family not to wait, for both Seamus and Shona had had to ask for time off work to accompany them to the docks. They would probably never have seen them from the ship anyway, Fiona commented consolingly to her father, for the quayside was still packed full of people waiting to see the great liner leave at the scheduled time of 12.30 P.M.

Three nerve-shattering blasts of the ship's foghorn marked the moment and had children screaming, and the passengers lining the rail clapping their hands over their ears at the almighty din. Fiona was convinced her eardrums had burst as she looked over the side to see that all those standing on the dockside were forced to do likewise.

She glanced at her father and his eyes were aglow with excitement as he watched the dockworkers on shore heaving at the massive ropes attached to the gangplanks, which inch by inch were being drawn back. Then the hawsers were cast off to come snaking up the ship's side.

The ship's orchestra was playing 'It's A Long Way To Tipperary' and the jaunty rhythm vibrated in the heads of all those on deck, as the small flotilla of tug boats eased the great ship out into the Hudson, to slowly swing her round in the direction of the Atlantic Ocean and England. Then the mighty engines took over and they too roared their goodbyes to New York.

'We're on our way, Pa,' Fiona said excitedly, as she clasped his arm that bit tighter. 'We're going home.'

As the grey waters of the Hudson were whipped to a white foam by the powerful propellers and the great ship headed out to sea, Finbar was content to rest quietly in his cabin while his daughter went back on deck to watch them glide through the lower bay and make their way down to Sandy Hook, where they dropped the pilot and were really on their way. And there were tears in her eyes as she watched the Statue of Liberty lift her torch in silent salute in the distance to those departing once more from the peace and security of the New World to the trouble and uncertain future of the Old.

> 'Give me your tired, your poor,
> Your huddled masses, yearning to breathe free,
> The wretched refuse of your teeming shore,
> Send these, the homeless, tempest-tossed to me:
> I lift my lamp beside the golden door.'

She repeated the last lines of words she knew to be written

there on that great symbol of her adopted country, and tears came to her eyes. Her family had been just such people once, who along with millions of others had made this crossing from the Old World to the New, in search of that possibility – the opportunity to breathe free.

And in their own way, they had found it. And she thanked God that her young brother, Seamus, was now an American citizen and could return today to his place of work, to bring his family up in peace and security, and not have to face the slaughter of the trenches as so many family men back in Europe were doing on this lovely spring day.

The first seven days of the voyage proved to be some of the happiest in the lives of both father and daughter. A plentiful supply of good food, plenty of rest, and bracing sea air combined to make it a voyage to remember, and Fiona even took to writing a daily report in a child's hardbacked jotter she bought in one of the ship's shops, for Mhairi to read when they got back.

There were so many exciting things to remember: dining at the Captain's table, passing the time of day on deck with such people as Alfred Gwynne Vanderbilt, the millionaire, and Charles Frohman, the famous theatrical impresario, who told her that he had it in mind to talk to George Edwardes, while in England, with a mind to signing up Mhairi for an American tour . . . Yes, she wanted to share every moment with her cousin; after all she was the one responsible for them being fortunate enough to make the journey in the first place.

By the afternoon of Friday, 7 May, they were informed they were now off the south-west coast of Ireland, and after lunch Finbar left Fiona writing up her report in her cabin as he came up on to the boat deck to see if he could catch a glimpse of his old homeland. They were about ten miles off County Cork, and to his delight the Old Head of Kinsale was just visible in the distance.

'Ireland . . .' He whispered the word aloud into the wind as tears sprang to his eyes, as they peered into the distance at the low green hills. Sure and it was still God's own country to him, and to every Irishman, no matter how long it was since they had left its shores.

His eyes were still on Kinsale when the first explosion occurred.

'What in the name . . . !'

It threw him backwards into the arms of a passing steward and sounded like a heavy door banging somewhere in the vicinity. 'In the name o' the wee man!'

Then another blast followed almost immediately, and this time the whole deck seemed to rise up to meet them.

'Jesus, I think we've been hit!' The white-coated young man into whose arms he had fallen, deposited him on the deck as he ran off towards the starboard side of the bridge, where the noise appeared to have come from.

As he did so a huge plume of water, smoke and flame soared into the air from just beyond the bridge. Then, as Finbar lay helpless on the deck, the flaming debris appeared to hang in the heavens for a moment, then began to slowly float down to settle all around him. And as he lay there it continued to fall like some strange celestial rain, the water soaking his hair and clothes, and the splinters of glass and flaming pieces of wood landing on top of him and on the surrounding deck.

The whole vessel shuddered, then began to list to the starboard side. For a few seconds there had been an uncanny silence, then all around him people began shouting, and running. Some were screaming. There were cries of, 'Torpedo!' and 'It's the bloody Gerries!'

He tried to pull himself to his feet, but the ship was listing too badly to get a grip. Like himself, the deck was now covered in a mixture of soaking wet soot, splinters of glass, and burning pieces of debris.

Passengers just as dazed and bewildered as he was were

pouring on to the filthy boards beside him. Smoke and steam were spewing from the ventilators around the ship's two central funnels and swirling around the boat deck like some hellish fog.

His weakened lungs rebelled and he began to cough and gasp for breath, then out of the murk the young steward appeared into whose arms he had fallen when the first explosion occurred. The young man took one look at Finbar still lying helpless on the deck and bent down to hook one arm around his waist. 'You stay with me, Dad,' he told him. 'You'll be OK.'

Finbar's eyes were wide with fear. Where was he taking him? He could not go anywhere without first finding Fiona. 'But my daughter,' he gasped. The words came with difficulty from his choking lungs. 'My daughter's still in her cabin.'

'Don't you worry about her. She'll be OK.' He had short sandy-coloured hair and a Liverpudlian accent. 'The bloody Gerries have knocked a ruddy great hole in our bows. It's you old 'uns and the kids we've got to worry about now − the rest of them can take care of themselves.'

About twenty feet from where they were standing, two deckhands and a couple of passengers were attempting to lower a lifeboat. It was already full, but the young man beside him began to pull him up off the deck, where he had slipped back down. 'Come on, Dad, for Christ's sake, make a move!'

Half-stumbling, half-running, he was propelled along by a much younger and stronger body, which seemed to impart some of its own strength into his own. 'Gi's a hand here!' the young man yelled up at one of the deckhands. 'Get the old boy aboard!'

And so Finbar found himself hauled on board, to land awkwardly between the hobble-skirted legs of a young woman who sat, white-faced, clutching a baby. 'My husband's still in the dining-room,' she cried, to no one in particular. 'Please someone get him!'

Finbar struggled to squeeze himself on to the wooden bench nearest him and he turned to thank the young Liverpool lad, but he had already disappeared back into the crowd milling around in the fog on the deck.

Then everyone screamed as the ship's timbers gave an ominous creak and the whole deck lurched forwards, tipping the passengers on top of one another, as the bow sank further into the grey waters. Shrieking passengers scrambled frantically in the direction of the stern, their feet and hands slipping on the soaking filth covering the deck beneath them.

The sudden movement had wrenched their own small craft out of the hands of the men at the davit and all aboard shrieked as the twin supporting ropes began to race through the block and the lifeboat hit the water at an angle that sent everyone flying to one side.

The waves crashed over them, soaking the young mother with the baby and washing a small child overboard. They all watched helplessly from their tangle of bodies, as the infant was swept up on the crest of one wave to disappear beneath another.

Horrified, Finbar waited for the cry of anguish from one of the women in the boat, as he attempted to right himself, but its mother was not aboard, and the few women who were clung all the tighter to their own bewildered offspring. Many had blood oozing from cuts and grazes that had occurred as they were thrown to one side, but no one appeared aware of their injuries as they clung, numbed with horror, to their rescue craft.

'Dear God, save us . . .'

Above them the sun broke through from behind a cloud as their small boat bobbed around in the water. 'Holy Mary, full of grace . . .' All around them prayers were being said, but no one quite knew what to do as they stared helplessly at the side of the ship towering above them.

It was now listing at a forty-five-degree angle, the bows completely submerged and the water lapping as far up as midships. Frantic passengers were clinging to the rails, their screams echoing in the ears of all those already fortunate enough to have got into one of the lifeboats. By now there were at least three other boats bobbing in the water alongside them. Like their own, all were full to overloaded, but in desperation people were still throwing themselves from the rail of the ship into the water in the hope of being hauled aboard one of them.

Heads and thrashing arms were all around them, and hands that reached desperately for the sides of the small boats that meant life were pushed away by the terrified occupants within. 'Any more and we're all a'goner!' someone shouted, but still the imploring fingers reached out.

As the ship's bows sank deeper into the water, people were clinging like flies to the listing stern deck. Above their screams could be heard the creaking of timbers and crashing of machinery from inside the stricken ship, while above them fire and water was still spewing into the afternoon sky and showering down on them in a deadly rain.

The young and more able were attempting to clamber over the rail to take their chance in the water. A young woman attempted to slither down the log line, and others watched in horror as after a few yards the wire rope ripped the flesh from her hands and she plummeted downwards to disappear beneath the stern of one of the lifeboats.

Finbar's eyes searched the faces of those hanging over the rail, peering down at them from the sinking ship. Eyes wide with terror stared back at him and hands reached out imploringly, to God or himself he could not be sure. He even recognized a few from the first-class cabins. Little had they dreamt what their hundreds of dollars would buy. But there was no Fiona. 'Please let her appear. Please God, make Fiona appear . . .'

Then, just as he was giving up hope, he caught sight of her in the crowd pushing and shoving above them. Her greying hair was dishevelled and her eyes were staring blankly ahead.

'Fiona . . . ! Fiona . . . !' His voice was hoarse and totally inaudible amid the cacophony of screams and shouts all around him. He could hardly see her now for tears were streaming down his face as he attempted to stand up in the boat. 'It's my daughter! My daughter's up there!'

'Sit down, you old fool!' Frantic hands clutched at him and dragged him back down on to the wooden board as the lifeboat lurched frighteningly to one side. 'Bloody idiot! You'll have us over!'

Whether it was the yells of the other passengers as he attempted to stand up, or the struggling bodies as they hauled him back into his place, he never knew, but something made her look down at that moment. 'Pa! Oh, Pa . . . !'

For a few seconds their eyes met, then he saw her struggle forwards to get to the rail. She was almost directly above them as their small boat bobbed some thirty feet below the listing metal bar to which she clung. Then something came sailing down through the air to land almost in his lap. A small boy made to grab at it, but he snatched it out of the child's reaching hands. 'It's mine!' he cried. 'It's from my daughter!'

It was her precious notebook, with her record of the trip, and neatly inscribed in her neat script on the front cover was the name: 'S.S. LUSITANIA'.

Chapter Twenty-Two

Mhairi gazed down at the water-stained notebook in her hands and slowly flicked through the pages. Most of those written in ink were now unreadable, but on the ones where Fiona had written up the day's events in pencil she could still make out the joyous comments they contained.

She closed the book and held it to her breast, shaking her head. 'I can't bear to read it. Maybe later – when I've got used to her not being here. But not now.'

She still could not bring herself to use the word 'dead' or 'death', for it was impossible to believe she would never see her cousin again. But it was true all the same; Fiona, who had been closer to her than a sister, was gone never to return.

Finbar nodded his head in understanding. It was hard enough for him to come to terms with it, and he had been there.

The death toll from the *Lusitania* had been 1,198 out of a total of 1,957 on board. The whole country was stunned, and the United States even more so. There was even talk of America entering the war against Germany, so incensed was feeling over there over the torpedoing of the great ocean liner.

Mhairi opened her desk drawer and tenderly laid the notebook inside. She was touched beyond measure that her uncle should have given it to her.

'She wanted you to have it,' he said quietly, as if reading her thoughts. 'It was only written for you, you know . . .

That week on board ship, I do believe it was the happiest in either of our lives.'

Mhairi came over to his armchair and knelt down beside it, taking one of his hands in hers as she shook her head. She gazed up at him. He looked tired and drawn, but that was understandable after all he had been through. In fact it was a miracle he had survived.

She reached up and gently touched his cheek as she thought of the young red-headed man who had stood so perplexed on Manchester station all those years ago as a small child had vigorously denied any knowledge of him. What little hair he had left now was the colour of old pewter and was confined to a few whiskery tufts in the region of his ears and round the back of his head. His bald pate was bright red from the hour or so adrift in the lifeboat under the afternoon sun, and ever since he had arrived in her home this afternoon his face had worn a look of such indescribable sadness that she knew no words of comfort could make good their loss.

'I wish it had been me,' she said quietly, meaning every word. 'I have had so much more out of life than poor Fi — why couldn't it have been me?'

'None of us have the luxury of choosing our fate, lass. That's in God's hands.'

She rose wearily and looked out of the window to where the pale evening sun was highlighting the white lilac blossom on the bush in the front garden. She had been arranging a vase of it in the hall to welcome them both home when she had heard the news. 'Perhaps you're right,' she sighed. 'Perhaps we're all of us in the hands of the Almighty — or Fate — whatever you want to call the unseen hand that shapes our destinies.'

'I hope they don't find the body,' Finbar said suddenly, and Mhairi was taken aback by the strength of the conviction in his voice. 'I pray to God they don't find it.'

371

She looked round at him in astonishment. 'Why on earth not?'

'Because she would want it that way, that's why,' he replied. 'She will rest easier knowing she's with her Bobby.'

And Mhairi knew it was true. Little Bobby lay buried in those cold grey Atlantic waters, and there was no resting place Fiona would rather have had than to be with her son. 'I hope they don't find her too,' she said softly.

They never did, and although bodies were fished from the waters around the Irish coast for some time to come, they never found Fiona, and the knowledge brought a curious comfort to her family. None of them had any doubt that was how she would have wanted it.

About two weeks later they got letters from Shona and Elise, Seamus's wife, in New York, telling them that memorial services for those who had perished on the ship had been held in Manhattan's Cathedral of St John the Divine, which they had all attended.

And as Mhairi read the letters aloud to Finbar over the breakfast table he had nodded and given a tired smile. 'I'm glad they have had the chance to say their goodbyes in God's house too,' he said quietly, thinking back to that happy group who had hugged and kissed at the dockside just a few short weeks before. 'It's just as well we can't see what's ahead of us, isn't it, Mhairi love, or we'd never get out of bed in the morning!'

She had given a wry smile as she poured them both another cup of tea. How many times could she have said those words herself in the past?

After the initial shock of the sinking wore off, Finbar settled in well into his quarters on the third floor. He very soon became a firm favourite of Mrs Chambers, the cook, and of Annie, the maid, who were kept entertained for hours as he sat in the kitchen drinking tea and telling tales of life in New York that bore little resemblance to any of

Mhairi's own memories of the city, but she would never have dreamt of saying so.

He even came to see her shows occasionally and was given the best box in the house, next to the King's. But the link between royalty and the Gaiety had never been the same since King Edward died; his son George had neither the same eye for the ladies, nor the love of the good life that had characterized those golden years now gone that they were already calling 'The Edwardian Era'.

And as the summer wore on and the news from the trenches got no better, names like Arras and Ypres became as familiar as Harlow or Southend. Almost everyone you met had a loved one over there, and knew of someone who had either been killed or wounded. It seemed as if the war had taken all the colour out of life. No one wore evening-dresses to the theatre any more, and night or day no more gay hues were seen in the ladies' dresses. All wore sombre clothes; it would have seemed an insult to the untold thousands who had died to do otherwise.

It was not until the first week of October that the postcard arrived that brightened up life the moment she read the familiar scrawl. Rob was coming home on a forty-eight-hour pass, before heading back for France. It would be the first time she had seen him since Fiona's death.

Her excitement was short-lived, however, for some other news was waiting for her when she arrived at the theatre that night: George Edwardes, her producer and dear friend for so many years, had finally passed away. He was buried at Kensal Green Cemetery on 4 October, and she attended the ceremony on the arm of her uniformed son.

Rob had arrived early that morning as she was finishing breakfast with Finbar. 'It's Mr Rob, ma'm!' Annie had shouted excitedly from the hall, and Mhairi had turned to see the tall kilted figure, with the glengarry bonnet, already in the room.

'Hello, Ma.' He stood there looking across at her, his kitbag at his feet. He was the same height, the same build, and the same grey eyes were smiling back into hers, but he was no longer the same young man she had seen off to Officer Training School that cold autumn day, late last year. In fact, he was no longer a young man. It was a young man with an old man's face who looked back at her.

She had rushed to his arms and his cheek had felt rough against her own. 'Oh Rob, Rob . . .' No words could express her feelings. She took his hand and led him across to where Finbar was sitting.

The older man rose from his seat at the table and bowed his head, almost deferentially, to the much younger one. 'It's right pleased I am to meet you at last, son.'

Rob gazed down at the great-uncle he had never met, yet had heard so much about. 'The pleasure's all mine, I can assure you, Uncle Finbar.'

Another place was laid and Mrs Chambers, the cook, set about frying two new rashers of bacon and a couple of eggs in the pan. These Rob devoured with relish as he sipped his tea and listened to what his mother and uncle had to say about life in London over the long, hot summer that had just gone.

Then, as he sat back and lit a cigarette over his last cup of tea, they could avoid the subject no longer: 'It must have been terrible for you reading about Fi's death in a letter like that,' Mhairi said quietly, and her eyes dropped to her own cup of tea on the table before her, for she could not bear to see the hurt she knew would have come into his eyes.

There was a long silence, then he said quietly, 'I'd rather not talk about Fi, if you don't mind, Ma.' So many of those close to him had been killed tragically this past year that to risk crying for his aunt would be to open the flood gates for so many other such pointless deaths brought about by this bloody war.

He stared into space as the smoke from his cigarette rose lazily towards the ceiling. They knew almost nothing of his life this past year. He had been in France for almost six months – the longest six months of his life – yet his family knew nothing of what had happened to him over there, other than the odd postcard or letter which did not mean a damned thing once the censor had got his pencil out.

Yet neither could he tell them. How could you describe to someone how it felt to watch your best friends die? To be there as a young man's head is blown off just a few yards in front of you, or to see another lose his legs in that same attack? And so the gory list went on. And they were all his friends – closer often than brothers, for you could not eat, sleep, and wake with the same bunch of men for as long as he had, and look death in the face every single day of your life, without becoming as close as it was possible to get to other human beings.

Ypres – or Wipers as his men had called it – the name of that place was engraved on his soul. Then, in the quietness, his lips took on a bitter twist as he began to hum:

> The bells of hell go ting-a-ling-a-ling
> For you but not for me,
> The angels they sing ting-a-ling-a-ling
> They hold the gates for me.
> O death, where is thy sting-a-ling-a-ling
> O grave, thy victory?
> The bells of hell go ting-a-ling-a-ling
> For you but not for me . . .

'I hope you're not singing any of those bloody, nauseating enlisting songs in your show?' he suddenly asked, with vehemence. It was the first time he had sworn to his mother.

Mhairi shook her head emphatically. 'Oh no, Rob. I couldn't!'

'Thank the Lord for that.'

A silence fell once more and Finbar lit his pipe. He puffed the tobacco thoughtfully into life, then said quietly, 'Don't think we don't know, son. We do, you know. You just have to look at those lists in *The Times* every morning to know it ain't quite the picture the big wigs are painting over there.'

Rob nodded, but said nothing. He reached inside his tunic and took out a cigarette case, which he opened and extracted a cigarette from. It was made of silver, beautifully engraved with a design she could not quite make out, and it had the initials 'R. MacL.' engraved in the centre. Mhairi looked at it curiously, then at her son as he struck a match and inhaled the smoke deep into his lungs. He had not even smoked before he joined up. 'That's a lovely case,' she commented. Had a girlfriend bought it for him?

Rob glanced down at it before returning it to his pocket. 'Yes, yes, it is, isn't it. It was given to me in France . . .' His eyes took on a distant look as he drew deeply on the cigarette once more and let the smoke out in a slow thin stream.

Mhairi sat looking at him across the table. There were so many questions she longed to ask, but now was not the time. She could see by the look in his eyes he was already far from the homely comforts of the breakfast room; he was in another time and another place altogether.

Rob blinked his eyes through the smoke. He could see it still – that crucifix silhouetted against the night sky, with its lifesize figure of Christ, hanging there in agony for the sins of his fellow men. It was 9 March 1915, and he was in the little roadside village of Neuve Chapelle. It wasn't much of a place really: apart from the church with its crucifix, there was a brewery and a few houses, that was about it. Behind the village the ground rose slowly towards the hamlet of Aubers, and about nine miles beyond that was the great city of Lille. The object, they were told, was to get to the high ground at Aubers Ridge and from there to take command of the approach road to Lille itself.

It was bitterly cold and snowing that night before the attack. The trenches were knee-deep in freezing water, and as they waited for the zero hour of 7 A.M., each second seemed an hour, each minute an eternity.

Then the first faint streaks of dawn appeared in the night sky; there was a half-light in the east, and as the greyness grew to suffuse the surrounding countryside with its eerie glow, a deathly silence seemed to enfold the world and he had felt the first tremor of real fear through his body. It was a sensation he remembered from the few days he had spent at the Front just before Christmas. But then, he had not been personally involved in the hand-to-hand fighting. This time it was for real.

Officers buttoned their tunics and loaded their revolvers. 'Fix bayonets!' he commanded his men. There was the cold sound of metal on metal and six hundred blades glinted in the pale morning sun. What followed still brought him out in the cold sweat of fear only those who had gone through it can know.

He had been surrounded by Scottish regiments that day and one of his most vivid memories was of saving the life of a major and a handful of NCOs by killing his first German. By shooting his first German in the back. And he still felt sick at the thought.

He could see it yet, that ploughed field immediately in front of him, with the only visible cover a group of buildings surmounted by a tall redbrick chimney known as the *Moulin du Piètre*. It took him and his men a suicidal advance through a hail of bullets to take it. But once inside, to their astonishment they were not the first. A handful of Black Watch had got there before him. They could just make out the small group in their dark green and black kilts in the chamber beyond. From the looks of it they were tending to one of their number who had been hit in the neck.

The outer chamber where they now stood had obviously been used by their own men in the recent past, for tangles of equipment hung from nails in the walls: helmets, haversacks, revolver cases and water-bottles. A steel helmet and a couple of Mills bombs lay in one corner next to a half-flattened petrol can.

At first he did not see the Gerry, for the man was hidden in the shadows about twenty feet in front of them, in the narrow passage that divided the two chambers. His back was to them and his attention totally on the small group within. In his hand was a grenade aimed at the men tending their wounded comrade.

His own arm went out to halt the advance of his men as he drew his revolver. There was no question but he had to fire. He could remember nothing of the bullet finding its target, for almost simultaneously the grenade fell to the ground at the man's feet and was detonated. It blew its owner to pieces and knocked holes in the surrounding brickwork. It showered them all with debris. Then, as the air cleared, and they coughed and blinked their eyes free of the red dust, they could make out the figures of the other Scotsmen, beyond the debris, staring at them in a mixture of shock and panic.

'Thank Christ you're ours!' the major said, relief written all over his face at the sight of their kilted figures. 'The bastard almost had us there.'

The German's tin helmet was embedded in the masonry above their heads and pieces of the man's body were strewn around them. A piece of bloodied hair was stuck to the sole of Rob's shoe as he walked over what was left of his enemy to shake the other officer's hand.

The major pumped the younger man's hand with some feeling. 'Well done, Lieutenant. I'll see you get a mention for this.' He took a cigarette case from his tunic pocket and handed Rob a Goldflake, before taking one for himself.

Both had been shaken by the experience, and Rob drew deeply on the cigarette as his eyes scanned the room. A wooden bench ran round the side of one wall. Beneath it lay the remains of an arm with a hand attached, and on the hand was a wedding ring. Suddenly he felt violently sick.

When he returned the major was looking at him in a most peculiar way, and he immediately felt ashamed. True soldiers did not vomit at the sight of death; they took the killing of their first enemy in their stride. 'I'm sorry, sir,' he began. Should he explain it was his first day at the Front? But the older man was shaking his head. While he had been vomiting his guts out in another corner of the mill, the Black Watch major had asked one of the young lieutenant's men his officer's name.

'Your name – it's Lieutenant Robert McLeod, I believe?' he now said, in a curiously hoarse voice.

Rob nodded.

'You wouldn't by any chance be related to Mhairi Cloud, the actress?'

Rob's brows knitted. 'Why, yes, she's my . . .' No, why the hell should he lie at a time like this? 'She's my mother.'

Then to his astonishment, the major gripped him by the shoulders, and his eyes had a strange intensity to them as he said, 'Remember me to your mother next time you see her, won't you, lad? The name's MacLachlan. We first met in New York many years ago.'

Then he had taken the cigarette case out of his pocket once more and pressed it into Rob's hand. 'Keep that,' he had said. 'Keep that and remember how you saved our lives here this day.'

It was funny how things suddenly came back to you like that, out of the blue. He had rarely given the man a second thought until now, and had certainly never run into him again. But he had kept and used the cigarette case. It was quite lucky really, for the initials were almost the same; only the way of writing Mac was slightly different, but not enough to notice. He looked at his mother across the kitchen table. 'By the way, Ma, a bloke by the name of Major MacLachlan sends his regards. He says he met you once back in New York.'

Mhairi dropped the cup with a clatter into her saucer, spilling the tea on to the clean white damask of the tablecloth. She dabbed at it in confusion with her napkin, as her son looked at her curiously. 'MacLachlan, you say?' The words came out in a curious high-pitched tone. 'You – you met him, did you?'

'In the passing,' Rob replied, reaching for a copy of that day's *Times*. 'I think he was the one responsible for me getting mentioned in dispatches.'

'Oh.' He had never even mentioned in any of his letters he had been commended for bravery. 'He's in the Army, then?'

'He's a major, if I remember rightly. In the Black Watch.'

The Black Watch . . . The Black Watch . . . So she had been right all those months ago in Harrods. He *was* in the Black Watch. Arguably his country's greatest regiment. It was right somehow. 'And he knew you were my son, did he?' she mused softly. But she already knew the answer, for she had read it in Ralph's own eyes in the luggage department of London's most famous store.

She looked across at her son – *their* son – but Rob's mind was already on other things. Had she been right to accept his silence on the subject of his father over all these years? Certainly he did not appear to have set any store by the major he had met so fleetingly that day having the same surname as his own middle name. But then why should he? This was just her own conscience getting the better of her. MacLachlan was a common enough Scottish name, and since childhood he had simply accepted he had been given an old family name as part of his own.

She found her eyes misting as she looked at the deep furrows etched across his brow and the dark shadows that shaded the skin beneath his eyes. Her son was a man now. A man doing a man's work. He had more on his mind these days than puzzling over his parenthood. With death as your constant companion, why spend precious moments agonizing over the man who gave you life?

As she continued to look at him, the tense face of the young man seemed to fade into that of the eager young boy of adolescence, then change again into the bright-eyed child who had sat on her lap, not so very long ago, and lisped, 'I love you, Ma,' into her ear.

'I love you, Rob.' The words burst out of her and she looked away, flustered, as he glanced across at her, a look of surprise mingled with tenderness on his face.

'And I love you, too, old thing,' he smiled. Then he blushed and threw an embarrassed glance at Finbar. 'You'll be thinking we're a couple of ninnies, and no mistake,' he laughed.

But his great-uncle was not laughing. Instead he shook his head. 'If you ask me, this old world could do with a lot more of that these days, lad. If we all admitted to loving our own families a bit more, then maybe it would spill over to our fellow men and there might just be a chance to end this bloodbath that's going on over there across the Channel.'

'And amen to that,' Mhairi said, reaching for the teapot, as a great warmth enveloped her. She had never felt closer to either of them and in that moment she knew she was truly blessed. She had the love of two good men, what more could she want?

But Rob's two-day pass was over all too quickly and the parting from him was every bit as painful as she imagined. 'Keep smiling for me, Ma,' he said, at the station. 'Keep smiling for me, and for all the chaps who come to see you on those precious forty-eight-hour passes.' And she attempted to do just that. She threw herself into her work at the theatre with even greater vigour, and tried with all her heart not to dwell too much on what he was going back to in France.

In London itself the Zeppelin raids were becoming more frequent and you could feel the tenseness in the air as darkness approached. The fear was most intense on moonless nights, for those were the nights the Germans chose to let loose their bombs. Zeppelin raids on the capital during the last moonless period accounted for forty-four lives, and had maimed almost two hundred.

The evening of Wednesday, 13 October was overcast, and Mhairi looked with some trepidation out of the drawing-room window as she pulled on her gloves. 'What do you think, Uncle Fin? Will we be having some unwelcome visitors tonight?'

Finbar looked up from his armchair by the fire. 'I shouldn't worry too much if I were you. You'll be safe enough. I should think old Gerry's got his eye on more important targets than the stages of the West End right now!'

Mhairi hoped he was right as she gazed out of her taxi window as it made its way along the Strand. And certainly by the looks and sound of things, not too many people were worried about a lack of moonlight. On their usual corners, the barrel-organ grinders still churned out 'Keep The Home Fires Burning' and 'Goodbye Dolly Gray', and the newspaper boys were still calling out the latest headlines to passers-by. Tonight it was: 'Gallant Serbia Hard Pressed'. And everywhere there were soldiers, with their girls on their arms. The feeble glow of the oil lamps might do little to light the life of the capital, but it did wonders for romance.

Yes, despite the shadowy streets required by the Defence of the Realm Act which prohibited bright lighting, the capital of the Empire still had a great deal to offer her sons on leave. The restaurants were crowded, and from behind the heavily-curtained windows of the hotels and dance-halls came snatches of dance music. Inside she knew there would be the clinking of glasses, tearful toasts, promises made – some broken, kisses and hugs, hellos and farewells. And yet more farewells . . . Whilst in the skies above the teeming city, the velvet darkness was criss-crossed by the glaring beam of the searchlights. Yes, London at war had an atmosphere all of its own.

And at least the theatres were still full, even if they had lost a lot of their glamour. A 'House Full' board hung as usual outside the Gaiety as the taxi swept past to deposit her at the stage door. Soft lights glowed from inside the foyer, and people were already thronging up the front steps. Inside she knew, in stalls, pit and gallery, there would be the familiar sea of khaki.

As she got out of the taxi, there was the usual cheer from the crowd always gathered there on the pavement, and she paused to scribble her name on a couple of programmes and an odd envelope or two, before hurrying on into the theatre. Mr Jupp, the heavily moustached head door-keeper greeted her with his usual tip of the hat and 'Evening, Miss Cloud,' as she hurried on past.

She was late tonight, 'Overture and Beginners' had already been called, and the curtain had risen on Act One. As she hurried down the corridor to her dressing-room she could hear the waves of laughter greeting the jokes of Leslie Henson and George Grossmith, the two leading men.

Jimmy Wickham, the call-boy, lifted his cap to her as he passed, 'Evening, Miss Cloud. Any letters for posting?' He made a regular trip to the nearest pillar-box at the top of Catherine Street at this time each evening.

'Oh yes, Jimmy, if you don't mind.' She reached inside her bag and took out two letters, one addressed to Rob and one to Seamus and his wife in America.

The lad disappeared, and she made her way into her dressing-room and closed the door. In a silver frame on her make-up table a photograph of Rob smiled up at her. It was the only one she had of him in uniform. He had had it taken specially to please her shortly after he enlisted. She glanced at her watch. It was another half-hour before she was due on stage. Hers was the last act before the nine o'clock interval.

The roar of recognition and the wave of applause that greeted her when she finally swept on stage at a little after eight-thirty was as great as ever. But she had not even launched into her first song of the night when the explosion occurred. It seemed to come from somewhere outside the area of the front door and the whole building shook to its foundations.

Most of the audience jumped to its feet, and as Leslie Henson and Mhairi tried in vain to calm them, many of the chorus girls fled in panic.

The painted back-drop of the Covent Garden Ball was flapping wildly now, having come loose from its fixings, but the orchestra was continuing to play: the romantic notes of the new Jerome Kern hit written specially for the show wafted up from the pit below them. 'Carry on singing!' Leslie shouted to Mhairi above the din, and this she did, catching up with the ballad halfway through:

'. . . And when I tell them —
And I'm certainly going to tell them
That you're the guy whose wife one day I'll be,
They'll never believe me,
They'll never believe me,

384

That from this great big world
You've chosen *ME*!'

The full extent of the tragedy was not known until she came off-stage some fifteen minutes later. The whole area surrounding the theatre had been heavily bombed. One had landed just outside the Lyceum Theatre just across the road, and this had been followed by another which struck the Bell public house on the corner of Exeter and Wellington Streets. A third bomb had landed right between their own Gaiety and the Strand Theatre almost next door, and poor little Jimmy Wickham had been caught in its blast.

'One of our electricians is a-goner and "Nelson's" copped it too!' she was informed by an almost hysterical chorus girl as she pushed her way through the crowd gathering backstage.

'God help us!' 'Nelson', the one-eyed messenger boy, had been everyone's friend. Then, as she stood there, in the middle of the commotion, Withers, the Gaiety's cellarman was carried out on a makeshift stretcher. He had had one leg and part of an arm blown off.

'I'm getting out of here!' George Grossmith, one of her co-stars, shouted, and Mhairi followed him into the street, to find things even worse outside. A London General omnibus full of passengers had been blown to bits, and it seemed there was death and destruction everywhere you cared to look.

All around them was the clanging of fire-engine and ambulance bells as the rescue services rushed into action. But it seemed there was just too much for even the professionals to cope with: all the pavements were ankle deep in broken glass, with wounded and dying people everywhere.

The old axiom of 'the show must go on' was forgotten as every theatre in the vicinity became a temporary dressing-station, and the cry went out for bandages and hot water. The worst of the destruction seemed to be in the little street that ran parallel to the Strand, between the Lyceum and Covent Garden. It had been crowded at the time the bombs fell, and, as Mhairi ripped up petticoats to tend the wounded, she listened in horror as witnesses recounted the sight of seeing one woman blown to pieces before their eyes, and another cut in two by a sheet of glass blasted from a shop window.

Another woman who had been watching their own show in the Gaiety was in hysterics and could not be comforted. Her husband had rushed down the staircase and into the street to help when the first explosion occurred, leaving his wife in her seat. He had been killed instantly he set foot outside, by a flying fragment of metal from one of their own anti-aircraft guns.

In the Bell pub next door, nine people including the barmaid had been killed, and as Mhairi rushed to aid those still capable of being helped, she froze in horror. In what was left of the doorway, a man stood there still clasping his glass of beer and sandwich. He was mutilated beyond all recognition. 'Help me . . .' he gasped.

And she had taken his arm and led him gently to a stretcher. 'Get him to an ambulance!' she ordered Jimmy Jupp, the door-keeper. 'He's far beyond anything we can do here.'

In fact, by the end of the night, she had amazed herself at her ability to cope with the horror she had witnessed. Despite the blood and gore, the dust and debris, she felt cleansed somehow. As if the part she had played here this night had somehow atoned for the nights she had merely sung as the rest of mankind over there in France went to hell and back.

It was late – well after one in the morning – before she got back, filthy and dishevelled, to her home. Finbar, Mrs Chambers, the cook, and young Annie, the maid, were still up. They greeted her, white-faced with worry, in the hall as she wearily closed the front door behind her.

'Oh, ma'm. Thank God, you're alive. You've had us so worried!'

She stared at them dully for a moment. Then realization dawned at what they must have been going through. 'Oh Lord, I'm so sorry,' she groaned. 'You must have been going through hell.'

'Not half as much as you, by the looks of it,' Finbar said, his eyes on her blood-stained clothing. 'Are you sure you're all right, love?'

He took her gently by the arm and led her through to the drawing-room, as Mrs Chambers hurried off to put the kettle on for the umpteenth time that night. 'Now then,' he said, sitting down in the armchair opposite her. 'Tell the old man all about it. What on earth have you been doing with yourself out there tonight to get into a state like that? Not singing, that's for sure. We heard about the bombs in the Strand, though, and thought you might have stayed to help.' He could not tell her of the hell they had also been going through imagining she might be one of the dead or injured. He gave a quiet smile. 'You'll be asking them to write a Florence Nightingale part for you now, I'm thinking!'

Mhairi gave a wry smile in return. 'And you might very well be right. But it wouldn't just be a part on the stage any more, Uncle Finbar. I've had enough play-acting in my life now. I think it's high time I began experiencing the real thing.'

He looked at her quizzically over the top of his glasses. 'Meaning?'

'I mean, once this show's over, I think it's high time I did my bit for the war effort that doesn't entail strutting the boards every night, don't you?'

Finbar smiled and reached for his pipe. Whatever his niece decided, she would make her own mind up, with no help from him, he had no doubt about that.

Chapter Twenty-Three

The white body of evening
Is torn into scarlet,
Slashed and gouged and seared
Into crimson,
And hung ironically
With garlands of mist.

And the wind
Blowing over London from Flanders
Has a bitter taste.

Richard Aldington

Mhairi left the cast of *Tonight's the Night* at Easter 1916, to gain the first-aid certificates necessary to enlist as a nursing auxiliary in one of the Voluntary Aid Detachment units destined for France, and the Western Front.

It was not a decision she took lightly, but it was the only one which she believed could give her the peace of mind to live through the remainder of this bloody war that seemed to have no end in sight.

To her great relief, in spirit at least, Finbar was with her every step of the way. He had by now settled so comfortably into life in her Bloomsbury home that she had a sneaking suspicion he might just enjoy himself even more with the undivided attention of Mrs Chambers and Annie to see to his every need. At any rate, he supported to the hilt her decision to enlist and appeared to be in the best of spirits as he watched her make the last-minute adjustments to the black straw bonnet of her uniform before they set off for the boat train at Victoria Station that sunlit summer's morning in late June 1916.

'Sure and nobody would recognize you now!' he declared, his eyes bright as he regarded her with pride, and she knew it to be true. Dressed in the VAD uniform of long black cloak, black shoes and black woollen stockings, and her long hair tied back in a neat bun beneath the small black straw bonnet, she could have been any one of the hundreds of women up and down the country who were volunteering for such work. 'You're a treat to the eyes. I only wish I'd had someone like you to look after me when I was laid up last year – sure and I would have been back on my feet in record time!'

'Away with you, you old flatterer!' she laughed, but inside his approval meant a great deal. He was the only one of her family she had left in Britain to give an opinion on her decision to leave the stage, and it was not one she had taken lightly. The stage had given her everything: success, financial security and the love of millions. The only thing it had not given her was the love of the only man she had ever really wanted. But that was one of life's tragedies she had had to learn to live with over the years. And God knows, she was not alone. Countless others had suffered the same fate in the past, and legions more would do so in the future. And, as for the present day, this war had already witnessed more human heartache and misery for so many people that her own secret sorrow seemed to pale into insignificance in comparison. Never had there been anything like it, and she could only pray to God that there never would be again. But prayer was one thing, and concrete action was something else. Not one day longer could she have remained safe in London. The time for dressing-up was past, the party was over. And she did not regret it one bit.

They set off for Victoria just after seven-thirty, for the

boat train was due to leave an hour later. The whole area round the station was a mass of khaki when they arrived – men going back to the Front after all too short a leave with their loved ones. The authorities had taken to disembarking the wounded from the battlefields from the boat trains in the middle of the night, so as not to lower public morale too much by their ever-increasing numbers, and that meant the men who now filled the station during the day were virtually all going one way – into battle.

How many of *them* would be sent back under cover of darkness, she wondered, as, weighed down with kit and rifles, they called out to one another and joked as they waited to report to the Railway Transport Officer on duty. Others preferred to ignore their comrades and cling on to home as long as possible; they stood to the side in small family groups, usually holding their youngest infant in their arms, whilst the older ones clung to their rough khaki tunics. Beside them, their wives stood in numbed silence, with not even the pretence of a brave smile on their lips.

Here and there, to Mhairi's great relief, she saw a glimpse of the black or grey of the nurses' uniforms, and she thought wryly of Finbar's remark that there wouldn't be a single one of the men on that station who would recognize her now as one of their favourite pin-ups. She had been told often enough by soldiers home on leave that hers was the most popular picture postcard in the dugouts and the knowledge had given her a warm glow. But now she was simply one more VAD amongst many, and that was the way she wanted it. Her identification card said, Mhairi Anna McLeod, and from now on, as long as this dreadful war lasted, that was how it was going to be.

She had not even told her colleagues at the theatre of her decision to join the VAD. They all thought she was off to visit her family in America for the next few months. She had even made sure that that was the story leaked to the newspapers, and what would happen if they found out the truth she shuddered to think. The last thing she wanted was to be thought of as some sort of heroine.

On Platform 7, a newspaper stall had been given over to a Bureau de Change, with a large notice stating: FRENCH MONEY EXCHANGED HERE FOR TROOPS IN UNIFORM ONLY, and she turned to Finbar at the sight of it. 'Do you think I count as one of the troops?'

'There's only one way to find out.'

And to her delight, she did indeed count as one of His Majesty's Forces, for the purpose of changing her pound notes into French francs at least.

'I doubt if there'll be much over there for you to spend your money on,' Finbar commented, as he carried her bag to the open door of the waiting train. 'But remember now, keep those postcards coming. And if you run into that young lad of yours, you tell him not to forget his old uncle, although his Ma's on the wrong side of the Channel now!'

'I will. I promise I will.' She knew Finbar's postcard album was one of his greatest joys and she resolved to make sure she sent plenty of colourful cards to fill its pages whilst she was gone. She also prayed to God that Rob stayed fit and healthy enough to do the same. It was weeks now since they had received their last card from him. She presumed he was still in France, for the fighting there was still intense, and just being on the same side of the English Channel to him would be of some comfort. At any rate, she should hear more over there as to his regiment's whereabouts than back in London. And she should at least learn the truth about what was happening out there in the trenches. If only half the victories the newspapers claimed were true then the war should have been over months ago.

Solitary soldiers stared at them from out of the carriage windows as they approached the waiting train. She presumed that many, unable to bear station farewells, had got here early and those were the ones already in their seats, most puffing impatiently on their Woodbines as they waited for the final whistle. And quite a few were in kilts. Their goodbyes must have been said north of the border long ago.

The guard passed them, his flag at the ready. They watched as he took his place outside the guard's van and gripped the whistle between his lips. Its ear-piercing sound was followed by an enormous hiss of steam from the engine, and the clanking of pistons. There was a last-minute opening, then banging of doors as kitbags were thrown aboard. Wives, mothers and girlfriends were kissed for the last time, and Mhairi clasped Finbar to her in a final embrace. 'Take care of yourself,' she pleaded. 'Take care till I'm back!'

'God bless you, Mhairi love. And God bless that young lad of yours and bring him back safely too!'

Then she was on the train and straining for a last glimpse of him out of the crowded carriage window as, to a barrage of yells and cheers, the wheels clanked into life and they began to pull slowly out of the station.

She was headed for the French province of Champagne, and it turned out to be a long and tiring journey; it was late at night before she arrived at her destination in the small village of St Savine, just outside the historic old town of Troyes.

The Matron, a Mrs Harley, otherwise known as Madame la Directrice, who greeted her arrival at the hospital, was a daunting figure, in full dress uniform. Her piercing blue eyes dwelt meaningfully on Mhairi's own travel-creased cape and dusty shoes. 'I think you should know I expect my staff to be immaculately turned out at all times, my dear. Some may say VAD stands for Virtually All Duffers, but I'm willing to give everyone a chance, if they're keen to do their bit.' Then her eyes softened. 'I'm just on my way out for my last round of the evening. Would you care to join me? It'll let you get your bearings before you turn in and so save precious time in the morning when you come on duty.'

Although dead on her feet, Mhairi accepted the offer with a brave smile. She had neither the heart nor the courage to turn it down.

The hospital was in fact a requisitioned country house, the Château de Chanteloupe, and had been set up the previous year by the Scottish Women's Hospitals Unit as the first tent hospital on the Western Front. And, the Matron was proud to point out, it was also the only one in France to be staffed entirely by women.

The château itself was a white, rambling building, with lots of tall shuttered windows, in front of which potted palm trees swayed in the breeze.

'It's in the main building here that the hospital's administrative offices are situated, and of course I spend most of my time in here, but it will be out there on the lawns where most of your own work will take place,' Mhairi was told.

The wards were, in fact, a collection of marquee-like tents, the walls of which Matron explained could be rolled back in the daytime to take full advantage of the sun. And as they walked round in the warm dusk of the summer night, Mhairi found it hard to believe they were so near the Front; the surroundings were pleasant and green, and the nurses who moved silently between the tents were as professional as any she had left behind in London.

By the time they had completed their round it was almost midnight, and it was an hour after that before Mhairi finally got settled down in the bed that had been allotted to her in one of the dormitories. More than half the other beds were occupied, their inhabitants already fast asleep, as she carefully stowed her few belongings into the metal cabinet assigned to her, then slipped between the white cotton sheets. She was so tired she could not remember falling asleep, and it seemed she had barely got to bed when she was rudely awakened at a little after five in the morning, by the sound of running feet and raised voices.

For a moment she thought she was back home in her own bed in London as she struggled back to consciousness and pulled herself up on the pillow. But the sight that met her eyes told her otherwise. There were hurrying female bodies everywhere, all in various stages of undress as they rallied to the call. A convoy of field ambulances was arriving from a skirmish that had taken place during the night, some twenty kilometres or so to the north. All hands were needed to deal with the wounded.

By the time Mhairi had dressed and run down the marble staircase to join the others, the first trucks had already arrived with their bloodied cargoes, and to a raw VAD recruit such as herself, the sight that met her eyes was both awesome and terrifying.

Her first instinct was to hang back and let others with more experience take the lead, but she soon realized this was no ordinary hospital, it was as much a part of the war zone as the battlefields themselves, and there could be no question of not pulling her weight, no matter how terrified she might be of the task that awaited her.

As the nurses clustered round, the male attendants who had accompanied the convoy were unloading heaps of mud-caked clothing, bandages and blood from the trucks. Then to her horror, she realized the heaps were in fact human beings – young men, most barely older than her own son. And in the middle of it all a middle-aged lady doctor, with an Aberdeenshire accent, was calmly giving orders as if it were an everyday occurrence. Then the awful thought occurred – perhaps it was.

Mhairi was sent downstairs with several others to get on with the first truckload as soon as possible; they had been told to expect at least several more within the hour.

The first priority, she was told, was to slit the blood and mud-caked uniforms from the mangled limbs. This unenviable task was done in the basement of the château, where fresh hot water was readily available to cope with the influx. The big basement room reeked of ether and iodoform and it made a heady mix with the stench of dried blood and other mucus that was emitted from the new admittances. Most of the victims were still conscious and moaned in agony as the huge scissors cut their way painfully through the blood and gore.

'Here, you take these and get on with that young lad in the corner.' The staff nurse who issued the order barely gave her a second look as she thrust the scissors into Mhairi's hands and nodded with her head in the direction of a freckle-faced, tow-headed youth who had been one of the first to be brought in.

Mhairi balked when she gazed down at what looked like a pair of gardening shears in her hands. And she felt even worse as she approached the young man and saw his eyes regard them with even greater terror.

'I'll be as gentle as I can,' she promised, as she stuck the steel blades into the clotted material that had once been a trouser leg. The stench was almost unbearable and to her horror she saw almost immediately that the bottom half of his leg below the knee had been shot away.

He was from Eccles, in Lancashire, he told her. 'The same place as the cakes.' She forced a smile to her lips and murmured something about being very partial to an Eccles cake now and then. She was certain he did not know his lower leg was missing.

It was much harder work than it looked and within a few minutes her own hands were red and swollen from the pressure she was having to exert on the scissors. With every snip of the blades the young man inside the bloodied clothing would wince and moan, or occasionally scream out in pain.

'Bloody hell, nurse, go easy . . .'

It was a nerve-racking business for a VAD fresh off the boat from England, and, to her great embarrassment, she found herself weeping tears of frustration and sympathy into the caked blood as she forced her painful hands to do their awful work.

Once their clothing was removed the wounded were left lying naked on their stretchers whilst other attendants dabbed at their wounds with sponges soaked in hot water and disinfectant. As they did so the blood ran in rivers from the naked flesh, through the stretchers, to stain the floor beneath and seep into the cracks of the marble tiles.

They made a terrible and awesome sight lying there, the relics of battle, their young faces and hands brown with mud, their hair tangled and matted, their cheeks un-shaven and bloodless – the colour of parchment. And their bodies – their once strong young bodies – naked and mutilated beyond belief.

It had been a hot night, and the day that followed was hotter still, the sun beating down from out of a cloudless sky. Some of the casualties had been gassed, and the stench from their choked, fluid-filled lungs, and the gangrenous wounds of some of the others, was almost unbearable. Some had already choked to death before reaching the hospital and had arrived with faces blue and bloated beyond recognition. These, along with those beyond help, they assigned to the Moribund Tent. Others headed for the same tent had arrived with limbs mangled beyond repair, or nerves shattered beyond redemption. For these, she knew, the best treatment in the world would not be enough, and her heart went out to them as they lay there and waited for death.

By lunchtime all the casualties had been stripped and cleaned as best they could be and transferred to the Dressing-tent, or the waiting-room for theatre. And it was only then that she found herself enjoying her first break of the day. Half a glorious hour to have a cup of tea and a bite to eat. But the sliced sausage and cold potatoes were left on her plate. After a morning like that she could not face the tiniest morsel.

'Don't worry,' a pretty dark-haired Glasgow girl told her. 'It gets all of us like that the first day, but you soon get used to it.'

Did you?

After lunch things were not quite so hectic and she found herself in the charge of a cheerful young nurse from Galashiels, in the Borders. Peggy Moffat taught her how to recognize which casualties required to have the label with the red stripe pinned to them and which didn't. 'The "Red Labels" are those lads most likely to haemorrhage and we have to keep a special eye on them for obvious reasons.' She grinned. 'The others say it's favouritism, nothing else, but they're always pulling our legs.'

They could lie there so badly mutilated and still make jokes? Mhairi listened and nodded, and hoped everything became 'obvious' eventually. Right now it seemed there were a hundred and one things to learn and remember to do.

'Do you fancy a wee stint in the Dressing-tent?' Peggy asked halfway through the afternoon. 'I'm sure they can do with the extra pair of hands.' This time Mhairi did not even bother replying, but merely followed her young mentor across the grass in the direction of the tent where most of the activity was going on.

The Dressing-tent had a stomach-turning smell which met you at the door, despite its rolled up sides. Peggy saw her wrinkling her nose and sympathized. 'You soon get used to it,' she said brightly. 'It's a combination of chlorate of lime and gas gangrene from the wounds.'

Mhairi nodded and wondered if that knowledge would help her bear it any better, as her companion went off to talk to the staff nurse in charge.

When Peggy returned she informed Mhairi she was to be put on one of the most menial, but also one of the most important jobs: 'It's making up the big demi-johns with gallons of the solution of a quarter per cent Hypochlorous Acid that we use to cleanse the wounds.'

Mhairi gazed down at the array of huge bottles waiting to be filled. The hospital was obviously short of supplies, for she recognized some of them as having once contained her favourite champagne and she thought of the young German count who had once drunk just such a brand from her own slipper. Where was he now? Somewhere out there in this hell they called the Western Front, no doubt. It was a sick world, all right.

The Dressing-tent was also, she discovered, one of the most harrowing duties to be assigned to, for having their wounds cleaned and dressed was often more painful for the patients than receiving the initial injury. The treatment for the less serious wounds consisted mainly of swabbing with lysol, then gauze dipped in tincture of iodine, and when available spaghnum moss dressings were used on the worst cases, with a final binding of Jackinette, a waterproof material that helped keep the beds dry should the wounds suppurate. The very worst cases had to have their injuries irrigated by fixing tubes of the cleansing solution into the open wound. This was an extremely painful procedure, she discovered, and it had to be done every three hours, even waking men up throughout the night to do it.

She had just finished working on one of these irrigation cases when she noticed the young man being brought in whom she had cut the uniform off first thing this morning. His face had been washed since she last saw him, but he was pasty-white beneath his freckles and she could see he had been crying, for his long fair lashes were spiked and wet.

'VAD – yes, you – over here, please!' The staff nurse's voice was impatient.

Mhairi obeyed immediately, hurrying to the side of the dressing-trolley that stood between herself and the patient.

'His leg's been suppurating,' the staff nurse informed her. 'It needs redoing.'

The young man winced and bit his lip, then stifled a cry as the old dressing was ripped off to reveal the bloodied stump from which the pus was still oozing. 'Hold the stump!' the nurse commanded.

Mhairi balked.

'Get hold of that leg!'

Mhairi put her hands out and, averting her face, gripped what was left of the young man's leg above the knee as a pint of Hypochlorous Acid she had just mixed was poured over the raw flesh. She could feel the pus from the wound ooze through her fingers, along with the blood and cleansing fluid.

'Be particularly careful of any cuts or grazes you may have,' she was advised by the Sister in charge, who had come to take a look. 'Changing dresses on a septic wound is highly dangerous. Sepsis is most contagious and I've already lost too many of my girls after having to be sent home with badly swollen hands brought about through their own carelessness!'

Mhairi listened, then dared a look down at her own hands which were still gripping what was left of the young man's leg. What she saw made her stomach well up into her throat. Then the Sister's voice became fainter and fainter, and she was seeing two stumps, and four hands were gripping the bloodied flesh. She began to sway and was conscious of no more.

When she came to she was outside the tent and the young nurse from Galashiels was holding a cup of hot tea to her lips. 'There you are,' Peggy Moffat was saying. 'You'll be feeling better in no time.'

Mhairi gazed up at her as the sweet tea found its way over her throat. 'I'm so sorry . . . I'm so ashamed.'

'Och, there's no need to be that. They do say you can't call yourself a real nurse until you've ended up on the floor!'

It was meant well but was small comfort, and as she tumbled, exhausted, into her bed late that night, Mhairi wondered if she would ever get used to this strange, hellish world in which she had found herself – if she would ever call herself a 'real' nurse. What she was doing now seemed a million light years away from London and the nightlife of the Gaiety Theatre.

It was astonishing how quickly you did become accustomed to the most awful things, however, and the following days found her coping with situations she had never even dreamt of on the train journey and voyage over from England. She was also becoming personally involved with almost every one of the young men she found herself assigned to take care of, no matter how often she was told not to fraternize. It was impossible not to listen as they talked wistfully of wives and sweethearts left behind, and of their hopes of seeing them again. For so many she knew this was a dream that would never come true and she did her best to lighten their remaining few hours or days with as many jokes and quips as she could remember from her life on the stage. This was something she had to make sure never got to her superior's ears, however, for as one 'Jock' put it: 'Laugh and the nurse laughs with you. Sister enters and you laugh alone!'

It was during her second week at the Château de Chanteloupe that she found herself tending a young officer from the Public Schools Battalion of the Middlesex Regiment. Although she did not recognize him, to her consternation he recognized her. Second-Lieutenant Hugh St Just had known Rob at Harrow and to her delight it transpired he had run into him only the week before.

'You mean Rob's here – he's in this area?' she asked

excitedly, trying hard to keep her voice down so the Sister would not hear.

The young man shook his head on the pillow. 'The London Scottish are about a couple of hundred kilometres to the north-west of here – along the banks of the River Somme . . . It's not just his regiment – they're all congregating up there – thousands of them.' His voice dropped. 'They say there's going to be a big push up there before long.' His eyes darted to either side. But thankfully nobody was listening. 'I can't really say any more.' He had already said too much. 'By the way, nurse, how're the other two from my unit? Did they make it here?'

Mhairi scanned the admittance list in her hand, trying hard not to let her excitement at hearing about Rob distract her from the job on hand. 'I'll find out for you.'

She found the two young men in question in the basement of the château: one was a young slightly-built boy called Hunter-Jones, whose face they had already covered with a red blanket, and the other a fair-haired, good-looking young man waiting to go to theatre. She walked to the side of his trolley and smiled down at him. 'Your friend Hugh St Just has been enquiring about you.'

The young soldier attempted a weak smile. His face was ashen and blood was still oozing from his abdomen, despite the makeshift padding strapped to it. 'Tell him I bet I'll see Manchester before him.' His voice was so faint as to be almost inaudible.

Mhairi bent nearer the trolley. 'You're both from Manchester?'

'You know it?' Despite his obvious pain, his eyes lit up at the thought of someone who might know his home town.

'Oh, not very well . . . I lived in Ancoats once for a short time, a long time ago.' She attempted to ease his head into a more comfortable position on the pillow.

There was a moment's silence as a wave of pain passed over the young man's face, then he nodded. 'Our family's had mills there for years . . . Ashton's "Red Rose" mills, you might remember them?'

The beauty of the name stirred her memory, and she looked once more at the admittance sheet in her hand: Second-Lieutenant Ashton B.E., she was talking to. She drew in her breath. 'Your father wouldn't be a Barnaby Ashton, by any chance?'

Young Barnaby Edward Ashton Junior's eyes lit up. 'You know Pa?'

Mhairi gave a wan smile. 'I knew someone once who knew your father, and I knew your half-brother Bobby.' She didn't know why she said it, but she did.

Disappointment welled in the soldier's eyes. 'I think you must have the wrong Ashton, ma'am. I'm an only child. I have no half-brother called Bobby.'

She looked at him without speaking for a moment or two, then shook her head. 'How silly of me . . . Of course you don't.' After all, Bobby had died almost thirty years ago, hadn't he?

She turned from the trolley as the theatre sister hurried in with an orderly in her wake and the young man was whisked away for surgery. Mhairi was still in the waiting area when the orderly came out several minutes later. 'Funny how some of them don't last long enough to even go under,' she said, with a shake of her head. 'But then it wouldn't have been much of a life for the poor blighter, anyway, with half his privates blown away.'

Mhairi turned to stare at the swing door to the theatre as the attendant's words echoed in her head. Barnaby Ashton had just lost his only surviving son. She looked fiercely at the orderly who was pushing a pile of soiled sheets into a laundry bag. A deep anger welled within her that would not be controlled. 'This is a bloody awful war, isn't it?' It was the first time she had sworn in public.

'Yes, it is,' the woman agreed, without even looking up.

'We all know that. It's high bloody time that somebody told the Brass Hats!'

Mhairi made no reply as she walked from the room, but she heard the words and remembered, and she also remembered what young Barnaby Ashton's pal Hugh had told her about Rob.

She was back in the theatre that evening with Dr Louise McIlroy, the head of the surgical unit, someone she liked a great deal, and who was known to be understanding. An idea had been fermenting in her head all afternoon. Dare she ask her? She had to, for, if the truth be known, the thought of moving further up the line to be nearer the Front had been on her mind ever since she arrived; it was just a matter of when.

Nevertheless it took her all her courage to broach the subject as she stood at her superior's side by the operating table that evening. She could feel herself sweating beneath her uniform, for the air in the theatre was stifling; it reeked of ether and iodoform, and she felt sure she would faint, either from nerves or from the smell, as she waited for the reply to her request to leave the hospital.

Dr McIlroy did not take her eyes off her patient for an instant as she queried, 'So you've heard they're to be asking for volunteers, have you?' She herself had only got wind of it the previous day. Rumour had it they would be asking for more volunteers to man the Casualty Clearing Stations further up the line, for there was a major offensive about to be launched in the north-west. The French Army had been undergoing a traumatic time since February with the big German offensive at Verdun earlier in the year, and it was said that a major attack by the British was needed to distract the enemy. She had been expecting requests to transfer up the line any time now, for there were always those who wanted to be where the action was. 'Are you sure you want to go? There's plenty of work for you here, and the Front in any major offensive is not exactly the safest place to be, you know.'

'I'm sure. And I don't mind the danger.'

Dr McIlroy sighed; a distinguished gynaecologist and obstetrician, she was one of the few who were aware of Mhairi's previous identity, and as she too had left a successful career to travel all the way to France to tend wounded men, she could appreciate what drove those who felt that to be even here in St Savine was not enough. 'Well, if it's nearer the Front you're set on, then I'll have to see what I can do . . . Sutures, please.'

Mhairi handed her the threaded needle and watched as the older woman began to sew the torn flesh together. A tremor of excitement and not a little fear ran through her. She could be up there in the firing-line herself any day now.

Chapter Twenty-Four

How long, O Lord, how long, before the flood
Of crimson-welling carnage shall abate?
From sodden plains in West and East the blood
Of kindly men streams up in mists of hate,
Polluting Thy clean air; and nations great
In reputation of the arts that bind
The world without hopes of Heaven, sink to the state
Of brute barbarians, whose ferocious mind
Gloats o'er the bloody havoc of their kind,
Not knowing love or mercy. Lord how long
Shall Satan in high places lead the blind
To battle for the passions of the strong?
Oh, touch Thy children's hearts, that they may know
Hate their most hateful, pride their deadliest foe.

Robert Palmer,
killed in action, 1916

It seemed as if the journey to the Front would never end. Since early morning the field ambulance, empty save for herself, the driver, and one attendant, had battled over the dry dirt tracks they called roads on its way back to the green fertile valley of the Somme.

It was a land of soft rolling downs, of green woods and meadows, of sweet-flowing streams and slumbering villages, and on the last day of June, with the still air heavy with the sights, sounds, and smells of high summer, for a few short miles it was almost possible to believe there was no such thing as a war going on somewhere over the horizon – until they got to within fifty miles of the guns. Then it became a different sight altogether, and Mhairi's courage began to wilt along with her body as she sat alongside Ned, her driver, and peeped out through the dusty windscreen.

Suddenly soldiers began appearing, long weary lines of them, stretching as far as the eye could see along the road that cut across a countryside now scarred and mutilated beyond recognition. They first ran into them around midday, and by teatime their numbers had increased, as battalion after battalion headed for the battle zone.

Mhairi found it hard to relate the handsome young men in khaki who had thronged the Gaiety to hear her sing to these strange creatures who dragged their bleeding feet mile after dusty mile along the rutted road. They seemed to move permanently in a cloud of white dust kicked up from the dried chalk surface. Their faces, slack and haggard with fatigue were caked with it, save for the lines made by the rivulets of sweat that ran from their brows down their sunken cheeks, to disappear beneath the collars of their tunics.

'It never ends, you know,' Ned commented. 'This bloody procession, it goes on night and day. The road never sleeps – like the poor buggers whose feet are pounding it.'

And as she gazed out of the window, she could almost feel the surface groan under the weight of the millions of iron-rimmed wheels of the ammunition trucks, armoured cars, limbers, GS wagons, and those endless lines of constantly marching feet. Its surface was cracked and crumbling, with potholes of every size pitting its entire length, and every so often the wheels of their ambulance would judder into one of the craters, but, thankfully, they always came out the other side. Others had not been so lucky, for several times they were held up by blockages caused by overturned vehicles. When that happened the whole slow-moving caterpillar, of which they were now part, could be held up for anything up to an hour at a time until the blockage was cleared and they could continue their slow crawl.

'Don't ambulances get priority at a time like this?' Mhairi asked, as they began to inch their way forward once more.

'God love you, no!' Ned laughed. 'It's quite the opposite – even when we're full. It's the ammo and healthy men that get the priority. The *déchets* are bottom of their list!'

'The *déchets*?' she queried.

'The wounded – the "has beens", the Froggies call 'em. And that's how our Brass Hats think of 'em too. Rate for nothing, they don't – the wounded. Can't fight any more, you see. They're finished with as far as the Army are concerned – *kaput*!'

Then, to the familiar strains of 'Onward Christian Soldiers', a voice began to sing softly in the rear:

'Onward Joe Soap's Army
Marching without fear,
With our own Commander
Safely in the rear.

He boasts and skives from morn till night
And thinks he's very brave,
But the men who really did the job
Are dead and in their graves.

Onward Joe Soap's Army
Marching without fear,
With our own Commander
Safely in the rear . . .'

There was a silence as Taffy Howell, the young lad from the Rhondda, finished the song, then Ned said quietly, 'He could be court-martialled for that, you know. Bloody shot,

407

he could be.' Then he added, so quietly she was sure only she could hear, 'But it's bloody true. Every last word of it.'

Mhairi said nothing, but continued to stare out of the window. A burnt-out ambulance lay on its side on the grass verge, an abandoned stretcher propped up against the front wheel, the bloodstains that covered the canvas now caked brown and flyblown.

She averted her eyes to the stagnant dust cloud ahead; they were coming up to a column of 'Jocks', but the tartan of their kilts was so mud-caked and filthy it was impossible to tell which regiment they were from. Could it be Rob's London Scottish? She craned her neck to see, but every one of those exhausted, dust-caked faces looked like the other.

To the left of them was what appeared to be a field of extinct volcanoes. 'They're shell craters,' Ned said. 'You'll be seeing a lot of them. That was the field that accounted for that lot we brought down to you at St Savine last week.'

She thought momentarily of the young lad from Eccles. He had gone into shock on the second day and was dead by the third. She gazed out at the acre of pitted earth. Had it been worth it? She already had a good idea what Ned and Taffy's answers would be.

They reached their destination at a little after eight in the evening. In the gathering dusk she could just make out the tents that were to be her new home. The ambulance ground to a halt next to a wooden notice-board with an arrow and red-painted letters stating: WALKING WOUNDED. Where it was pointing them she was not quite sure, but had no time to dwell on the matter for Ned was already opening her door.

'You'd better report first to the MO,' he advised her. 'He should be in that tent over yonder.' He indicated with his head in the direction of a smallish erection to their right.

As Taffy handed out her bag from the back of the

vehicle, she thanked them both for the lift and the company, and, feeling more apprehensive than she had anticipated, she made her way across the scrubby earth in the direction of the Medical Officer's tent.

The officer in charge that night was a Major Harry Evans, a jovial Welshman, with a dark handlebar moustache and a monocle in his right eye. He eyed her curiously through it. 'Well now, Miss McLeod, is it? You're a bit older than the usual VADs we've been getting out here, but if that means you're also a bit more sensible, then I'm not complaining.'

Mhairi opened her mouth to say something, then shut it again. Was he inferring she was over the hill? It was the first time anyone had made any sort of remark about her age and she found it more amusing than anything else. It was a far cry from the adulation she was used to receiving from the opposite sex, that was for sure.

'Been at the Front before?'

'No, this is my first time.'

'Aaah! A Frontal virgin!' He sighed and pushed his pen into the breast pocket of his tunic. 'I'd get a good night's sleep tonight, if I were you, Miss McLeod. It might be the last one you have for quite some time to come.'

She stared at him. He obviously knew something she didn't. Could it mean this new offensive everyone was talking about, but no one was supposed to mention, was to be tomorrow morning? A shiver ran through her.

'Fancy a breath of fresh air before you turn in?' He had eased himself out of his canvas campaign chair and was stretching his arms; they almost reached the sides of the tent. He yawned and shook his head. It had been another full twelve-hour stint. 'A few less Brass Hats and more blooming doctors is what this Army needs, if you ask me!'

They walked together to the door of the tent, then she accompanied him to the edge of a small copse that shaded the field dressing station from the expanse of No Man's

Land and the Front-line itself. As they stood there in the gathering dusk they could see the outlines of German soldiers mending their defences silhouetted against the night sky about a quarter of a mile away.

'Poor beggars,' her companion said. 'Their time's not long now.' There was a weariness in his voice that seemed to come from the depths of his soul.

'Have you been out here long – at the Front itself, I mean?' she asked.

He took out his monocle, wiped the dust off it and replaced it in his eye. 'From the beginning of time, Miss McLeod . . . From the beginning of time. But then every poor blighter over here feels like that, not just me. You begin to wonder if there ever really was another world out there where sanity prevailed and people were nice to one another and said Please and Thank You, and gave up their seats on buses to old ladies . . .'

His voice trailed off as his eyes once more wandered over No Man's Land to the small specks in the distance, that they knew to be the enemy. 'It brutalizes you – war, my dear. It brutalizes everyone eventually. Just look at Fritz over there, brewing up for the last time tonight. Smoking his last fag of the day, no doubt, and writing to Gretchen or Liesel back home in Hamburg or Berlin, just like the Jocks in our own trenches over there writing to Nellie or Mary back home in Dundee or Edinburgh . . . Poor blighters, poor old blighters.'

He thrust his hands deep into his pockets and began to walk slowly back towards his tent. When they got outside, he turned to her. 'Do you pray, Miss McLeod?'

She looked up at him in surprise. 'Well, yes. Yes, I do.'

He nodded thoughtfully. The answer seemed to please him. 'Then pray for us tonight, my dear. Pray for all of us . . .'

His eyes strayed back to the German trenches beyond the line. '*Gott mit Uns*, Miss McLeod . . . And God with

Them, too. In fact, God with every last one of us . . . Yes, God help us all when daylight comes.'

He disappeared back inside the tent, and the flaps dropped into place behind him. She could see him silhouetted in the light of the paraffin lamp on his desk as he sank back down wearily in his chair. She stood there outside, her bag still on the ground beside her, where she had left it when she got out of the ambulance. What a strange man. What a strange, but nice man. His words repeated in her head as she gazed about her. A shiver ran through her. It was obviously a busy station, but almost nothing stirred. It was as if the whole world was waiting for something to happen. Something big.

She picked up her bag and walked in the direction of another tent where she could see a light on inside and figures in nurses' uniforms gathered around a small table.

All eyes turned to her as she appeared at the door of the tent. Then a tall, stout woman spoke. 'You must be the new helper from St Savine.' She gave a dry laugh. 'Another glutton for punishment to join the merry band.'

She found herself billeted in a small tent containing just three other nurses. There was one other VAD like herself, a young woman by the name of Marjorie Duncan from Sheffield, and two trained nurses, Jane Digby from Walsall, and Freda Stewart from Halifax. The four camp beds were arranged two along each side of the tent and Mhairi found hers had a broken leg.

'A compound fracture of the femur,' Madge Duncan grinned, by way of apology. 'We're sorry about that. Dolly, its last occupant, was a bit on the hefty side and the poor old thing just couldn't take it any longer.'

'You mean the bed or Dolly?' Mhairi asked, investigating the pile of books propping it up at the broken end.

Madge's grin grew broader. 'Well, both actually. Poor old Doll got invalided back to Blighty herself the other day with a septic hand.' She looked at Mhairi investigating the books. 'If you're looking for something to read, they're a pretty boring lot, actually. Anything that arrives with any spice in it, we read then hand straight over to the boys. There's little enough we can do to lighten their lives out here as it is.'

Mhairi sat back up on the bed with a sigh. She felt hot and sweaty and would have given anything for a bath. 'I don't suppose there's an ablutions tent?' she asked tentatively. She had vaguely heard of such a thing.

All three laughed in unison and Madge pointed to a small collapsible canvas trough that lay against the back of the tent. 'We use that to wash in,' she said. 'It'll hold about a jug of water before it starts leaking through.'

'And if you want a bath?'

'A bath!' Madge looked at the other two in mock confusion. 'Have we heard of such an exotic thing around here, girls?'

They shook their heads, then Jane, the smallest, said wistfully, 'I dream of that with a passion every night. Others may yearn for their knights on white chargers as they lie down to sleep – me, I yearn for a humble tin bath and lashings of hot water to go in it!' She jerked her thumb in disgust at the canvas sink a few feet away. 'We seem to spend our lives bent over that thing when we're not working. When we're not trying to wash bits of ourselves in it, we're washing collars, and cuffs and caps, which they expect you to keep spotlessly white in this dust-bowl they call a camp! I tell you lot, one day I'm going to personally make a funeral pyre of that thing and sing and dance around the flames!'

'Well, just hang on till I've had a chance to use it, will you?' Mhairi said wearily. It looked like that awful canvas object was the nearest thing she would get to a proper wash for some time to come.

Reveille woke them at 5 A.M. and they had to take it in turns to wash in the detested canvas sink, then get into their uniforms as best they could in the confined space. When they emerged from the tent it was obvious that 'the cooker', as they referred to the cookhouse, had already been serving breakfasts to the men for some time. Too excited to be hungry, Mhairi only managed to nibble a piece of bread and sip a mug of tea as she attempted to get her bearings in daylight.

The main field hospital itself was further down the line, about half a mile away, she was told, but their advanced dressing station was impressive enough. It consisted of about a dozen tents and she was told there were several more of them running the length of the Somme, with well-sandbagged casualty collecting centres in between. As well as their complement of nurses and auxiliaries, they had their own specialist surgical teams of doctors, nurses and anaesthetists on stand-by to rush to wherever the need was greatest. Operating centres could be set up anywhere near the line to deal with the most seriously wounded who would not survive even the ambulance journey to the casualty clearing stations. The nurses who explained things to her as she wandered round, her mug of tea in her hand, were curiously tense, and when she got as far as the main MO's tent and found her Welsh major there once more, she could not resist asking the reason. 'Is the big push, as they call it, really to be this morning?'

Major Harry Evans looked up from his desk, and got up and walked to the door of his tent. His eyes turned to the east where the first faint streaks of dawn were appearing in the sky. 'It'll be full daylight soon,' he said. 'And I doubt if we'll ever know another first of July like this one in our lifetime.'

She knew it was all the answer she would get, but it told her all she wanted to know. And shortly after that she was told the time of the attack. The men were to go over the top at 6 A.M. precisely.

As the hands of their watches ticked round to zero hour,

a tangible tenseness crept into the air. The quips and jokes ceased, as each man came to terms with fear in his own way. A whisper here and a cough there were the only sounds, then even they ceased, and for the final few minutes no one spoke. It seemed as if the silence of the grave was enfolding the world. Their world, for no other existed beyond the barbed wire. Out here on the edge of No Man's Land she was as far away from the Gaiety Theatre and her previous life as it was possible to be.

But worse than the waiting, much worse than anything was the knowledge that somewhere along this line, waiting for the signal to go over the top was Rob. Her son was here somewhere. And suddenly she knew she had to find him.

She turned back and headed for the MO's tent. To her relief, Major Evans was still there. 'I'm terribly sorry to bother you again, sir, but could you tell me . . . are the London Scottish anywhere near here?'

He looked at her curiously and scratched his head beneath his cap. 'The London Scottish, let me think . . . Aren't they part of that new battalion that's just been formed . . . The 168th Brigade, if I remember rightly? . . . Yes, that's it, they have the Fusiliers and the Kensingtons in there too. The Rangers too, most probably.'

'But are they near here?' She tried to keep the desperation from her voice.

'About a mile up the line, I'd say. Around the Gommecourt Wood area.' He indicated with his head the general direction.

'Thank you. Thank you, so much.'

And then she was running, lifting her skirts well above her ankles so that she did not trip on the rough ground.

Men were dug in all the way along the line. She could see them all, white-faced and tense as they waited in their trenches for the signal to go over the top. Over the top. The very words struck terror in the soul.

After running for almost five minutes she glanced at her watch. It was almost six. There were 'Jocks' in the trench to her left. Lines and lines of young kilted soldiers, most no older than her son. Were they the London Scottish? She paused to catch her breath against the stump of a tree. A captain was standing just above the trench with a white handkerchief in his hand. He was looking at his watch. She glanced once more at her own. There were only seconds to go.

She listened to him count out loud. 'Five – four – three – two – one.' His face was ashen as the handkerchief came down. 'Zero . . . NOW!' He barked the words in a hoarse croak, then a whistle blew.

To a man, the soldiers in the trench rose to their feet, their bayonets gleaming in the strange half-light. Then, as they swarmed up the ladders and over the tops of their trenches, suddenly the ground around began to rock as the men went over to dash headlong through the smoke and flame of the German flares.

As she clung petrified to what was left of the tree, as far as the eye could see the earth was writhing in a spreading shock wave. Like the ripples on a stream it rose and fell, as from across No Man's Land came a sudden rush of wind – the hot breath of Satan himself. Then came his roar as the guns opened up all along the line. Louder and louder it grew, battering the eardrums, as bigger and bigger weapons opened up from behind. Very soon the whole Front was one crescendo of sound and the very air she was breathing was vibrating in the lungs.

The countryside that only moments before had been hushed in the coming dawn was an inferno of flames, as flashes from the cannonading raged and thundered around her. The very earth itself was opening and spewing its contents into a black pillar that was carried heavenwards in one gigantic flame. It seemed to hang there suspended before dropping on to the thousands of khaki-clad figures that swarmed over the ground, racing half-bent across the tortured earth, which beneath their booted feet continued to heave and shudder.

Great sods were hurtled through the air to fall, along with the exploding shells, on the soldiers beneath. Already bodies were strewn across the landscape, and still the cascade of death continued to bear down on the men beneath its deadly rain, battering bodies to pulp and sending dismembered limbs high into the smoke-filled air.

Aghast at this living hell that had broken out around her, Mhairi pressed her hands to her ears in a useless gesture as tears streamed from her eyes as she thought of those young men caught in the middle of this holocaust.

Suddenly the first of the sun's beams broke through the smoke-veiled flashes. It seemed as if the finger of God was pointing to man in his utmost folly. The morning air hung heavy with the acrid smell of cordite.

Overhead she could hear the drone of aircraft and caught sight of the glint of silver wings. Were they on their way to seek yet more targets for the hungry guns?

There was a small hillock just ahead and she clambered up it, shielding her eyes from the sun and the glare of exploding shells as she looked out over the scene of battle. Across what had a few short minutes ago been a green and pleasant cornfield, Death had cut with his scythe; his foul breath wafted towards her on the breeze, nauseating her with the stench of blood and gas; it sickened the throat and clutched tightly at the lungs so every breath was an effort, and in her ears his harsh voice rang out in the dreadful roar of the guns.

Below her in the abandoned trenches she could see letters lying, alongside empty bully beef tins and discarded cartridge-clips. There were picture postcards of popular beauties pinned to the wooden supports. Was hers down there?

A horse and wagon carrying supplies was trundling

down the road behind her. A shell screamed overhead and the animal whinnied and put its ears back as if to switch off flies; there was real fear in its eyes as it pawed the hard ground. Poor animal, she thought, to be caught up in this.

In the distance to her right she could see activity around the medical tents. They must be bringing the wounded in already. Suddenly making her way along the line to where she hoped Rob's battalion might be seemed too great a luxury at a time like this. She was on the verge of returning to her station when a shout had her whirling round in the opposite direction.

'Hey, nurse, over here!'

She ran down to the side of the trench where a frantic looking medical orderly was standing alongside a stretcher.

'Do you reckon you're up to taking the back end of one of these?'

He sounded desperate, and she glanced down at the empty stretcher, then back at him. She was taller than he was, if not as broad. 'I can try.'

'Good girl!' Relief flooded his face. 'My mate's copped it and there's been a hit on one of the aid-posts. We'll have to get the wounded out of there.'

She needed no further encouragement, but bent to pick up the back end of the stretcher and followed him, half-running, half-stumbling over the pitted ground.

The aid-post was a half dug-out, half lean-to building, built into the side of a trench and supported by sandbags. Half the wall supports at one side had collapsed and what had once been the entrance sagged at a forty-five-degree angle. They had to bend almost double to get inside, and to Mhairi's amazement the interior was quite large. But, despite the sun outside, visibility was limited. She could just make out a figure lying on the floor, and several less seriously injured, shadowy forms sat slumped around the walls.

'It's the Brigadier,' she heard her companion say, indicating the figure stretched out on the floor in front of them. 'We'll have to get him on to the stretcher.'

As she got nearer she could see his whole body was trembling violently and he was making incomprehensible gibbering noises.

'It's shock,' the attendant said.

He must have weighed around ten stones and, grabbing him by the ankles, she had to strain to heave him on to the waiting stretcher. It took some difficult manoeuvring to negotiate it and its new load out of the confined space, and once out in the open air, it was useless trying to keep to the regulation broken step advised to avoid swaying the patient too much for the ground was too rough to do anything more than attempt to keep on your feet.

It seemed to be taking forever as they carefully picked their way over the duckboards, and slowly wound their way through the deserted trenches in the direction of the field dressing station. Her arms, almost stretched out of their sockets, were growing more leaden by the second, and seemed as if she was bearing the whole of the Brigadier's weight on the slings which were biting painfully into her stooped shoulders.

By the time they had reached their destination she was slumped forwards so much that the sling had worked its way up to the back of her neck, half strangling her, and her arms felt as if they had been pulled half out of their sockets.

The first person she saw was Harry Evans, the Welsh doctor, who had his sleeves rolled up to the elbow; beads of sweat stood out on his brow. There were wounded everywhere. He looked askance at the Brigadier who had his eyes open and was staring vacantly at the roof of the tent. 'What's wrong with him?'

'Shell shock mainly, I'd say, sir. At any rate he can't walk or talk.'

'Put him down and I'll take a look at him when I get the chance.'

There was no space inside the tent so they laid the stretcher just inside the open doorway. Mhairi groaned aloud with relief as she at last let go, and as she did so Madge Duncan, her fellow VAD, appeared round the corner of the tent.

'Oh, Mhairi, Sister's been looking everywhere for you. You're needed in the dressing-tent, toot sweet! It'll probably only be for a short time 'cause they're calling for help further down the line and you might be assigned to that.'

Mhairi's spirits rose. Did she mean around the area of Gommecourt Wood? Her prayers could be answered sooner than she anticipated.

It was not to be, however, for she was still working in the dressing-tent as the shadows of evening grew long on the scrubby grass outside the tents, and the numbers of casualties grew so large they were spread out on the ground all around. They had long passed the time when there was room for them inside the tents. And they said that the dead still lying there unburied on the battlefield even outnumbered the living.

It was around seven-thirty when she ran into Major Evans, again at the 'cooker'. Both were having their first mugs of tea in almost four hours. He looked at her quizzically through his monocle. 'You're the young woman who brought the Brigadier in, aren't you?'

'Well, yes. How is he?' It was only polite to ask.

The Major was silent for a moment or two. 'It's more mental than physical,' he said at last. 'I reckon it's time he was taken back to Brigade HQ. His chances of recovery will be a darned sight better there.' He took another sip of tea. 'It would be better if somebody accompanied him in the ambulance . . . I mean, we don't want him suddenly raving and accosting the driver. It's happened before, you know.'

She didn't know. In fact there was a whole lot about war and what it did to people that she hadn't known until today.

'I know it's a lot to ask. You've been on duty as long as anybody today, but would you mind very much accompanying him? It shouldn't take too long. Headquarters is only a couple of miles or so down the line, at Sailly au Bois.'

Her heart sank. Just when she thought she might be in for an hour or so's break, she had to hold the hand of some Brass Hat in case he went off his head. It was almost like rubbing salt into an open wound, for her opinion of the calibre of those in charge of this war was even lower than that of the men's after today — and that was saying something. 'If it'll help you, Major, then yes, I'll do it.'

'Bless you, Miss. You should be back within an hour or so, and I'll personally see to it that you're relieved.'

The journey to Sailly au Bois was over a road that was now almost non-existent, blasted out of recognition with the constant barrage of shelling throughout the day. There were more craters than solid surface and the driver had to use all his skill to manoeuvre his way around the holes as they crawled their way towards their destination.

A mile or so from the camp they came upon a weary column of German prisoners, escorted by a handful of equally exhausted British soldiers. They were a mixed bunch: some appeared to be too old to be there at all, some were mere boys. A few were walking wounded, whilst others carried their more badly injured comrades on stretchers heavily stained with blood. Those who were able were attempting to keep their spirits up by singing, and a few bars of the sad old refrain of '*Morgenlied*' wafted in through the open windows of the ambulance.

The noise from the guns had abated somewhat now and only the distant sound of sporadic firing could be heard from the direction of the Front. Was there anybody alive out there to still carry it on, Mhairi wondered bitterly, as the pathetic little group of ex-combatants disappeared down the dusty road behind them. And once again her thoughts turned to Rob. She simply had to find out how and where he was. But then she brightened visibly. Brigade Headquarters would be exactly the right place to find out just such a thing.

There was much consternation after their arrival at Sailly, for, although Headquarters had been informed that the Brigadier was slightly wounded, they were not prepared for the gibbering, nervous wreck who was carried in on the stretcher.

Mhairi accompanied the patient into the building, while the driver waited outside in the ambulance. And, once inside, she suddenly had a thought. Why not make the most of the trip? They might even have running water here! As two corporals carried the Brigadier off on the stretcher, she asked a passing captain if there was a toilet in the vicinity.

'Up those stairs and second on your left, through the main door,' she was told.

Thankfully she hurried up the staircase and followed the directions indicated. They led to a large tiled bathroom, and the mere sight of such a place lifted her spirits as nothing had done since her arrival at the Front. It took her less than ten minutes to freshen up, and with a clean face, hands, and newly combed hair, she felt quite rejuvenated as she began to make her way back downstairs.

As she passed a half-open door at the top of the stairs she could hear voices within. She paused, her pulse quickening; someone was talking about the London Scottish. Rob's battalion! They were talking about Rob's battalion!

She moved nearer and pressed her ear to the crack. They had gone into the attack with 856 officers and men, the voice was saying, and had taken four lines of German trenches. But casualties had been heavy . . .

Her heart was in her mouth as the voice continued: 'We estimate the dead or wounded at over 600 – we're down to about one-third of our strength.'

Her stomach turned over. Two-thirds of the battalion wiped out to gain four lines of trenches: a few hundred yards of land at the most! Two-thirds of the best and finest, dead or wounded – for what? For a few hundred yards of shattered earth? And Rob –what of Rob? Was he one of those casualties so casually referred to by that disembodied voice in there?

The voice was still continuing, he was talking about the Serre Front now: the Pals Battalion from Yorkshire. She could listen to no more.

Half-dazed with grief, and half-crazed with anger, she made for the stairs. At the foot was a door marked: Duty Officer.

She stared at it for a moment. Someone ought to know. Someone should be told that this slaughter must not be allowed to continue. It was a whole generation they were murdering out there – and for what? A few hundred yards of shattered earth!

She did not even bother to knock, but threw open the door and slammed it behind her. The Commanding Officer was seated at his desk, head down, writing something on a pad in front of him. He looked up immediately the door slammed behind her.

He stared into the distraught face of the woman in the VAD uniform, then let out a gasp. 'Good God!'

Mhairi stared back. Then slowly the blood began to drain from her face. The soldier in the Major-General's uniform began to walk round the desk towards her.

She continued to stare at him, then silently her lips formed his name: 'Ralph . . .'

Chapter Twenty-Five

'You!' Mhairi gasped in astonishment at the man who was looking with equal surprise into her own eyes. 'You're in charge here?'

He came round the desk and, taking both her hands in his, he pressed them to his lips. 'Mhairi . . . Mhairi . . .'

Major-General Ralph MacLachlan shook his head as he gazed down at her. He could not believe the sight of his own eyes. Her – out here, of all places . . .

He shook his head once more, and kept on shaking it. He longed to take her in his arms, but so many years had passed, so much water had flowed under that old bridge . . . 'What on earth brings you, of all people, out here to this hell?'

Mhairi extracted her hands from his and took a step back. Her heart was pounding as she looked at him, her eyes taking in the greying hair at the temples, beneath the braided cap. He looked older – and tired. Very tired. There were dark shadows beneath the grey eyes. 'My son,' she said softly. 'My son is out there, in that hell as you so rightly describe it.'

He caught his breath. 'Our son.'

She whirled around and walked to the window. She could see her driver sitting in the cab of the ambulance, smoking a cigarette as he waited for her. '*My* son,' she corrected. 'You had nothing to do with him, other than the fact that one night we made love together . . .' Her voice trailed off. 'If you could call it "love".' Her voice had a bitter edge as she continued, 'For is it not a funny kind of love that professes itself one night, to totally disappear out of one's life the next day?'

He came up behind her and caught her arm, turning her round to face him. 'Whatever I said to you that night, Mhairi, was the truth. I meant every word. I did not lie to you. You do believe that, don't you?' There was a desperation in his voice that was mirrored in his eyes. It was as if he had been mentally asking her this question all the days of his life.

She looked at him steadily as she fought to keep her voice from rising. 'Perhaps – perhaps not,' she said softly. 'But you never came to my room again, did you, Ralph? Not once, in the rest of my life.'

He made a despairing gesture with his hands. 'You know what happened that day, Mhairi. You know as well as I do.'

His eyes clouded at the thought of Effie's death. He had tried so hard over the years to put that whole nightmarish episode completely out of his mind. His shock at being told of what had happened was only surpassed by his horror at being told that Mhairi had been with her, and that one of the maids was accusing her of having pushed Effie over the edge of the cliff.

'You never thought to ask *me* what really happened that day.'

'By the time I got back and learned of what had happened, you had already gone.'

'And you made no effort to come after me.'

His eyes darkened. It was true and that one failure to act had haunted him ever since. He shook his head as he took a crumpled packet of cigarettes from his pocket and lit one. His fingers trembled slightly as he blew out the match with the exhaled smoke. 'I couldn't begin to explain to you what I have been unable to explain fully to myself,' he said, in all honesty.

'Try me.' She wanted with all her heart to understand.

He looked past her, out of the window, his eyes on the far horizon. Smoke was rising, drifting almost lazily on the evening air, beyond the small copse of trees that divided the headquarters from the battlefield. Somewhere in the distance a lone round of gunfire sounded, then petered out. 'Gregor McGregor was my father's oldest and dearest friend,' he said quietly. 'Effie – his daughter – meant everything to him . . .'

He turned to face her, 'Good God, Mhairi, don't you think I felt bad enough? . . . That very morning I had told him I was denying him his greatest wish on this earth; I told him I was not going to marry his beloved daughter . . . I was rejecting Effie, who meant more to him than life itself, to marry you. Then when I get back from the hills I am met by him, more shaken than I have ever seen any man, outside this bloody war, and he takes me to his room to tell me that Effie is dead, and he believes you to be the cause.'

He looked across at her, and their eyes met and held. His face was transparent in its honesty, in its desire to be believed. 'I want you to know here and now that I never for one moment accepted you to be the cause of Effie's fall.'

'But you never came after me to tell me that.'

'I never came after you . . .' There was no denying it.

His broad shoulders seemed to slump inside the braided tunic as he mentally relived the anguish of that terrible day. 'I never came after you because I had a dying man on my hands – a heartbroken man – who was not only my father's oldest and dearest friend, but who came from a family whose whole history had been bound up with our own. He had saved my father's life at the Battle of Modder River in the Boer War, and there had been debts of honour owed and paid between the McGregors and the MacLachlans since time immemorial. Can you imagine the hurt – the anguish – it would have caused, if I had rushed off and left him there at that moment to follow you – you whom he believed was responsible for his daughter's death?'

Her eyes never flickered from his. 'Yes,' she said softly. 'Yes, I can imagine the hurt.' She could imagine it, but she had suffered too. She had known the anguish of giving birth to a child – his child – whom she knew would never know its father.

She dropped her eyes from his and glanced down at her right wrist which she held out towards him. She pulled up the white cuff of her uniform and the silver bracelet glinted in the lamplight. 'It's against regulations to wear jewellery,' she said quietly. 'But I have worn this since the day Fiona gave it to me the year before Rob was born. There is a quote from Shakespeare's *King Lear* engraved on it,' she continued quietly. 'You're a learned man – you went to public school. Perhaps you know it:

> I grow, I prosper,
> Now, gods, stand up for bastards!'

She gave a bitter smile as she pulled down her cuff and covered it from sight. 'I little thought when she gave it to me that my own child would be destined for just such a fate.'

He made to say something, but she held up her hand as if to silence him. The bitterness she had felt – had buried inside her all these years – had taken command. 'If I have learned anything in this life, it's that you are on your own. You must rely on no one. There are no illegitimate children in this world – only fathers who are bastards!' She could feel the hot sting of tears in her eyes, but she was determined not to break down in front of him. 'I had one – a father who was just such a bastard – who also just happened to be your dear and noble friend, the McGregor of Dalriada. And my son has one, for who else but a bastard would put duty to a family friend before duty to his own son?'

His face was ashen as her words sank in. 'The McGregor was your father?' The very idea was grotesque.

Mhairi's chin rose fractionally higher as she nodded the affirmation. 'It is a fact of which both of us were aware, but of which neither of us was very proud.'

He took a deep breath and let it out slowly. The news staggered him – staggered him almost as much as learning that day in Harrods that he had a son. He shook his head and drew deeply on his cigarette, then studied the glowing tip as he said quietly, 'Mhairi, I swear to God I never knew . . . I never knew. I had no idea you had a child until that day in Harrods. I swear to God it was the biggest shock of my life.' His insides still quaked when he thought of it. The knowledge had preyed on his mind for weeks after that, and if he had not been due to leave for France the following day, he knew he would have had to have contacted her.

'Ah yes . . . That day in Harrods! That was a surprise all round, wasn't it?' She attempted a bright smile that was at total odds with her feelings as she said lightly, 'Was that your wife you were with?' That cheeky hat haunted her still.

His jaw tightened and he lit another cigarette from the stub of the old, which he threw into the open fireplace. 'Yes, that was Grace.'

'Grace . . .' She tried the name out for size on her tongue. 'So you ended up with a Grace and Favour house, did you, Ralph? Grace came along and saved Craig David with her inherited wealth. She got the title – Countess Grace MacLachlan – and you got the money and Grace. Not . . .'

She got no further. 'Stop it, Mhairi! For God's sake, stop it!' He thumped his fist on to the edge of the desk, sending a pen bouncing from its inkwell. Ink spots peppered the scattering of official papers lying there; he stared at them with unseeing eyes. His nerves were already raw, without this. Everyone's were. But what she was saying was far too near the truth. Dear God, it *was* the truth! 'It's no good torturing ourselves like this. What do you want me to say? That I loved you then – that I love you now – and that I bitterly regret that things could not have been different for us? Is that what you want? If it is, then I'll say it! Yes, dammit, I'll say it! I loved you – I still love you. Dear God, I will always love you . . .'

His voice trailed off, as a look akin to real pain came into his face. His lips twisted as emotion charged through him and he fought to keep his reason, to resist his overwhelming desire to take her in his arms and beg her forgiveness for all the wasted years. He understood only too well the pain she had gone through – the pain she was still going through. He took a deep breath and when he finally spoke, his voice was calm, almost too calm, and betrayed nothing of the turmoil within as he stated truthfully, 'Yes, I will always love you, Mhairi McLeod. But if you ask me if I can do anything about it, then the answer is, No. I made my vows to my wife, and I will stand by them. If I cannot love her as she might have wished, then it is the very least I can do.'

She felt her legs go weak. His voice might be calm, but he was looking at her with such anguish in his face that she had to turn away. The cost of each of those words was writ large across his features. She stared with unseeing eyes out of the window beside her. Every dream she might have dreamt in all these intervening years . . . Every dream she *did* dream lay in pieces at their feet. His words had shattered everything – everything that might have been, and now, she knew from his own lips, never could be . . . 'You didn't have to say that,' she said quietly. 'You didn't have to tell me that. I never would have expected it any other way.'

But he had had to tell her. He had had to say it out loud. He had had to say it to her. Only then could his own mind be at rest. So many times over the past nineteen years he had dreamt of this moment: the moment he met her again. There would be just the two of them, and he could tell her of the agony he had gone through, of the anguish in his soul as he lay awake at night beside the woman he *had* married – as he lay beside Grace – and listened to her breathing in the wee small hours of the morning, and he had hated her because she wasn't Mhairi. She wasn't the woman he loved. And he had never known until this moment if he would have the courage to say what he had just said. The courage to claim his own happiness at the expense of another's – a woman who had stood by him for the past sixteen years, who had helped him rebuild Craig David, and restore it for the good of future generations.

His eyes darkened in the lamplight. That had been the one cloud hanging over their married life. There had been no children. Unable to accept that she could not give him what his heart desired most – an heir for Craig David – she had blamed him, and he had even been prepared to accept that blame, for he had not known of his son's existence till that day only last year in the luggage department of Harrods. He gave a bitter smile as he drew deeply on his cigarette. What a place to learn the truth.

Then, as he looked at Mhairi, his grey eyes took on a different hue. And, for the first time in his life he realized the real irony of the situation. His soul was laid bare as he looked at her across the lamplit room. 'I married Grace to save Craig David,' he said huskily. 'I admit it. I married her to save the castle that has been in our family for generations. More than anything else I was afraid of being the one who lost it – who broke that sacred trust. And when I married her, I admit that her money saved the castle and its lands from passing out of the family. But we have had no children. My parents are dead. My brother Davey is dead. There are no cousins to inherit the title . . .'

'There is only your son.' Their eyes met and held once more.

'There is only my son.'

As he said the words, the tears that had been lurking beneath the surface trembled on Mhairi's lower lashes and began to trickle slowly down her cheeks. So he would not do what her own father had done. He would not reject his own child. He would recognize Rob. And Robert Ralph MacLachlan McLeod would one day be the Earl of Inverbervie.

But his mother would remain alone.

What was it again – the MacLachlan clan motto? 'Brave and Faithful.' She whispered the words aloud, beneath her breath. It would be a brave decision all right, to recognize a bastard son, but she knew he would do it. And he had taken an equally brave decision in remaining faithful to his wife.

And, as she looked across at him, standing there in the lamplight of the room in this foreign place, with the sounds of battle still raging out there in the gathering dusk, she knew she loved him now as she had never loved him. She loved him with the love of a woman for a man. They had been little more than children when they first met. And they had come down a long road since those heady days in New York, when they and the world were young and carefree. But the world was different now; that world they once knew now lay in bloody pieces all around them. And they were different. They had grown up. She could not beg him to change his mind. She could not add to his agony.

'I must go,' she said softly. 'I must get back.'

He put out a hand, as if to stop her, then drew back. He must not touch her. To touch her would be to beg her to stay. He must let her go. For both their sakes, he must let her go.

She turned and walked quickly from the room. The door clicked shut behind her, and she did not see the tears that had sprung to his eyes, nor hear the low moan that seemed to come from the very depths of his soul as he slumped down at his desk and buried his head in his hands.

She did not speak on the journey back to the hospital station. The driver in the cab beside her took her silence for exhaustion and did not press for conversation.

She could not face going back to the company that awaited her in her tent; the banter of her fellow nurses was the last thing she needed right now, and she was far too tired to report back for duty. It was a bright moonlit night and she found herself wandering over to gaze at the wide expanse of shattered earth that was No Man's Land. A figure was already standing there, his eyes on the distant horizon. He turned as she approached.

'Ah, Miss McLeod – you're back.' Major Harry Evans was taking a moment out of the frenetic activity that was still going on in the medical tents, to collect his thoughts and gather his energies for what was going to be a long night. But if he was exhausted, he knew just how tired the nurses must be. There was sympathy in his eyes as he looked at her. 'Are you turning in now?'

She was on the point of saying, yes, when she suddenly shook her head. 'No, if you don't mind, sir, I think I'll take a walk down the line to around Gommecourt Wood, before getting some sleep. I want to find out if my son is safe.'

He looked at her in surprise as she turned and made off in the direction she had just mentioned. He had had no idea she was old enough to have a son in this hell.

She was not alone on the road to Gommecourt, for columns of battle-weary men shuffled past her in both directions. Many had no weapons; their bloodshot eyes looked at her dully out of haggard faces, their shoulders drooping with the weight of kitbags and equipment long since lost in the scramble to get over the top. Once spotless puttees were mud-caked and coiled around boots in which feet were swollen beyond pain.

And every so often the shell-shock victims would pass, supported by their comrades. You could recognize them immediately by their slavering mouths, and rolling, bare-teethed heads. Some clawed their mouths incessantly and made animal whimpering noises as they stumbled on towards their destination. But for others even that was too much and they sat by the roadside, rocking backwards and forwards like demented infants. They leered at her as she passed, with eyes that rolled in red-rimmed sockets, and called out with tongues that lolled from vacant mouths. And past them, the stretcher-bearers plodded on their never-ending journeys with their bloodied cargoes. She could feel their pain and exhaustion. She could feel the pain for each and every one. They were all somebody's sons, somebody's brother or husband. And tears burned hot and bitter in her eyes for everyone caught up in this hell they were calling the Great War.

It took her almost an hour to find the spot where the London Scottish had gone over the top. Although the line itself stretched for around twenty miles, the area she was looking for was not much more than a field's width. What had once been a pleasant wooded meadow was now nothing more than a deserted stretch of tortured earth, with here and there a mutilated tree pointing accusing fingers to heaven.

Every few yards were bomb craters and mounds of bloodied clay. The dead, and dismembered parts of bodies, lay scattered all around her, as far as the eye could see. The main concern since the lull in the fighting was to bring in the wounded, but now some attempts were being made to bury those of their comrades who had not made it back. Already the ground was scattered with small wooden crosses. And how many hearts were broken for each one, she wondered as she surveyed the scene with a feeling of mounting desperation?

About twenty yards ahead of her, in the moonlight, she could see two soldiers filling in what she could only imagine to be a grave. Every spadeful of earth was an effort, and they paused between each one to summon the energy for the next. She would ask them about Rob. Perhaps there was a company headquarters around here. He would be sure to be in that.

Her heart was in her mouth as she approached them. Their ears long tuned for the slightest noise, they turned in unison as she approached. 'Can we help you, nurse?' the tallest said.

She took a deep breath. 'I hope so. You are the London Scottish, aren't you?'

'Aye, we are that.'

'I – I'm looking for a Second-Lieutenant Robert McLeod. Do you know where I'm likely to find him?'

The two privates looked at one another, then the tallest one spoke again. 'You must mean Captain McLeod . . . He was promoted twice in the past month.'

'Oh really! I didn't know that . . .' Pride rose alongside the excitement that welled within her at their recognition of his name. 'We *are* talking about the same one, aren't we? He – he's from London, from Bloomsbury – tall with dark auburn hair and grey eyes.'

'Aye, that's him all right.'

Her breathing quickened. 'Well?'

The men looked at one another again. 'The Captain's been reported missing, ma'am.'

'Reported missing?' She looked frantically from one to the other. 'What do you mean, reported missing?'

'Just that, ma'am. He went over the top with the rest of us this morning and hasn't been seen since.'

She stared at them both in turn, her eyes wild as panic

gripped her. 'But where – where could he be?' She already knew the answer but nothing on God's earth could make her admit it.

The man looked uncomfortable. Their bodies ached with fatigue, and their hearts ached for the woman in nurse's uniform who stood before them, despair writ large across the fine-boned features of her face. Whoever she was, she was feeling it – the pain – the unutterable agony felt by each and every one of them, and all those other ordinary people whom this bloody war was sending to hell and back.

'Where, oh tell me where he can be . . .' Her voice faded to a whisper, then the tall one turned to look meaningfully at the waste of No Man's Land behind them.

Mhairi's eyes followed his gaze. Then, not stopping to ask anything more of them, and half-blinded with tears, she lifted her skirts and ran out into the emptiness. He was out there somewhere. He had to be out there somewhere. And still alive. Please God, let him still be alive!

Her booted feet stumbled over the rough ground. An eerie silence filled the air. The stretcher-bearers had removed most of the wounded long ago, and now, apart from the odd burial party, her only companions were the bloodied corpses of the young men who lay unrecognizable where they had fallen just a few short hours ago; young men with mothers back home who loved them, just as she loved Rob. Young men with the whole of their lives before them. Until today.

Her foot caught in a shred of tartan. Never had there ever been so much blood spilt on her country's cloth. And for what? What in the history of creation was worth this sacrifice? A whole generation wiped out in the blink of an eye.

Her own eyes filled with tears which ran in salt-tasting streams down her cheeks, but she made no attempt to wipe them away. She was no longer aware of her own body, or of the fatigue that made every step an effort as she stumbled on in search of her son . . . Her son . . . 'Rob . . . Rob . . .' His name was spent like a sigh in the cool night air. 'Dear God, help me. Help me find my son . . .'

They were all around her – his friends and comrades. Those still recognizable stared back at her, their unblinking eyes gazing upwards, towards a god who mocked their suffering and death in this foreign field; a god who allowed such atrocities to take place on a fine summer's day, in a green meadow where poppies as red as blood lifted their heads and danced amid the mangled specimens of the finest flowers of a nation's youth.

She had no idea how long she had been searching when she was aware of someone behind her. She did not have to turn to know who it was.

He had followed her. Despite his resolve to stay out of her life, he had followed her, and had asked at the MO's tent where he might find her. The officer in charge, Harry Evans, had been puzzled by the enquiry from one of the Brass Hats. But he had told him all the same. 'Gone to look for her son around Gommecourt Wood,' he had said. And Ralph had got back into his vehicle and followed her.

'They say he's missing,' she said, her eyes frantically searching the emptiness. There was real desperation in her voice. 'I have to find him . . .'

He looked down at her and laid a hand on her shoulder. She turned her face to his and their eyes locked. Whatever had gone before, they were now as one. One heart, one soul.

And so they searched together, two very different figures – the tall, kilted frame of the Major-General dwarfing the much slighter female one in the flowing nurse's cloak as they moved forward slowly over the tortured earth, to be glanced at curiously now and then by the small burial parties still carrying out their grisly tasks of collecting anything that was recognizable of their dead comrades. Now and again a shout would break the silence when one of the corpses was found to still possess a breath of life. Such moments raised their spirits and put fresh hope in their hearts.

Occasionally she glanced across and caught sight of Ralph's face. Despite his years of soldiering, the agony she herself was going through was mirrored in his eyes as they continued their awful quest. Had he found his son – his only son – only to lose him again? They paused on the edge of a small copse to gaze about them. Mhairi felt physically sick at the sight spread out before them. Surely this was the most terrible place on God's earth. Never had she seen so many kilted soldiers – all dead.

'Will the world ever know?' she whispered. 'Will they ever know the cost? They have wiped out a whole generation of young men here today. And will do the same tomorrow, and the next day, until someone ends this ungodly massacre, this slaughter of the innocents.' For that was what they were – most of them little more than children, like their own son . . .

He had no answer for her, for he was part of it. He was one of those men whose task it was to send these young men to their deaths. 'May God forgive me,' he said softly. For surely he would never forgive himself.

She had paused to stretch her aching back when he called her over, and at first she wondered why. There was no sign of a body on the pitted ground. Only a fragment of tartan and what looked like a heap of bloodied clothing. From the middle of the heap something glinted in the moonlight, and as she approached, Ralph bent down and picked it up.

He held it in the flat of his hand. It was a silver cigarette case with the initials 'R. MacL.' engraved in the centre. He had not set eyes on it since the day his life was saved in that old mill at Neuve Chapelle.

She gazed down at it in the palm of his hand, and her

fingertips reached out to touch the wreath of leaves that surrounded the initials.

His arm went around her shoulders and a mist came to the grey of his eyes, as his grip tightened around the woman he loved. The woman he would always love as long as he walked this tormented earth. 'It's a Rowan tree,' he said huskily. 'It's the MacLachlan clan crest.'

And spotted across the shining metal were tiny flecks of blood as red as berries. The sacred tree of his clan had born a bitter fruit.

Epilogue

Backward, turn backward, O Time, in your flight,
Make me a child again, just for tonight!

Backward, flow backward, O tide of the years,
I am so weary of toil and of tears –
Toil without recompense, tears all in vain,
Take them, and give me my childhood again!

It is one of the joys at the end of one's life to find how clear our childhood becomes. And it was this that prompted me to buy Dalriada when eventually it came on the market.

Little did I imagine when I returned to London at the end of the Great War that I would ever return to Skye. Meeting, then losing Ralph again, then the death of my beloved son, Rob, in the trenches of the Somme meant that almost all I had held dear in my life had been taken from me. Almost all. For it was then that I remembered my Great-aunt Jessie McLeod's words: 'You are thistle-down, Mhairi. Fly on the winds, lassie. Fly on the winds . . .'

Was I really destined never to have a real home – a people that belonged to me? I could not believe that it was my fate to remain a stranger in a strange land. For even thistledown takes root.

Then it appeared in the paper: 'Remote Scottish castle, in need of restoration and love.'

In need of restoration and love . . . Those words could have been written about its new owner, when I finally signed the deeds that would buy the inheritance that Fate had denied me.

After Gregor McGregor's death — I still cannot refer to him as 'my father' — as far as his executors were concerned, he left no living relative to inherit Dalriada. The castle was willed to the safekeeping of his butler and valet, Hamish Mhor, for the old man's lifetime. They breed them strong in the Highlands, for Hamish Mhor lived to see the year of his hundredth birthday, dying in the late spring of 1945, in the closing months of yet another World War.

I had long been living alone in London, still in the same Bloomsbury house I had shared with Finbar. My uncle passed away peacefully in his sleep during the night of 20 November 1925, the same day King Edward's widow, the dowager Queen Alexandra, died at Sandringham. It seemed symbolic somehow. That chapter of my life was finally closing. My best friend in London, Jennie Churchill, had died after a fall in 1921. A sad loss, and sadder still that she did not live to see her son Winston inspire his country in the Second World War we were all to endure within a generation. As for dear George Cornwallis-West, after a miserable marriage to Stella, Mrs Patrick Campbell, he married his third wife in 1940 — the very day Stella's obituary appeared in *The Times*. Stella would have been outraged by his timing, and regarded it as the ultimate in upstaging, and she would have been right. But she was sadly missed by all those who retained a love of the stage. And I still counted myself as one of those, although I never sang again after returning from France in 1918.

I did not miss the stage, for in those years spent in the bloodied mud of Flanders' fields I had played a far greater part than could ever have been written by any playwright. I did not regret my years in the theatre, however, for success on the stage had opened doors on a world that would otherwise have remained firmly shut to a young girl such as I.

But it was not the real world, and I think I had always been aware of that. Reality for me would always remain firmly embedded in the dark, peaty turf of my Highland home, where, as I reached young womanhood and strutted the boards of Broadway and London's West End to receive the applause of the rich and famous, my people still toiled on their small crofts as they had done since time immemorial. The real world was the dark, mean streets of Manchester where young lives grew old in the pay of King Cotton. It was the back streets of New York, where for so many Uncle Sam had not turned out to be the much hoped for benevolent relative and poverty was still a life-companion.

Yes, inside the Other Woman the world came to know as Mhairi Cloud, Mhairi McLeod, the Child of the Mist, still lived, and knew in her heart that one day she would know that the make-believe would be over. One day she would know that the time had come to say goodbye to the glitter and the glamour. And there would be no regrets, only a profound gratefulness for the many joys it had brought. That day came for me amid the horror and heartache they called the Great War, and, when it was all over, and the world came to count the cost, I knew that the life of service I had known during those dreadful days must go on. From then on my life would be dedicated to helping others who had not been as fortunate as I had been.

Money I had in plenty, and after financially taking care of what was left of my own family, I spent most of my time, and a good deal of my fortune giving other young children the chance to spread their wings. The Mhairi Cloud Foundation was set up in the hope that as many as possible would benefit, and one or two might even learn to *fly on the winds* as I had done all those years before.

Of the Gaiety that had been part of my life for so many years, all that remains for me is an oil painting they presented me with, of a young woman they once knew as Mhairi Cloud. It hangs alongside all those generations of McGregors, in the great hall in Dalriada. I often wonder what they, my illustrious ancestors, make of their new companion: a young woman in a big picture hat, with a feather boa slung round her shoulders. And engraved on a brass plate along the bottom are the words:

MHAIRI CLOUD

She was a peal of laughter ringing its way through life:
She was the Gaiety's censure of London's toil and strife.

But those days are long gone, and one by one over the years my ties with the past have been severed; another World War has come and gone, and now my restless soul longs for peace. The Foundation I set up just after the Great War, and that had taken up most of my time over the next twenty years, is now run by experienced, capable people who are doing a far better job than I had ever done. After two decades of dedication, with love and pride, I stepped aside in 1939, to hand over to those I had trained and trusted to carry on the work. Now, less physically involved, I became more of a dedicated figurehead and benefactor, grateful that most of what remained of the fortune I had earned from the love of the public at large, could now be given back in the form of aid to enable their children and grandchildren to pursue careers that would otherwise have been far beyond their reach.

It seemed right somehow, it was in the scheme of things that I would return to Skye. I think I always knew that some day I would go home.

I returned to my island one day in 1945, as the green tides of high summer were passing into the golden glow of late September — that special time in the Western

Highlands when at the rising of the moon we hear the falling echo of a song, and the earth sighs and yearns for the passing of all that is young, all that is golden. And on the moors, and in the hills, and along the wave-whispering shore, the air is filled with the sound of the coming dark, and sweet remembered fragrances of flowers long dead.

The month of peace, it is called in Gaelic song – the month when a golden haze lies over land and sea like a benediction. When in the morning a delicate frost lingers after a rose-flushed dawn, and beyond the gates of Dalriada, sombre clouds drift in from the great Atlantic, and we must look into the firelight of our own hearts to recapture what has gone, for it is there in the human heart, whose lands are lit by neither sun nor moon, that lie those secret places where old dreams never die.

And alone I sat on that desolate shore and gazed out to the far horizon. I sat at the edge of the world and breathed the air in the cool green wind that eddied up the grey waters of the loch. And I thought of Effie, and all that had gone. All who had died, whilst I remained. I thought of Ralph, and that castle, Craig David, on its cliff overlooking the grey North Sea, and I remembered the words of my old friend Willie Honeycomb who once told me that the tragedy in life is not what we suffer, but more often what we miss. And I knew that in the missing was the suffering. To desire something – or someone – with all one's heart and to be denied leaves an emptiness, an ache deep in the soul that remains with us all the days of our lives.

And as I sat there and thought of that other woman and the life that had been, the rain of the day gave way to a rainbow mist, a mist that drifted across the desert of that human soul as it surrounded Dalriada, and crept into every haunted valley of my defeated dreams. But the mist brought comfort too. For I was back in *Eilean a' Cheo*. I was back on my island. I was myself again. Her Child of the Mist had come home.

And today, in the evening of my life, I stand by my window, and in my hand there is clasped a small silver cigarette case, engraved with the initials of the two men I have loved. They are with me still, in the secret places of my heart, and I speak their names in the stillness of the night, when no one but me can hear, and no one but me can know . . .

And beyond my window there is a tree. It was planted there that September, in 1945, when the tides of war were once more receding across a bloodied world. It was planted there in remembrance of another war, the one they called the Great War, which robbed the world of a whole generation of its young men. It was planted there in memory of two men, a father and son. And there it will stand long after I am gone to join them in our Gaelic heaven of *Tir-nan-Og*, the Land of the Ever Young.

It is planted here, in front of my window: a tall Rowan tree, with leaves as green as springtime and berries as red as blood. My eyes and thoughts linger on it now, then move heavenwards to the blue of the sky, where, far above the clouds a white bird circles and waits.

It is the white merle I have been waiting for all the days of my life . . .